SUBMARINER

SUBMARINER

A novel by

Alexander Fullerton

SPHERE

First published in Great Britain in 2008 by Sphere

A CIP catalogue record for this book
is available from the British Library.

ISBN 978-1-84744-175-1

Typeset in Bembo by Palimpsest Book Production Limited,
Grangemouth, Stirlingshire
Printed and bound in the UK by
CPI Mackays, Chatham ME5 8TD

Sphere
An imprint of
Little, Brown Book Group
100 Victoria Embankment
London EC4Y 0DY

An Hachette Livre UK Company

www.littlebrown.co.uk

To Andrew Hewson, with thanks for heaven knows how many years of support and friendship.

1

Home, sweet home, he thought – might even have murmured it aloud – and it certainly looked a lot less *un*sweet than it had when he'd last seen it. Distant, still, but in the periscope's quadruple magnification clear-edged in the evening sun, and a lot easier on the eye than it had been ten or eleven weeks ago when the air assault had been at something like its worst, that image of towering stone walls, ramps and bastions shrouded virtually from dawn to dusk in the smoke and drifting stone-dust of Fliegerkorps II's virtually incessant bombing. Which, remembering not to count one's chickens, might be resumed of course, might well . . . He was searching the air now, the top lens tilted and himself circling, darkly furred forearms draped over the periscope's spread handles, longish legs necessarily bent slightly at the knees, plimsolls' scuffed toes against the rim of the well in which the long brass tube lived when it was not in use. A moment ago he'd spotted what he'd guessed would be the promised minesweeper on its way out to meet him, had studied it for a few seconds, confirming this – greatly appreciating it, such unaccustomed pampering – then left it to spend this half-minute on a slower and more concentrated air-search than he'd made initially.

Clear, empty sky, except for streamers of white cloud. Focusing back on the minesweeper that was fine on *Ursa's* bow and truly a most welcome sight – could only be one of the four modern sweepers which as one had heard had somehow managed to sneak through from Gibraltar during the flotilla's absence, and would have been working flat-out ever since. Mines had been as much of a bloody menace as the bombing, some of them parachuted by night into the harbours and approaches – because mines drifting down on parachutes in daylight were vulnerable to the gunners onshore, whereas at night searchlights had to find them first – and others laid in dense fields offshore by E-boats out of Syracuse or wherever – Syracuse and Augusta, Licata maybe. They'd played as big a part as the Ju 87s and 88s in rendering Malta unusable by the 10th Flotilla.

Temporarily unusable. Flotilla reassembling, back on the job now, with plenty of catching-up to do. Job being to disrupt the flow of war supplies from Italian ports to Field Marshal Rommel's Afrika Korps. A week or two ago Rommel in his drive westward had taken Tobruk, then Mersa Matruh; the British Eighth Army were holding him – for the moment – at El Alamein on the Egyptian frontier. Alexandria had been evacuated, being by then in Stuka range from desert airstrips. As it still was. Rommel had in front of him the Canal, the Middle East and its oil, prospects of linking up then with German forces in southern Russia.

Mike Nicholson pushed up the periscope's handles, and Ellery, Engine Room Artificer, depressed the lever that sent it hissing down into its well. Ellery – a tallish man, pale, thin-haired, watchful – was the Outside ERA, responsible for all machinery outside the engine-room itself. Like everyone else, he'd actually shaved today, had that odd, spruced-up look about him. Mike said, 'Stand by to surface', and Jamie McLeod – first lieutenant, second in command – ordered quietly, 'Check main vents.' Familiar routine now: obviously, to blow the water out of ballast tanks the vents in their tops had to be shut, otherwise the air would be blasting through and out into the sea. McLeod – lieutenant RN, same rank as his captain but a few years younger – Mike at twenty-eight looked more like thirty, thirty-two – had his narrowed eyes on the depth-gauges, the bubble in the spirit-level and the positions of the hydroplanes, all indicative of the state of the boat's trim – weight and balance in the water – which was his responsibility. Glancing at Mike, enquiring, 'You doing this, sir, or –'

'Might just risk my precious neck.'

Joke: raising a smile here and there, but only a nod from McLeod – whose query had been whether Mike himself would surface the boat, be first up through the hatch – normal procedure, of course, for a skipper to surface his own submarine – only in question now because since about the start of this year 'Shrimp' Simpson's orders had barred COs from appearing in their bridges until boats were actually inside the harbour. First lieutenants or even third hands were to con them in, wearing tin hats as protection against Messerschmitts and Heinkels who'd taken to haunting the harbour approaches in the hope of catching submarines at their most vulnerable – in the act of surfacing, in those few minutes stopped and wallowing, blind – the Germans diving on them with machine-guns and cannon blazing. It had happened more than once, and submarine COs were too valuable to be put at such risk unnecessarily.

Admiral Max Horton's orders to Shrimp Simpson had included the instruction to treat his COs like Derby winners, and Shrimp, a very experienced and successful submarine CO himself, now approaching forty and commanding this flotilla, wasn't putting them at unnecessary risk if he could help it.

Things clearly had taken a very sharp turn for the better though, in the course of just ten, eleven weeks. Touch wood: and, according to Shrimp, in Haifa recently. For one thing Fliegerkorps II, who'd been transferred from the Russian front to Sicily with the object of neutralising Malta, were being kept busy in support of Rommel, operating mainly from the desert and from Crete. For another, the RAF now had a substantial force of Spitfires on the Maltese airfields. No fewer than sixty-five had been flown in from the *Eagle* and the USS *Wasp* during the flotilla's absence – and mostly survived, as distinct from being destroyed on the ground within hours of their arrival, which was what had happened to previous consignments. On top of which one now had these minesweepers with their magnetic sweeps – as distinct from just one fairly ancient vessel, the poor old *Abingdon*, which having been strafed at every daylight appearance had been obliged to do her sweeping – as well as she'd been able, with the gear she had – by night.

To do her justice, she'd done wonders too. The job had been too much for her, that was all. It would have been too much for half a dozen of her.

'Ready to surface, sir.'

Vents shut, blows open at the tanks. Lower lid – the hatch, here in the control room – open too. Mike moving to the ladder, with the signalman, Walburton, ready to follow him up. Both in tin hats, and Walburton with a White Ensign and *Ursa*'s Jolly Roger stuffed inside his shirt, leaving his hands free for the climb and for collecting the six-inch Aldis lamp from its stowage on his way up through the tower. Mike said, with one foot on the ladder, 'Surface', McLeod told Ellery, 'Blow one and six', and the artificer jerked those two valves open on his control panel, sending bottled air at

4,000 pounds to the square inch ripping noisily to the tanks right for'ard and right aft. Rush of air through one-inch-diameter piping loud in Mike's ears as he went fast up through the tower — not all that much more than shoulder-wide internally, for him at any rate — and paused under the top hatch, McLeod intoning loudly for his information, 'Twenty feet, sir. Fifteen. Twelve —'

He'd taken the cotter-pins out of both clips. Had one clip off and swinging free now, waited with a hand on the other.

'Ten feet. Eight —'

Second clip off, hatch lifting, internal pressure of somewhat foul air venting, hatch crashing back, a gallon or two of salt water splashing in as he clambered out and into the bridge's forefront. *Ursa* wallowing with the sea sluicing down out of her free-flood bridge and casing — at half-buoyancy initially, the other main ballast tanks could be blown when Mike was sure he was *staying* up. OK this far: all clear all round, in the *immediate* vicinity, beyond the foaming area of her emergence. Sky clear too. Behind him, clack-clacking of the Aldis, Walburton giving the minesweeper *Ursa's* pendant numbers, confirming her identity. Answering flash from the sweeper's bridge: she had her wheel over, turning to lead them in: you saw the shift in the white flurry at her forefoot, then her low, grey shape lengthening as she swung. *Ursa's* diesels pounding into thunderous life, driving generators that powered her batteries, and in the process sucking a flood of clean, sweet air down through the tower. He'd opened the voice-pipe cock meanwhile, called down, 'Lookouts on the bridge.' To look out for aircraft, mainly; even with the sweeper and her Oerlikons in close company it would take only one Stuka, one pair of bombs from the bottom of its screaming dive, banshee howl of the kind of which there'd been about one a minute throughout all the daylight hours, day after bloody day from March into early

5

summer. Best of reasons not to have spent a day more than necessary in harbour: safer outside, at sea — at least, arguably so — and Shrimp well aware of it as well as wanting you out there on the Axis convoy routes. Shrimp also wishing, as Mike knew well, that he could have been out there himself — which he could not, on account of his age, forty or near it being too old for submarine command anywhere, let alone in these waters and circumstances. Shrimp would have given his right arm to be out there doing it himself, *not* to be limited to sending his young Derby winners out, most of them still in their middle to late twenties.

It was a young man's job, was all. A very fit young man's, at that. And in Malta even harbour-time had had its acute anxieties. In fact, that the blitzkrieg should have ended so suddenly wasn't all that easy to believe, trust in entirely. Possibly not all that wise to either, Mike told himself, *so let's not.* He had three officers and twenty-eight ratings in this fairly minuscule, under-armed and frustratingly slow submarine, he'd had her and them out here with him for well over a year — sixteen patrols in that time — or was it seventeen? — and touch wood might not be many months before he took them home again. All of them — the boat intact and her men alive — also, in his own view, bloody marvellous. Despite there having been times that had taken a bit of getting through. They'd stood up to it and learnt from it, that was the thing, they knew their business and were proud of it, weren't going to let either him or each other down. *Ursa* could count herself as one of the flotilla's veterans and top scorers now; there were new or newish boats and faces, and yet newer ones on their way, replacements for those who'd come to grief or — the lucky ones — done their time and gone home for refit, but of the really old guard, the *crème de la crème* — well, there'd been two grievous losses in very recent times. Not that any loss was anything less than grievous: but David

Wanklyn VC and *Upholder* had been lost at the end of April, on what was to have been his last patrol before going home, and his close friend, the equally successful and well-liked 'Tommo' Tomkinson and his boat *Urge*, a fortnight later.

Flag Officer Submarines Max Horton was sending replacements all right, maintaining or even increasing the flotilla's strength, but neither of those two individuals or their crews could ever be thought of as replaceable.

The lookouts – Barnet, a torpedoman, and Brighouse, stoker – were on the job now at the after end of the bridge, searching the sky bare-eyed, out of long habit and common sense dividing it between them, and Mike had passed the order down to completely empty numbers two, three, four and five main ballast. Walburton meanwhile had the ensign flying from its staff, and was up on the gleaming-wet periscope standard bending on the Roger. Jolly Roger, *Ursa's* own record of her successes, a black flag with a somewhat crude white skull and crossbones central, bars in the fly for ships sunk by torpedo, stars under crossed gun-barrels for enemies dispatched by gunfire. White bars for merchantmen, red for warships, dagger symbols for special operations such as train-wrecking and landing/embarking agents or commandos. *Ursa* had plenty to her credit, and for this last patrol a new white bar that Walburton had painstakingly stitched on last night. Making – Mike had forgotten how many torpedoings. A round dozen, roughly. Tonnage in any case was now over thirty thousand. Thirty-two or -three, probably. It was tonnage you went by: the flotilla's score was around the half-million mark at this stage.

He lowered his glasses, stooping to the voice-pipe: 'Come five degrees to starboard.'

'Five to starboard, sir!'

Voice of Able Seaman Smithers, gunlayer. Glasses up again: the sweeper calling them up and Walburton, down from the

7

periscope standard, grabbing the Aldis and flashing a go-ahead. Mike read the incoming message for himself: 'Looks like your Jolly Roger flying. Good bag, I hope?'

'Tell him, one fair-sized transport, laden.'

Fair-sized and *well* laden. Eight or nine thousand tons, at any rate. So how many *Soldaten* who wouldn't be joining Rommel – five thousand? Twice that number? Germans, for preference – one dead German being worth ten Italians. Destroyers had picked up quite a lot of them; and one of the destroyers would have gone too, complete with its load of rescuees, if *Ursa* had had the right torpedoes, the Mark VIIIs she should have had. Torpedoes had always been in short supply, and the shortage had become substantially worse when a U-boat had torpedoed the submarine depot ship *Medway* on her way from Alexandria to Haifa during the evacuation. She'd had ninety spares in crates on her upper deck; destroyers out of Haifa and Port Said had recovered about forty floaters the next day, but it was still a serious loss. As had *Medway* herself, of course – actually a shocking loss.

The sweeper had replied, 'Well done you.' Maintaining her distance ahead – *Ursa* making about ten knots, which was her best surfaced speed. Malta dramatically aglow with the lowering sun behind it: Fort Ricasoli off to port, then the entrance to Grand Harbour darkening in a haze that was not far short of purple, Fort St Elmo's façade and foreshore more rose-tinted. No red flag flying on the Castile: no enemy aircraft around, therefore. And from there, now training his glasses right – past the St Elmo lighthouse, then Point Sant'Jiermu, less distinct from this bearing and distance – inside Point Tigne was the entrance to Marsamxett Harbour and Sliema Creek. Those two waterways being separated once you were inside by Manoel Island, with Fort Manoel at its eastern end and Lazaretto, the 10th Flotilla's base, facing directly on to Lazaretto Creek running northwestward out of Marsamxett.

Visualising it, of course, not seeing it yet – not for about twenty or thirty minutes yet. Actually, looking forward to the sight of it: not home *sweet* home, exactly, but having been forced out, and returning now – there was a pleasure in *that* – and anyway with all the memories good and bad, a *kind* of home – even though last time one had seen it, had been largely rubble.

Clear sky, still. Darkening, colours deepening, still no hostiles in it. There'd be Spit and/or Hurricane patrols in northern offshore sectors, he supposed. Although the RAF wouldn't be burning up aviation spirit any faster than they had to. Petrol did come in by submarine – the larger boats, such as the minelayers and the River-class – and even T-class visiting with loads of it in their ballast tanks – but in relation to actual requirements it could only be a trickle, nothing like enough to satisfy the Spitfires' thirst. The so-called 'Magic Carpet' boats brought other stuff as well, of course – medical stores, for instance, or special foods for invalids and babies – whatever was most urgently required and they had room for.

A convoy operation would be the priority now, Mike thought. Shrimp had in fact said as much, when they'd been in Haifa; he'd been desperate to get his submarines back where they belonged.

The sweeper was flashing: *Can you find your own way from here to Lazaretto?*

'Make to him, "Might just stumble on it. Thanks for your company."'

Walburton muttering the words to himself as he aimed the lamp and started sending. Mike stooped to the pipe: 'Starboard ten . . .'

Entering harbour, finally. McLeod with him in the bridge, also the coxswain, CPO Jacko Swathely – steering from the wheel up here in the bridge now – and casing party down

on the casing, five men for'ard and three aft, under the supervision of Sub-Lieutenant Tommy Jarvis RNVR and the
second coxswain Petty Officer Hart, known to his friends as
Tubby. You could see why they called him that, but he was
a big man, could manage his avoirdupois all right. Also in
the bridge was *Ursa*'s fourth hand and navigating officer, Sub-
Lieutenant Pete Danvers RNR, who'd come into the RN,
and after a year or two into submarines, out of a Merchant
Navy cadetship. *Ursa* motoring into Marsamxett now with
Fort Manoel to starboard and Valetta to port, and a *dghaisa*
ferryman in his gondola-shaped craft waving his hat and
screeching with joy, one scrawny sun-blackened arm pointing
at the Jolly Roger flapping from the after standard. Mike and
others gave him a wave. It did feel like a homecoming now:
in water in which, in the final month or more before pulling
out, submarines in harbour between patrols had had to spend
their days lying on the bottom in fifty or sixty feet of water,
surfacing at dusk to resume necessary maintenance work and
other preparations for patrol.

Lazaretto in clear sight to starboard, finally. Two U-class
lying between buoys, with floating brows connecting them
to shore, and what was known as the wardroom berth, right
alongside the old building, vacant, reserved for the new arrival.
Mike said, 'Group down, slow both', and while McLeod was
passing that order down told CPO Swathely, who was about
shoulder-height to him, 'Put her alongside, Cox'n. And stand
by to pipe.'

'Aye, sir . . .'

Swathely with a look of satisfaction on his well-weathered
features: bosun's call ready in his palm, ready to sound the
'Still' and bring all hands to attention in salute to the boss,
old Shrimp.

2

Shrimp shook his hand. 'Nice work, Michael. And good to be back where we belong, eh?'

'Is indeed, sir. Good to see you too.' Mike in khaki, Shrimp in white shirt and shorts and the four stripes of a captain on his shoulder-boards. Not all that tall – hence the nickname – but stocky, solid, with a broad face and strong jaw: a fighter's face, although the truth was that he was a kind man, thoughtful and easy-going, as well as highly resilient and innovative in his approach to the problems of command in exceptionally haphazard circumstances. Tailor-made for the job, in fact. They were old friends, Mike having served under him in the Harwich flotilla in 1940, Mike then with his first command, one of the old H-class, on anti-invasion patrol on the Dutch coast mainly, and Shrimp with only three stripes but commanding *that* flotilla – which like this one had been scrambled together in a hurry and with few facilities beyond those of Shrimp's own devising. Anyway – *had* known each other quite a while: and meeting now on the arcade on the Lazaretto waterfront, outside the wardroom, *Ursa* secured alongside right there on the harbour side of the low, yellowish limestone wall and series of arches; Shrimp glancing up at *Ursa*'s Jolly Roger, becalmed and drooping over her blue-painted hull in the lee of the fine old building.

Hull, casing and bridge blue-painted for camouflage when dived. Italian Cant seaplanes flying so slowly that they were almost hovering could see you seventy feet down, when there was no lop on the surface.

Shrimp commented, 'Roger getting a bit full, eh?'

'Oh – still a *little* room, sir . . .'

Gear was being brought ashore over *Ursa*'s plank – sailors' own gear, bags and hammocks, some cargo too, crates of stuff from Haifa – amongst it a few cases of gin for the wardroom mess, as well as items that were perhaps more obviously essential – medical stores, so forth. There wasn't much room to spare in a U-class submarine: in fact there wasn't *any*. Anyway McLeod and the coxswain would be supervising all that, McLeod assisted of course by young Jarvis, and with base staff on hand to show them the layout of the place as now revamped during the flotilla's absence. Mike had been greeted by the COs of *Ultra* and *Unbowed*, and others too, a whole bunch of them, as he'd come over the plank, but they'd left him to Shrimp now, of course. Those two, Jimmy Ruck and Guy Mottram, would be sailing for patrol before first light, he'd gathered in those first exchanges, and as they could only have been here a day or so it seemed likely that Shrimp would be pushing *Ursa* out fairly smartly too. Which was fine, what one was here for, but her officers and crew would meanwhile be wanting to know the form, how long a respite they'd be getting. Mike didn't even have to look round to know that McLeod, for instance, would be on the casing with an eye on him, waiting for the word – which Shrimp would come out with soon enough. Telling him meanwhile that the care and maintenance team had done bloody wonders during the flotilla's absence: 'I'll show you. Tunnelled-out new

12

sleeping quarters – and sickbay, ops room, staff office etcetera – new bathrooms right beside the mess-decks – well, blooming luxury! The cabins up there are habitable again, incidentally.'

Above this arcade, which ran the full length of the building, was a first-floor gallery – balcony – with COs' cabins leading off it, under the building's flat stone roof. Ten weeks ago, a lot of it had been open to the elements – stone blocks blown out of the roof, all the glass and timber frames out of every window, COs and everyone else sleeping – living, more or less – in rock tunnels in the limestone cliff that backed the building itself. It was a saving grace in fact that tunnelling was so easy – not only here, but all over the island. Shrimp added, about the cabins, 'As long as when the sirens go you leg it down into cover right away – no hanging around, no excuses accepted, alternative's to sleep in the tunnels as before – all right?'

'Aye, sir.'

A bit of a threat in that, too. The cavern used as officers' sleeping quarters, at the height of the blitz here, had originally been an underground oil storage tank – with oil sludge on its uneven flooring, planks put down on and in that as walkways, and the most God-awful stench. But the maintenance people would have done something about it by now, he guessed. *Must* have . . . Asking Shrimp, 'The bastards *are* still at it, then?'

'Lord, yes. Couldn't expect 'em to ignore us altogether. It's roughly like it was in January – a raid or two most days, nights too. But the RAF's coping well now, and quite a bit of it's not Luftwaffe but Regia Aeronautica.'

Italian air force. They were less like mad dogs than their German allies. Tended to stay high, and to beat it when powerfully discouraged. The island's gunners, Royal Artillery and Royal Malta Artillery, were pretty damn good by this time, despite a high rate of casualties. They were a splendid lot: a diving Stuka took a bit of standing up to. Shrimp had changed the subject: 'There's mail for you, I think. Might as well pick it up while we're here.' Leading the way into the wardroom – which was unchanged. Spacious, cavernous, darkish by virtue of the covered arcade outside it, its most striking feature was the big fireplace at its centre, with an open hearth in each of its stone chimney's four sides. But also, inside the archway entrance, on the right, the flotilla's scoreboard, a chart-sized square of board with submarines' names and/or numbers down the left-hand edge, ruled columns allowing a small rectangle for the results of each patrol, little thumbnail sketches in it of targets sunk or damaged. In some cases – far too many – the 'strip cartoons' terminated in a space blanked-off with diagonals. Making it as much a memorial as a scoreboard. Mike's eyes moving from *Ursa*'s to *Urge*'s and *Upholder*'s – both of those blanked off. By very recent hand of one of Shrimp's staff, probably; *Urge* had been lost during the general exodus, on her way to Alex, and Shrimp plus staff had flown in from Cairo only a few days ago, ahead of all returning boats.

Shrimp had turned from his own brief perusal of the board. 'Your estimate of eight thousand tons for this troop-ship – reasonably sure of that, are you?'

'Could have been nearer eight and a half, sir.' A shrug. 'I'd settle for eight, though.'

'The true figure's eight seven-fifty. Forget her name, but we have it – show you, in a minute, in the office. There was an RAF report – they'd been after her earlier in the day, a Blenheim got shot up apparently. Escort of two destroyers – right?'

Mike nodded. 'One of 'em put me deep just as the DA came on – on an eighty track, rather close inshore. I'd got one fish away, fired a second by asdic on the way down, heard one hit, and held on – didn't have room to do much

14

else, must've passed just about right under him. HE had stopped, but I knew pretty well where he was – wasn't all that much water in there though, so I turned sharpish, came up for a look and there he was, already bow down. I thought one more'd make sure of it, used number three tube and hit amidships. Well – would've been a disgrace if I hadn't, frankly.'

'The escorts meanwhile not troubling you?'

It wasn't an *idle* question: Shrimp's eyes were hard, analytical. Mike told him, 'They were both to seaward of him. If they'd had much savvy they'd have had me boxed in – couldn't have realised the last hit had been on his starboard side. Extraordinary, but – anyway they were picking up survivors, troops going over the side in droves, and maybe they didn't want to know – any charges they dropped – well, must've been hundreds still in the water. I gave it a few minutes, couldn't go deeper than forty feet, came up for another shufti and the bugger was still afloat – *just* – one destroyer practically alongside his after-part – by the look of it still getting men off as well as out of the drink – and his mate out in the deep field somewhere – transmitting, incidentally, which goes to show –'

'Not the first eleven exactly. But the near one a sitting duck meanwhile?'

'I know, sir. Would have been. But – I've explained it in my report – highly frustrating, but –'

Shrimp's eyes on his, waiting to hear why he hadn't used the last of his four torpedoes on this destroyer – in easy range, lying stopped, unmissable, and by that time its decks crowded with survivors. He – Shrimp – had strongly disapproved of another CO's decision in similar circumstances a few months ago to leave escorts to their rescue work when he'd have had a good chance of sinking at least one of them. He'd pointed out to an assembly of his COs – staff conference – 'Those destroyers – who'd do for *you* in two shakes if you gave 'em half a chance – and the pongos they're picking up – hell, tank crews, gunners, SS, whatever – Afrika Korps anyway, for God's sake!'

Mike had known he'd be called on to explain this. He said, 'The one fish I had left in a tube, sir, was a Mark IV.'

'Oh. Oh, *was* it . . .'

With Mark IVs, 1914–18 vintage, you couldn't alter the depth-setting, as you could with Mark VIIIs, once they were in the tubes. So that deep-set torpedo would have run under the shallow-draft destroyer and been wasted, pointlessly. He added to Shrimp, 'I thought of bottoming and putting a shallow-set reload in – would have taken half an hour though –'

'By which time they'd have cleared off. The transport having sunk.' A nod. 'Only reason for hanging around would have been to hunt *you*. And they could have had others join them and take over.'

'Did seem wiser to skedaddle. I was a bit nervous of the air too – in those shallows. And as you say, sir, that close to Benghazi. I've roughed out a patrol report – only in long-hand so far, but –'

'I'm sure Miss Gomez will help out.' Shrimp glanced at the sheaf of signal-pad pages in Mike's hand. Miss Gomez was Shrimp's secretary. 'In the morning. She'll have gone home by now. What about your mail?'

'Hell, yes . . .'

As if it hadn't been in his mind, at least in the back of it, from the moment he'd walked in here. Well, for *weeks*. Only exercising restraint – whether or not Shrimp would have given a damn. But delving now in *Ursa*'s pigeon-hole, shuffling the pack and dealing out his own, two air-letters and a bill from Gieves the naval tailors – instantly recognisable, they'd been sending it repeatedly over recent months. With all respect to them, they rather encouraged late payment, by having allowed it to be known that when an officer who owed them money was killed on active service his debt was automatically written off.

The air-letters were from his father, and Ann Melhuish. Hers familiar enough to him despite her having scribbled a fictional name and address as 'Sender', in that space on the back.

He poked the Gieves envelope back into the hole, folded the air-letter forms together and stuffed them in a pocket. She was taking a hell of a risk, he thought. Might not have appreciated the degree of it, if she'd written this a few weeks ago – which she might have done, it could have been lying here, courtesy of Fleet Mail, while they'd been disporting themselves in and around Haifa. He followed Shrimp out into the arcade and to the right. 'You mentioned not long ago, sir, that Charles Melhuish was joining us with a new U–class?'

'Melhuish . . .'

Giving it thought, the name as yet unfamiliar. Then getting there: 'Melhuish – yes. *Unsung*. Sailing from Gib tomorrow, as it happens. Yes, that's another.' Counting on his fingers: 'Three already out, those two on their way, three still to come from Aegean patrols – then *Tango* passing through and *Swordsman* on loan from the 8th Flotilla – and you, of course. Is Melhuish a contemporary of yours?'

'Two or three years junior to me. Roughly that. Since his Perisher he's had a training boat based on Campbeltown. Well, last I heard –'

'*Unsung*'s his first operational command, then. Good Lord, hang on . . .' Stopping, pointing at a Chief PO who'd saluted him in passing. Shrimp staring for a moment, then his face clearing.

'Dennison.'

17

'Spot on, sir.' Broad smile. 'Served with you in *Porpoise*. Killick torpedoman I was then, you put me through for PO.'

'Haven't wasted your time since, have you. Well done.' Shaking hands. 'What are you doing now?'

'TGM in *Unbowed*, sir.' The letters stood for Torpedo Gunner's Mate. 'Joined her in Haifa. Got sunk in *Medway*, then in Haifa so happened *Unbowed*'s TI got 'isself landed to hospital, so – pierhead jump!'

'Sorry for the other chap, but lucky for you and for *Unbowed*, then. You're off at cock crow, eh?'

'We are that.' Smiling again: 'Good seeing you, sir!'

'Very good to see *you*, Dennison. We'll meet again before long.' Returning the CPO's salute, then rejoining Mike. 'Small world, ours. Look here, you haven't asked what's lined up for you next, but how long d'you need?'

'Store ship, fuel and water, torpedoes – make good a few minor defects –'

'No dockyard assistance?'

'No sir, we're –'

'Twenty-four hours then?'

'Might I have thirty-six?'

'All right. Sail first thing day after tomorrow. How'd Palermo suit you?'

To which the answer might have been 'as well as anywhere else'; but Shrimp would no doubt explain presently why a patrol somewhere off Palermo on Sicily's north coast might be productive at this juncture. Mike called to McLeod, who was still on *Ursa*'s casing – in conversation now with the fourth hand, Danvers – 'Thirty-six hours, Number One. Push off at first light Wednesday.'

'*Right . . .*'

Saluting Shrimp then – since he happened to be looking at him. Shrimp returning the salute and not having to be told his name: 'How's the battle, McLeod?'

'I *think* we're winning it, sir.'

'About bloody time we did.' A jerk of the he., then: 'Come on. Ops Room.'

He'd been deep in thought on the way to it: as had Mike in his own case, thinking about Ann and the letter in his pocket, and her husband Charles who if he was leaving Gib tomorrow should be here in five or six days. Question being – at least, the immediate one – whether she'd be crazy enough to go on writing: how boring it would be if she stopped and how dangerous if she didn't. Passing meanwhile through the barracks end of the old building – in which, when it had been Malta's quarantine station, the poet Shelley had been incarcerated at one time and had gone so far as to carve his name and a couple of lines of doggerel in the soft stone up there – through to the tunnelled-out bomb-proof quarters and new Ops Room.

'So here we are.' Shrimp offered him a cigarette, and they both lit up. 'What d'you think of it?'

'Well – in just ten weeks –'

'Deserve medals, all of 'em.' Swapping one chart for another on the table-top, and reaching for dividers to use as a pointer. 'Several factors relevant now. One – not immediate but by a long chalk the most important, convoy operation from the west, code-name "Pedestal". Not immediate, ships are only now assembling in the Clyde, but it's going to be an all-out effort – escort from Gib eastward to include two battleships – *Nelson* and *Rodney* – and no less than three aircraft carriers. Unprecedented – simple reason being that if the siege isn't lifted, Malta starves. This flotilla's contribution will be eight or possibly even ten boats. And meanwhile – week, ten days, fortnight even – might as well use the time, eh, let the buggers know we're back?'

Mike nodded. 'Right.'

'Palermo, now.' He'd swung a lamp over the chart, and switched it on: the overhead light wasn't all that brilliant. Continuing: 'I'd say it's not unlikely the Wops'll be expecting a convoy operation now. One's very much overdue, last attempt failed miserably, and they aren't stupid, must know we're not far off starvation – so we might reasonably expect fleet movements, deployments in advance. I'd guess particularly of cruisers, and in this bailiwick as likely as anywhere to Palermo – Cagliari, for that matter, but –'

Glancing round – Mike too – as a door was opened and Hugo Short, Spare CO – he'd been on the arcade steps earlier to see *Ursa* slide in and tie up – told Shrimp, 'Those orders are ready for your signature, sir. Want them now, or –'

'On my desk, I'll sign 'em when we finish here.'

'Sir.' Gone, door shut. Spare COs were there to stand in for other COs when they needed a break, were sick or otherwise indisposed; and between such outings worked as staff, Shrimp's back-up. Shrimp back to Mike's briefing, however: 'So – *might* find a cruiser or two coming your way. And of course their convoys to the desert are still running – Tripoli, Homs, Misurata, as well as Benghazi, I'm deploying boats accordingly. Here, see for yourself.'

Off Crotone, he saw, and Cape dell'Armi. Those were to be Mottram's and Ruck's billets: Ruck watching the Messina Strait, Mottram with a longer haul in front of him, to Crotone and the route south from Taranto. Other boats already on patrol were disposed between Pantellaria, Lampedusa and Tripoli – from where they'd be readily enough redeployable to other convoy-covering positions south of Pantellaria and west of Marettimo. Distances – well, with the U-class boat's regrettably low surface speed of ten knots flat out a good night's progress – *if* uninterrupted – was something like seventy nautical miles.

Feeble enough. But Shrimp would have adequate notice

20

of the need to redeploy. And might leave those two where they were, he guessed. Especially if he had as many as ten boats at his disposal by that time.

Touching the Menorca to Malta chart with his dividers. 'I'm putting you twenty miles northeast of Cape San Vito, Michael. Prime position for anything coming down from Naples either for Palermo or to pass west of Marettimo. You could move in closer to Palermo if you had reason to; alternatively, withdraw north or northeastward, vicinity of Ustica. But stay to the west of Alicudi – otherwise you could fall foul of *Swordsman* – Dan Gerahty, d'you know him?'

'Lord, yes.'

'He's between Lipari and Cape Vaticano – northern approaches to Messina, of course.'

Swordsman, S-class – on loan from the 8th Flotilla in Gibraltar, Mike guessed. Gib flotilla temporarily expanding eastward during the 10th's absence, no doubt: and when she left her billet, might well be passing through or close to *his*. A point to check on, before departure. Nodding, mentally crossing fingers. Shrimp hadn't of course needed to mention that to get round to Sicily's north coast in the first place *Ursa*'s track would be through – or rather under – the QBB 255 minefield. There was no great problem about that, nothing in the least unusual; the established routine was that you dived to 150 feet off Cape San Marco and paddled northwestward on course 300 for fifty-five miles under the bloody mines before turning up around the island of Marettimo. Alternatively – shortcut to where *he* was going – inside it, through the channel between those islands.

Do that, he thought. Get on the billet sooner. He nodded again. 'Clear enough, sir.'

'We'll give it to you on paper in the morning. And – fuel, stores, water-barge and Msida, all of that by noon – right?'

'Yes.' Msida Creek had the torpedo depot at its head. *Ursa* would be embarking three, to replace the three she'd fired. Mark VIIIs, he hoped – but that would be up to 'Wiggy' Bennett, the base torpedo officer, and his right-hand man, Commissioned Gunner 'Sunny' Warne. Lick their boots, if that would help. Well, it wouldn't . . . Anyway, getting it all done by midday would be aimed at giving most of the lads the rest of the day to themselves, preferably for fresh air and exercise.

'See you for a gin later, sir?'

'My dear fellow, *that's* a novel idea . . .'

Visit the boat first, see McLeod had it all in hand and that Danvers had Sicily north-coast charts corrected up to date. Have a word with Chief McIver too. *Then* see to one's own gear, have a bath – first for twelve days – and read those letters.

In fact he'd decided, having attended to those and a few other priorities, to read his letters first. The Old Man's to start with. You could bet he'd have had news of Alan, Mike's younger brother who was flying Lancasters out of a field in Norfolk. When their father heard from either of them he invariably wrote to the other, passing on – well, effectively, implicitly, just reassurance. *Vital* reassurance. The Old Man having retired in 1938 was back in harness as a GP in the practice in Stony Stratford, Bucks, replacing two younger men now in the Army. He'd been an army doctor himself in 1914–18. Home was near Deanshanger, a village not far from Stony Stratford, and until quite recently he'd hunted with the Grafton. Which Mike had also done, when he'd had the chance.

'Bloomin' 'ell, the man hisself!'

Jimmy Ruck – and Mottram – at their ease in armchairs on the gallery, smoke from their cigarettes hanging blueish in the soft lighting that would be instantly extinguished if /

when the air-attack sirens started up. Elsewhere it was as good as dark now, moon no more than a sliver, vestige of the old one, and at that not far off setting; moonless nights in prospect therefore. Lights' reflections danced on the water where brows – floating walkways – led from shore to the submarines secured between their buoys – shadows with a glitter at their waterlines, yellow radiance spilling from open fore-hatches from which the sound of radio music emerged and where sentries lounged. Here, Guy Mottram on his feet with a hand extended – a big man, burly and affable with a prematurely receding hairline and prominent, beaky nose – 'Whopping great trooper you knocked down, Mike?'

'Fair-sized. Eight seven-fifty, according to Shrimp.' Shrimp had given him the ship's name – which *he*'d forgotten now. Asking them, 'Either of you get lucky?'

'Not me. Blank one.' Despondent tone and gesture from Jimmy Ruck. A blank patrol was one from which you came back without scoring. Mike asked him, 'How long since your last blank?'

'Well. A while, I suppose, but –' Another shrug, shake of the head: meaning *quite* a while. He was slightly senior to Mike, had been out here longer, and currently the flotilla's top scorer. He was said to have exceptionally fast reflexes, and tended not to miss. About half Mottram's size: compact, quick on his feet, impressive on a squash court. Mottram put in, as Mike glanced at him queryingly, 'Convoy of caiques in the Kithira Channel – gun action. No big deal, but they did have Germans in 'em. Bloody cheek, loosed off at us with Schmeissers. Next thing you know, they'll be chucking spuds. How about a gin, Mike?'

'Love one, but (a) priority's a bath, and (b) I told Shrimp I'd have a gin with him later. So if you're thirsty –'

'Guess who was asking tenderly after you last night?'

23

Ruck had asked him this. Mike asked *him*, after a moment's hesitation, 'Where were you, last night?'

'Gravy's.'

'Ah.' Sunday night, of course – this being Monday. He made his guess: 'Greta, perhaps?'

'She may have enquired as well, come to think of it – but come on now, who else springs to mind?'

'Well, just off the cuff – and not having seen all that much soap and water for damn near a fortnight, prospect of a hot tub occluding probably *most* other things in one's mind –'

'How about Abigail French?'

'Oh. *She* there, was she?'

'Certainly was. Came with her friend Nico, as always, but also bringing the new man who's taking over from him. Introducing him to the Gravies I suppose. Fat guy, younger than Cornish. She looked her usual cheerful self, but it must be a bit of a blow to her, wouldn't you suppose?'

'She'll miss him, obviously. Birds of a feather, those two, in a lot of ways. Yeah, poor Abbie.'

'Hah.' Ruck to Mottram: 'Ever see a man struggling to contain excitement?'

'Jimmy – I don't know what's given rise to this, but I can assure you I'm not deeply concerned, let alone *excited* . . . Why would I be? Mere fact of being acquainted with her – with *them*, if you like –'

'Well, I'd had a bit of an impression – OK, mistaken, if you say so –'

'So let's drop it.' Mottram the calming influence. 'Heck of a nice girl anyway. And incidentally the fact she and that Nico character were frequently to be seen together – at the Tenches', anyway . . .'

The Tenches – Wingrave Tench, hence the nickname 'Gravy' – had a large house at St Julian's a couple of miles up-coast from Sliema, were close friends of Shrimp's and kept open house for 10th Flotilla COs as well as others of the British community. Gravy was a retired businessman whom the Governor had appointed as a civil administrator overseeing all civilian food distribution – rationing, food supply in general – including soup-kitchens in all the island's villages, which had been his own brainchild and he still administered.

While Nico Cornish was – or had been – the island's Chief Information Officer. Pleasant fellow, and by all accounts extremely capable, not actually a soldier but carrying the rank of major, and according to local gossip Abigail French's lover. Abigail being unquestionably a dish; also, in Mike's view, based on no more than perhaps six or eight social encounters over the past eighteen months or so, extremely likeable.

Mottram was saying, 'I can confirm anyway, Mike, that she'd for some time been wanting to know when you'd be back – but also, getting what's left of a memory to it, that the enquiry was not unconnected with some party she'd been thinking of giving. *Not* therefore – at least not directly – with the imminent departure of Major Cornish.'

'So *that* threat's removed, you can breathe again.' Ruck chuckling at his own wit; and Mike on his way, excusing himself with 'Tub now. Mail to read, moreover. May see you later, otherwise good luck.' To Ruck then, on a second thought: 'This one likely to be your last, Jimmy?'

'Not quite. Last but one, in Shrimp's intention. Incidentally, neither I nor Guy will be burning much midnight oil tonight, Mike.'

'No. Very wise.' Seeing that they were both off at first light, respectively for Cape dell'Armi and Crotone. And *Ursa* to Palermo only a day or so behind them: Shrimp with his beloved flotilla reassembled, wasting no time at all, getting them all out there where they could do most good.

★   ★   ★

Mike's father had written that he was in good health: still getting around mostly by bicycle, which helped to keep him fit. Sure enough, he'd heard only the day before from Alan, who'd said he was about due for leave and promised to spend some of it at Deanshanger, and mentioned that he'd been busy lately – a euphemism for having been over Germany quite a lot. Poor old Mrs Hennings, who'd been cook/housekeeper since Mike's mother had died a dozen years ago, and cook before that, was suffering acutely from her arthritis, and was going to have to pack it in altogether pretty soon. And so forth; with a smattering of second-hand news of old friends' sons and daughters in their various locations and occupations – including one in the RAF who'd been reported missing, believed killed. *That rather cocky youth, remember? Used to pursue Chloe, and she couldn't stand him?* Chloe being Mike's and Alan's sister – now in London, in training as an orthopaedic nurse. Over to page three of the Old Man's letter now: news from the desert wasn't encouraging, was it? Auchinleck was going to have to pull his socks up, or we'd be in serious trouble, by the sound of it. And finally, *Look after yourself, old lad. May be a silly injunction to deliver, but you know what I mean . . .*

Ann's now. Allegedly 'Agnes Nicholson's'. She'd started calling herself that a few months ago, and suggested that if anyone enquired he should tell them she was his Aunt Aggie.

Hello, you!

Yes, chancing my arm while I can still hope to get away with it. Just have this irresistible urge to communicate with you. A more desperate one than that too, but unfortunately at this distance, however many hundreds of miles it is, I can only shut my eyes and think about it, relive our loveliest episodes while driving General Bloggs from A to B – as often as not having to stave off his paltry advances.

(She was in the MTC, Mechanised Transport Corps, spent most of her time driving brass hats around in khaki-painted Humbers.)

Perhaps this should be my last letter, Mike darling? His nibs being on his way within just weeks now? Isn't it an absolute sod? I suppose we have about a month or eight weeks before he can possibly be with you – wherever it is you are now, you rather implied some move being on the cards, in your last missive – although I may have got the wrong end of the stick and it's more or less illegible by now, after approx a thousand readings – but anyway he has not yet set forth, and I've gathered from him that those strange contrivances of yours are not all that speedy – right? But if I've over-estimated the margin of safety, can only trust to your innate sagacity and initiative, that you'll have moved like lightning to scoop this up and dash off to the lav with it. But Mike darling, listen – mightn't there be a great blazing light at the end of the tunnel very soon now? D'you think? Hang on a mo' with that, though – a minor point is that there's no reason you shouldn't write to me at least twice a week now, is there? I mean no one's looking over my shoulder. Will you, my darling – please? – and not be too damn stingy in what you say? You always are a bit careful, aren't you – which is a contradiction, considering that in other ways you're something of a desperado. Oh, maybe you have a censor to get by? Hadn't thought of that, until this moment: but I can see it might be tricky. And of course – seriously, I'm not an idiot – that at your end it would be difficult, in your circumstances and his – obviously could make for problems, if I did write – too often, anyway. But what I began to say about light at end of tunnel – ages ago you said you thought you'd be gone about a year, and Charles said maybe a year and a bit – 18 months max, could be? – so my dream now is of the doorbell ringing and it's you, suddenly blown in! You in person, here, large as life! Isn't it a dream that actually must come true? Only calling it a dream here because the actuality would be – will

27

be? – so absolutely blissful one hardly dares *believe in it – but write and tell me I can?*

Please? By return of post, my darling? I ache for you – literally, you know? There's more to this, though, and I've got to say it – simply that I also want you home because the longer you're out there the greater the chance you might not ever make it home. Horrible, unnerving truth, and you'd pooh-pooh it, but I most certainly don't and never have, and Charles told me when he was on his course that they'd heard the losses where you are were averaging out at about 50%, in other words every time you go out it's even-stevens whether you'll return or won't. And now we know he's likely to end up in the same part of the world – or at least I think we do – so then for you and me, the very best of both worlds?

Darling, please come home?

Folding it up small, crumpling it in his fist. Wondering what kind of censor let that 50 per cent stuff through. Figure near enough correct, but wrong message to be putting out. Charles again? It had been a total and most unwelcome surprise that following his Perisher course, and as usual a spell commanding a training boat, they were giving him a new 'U' and almost certainly sending him to join this flotilla; there were plenty of other places he could have gone, and surely more S-class being built than 'U's. But there it was – fact, apparently – and on top of that the virtual certainty that he, Mike, would pretty soon be sent home with *Ursa*, he and his crew and the boat having done their time here in the heat of it. *Almost* done their time: he hadn't done quite as many patrols as Jimmy Ruck, a couple of months' worth, maybe – but then – well, looking ahead, sharing that dream-scenario of hers, her answering his knock on her door etcetera – visualising her in close-up – fantastic eyes, irresistible mouth, cloud of marvellously soft, dark hair, enough of it virtually to cloak her lithe dancer's body – catching his breath at the thought and memory – the obsession that had possessed both of them right from the start resurgent now, having been as it were in abeyance for a while, hiatus following those final months in England and Scotland when they'd taken it as read that the affair would end with his own and *Ursa*'s departure for the Med; mutually accepting this as inevitable – which it had been, of course, neither of them speaking of it much, even – in his own thinking, incredibly, an element of Happy Ending – no tears, no blame, 'thanks for the memory', all that.

Shrimp announced, joining a crowd of them in the ward-room, 'Good news, chaps. Afrika Korps knocked back on its heels. Despatch received only an hour ago – I'm just back from Lascaris. Seems Rommel was probing Eighth Army defences on the frontier and got more than he'd bargained for. And as we're all well aware, his lines of communication are stretched very long and thin now.' Shrimp glanced around the big stone cavern, now probably better populated than it could have been for the last couple of months, with the offi-cers of the three submarines currently in harbour as well as this group of COs and flotilla staff. He added, 'In our court now, therefore. Good a time as any to starve *him* – especially of petrol, immobilise his bloody Panzers . . .'

'Here's to it.' Sam MacGregor, engineer commander, who since late 1940 when the flotilla had first moved in here had worked hand-in-glove with Shrimp, performing his own technical miracles in the most difficult of circumstances. Raising his glass as Shrimp took his own from a Maltese steward's tray. Shrimp certainly didn't spare himself: his visit to the Combined Services HQ in Valetta, since briefing Mike, would have meant crossing by *dghaisa* to Ferry Steps, climbing stone stairs to Palace Square, thence making his way virtu-ally the length of the bomb–blasted Strada Reale with the

29

stone wreckage of what had been the opera house at the end of it. Must have done it there and back at a trot if not a canter – *and* since then cleaned up and changed into Red Sea rig as he was now – despite, incidentally, there having been an air alert when Mike had still been in his bath – luxuriating in it, thinking mostly about Ann – all that – while knowing he *should* move, get down to the shelter.

There'd been no bombs, anyway. The RAF had no doubt chased the intruders off, the all-clear sounding while he'd been getting dressed. Italians probably, their approach picked up on the island's new top-secret long-range radar, and Spitfires intercepting. Things certainly had changed enormously for the better; as just minutes ago Mottram had remarked – 'Amazing. Leave rack and ruin and bloody chaos, and come back to *this*!'

'Could start up again, mind you.'

'I'd say they've missed the bus. Should have invaded when they had us on our knees.'

'When was that?'

A shrug, and the Robert Morley smile: 'You know what I mean. When we thought they were going to invade at any bloody minute?'

Twelve or thirteen months ago, the time of *Ursa*'s arrival – a month or five weeks in which the flotilla had lost P.32, P.33, and *Union* – and the supply-runner *Cachalot* – at that time an intercepted report from the German naval staff in Rome had warned Berlin: *The most dangerous British weapon in the Mediterranean is the submarine, especially those operating from Malta . . . A very severe supply crisis must occur relatively soon.* And there'd been an Intelligence leak soon after to the effect that the Führer had finally been persuaded by Grossadmiral Raeder to let him press ahead with an invasion plan – Operation 'Hercules' – and in the run-up to it have Kesselring move his Fliegerkorps II into Sicily in order to obliterate the island. That was when things had begun to get quite bad. Methodical twenty-four-hours-a-day smashing-up of the island, virtual elimination of the airfields and aircraft, wrecking of this base and dockyard, submarines between patrols having to spend daylight hours on the bottom of the outer harbour while the bastards probed for them.

Mottram had added, 'Weathered all that anyway, so —'

'Do so again if necessary.'

'Not if the population's actually starving.'

'Been at the point of it more than once, old man, haven't they. Not all that far off it right now, for that matter.' A shrug. 'OK just for the moment, but — hell . . .' He quoted Mona Lott of the *ITMA* radio comedy series, a whine of 'It's being so cheerful keeps us going, huh?' Mike meanwhile had spotted Wiggy Bennett; he excused himself and went over to him: 'How are you doing, Wiggy?'

'Why, Mike, hello!' To Hubert Marsham then — Commander, Shrimp's deputy — shouting, 'Another old lag back inside!'

'Wiggy — what are my chances of getting Mark VIIIs in the morning?'

'How many?'

'Three. Better still, four — then I'd land one Mark IV, straight swap. That'd give me four Mark VIIIs in the tubes, Mark IVs as reloads. Better still, of course —' holding up crossed fingers — 'if you possibly could manage it —'

'Up to old Sunny, Mike. I'm currently a bit out of touch in that area, tell you the truth it's entirely his pigeon. We do know *Tango*'s bringing us half a dozen Mark VIIIs — but Sunny's ashore tonight, and —'

'I'll get on to him first thing.'

Shrimp had mentioned that *Tango* (one of the T-class, of course, the largest submarines building in Britain at this time, twice the size of the little 'U's) would be passing through

31

shortly on her way east from Gibraltar to the Levant. The 1st Flotilla, formerly based at Alexandria and now working out of Beirut, was composed entirely of 'T's, who on their way from Gib routinely dropped off vitally needed cargoes here in Malta. Aviation spirit in their ballast tanks, for instance. If this one was bringing some Mark VIIIs – and neither *Ultra* nor *Unbowed* embarking torpedoes, not having expended any on their way here – maybe Sunny Warne *might* feel he could be generous. Bennett was explaining his own detachment from the subject as the fact that for several days he'd been preoccupied with efforts to get torpedoes out of *Pandora*, in French Creek in the dockyard. She'd been sunk alongside Hamilton Wharf by dive-bombers at the beginning of April, taking two officers and twenty-three of her crew to the creek's bottom with her, as well as the torpedoes in her eight tubes, if not the reloads in the racks. Parthian-class, completed in 1930, she was one of the large, cargo-carrying boats that had made the Magic Carpet supply run regularly; they might have used the space in her reload racks for other stuff, but otherwise it'd be a *real* bonanza, if all those fish could be got out of her. Bennett was saying what a tricky job it was to extricate them, warheads and all, from that heavy tangle of steel several fathoms down. Lacking more suitable diving gear, for instance, his artificers were using DSEA equipment – Davis Submarine Escape Apparatus – which allowed for only very limited periods actually on the job.

Mike moved on presently to where Jamie McLeod and young Danvers were in conversation with some of Ruck's and Mottram's officers.

'A word, Number One.'

A grin, as he joined him. 'Sounds ominous, sir.'

'Torpedoes in the morning. I want all Mark VIIIs, if we can get 'em, and it'll be up to Sunny Warne, who's ashore tonight. We'll be embarking three fish anyway, we've two

VIIIs and two IVs in the tubes at the moment, so if they only give us three VIIIs we'll load two of them in place of the IVs and settle for a mixed set of reloads. But I'll get on to Sunny first thing and try to improve on that. There'll be some reshuffling anyway, so warn Jarvis and the TI, huh?'

'Only thing is, we'd planned to start storing ship at 0800.'

'Msida Creek first. We'll leave the cox'n and a few hands here, they can have the stores ready for loading as soon as we're back alongside. Water-barge alongside while we're storing, then, and oil-fuel say mid-forenoon.'

McLeod shrugged philosophically. 'Dare say we'll cope, sir.'

'I'm sure you will, Jamie.'

Although it wouldn't be exactly like falling off a log. The fore-hatch was the only entry point for both torpedoes and stores, and the TSC, or fore ends, the compartment right under that hatch, would as always have crates and sacks of provender packed in around the reload torpedoes in their racks as well as filling every other cubic foot of space. That compartment was also where about a third of the ship's company lived, ate and slept. And moving torpedoes that weighed two tons apiece between the tubes and the reload racks wasn't either a quick or an easy job; the compartment had to be cleared of all loose gear and internally re-rigged with various special equipment before you could even start.

McLeod tossed his gin back, shook his head. 'Gawd 'elp us.'

Mike patted his shoulder. 'Nice rest at sea soon, uh?'

3

Ursa was sailing for patrol not at first light Wednesday but at midnight Tuesday – tonight, in about an hour's time. Shrimp had come up with this revised plan at midday, when Mike had been able to report her as ready for sea – torpedoes and stores embarked, oil-fuel and fresh-water tanks filled, CERA McIver's maintenance jobs either completed or satisfactorily in hand. Shrimp had remarked – on their way down to the deep shelter, as it happened, there'd been an air-raid and some bombs had fallen on Senglea – 'Your chaps have done well, Michael.'

'They're as good as any, sir.'

'Your first lieutenant about due for his COQC, you mentioned recently.'

'Coming up for it, yes. But as you pointed out, sir, as we're likely to be sent home before *very* much longer –'

'That's certainly on the cards. Yes . . . Home with a strong recommendation – which I'll gladly provide . . .'

COQC meant Commanding Officers' Qualifying Course – also known as the Perisher, periscope course. McLeod might be a little young for command as yet, but with the rate at which new submarines were being built, Flag Officer Submarines was concerned to find COs for them. He – Max Horton – having commanded one himself in 1914–18 and knowing very well the kind of men he needed. But then again, good first lieutenants didn't exactly grow on trees, and a ship's company like *Ursa*'s deserved the best officers you could give them. Added to which, Mike didn't much want to have to break a new man in: McLeod *was* good at his job, and he was used to him.

Anyway – advantages of this midnight departure were (a) *Ursa* would be on her billet that much sooner, and (b) two other 'U's were due in from Haifa and Aegean patrols at or soon after first light, and you'd be out of their way – making sure of it incidentally by turning sharp left out of the swept channel and heading northwest up the north coasts of Malta and Gozo, on a track which he'd been assured was being mine-swept *now*, at – checking the time – 2310 . . .

'One thing I had in mind to check on, sir – if *Swordsman*'s already on her billet north of Messina, odds are she'll be leaving the area before I do?'

'When the time comes, she'll be routed from the vicinity of Stromboli on a track north of Ustica. If you've had to withdraw northwards prior to that, don't worry, we'll keep you well apart. She's on loan to this flotilla, incidentally – be coming back here, not to Gib.' A gesture towards the chart: 'Your route now, Michael – thought about it?'

He nodded, having checked it over this forenoon during the loading of torpedoes. Several factors were involved: battery and air endurance, the need to get through that large minefield submerged, also to be dived throughout daylight hours – mainly not to be spotted by aircraft or become a target for some patrolling U-boat. He outlined his intentions: 'Reckoning to spend tomorrow dived 0430 to 2100, leaves us seven hours on the surface getting the box right up' – 'box' meaning battery – 'diving 0430 Thursday for passage of the minefield. Which I thought I'd curtail slightly by cutting up thisaway.'

A pencil-point on the channel through the Engadi islands, inside Marettimo. Adding then, since Shrimp wasn't showing any great enthusiasm, 'Out of QBB a bit sooner, and saving a few hours overall.'

'H'm.' Slight frown: and fingering his gingery-stubbled jaw. It had been an early start to the day, seeing off *Unbowed* and *Ultra* in the dawn. Wide-apart grey eyes on Mike's, now: 'Why not hold on past Marettimo? All right, by the time you're out of the mines the sun'll still be up, keeping you *down* – thinnish air and a low battery, obviously – but no lasting harm in that, eh?'

'Only thought to avoid the worst of it *and* get on the beat quicker, sir.'

'Could be making worse problems for yourself, though. In fact I'd advise you to stay well clear of those narrows. I know boats have slipped through there on occasion, but the buggers could mine them at the drop of a hat, couldn't they? E-boats out of Trapani here for instance. If they know we're back on the job and guess there has to be a convoy oper- ation soon, I've a hunch it's what they *might* do.'

You could see he meant it, *felt* it.

'All right, sir. I'll hold on past Marettimo, stay down until – well, nine-thirty, I suppose. Jesus. Well – for the battery's sake, I might make the QBB passage at two and a half or three knots instead of four – have a *little* more juice in hand.'

'That'd make sense. Don't let anything change your mind now, stay out of that channel. I've a feeling in my water about it.'

Mike looked awed. 'Certainly respect *that*, sir.'

'Bloody well hope so.' Sitting back from the chart, fumbling for a cigarette, 'We'll count on your being off Cape San Vito first light Friday – right?'

Charles Melhuish, moreover, would be here with *Unsung* by about the end of the week. Having about a thousand miles to cover from Gibraltar, and Shrimp had said he'd been due to sail today, Tuesday.

Hadn't answered Ann's letter. Not yet. *Had* written to his father – which would cover Alan, also Chloe. If fathers, brothers and little sisters didn't hear either from or of you, they worried.

He'd more or less packed his belongings away in the two green suitcases, and completed that job now, so they could be stowed out of the way of whoever used this cabin next – CO of one of the boats due in tomorrow maybe, but there'd be numerous other arrivals and departures in the course of the next week or fortnight, anyway. His seagoing gear went into an old rucksack he'd always used for this. Spare shorts and shirt, sweater, plimsolls, towel, shaving gear. Two books – Scott Fitzgerald's *The Last Tycoon*, which an aunt by name of Jennie – his late mother's sister – had sent him for his last birthday. She lived in America, invariably sent books both to him and Alan and was a fan in particular of Fitzgerald's. So – *The Last Tycoon*, for starters, and another American but published in England – John Steinbeck, *The Moon is Down* – which he'd borrowed from Hugo Short.

Write to Ann during the course of the patrol, he thought. Have it ready to bung into the post on return.

Eleven-forty now. He went on down to the boat. There was a berthing party of four men standing by to divest her of her ropes and wires, and at Mike's appearance someone in or close to the fore-hatch called, 'Captain coming aboard, sir!' Jarvis, third hand, emerged then, followed by McLeod;

Mike by this time halfway across the narrow, swaying plank, returning those two's salutes.

'Ready for sea, sir. All hands on board.' That from McLeod; Jarvis asked him, 'Single up, sir?'

'Yes please. We can do without the forespring.' He ducked into the hatch, swung himself down into the fore ends, the crowd and fug of it: torpedoes in the racks both sides, their bright-blue shellac paint almost dazzling where it wasn't hidden by mounds of gear around them. Men were still stowing gear, finding room for things there wasn't room for. When those hammocks were slung, you'd only get through this compartment on your hands and knees.

'Evening, sir.'

'Evening to *you*, TI.'

Coltart – Chief Petty Officer and actually Torpedo Gunner's Mate, TGM, but invariably referred to on board as the TI, which was the older term for it, the letters standing for Torpedo Instructor. Straightening, having come through the oval of the watertight door in the after bulkhead below this ladder: he was tallish – about Mike's own height and build – had boxed for the Portsmouth Division at one time. Mike asked him – knowing the answer but still asking, 'Routines done, I suppose?'

'All done, sir. Mark IVs an' all, but oughter run straight.' Touching wood, Mike agreeing that that was the main thing, and adding, 'Come to think of it, I've never known one of yours that didn't.'

It would have taken Coltart all afternoon and evening, carrying out maintenance routines on the fish they'd had on board to start with. He'd have had one or two of his torpedomen assisting him, but his own were the expert hands. The Mark VIIIs they'd embarked this morning would have been attended to ashore, and were now in *Ursa*'s tubes. Sunny Warne hadn't been all *that* generous with his fish, but at least had gone that far, you were no worse off than you had been when leaving Haifa. Mike heading aft now with McLeod on his heels, along the passageway down the boat's starboard side, passing on his right, port side, the POs' and Leading Seamen's mess, ERAs' mess, then the even narrower slot of the galley – in which AB Cottenham, loader in the gun's crew, also ship's cook – unqualified but not bad at it, considering the problems – paused in clattering his pots and pans around.

'Evening, sir . . .'

'All set, are we? Big eats?'

'Well – make do, I reckon –'

'Darned sure you will.' Moving on. A smallish but important element in submariners' rations came from the farm which Shrimp had set up on Manoel Island early in '41, using his own money to buy two pregnant Middle White sows and basic equipment such as troughs and the materials for building pens. At one time there'd been as many as seventy porkers on the flotilla's strength; nothing like that now, the blitz having taken its toll, but there was a lot of pork in cold storage and the farm had diversified into rabbits, poultry and at times fresh vegetables, all such produce being free of charge to the base and to submarines.

Wardroom, now: having exchanged brief greetings while squeezing past a few other individuals. The passage wasn't wide enough for two men simply to pass each other without manoeuvring. Wardroom now, anyway – about seven feet square, when you drew the curtain that screened it from the gangway. Square wooden table in the middle, settee berths around it, Mike's being the one on the for'ard bulkhead, with drawers and lockers fitted in below it and wherever possible, no inch of usable space being wasted. He slung his rucksack on to his bunk and went on through, past the chart table into the control room, where young Danvers was taking the wooden cover off what was called the 'Fruit Machine' – looked something like a one-armed bandit, was actually a calculating machine for the aiming and firing of torpedoes. Mike had a word with Danvers about their route to Cape San Marco, then moved on aft – passing the oily-shining pillars of the two periscopes on the centre-line, hydroplane controls and depth-gauges port side, diving and blowing panel starboard; at the compartment's after end he paused to look into the W/T office, chat for a moment with Lazenby the Petty Officer Telegraphist – grey-headed, former schoolmaster, married with three school-age children. All of them doing well, apparently, although Plymouth had come in for rather too much of the Luftwaffe's attention in recent months.

One knew about that. Including the fact they'd bombed the famous distillery, allegedly sending the best gin in the world running through the town's gutters and giving rise to jokes about Hun atrocities. But London had been getting it too, of course – as both Ann and Chloe had mentioned in letters.

He didn't go any further aft – eight minutes to the hour now, no point getting into conversations there wasn't time to finish. Looking aft from that latched-back bulkhead door though, past ERA Coldwell and Stoker PO Franklyn chatting there in the engine-room, the big Paxman diesels' glittering steel port and starboard, narrow steel walkway between them; motor room then with its rank of shoulder-high copper switches. PO Hector Bull and two of his LTOs there, smoking while waiting for the 'off' – and beyond *them* another watertight door giving access to the boat's narrowing aftermost compartment – known as the after ends – where stokers lived amongst a variety of auxiliary machinery.

Home, one might call it. Length just under 200 feet, beam 11 feet, displacement surfaced 600 tons, dived 800. Completed in the Royal Docks at Chatham about twenty months ago.

A brightly-lit, overcrowded, iron and steel tube, most of its interior surfaces finished in gleaming white enamel, polished brass hand-wheels here and there on the maze of piping; and in the control room and living spaces a deck-covering of brown corticene that was regularly buffed-up with shale oil. Shale was the fuel on which torpedoes ran; the boat reeked of it and so did her crew. All submariners smelled of shale.

In the control room, he checked battery readings – voltage, and density of the electrolyte – as recorded in chalk on a blackboard on the curve of deckhead. The submarine's huge battery – two sections of it, under this deck, each consisting of fifty-six four-foot-high cells weighing a quarter of a ton apiece, each section contained in its own tank – and electrics generally were another responsibility of McLeod's, as supervisor of electricians known as LTOs – PO Bull and his boys back aft there, denizens of the motor room. McLeod and CERA McIver had had *Ursa*'s diesel generators pounding away all afternoon and early evening, and the figures on the blackboard reflected this – readings well up, as they needed to be.

He checked the time. 'All right. Harbour stations.'

A quiet departure – few spectators, and certainly no brass bands; only Shrimp and a few others watching from the Lazaretto balcony while below them in the arcade the berthing party dragged the plank ashore and stood by to haul in the rope breasts when they were cast off. The only wire still in place being the back spring, running tautly from the boat's knife-edge bow to a point on shore level with her stern. Mike would turn her on it, the steel-wire rope restraining her from forward movement while a thrust ahead on the outer screw sent her stern swinging out into the stream. Coxswain Swathely at the bridge wheel, McLeod, Danvers and Signalman Walburton also up there with Mike, Jarvis on the casing with PO Tubby Hart and his henchmen. Shrimp had called, 'Good luck, *Ursa*!'; Mike thanked him, said to McLeod, 'Let go the spring' and to Danvers at the voice-pipe, 'Stop port, slow astern together.' On the fore casing, on McLeod's order they were taking that wire's turns off the bollard, to let it splash away. On war patrols you didn't take berthing wires to sea with you; even tightly coiled and lashed inside the casing they could be blasted loose by depth-charging, and loose wires had a tendency to wrap themselves around propellers and propeller shafts, which was – well, best avoided. Anyway, the berthing party ashore were hauling it in and *Ursa's* screws were imparting stern-way to her, a flood of black water washing for'ard along her slim, blue sides; Mike told Swathely, 'Port ten, Cox'n', and Danvers as she swung faster, turning near enough in her own length, 'Stop port.' The motors at this stage were 'grouped down', which meant the two batteries connected in series, as distinct from in parallel which provided more power but used the amps up faster. She was clear of the mooring buoys and the floating brow now, and pointing seaward: Mike told Swathely, 'Midships the wheel', and stooped to the voice-pipe: 'Group up, half ahead, start engines.'

Ursa on her way. Her seventeenth Mediterranean cruise, this would be.

He'd made by light to *Hebe*, the minesweeper which had taken them under its wing soon after they'd passed out of Marsamxett through the defensive boom, which by now its attendant trawler would have dragged shut again behind them, *Intend making trim-dive now before proceeding.* A trim-dive being essential in view of the entirely changed distribution of weights on board – stores, torpedoes, everything. McLeod would have got her as near right as he could, working it out with a trim diagram, established formulae and his own dexterity with a slide-rule, and putting things into balance by adjusting the contents of internal compensating and trimming tanks, but there were bound to be further small adjustments necessary, to get it exactly right. U-class were tricky beasts, tended to get out of hand if it *wasn't* exactly right.

Walburton had passed that message, and now took in the reply: *I'll stick around, see you on your way.* Mike too had read the flickering light. They were a mile down-channel, a mile from the Castile signal station, and it was Wednesday, half an hour past midnight. He lowered his binoculars, murmured 'Very kind of you.' *Hebe* was one of the four fleet minesweepers whose arrival had made such a difference here; the flotilla leader, who'd met them and escorted them in, was *Speedy*. Seemed more like an hour ago, than thirty. He told Walburton and Danvers, 'All right, clear the bridge.' The hands were already at diving stations, and McLeod was down there ready to control the dive, as always concerned to see how well or otherwise his trimming plan worked out. If he'd made a real cock-up of it, for instance, you could find yourselves nose-diving for the bottom.

Unlikely. Wouldn't be all that far to nose-dive, either – less than a hundred and fifty feet of water here. The only hazard anywhere near was the Dragut shoal with barely thirty feet on it, but that was a quarter of a mile back on the port quarter now. Mike glanced around the empty bridge and quiet, dark seascape: *Hebe* wallowing a couple of cables' lengths ahead, Malta's jagged black fortress shape two thousand yards astern.

Into the voice-pipe: 'Open main vents.'

Fairly quickly then shutting the voice-pipe cock. Vents crashing open, the rush and roar of released air, main ballast filling, hydroplanes hard a-dive to 'plane her down. He was in the hatch, on the vertical steel ladder in the tower, feeling the dive now as well as hearing it, grasping the handle of the hatch above his head and dragging it down shut on top of him. Clips now, to secure it . . .

43

'One clip on!'

For McLeod's reassurance that it was safe to continue the dive. Whereas if he'd somehow bungled it – been shot or had a fit, knocked himself out somehow – they'd either have reversed the dive – shutting main vents and blowing tanks instead of flooding them – or more likely by that stage had no such option, only time to shut the lower hatch, saving the boat but drowning him by the time they could get her up again. Second clip on, however – and finding the cotter-pins dangling on their short chains, shoving them in to lock the clips in place. Done – for the thousandth time – and clambering down to the hatch at the bottom of the tower, through it on to the control-room ladder. As he stepped off it, into the motors' hum, glow of lights and circle of familiar faces, Walburton shot up it to shut and clip what was known as the lower lid.

'Twenty-eight feet, sir.'

Periscope depth, that was. If he was holding her at that depth without much effort from the 'planesmen, the trim couldn't be too bad. Why make it too easy for him, though? Mike said, glancing at Barnaby – wardroom flunkey, a lad of about nineteen with the look of a startled rabbit, who was on the motor-room telegraphs – 'Group down, slow together.' The faster she moved through the water, the more effect the hydroplanes, which were effectively horizontal rudders, had in holding her at the ordered depth. Whereas if she was in fore-and-aft balance and neutral buoyancy – i.e. perfect trim – you might in ideal sea conditions achieve a 'stop trim' – screws stopped, the boat simply hanging, immobile, neither light nor heavy.

The motors' note had fallen to something more like a whisper than a hum. Swathely, on the after 'planes – controlling them by means of a brass wheel about eighteen inches in diameter, with an image in a dial in front of him showing the angling of the hydroplanes as he adjusted them, commented in a tone which in his own judgement might have been classifiable as *sotto voce*, 'Touch heavy aft, sir.'

'I'm pumping from aft, Cox'n.'

'Ah. Beg pardon, sir . . .'

Mock-reproving glance from Tubby Hart on fore 'planes – precisely similar controls, on the cox'n's right. Cox'n aware of the glance, ignoring it. McLeod with his hand up on the electric trimming telegraph, by means of which he'd ordered the stoker on the after pump to shift some ballast from the stern trimming tank to the midships one. Guessing that that should be about enough, switching to 'Stop pumping, shut "Z" and "O"' – and now assessing the effect of it.

Hydroplanes – fore 'planes and after 'planes – to all intents and purposes horizontal and barely shifting: depth-gauge needle flickering at 29 feet, bubble in the spirit-level one degree aft of centre.

Twenty-eight and a half feet: twenty-eight. Hart easing a few degrees of 'rise' off his fore 'planes. McLeod said, 'Twenty-eight feet, sir.'

'You've got her well trained, Number One.'

'Eats out of my hand, sir.'

It was as good as you'd get it anyway. One man coming aft from the fore ends now would be enough to upset it slightly, and if they'd been remaining submerged, all hands moving from diving stations to the routine state of 'watch diving' – one-third of them on watch, the rest with their heads down or playing Uckers, Cribbage, or whatever – the trim would be thrown out completely; whoever was taking over as officer of the watch would speed up enough to hold her close to the ordered depth until he'd got things back under control.

McLeod suggested, 'Want to tell 'em what we're doing, sir?'

It was a good idea – the right moment for it too, having

45

some peace and quiet, which presently on the surface with the diesels hammering away you wouldn't have. 'Yes.' Mike took the microphone of the Tannoy broadcast system from its hook on the deckhead and tested it for sound. Then – 'D'you hear, there? If you don't, get closer to a speaker. Listen – we've had darned little harbour-time, I know – sorry, fact is they want us out there on the billet. Had an easy enough time of it swanning around Haifa, Port Said and Alex, haven't we. And there's sound reason to be getting on with it now – Rommel on the Egyptian frontier – right? The more of his supplies we can deprive him of, better chance the Eighth Army has of reversing that situation. OK, that's nothing new, only happens to be about twice as urgent – hence the rush to get us out . . . So – our billet's off Palermo on Sicily's north coast – as you'll no doubt have heard. Means getting under the Marettimo–Cape Bon minefield – which we've done so often she'd practically find her own way under the bloody things if she had to.' He took a breath. 'And – well, surfacing now, three and a half hours at ten knots, we'll dive on the watch at 0430. Dived all day then, spend tomorrow night getting the box up for the minefield passage, should be on the billet first thing Friday.'

Looking around as he spoke – never all that keen on his own voice droning on – across the compartment he was face to face with CERA McIver. The Chief as he was known having no doubt been there all the time – one of the others must have moved sideways, as it were exposing him where he stood close to Ellery the Outside ERA, in *his* usual position at the diving panel. McIver being the best part of a foot shorter than Ellery – shorter than most, in fact – and dark-visaged, angry-looking – a permanent anger at being so close to the ground or deck-level? He and Ellery – who'd worked for the Austin Motor Company, at one time – were both extremely competent, and McIver was a highly efficient chief engineer. Still there and glaring as Mike finished with, 'Likely targets – toss-up, obviously, but anything south-bound, aiming to get round that end of Sicily – on its way to Tripoli for instance.' He shrugged – 'Just hope our luck's still running, uh?'

He switched off, hung the mike on its hook close to the trimming-order telegraph, and moved towards the big periscope – for'ard one – glancing at Ellery whose reaction was as always instant, bringing the glistening brass tube rushing up, shiny with grease and salt-water droplets, rivulets . . . Dark up there for sure, but it was routine and essential to take a pre-surfacing look around: even in pitch blackness you *might* catch sight of the white flare of an enemy's bow-wave, if there happened to be one and asdics for some reason hadn't picked it up. Mike throwing a glance at Fraser the asdic man – HSD, Higher Submarine Detector – as the periscope rose into his hands, 'Anything?'

Shake of the yellow head. 'Only the sweeper, sir – on oh-two-five, seven hundred yards, low revs.'

He found *Hebe* visually on that bearing, then made a circle with the 'scope in low-power first, then high, and found nothing else. As with *Hebe* in company one might have known there wouldn't be. Belt *and* braces, though . . . He pushed the big 'scope's handles up, and Ellery depressed the lever that sent it down, telemotor pressure achieving that. Mike nodded to McLeod. 'Stand by to surface.'

'Check main vents . . .'

En route, now, on one's own. Course 315 degrees, revs for ten knots but making about nine, diesel generators rumbling steadily, replacing amperes the motors were devouring. *Ursa* at half-buoyancy with 'Q' quick-diving tank, just for'ard of her centre of gravity, filled to its capacity of ten tons. With 'Q' to help her down, she could be under in less than fifteen

47

seconds – performing what journalists and script-writers liked to refer to as a 'crash dive'.

Jarvis had the watch until 0215. On Mike's left, bulky in sweater and weather-proof Ursula jacket, hunched in the bridge's port for'ard corner with binoculars at his eyes. Lookouts – Parker and another – further aft, one on each side of the after periscope standard, also with binoculars, searching their own sectors of the dark, lazily heaving seascape. Lookouts were relieved on the hour, officers of the watch at a quarter past – to reduce traffic in the tower and hatches and an overcrowded bridge, also to ensure there was always at least one pair of eyes up here adjusted to night vision.

Visibility wasn't bad. No moon, but a sky full of stars and very little cloud to hide them, wind no more than the Beaufort scale category of 'light airs'. *Ursa* pitching rhythmically as she drove across and through the swells, black Med surface broken only where her stem carved into it, whiteness rolling away left and right and flooding aft over her pressure-hull inside the casing, wake broadening astern where it fizzed away to nothing. Steady throbbing of the engines – audible to surface craft at maybe a thousand yards? Malta hidden in the night five miles to port, to be succeeded during the next hour by the smaller islands of Comino and Gozo at ranges of more like eight. Sicily – Cape Scalambri – forty miles due north.

Time to go down, anyway, leave it all to Jarvis.

'All right, Sub?'

'Aye, sir.'

'Call me for anything at all. *Dive*, for anything.'

He'd probably have given his sub-lieutenants that instruction several hundred times, he realised. They'd both, after all, earned their watchkeeping certificates seemingly so *very* recently. In fact, casting one's mind back, during the work-up period back home – in Scottish waters mainly – and a single work-up patrol off Norway, then the passage out, a week in Gib and a blank patrol from there off the French south coast, aimed at giving a new boat and its crew some initial Med experience. Admittedly neither of them had been *entirely* green when they'd joined him and *Ursa* in Chatham dockyard, they'd both put in at least *some* sea-time – in surface ships – before completing the submarine course at Blyth. And since then of course, on top of that period of what might be thought of as an extension of basic training, the real thing – sixteen patrols of it, some of them quite memorable, in conditions as tough as submariners had ever known.

Might say that made them veterans?

Might. Even in one's own somewhat rigorous view of it – stemming from long-term *total* responsibility as well as the isolation which in the function of command in stringent war conditions was inescapable. Plus maybe a tendency still to see them as one had a year and a half ago in that builder's yard – one trainee stockbroker from Colchester or thereabouts, and one former Merchant Navy cadet – Bristolian – then so recently promoted from midshipman to sub-lieutenant that you could still see where the blue patches of an RNR snottie had decorated the lapels of his reefer jacket.

It was a fact they'd both come through it all very well. Climbing slowly down through the tower, telling himself *So give the poor sods a break.*

Meaning, effectively, give *oneself* a break?

Which was not to say *relax*, exactly. Nor in fact that there could be any harm in telling them *Call me for anything, dive for anything* – basically a reminder that it was better to dive for a seagull than stay up and be bombed or strafed with cannon-fire.

In the control room now, off the ladder and out of the furious rush of wind the diesels were sucking in; taking in at a glance that it was Leading Torpedoman Brooks on the wheel, Ordinary Seaman Sharp control-room messenger – Sharp being a newish member of this crew, actually an SD, asdic rating, back-up to Fraser – although it was ERA Coldwell taking his ease on the asdic stool, cigarette in the fingers of one hand, tin mug in the other.

'Kye, sir?'

Hector Bull, PO of the watch. Pudding face – blunt nose, round chin – eyes questioning, with this offer of pusser's cocoa. Mike nodded, on his way to the chart table – to check the log, chart and whatever he'd noted in his night order book. 'Nice idea, Bull. Thanks.'

No problems here. Starting-point off Tigne Head where they'd surfaced within a few minutes of 0100 to start the thirty-five-mile run northwestward, hourly positions marked along the pencil track and culminating in the projected 0430 diving position: sunrise in fact nearer 0500, but false dawn putting a shine on the surface well before that. Danvers would have his head down now, would be shaken for his watch at 0200 and when relieved by McLeod at 0415 would have a quarter of an hour for starsights – if he found he had a usable horizon at that time.

'Thank you, Bull. All well with your lot?'

'All hunky-dory, sir, thank you.'

Home-town Cardiff, a fiancée who was a WAAF, two brothers at sea in the Merchant Navy – which by all one heard was *not* having anything like a hunky-dory time of it.

McLeod was at the wardroom table reading an Edgar Wallace thriller; Mike having removed his Ursula jacket joined him with his mug of kye. 'Thought you'd have crashed it, James.'

Meaning got his head down. McLeod nodded. 'Will do in a jiffy, sir. Thought I'd just read one chapter.' A shrug. 'Plenty of zizz-time between here and Marettimo, touch wood.'

If they were left to themselves, there would be. In fact any interruptions were most likely to be encountered tonight or tomorrow night. When you went deep for the QBB minefield, its borders extending from Marettimo to Cape Bon, thence down the Tunisian coastline to Hammamet and from there via Pantellaria to Cape San Marco, you were to all intents and purposes going into oblivion for as much as fourteen or fifteen hours – neither expecting interference nor thinking about mines. They were *there*, allegedly several thousand of them, but you'd be simply minding your own business, passing under them in the course of getting from A to B. *Thinking* about the bloody things didn't help. As McLeod had observed, it was 'zizz-time' when off-watch, dreamland while the hours crawled by.

He'd smoked most of a cigarette and about finished his kye when McLeod shut his book. 'Pretty good cock, but somehow holds one.'

'Courtesy of Eleanor again?'

'Well, yes. Small private library she uses.'

'In all that schemozzle you found time to see her.'

'Spoke briefly on the blower, was all. She'd left this for me – knew we were coming in, so –'

'Well.' A smile, more or less congratulatory. Eleanor Kingsley was a 3rd Officer WRNS, a redhead with a lot going for her. She worked in the Combined Services HQ in Valetta and was a frequent visitor to Lazaretto. Mike sent smoke pluming at the lamp that swung gently above the table: 'Lucky man, Jamie.'

'Competition's fierce enough, I may say.'

'That's what I meant.'

'Ah. Well.' A shrug. 'Turn in now, anyway.'

'Give me a shake, will you, before you go up at four?'

'Aye, sir. Incidentally, did I hear right, you mentioning a new boat joining us shortly, named *Unsung*?'

51

He nodded. 'CO's Charles Melhuish — know him?'

'Actually, I *have* met him — I think. Odd name though, *Unsung*?'

'Scraping the barrel for new U-names. Yes. Pleasant enough, in its way though — slightly poetic even?'

'Meaning uncelebrated. Unheard-of. How about *that*, though — *Unheard*?'

'Not bad at all. Might suggest it. After all, we've got *Unseen*. But *Unsung* — silent service, all that?'

He'd talked about U-class names with Ann, he remembered. The second night — the Sunday, when they'd been on the tiles on their own, and of course should not have been. November of 1940, when he'd been standing by *Ursa*'s building at Chatham, and Charles Melhuish on the point of starting his Perisher — Commanding Officers' course — at Blockhouse. Ann, though — it had been her suggestion, murmured into his ear in the Coconut Grove night-club, and he'd been rash enough to respond with something like 'Ann — *Ann* . . . You don't mean it — *do* you?' Whereas he *should* have said, 'Smashing idea, but of course we can't. You know darn well we can't!' Giving reasons then, if necessary — as indeed it *would* have been, since she certainly *had* meant it, was meaning it like nobody's business quite suddenly on that crowded, half-dark dance floor — smoochy saxophone, her bare arms tight around his neck, lips actually in contact with that ear and *in general* close contact suddenly, whereas until then everything had been quite proper. At any rate reasonably, normally so — with Charles most likely only a few feet away, dancing with Chloe, Mike's little sister, as it happened. He'd had her with him because some other girl hadn't been able to make it, and in any case having her along had fitted in with other plans. That was one reason he could have given her — given Ann — if he'd had his wits about him; the fact it was arranged that he'd be taking Chloe up to Buckinghamshire in the morning to stay a few days with their father, who'd be bitterly disappointed if they let him down. In the event he had been, too. In fact he *had* mentioned it to Ann, come to think of it: and might have thought better of himself if he'd told her more forthrightly, 'Because you're Charles's wife, and he's a brother officer. We'd be *insane!*'

Meaning that a night on the loose together would be insane. As he'd known for certain, even if she hadn't. She *had*, of course: had really had nothing else in view – no more than he'd had, by that time. From his first sight of her, earlier in the day, 'knocked for a loop' might have described it – long before any awareness of that total, instant reciprocity, lack of any hesitance at all . . . Answering her letter, might remind her of that. Obliquely – if he could find a way to do it. She was right, on paper one did tend to be cautious, not to stick one's neck out pointlessly. *Must* be firm about her not writing now: and yes, he'd write to her, you bet he would – but could not discuss any future comings or goings – not even if he knew of them, which of course he seldom did – beyond the fact that *Ursa* had just about done her time – and even that he couldn't mention . . . Stubbing out the cigarette-end, thinking to get a couple of hours' shuteye between now and four. Immediately, clean teeth and have a pee. The wardroom heads, WC and washbasin, was just across the companion-way, opposite the galley. Allowing his mind to drift back, though, to what had started him thinking about Ann again – the conversation about U-class names, which on the face of it might have seemed an odd subject to interest her much – in point of fact, that conversation must have taken place earlier in the evening of the Saturday, probably at the United Hunts Club in Upper Grosvenor Street – *his* club, the Melhuishes therefore his guests at that stage. The background to it all being old Billy Gorst's wedding that afternoon with the reception at the Dorchester, in the course of which Mike and sister Chloe had somehow teamed-up with Charles and Ann, and Charles had rather loftily invited them to dine with him at the Jardin des Gourmets in Greek Street; so there'd been time to kill, and Upper Grosvenor Street being just strolling distance from the Dorchester the Hunts Club had been an obvious port of call.

Billy Gorst was by this time a commander, aged about thirty-five, a submarine CO of considerable repute whom Mike had known for donkey's years, and under whom Charles Melhuish had served as fourth hand in one of the old R-class – Charles being then a mere sub-lieutenant, presumably. Yes, must have been. And had only been invited to Billy's wedding – Mike suspected – because a couple of years earlier he'd somehow persuaded the older man to attend *his* nuptials – in Edinburgh, where Ann's parents lived. It had been a fairly low-key affair, apparently – so Billy had intimated, in a brief, semi-coded chat at the Dorchester reception. Mike hadn't been asked to the Melhuish wedding, hadn't even known Charles, who at the time of his marriage had only recently become first lieutenant of an 'S', in fact was rather junior in the service to have been getting married, had only been able to do so through being personally well-heeled. Unconventional background, rather – mother an American who'd divorced his father and gone back to the States, father the owner of a chain of hotels; he was based somewhere in the Midlands and obviously rich.

How had Melhuish managed to get Ann?

Billy Gorst had touched Mike's arm, nodded in the direction of a group surrounding her. 'Knockout, uh?'

'Certainly is.' Introductions had been made earlier, to her and to her husband, whom Mike hadn't taken to enormously but envied, somewhat. She was *vibrantly* attractive. Changing

54

the subject slightly, in this chat with Gorst, asking him, 'Low key, you say — in Edinburgh?'

'Surprisingly so. Her father's a lawyer of some kind. Boss of some outfit, I don't remember, but — decidedly pompous, despite which definitely *not* splashing the stuff around — you know?'

'The champagne, you mean.'

'No, I meant the bawbees. There was a lot of very good champagne — which Charles had paid for, believe it or not. *And* told me he had! Extraordinary . . .' Change of tone: 'I take it *you*'re not thinking of getting spliced, old boy?'

'No such intention as of this moment.'

'Wise man, too.'The unblushing but radiant bride, returning from some solo mission and latching on to her brand-new husband's arm. Laughing: 'Crazy to give it even a thought, at this moment.' Sparkling, like the champagne; but now she'd come back there was a crowd closing in around her and Billy, and Mike looking for Chloe saw her in conversation with Melhuish.

Which putting things in their chronological order was where it had started, he supposed. Charles had taken a bit of a shine to Chloe, was the truth of it. Ridiculous, when one thought of Ann, visualised those two side by side. Chloe was quite easy on the eye, vivacious and very young — but in comparison with Ann, to whom the bugger was *married*, heaven's sake . . .

He'd finished in the heads. Didn't need to blow them, after no more than a pee. To blow them, the equivalent in ordinary life of pulling a chain, you operated certain valves and a lever like a gear-change, built up a head of air pressure that registered on a gauge, then let it go, blasting everything out to sea. OK as long as you kept your mind on the job, and did it right; if you put the pressure-charge on the wrong side of it, for instance, you got it all back, violently.

55

Undine was the boat whose name had triggered that conversation in the club. She'd been lost earlier in the year, and a friend of Charles Melhuish had been her third or fourth hand. *He*'d attended their wedding, and Ann had liked him; he and Billy Gorst had been the only submariners she'd met until now, other than Charles. She'd asked Mike whether he'd known this man – which he hadn't – and Chloe had asked what on earth did the name *Undine* mean. Mike had been able to tell her, Charles having admitted ignorance: 'Means a water-sprite who doesn't have a soul, only way she can acquire one is to mate with a human.'

'That true, or did you just make it up?'

'What's a sprite, when it's at home?'

Chloe suggested, 'A spirit, presumably. Same word, almost?' Ann thought it was a pretty name, dreadfully sad that she'd been lost. Did anyone know what had happened to her? No one did: Mike had said, 'One often doesn't', and Charles began to count off on his fingers the names of boats that had been lost, up to that time. Not 'U's, *Undine* had been the first of this class to go, but more than a dozen others – and Mike had cut in, putting a stop to the unnecessary recital by explaining that a lot of the U-class didn't have names, only numbers.

'The originals were given names in the usual way, but with the speed-up of war construction they did without them. Now they're having to find names for them all because Churchill's insisted no British submarine should go on patrol with just a bloody number. He said if the Admiralty couldn't think up names, *he* would.'

'Bet your life he would.' Ann asked Mike, 'What's yours called?'

'*Ursa*. Not a bad name – d'you think?'

'She-bear.' That smile of hers almost crippling, when she turned it on you at close range. '*Sweet* name. Don't you dare let *her* get lost.'

Mike had assured her, 'I won't, I promise.'

Certain of his ground. Believing in it. Had been then, and still was. At that time, though, he'd been irritated by Charles Melhuish having almost proudly reeled off the names of submarines that had been lost in the previous twelve, fifteen months. Boastfully, as if acceptance of such odds-against redounded to *his* credit, somehow. And feeding that stuff to his wife, for God's sake, when the normal and obvious thing was to provide reassurance.

Bunk now, anyway. Having turned the overhead lamp off, heaving himself up backwards and then swinging his legs up. Glow of light from the control room, but three-quarters dark in here with the curtain drawn; familiar rumbling of the engines, regular, gentle pitching – all cumulatively soporific, except there were men milling around out there: and now the helmsman's call of 'Bridge!'

Jarvis's answer, through the tube: 'Bridge.'

'Relieve lookouts, sir?'

'Yes, please.'

One of them at a time. When the first came down, the relief for the second would go up.

'Navigator, sir?'

At close range, this – Nat Sharp, SD, in the role of control-room messenger, stooping at Danvers' bunk. 'Sub-lieutenant, sir – two o'clock –'

'Right. Right . . .'

Sharp would wait until he saw the man he was shaking actually turning out, though. All too easy to say 'Right, thanks' and while mustering the necessary resolve slip back into dreamland.

4

Cessation of engine noise, replaced instantly and startlingly by the much closer sound of sea rushing over half-inch plating within a few feet of one's head, punctuated by the thuds of her butting through it, audible on its own now and triggering instant, auto-physical more than cerebral or truly *conscious* reaction of nerves and muscles – Pavlovian reflex to alarm, emergency. Brain waking to it maybe a second later, by which time one's in the control room, in the ringing echo of Danvers' 'Dive, dive, dive!' and standing back from the bruising descent from up top of lookouts Farquhar and Llewellyn. One of several queries in mind being why no klaxon, the usual eardrum-blasting signal to dive, emergency. All the rest pretty well as standard and simultaneous – CERA McIver having flipped back the six steel levers opening main vents, the sound of numbers one and six's high-pressure air escaping into the night, *Ursa* tipping bow-down, a yell from the tower – Danvers again – 'One clip on!' Second Cox'n Tubby Hart, PO of Blue watch – which succeeded White watch at 0200 and is now dispersed in the rush to diving stations. Hart temporarily on the controls of the after 'planes,

58

and messenger of the watch Barnaby briefly on the for'ard ones: depth-gauges showing ten feet – twelve – fifteen – down-angle steepening. Cox'n Swathely now on after 'planes, Hart's bulk displacing Barnaby and the latter transferring to the motor-room telegraphs, Danvers landing on his feet, slamming against the ladder – slim, broad-shouldered, head and face running wet from a small influx of sea – panting at Mike: 'E-boats, sir – two of 'em, port beam half a mile – lying stopped, so –'

'Slow both motors. Fifty feet.' Twelve or fifteen seconds maybe since being roused to this – and McLeod acknowledging, 'Fifty feet, sir,' and 'Slow both' having taken over the trim, taking her in hand as she approached periscope depth and passed it, for the moment carrying on down, and Walburton on the ladder shutting and clipping the lower lid. Mike telling Fraser the asdic man – on his stool at the set, one hand adjusting the headphones over his noticeably small ears, fingers of the other settling on the training-knob on a compass-dial at the top of the set – 'Port beam or thereabouts.'

'Fifty feet, sir.'

Hydroplanes having to work hard to hold her there. McLeod has the after ballast pump sucking on the midships trim-tank: at fifty feet she's heavier than she was at twenty-eight – periscope depth where she was when last submerged, before surfacing at 0100. The deeper a submarine goes the heavier she gets, since in denser water the hull's compressed, up-thrust thus reduced. Archimedes worked it out in 200 BC or thereabouts, his famous 'Principle' highlighting the ever-present danger that when a boat's going deep if you don't lighten her she'll continue deeper at an increasing rate until sea-pressure crushes her. U-class being tested only to 250 feet, it's a point to bear in mind. One does in any case, it's one of the things you live with. McLeod's lightened her enough now, anyway – hydroplanes approximately horizontal, needles in depth-gauges more or less static on the fifty-feet marks. Won't be staying at this depth for ever anyway, don't need to be *too* fussy: he's switching the order-instrument to 'Stop pumping' and 'Shut "O"', the stoker at that after ballast pump responding with 'Pump stopped' and '"O" shut'.

The clock on the for'ard bulkhead's showing five past three. Mike asking Fraser, 'Anything?'

Negative. Fingertips shifting the knob a degree or two this way and that. Narrow face damp-looking, taut with concentration. 'Foxy' Fraser, his mates call him. The E-boats must still be lying stopped, probably listening on hydrophones but presumably not hearing *Ursa*'s HE. Not yet: they wouldn't be just sitting there if they had. HE meaning Hydrophone Effect, propeller noise. All one can do at this stage is wait, strain one's own underwater ear while continuing to paddle quietly away. Certainly wouldn't contemplate doing battle with *two* E-boats, with the weaponry they carry.

Might be German-manned, might be Italian. The Germans have supplied their Wop allies with a number of E-boats recently. The Italians' own equivalent are called Mas-boats.

Anyway, the flurry's over. Mike joining Danvers at the chart table.

'No doubt of them being E-boats?'

'None at all, sir. Silhouette of the nearer one was clear enough by the time I was on him. It was Llewellyn made the sighting.'

'Good for him. Ambush ploy, presumably.'

'Seemed the likely thing, sir.'

Two of them lying stopped and silent – no bow-waves, not much danger of being spotted by the victim before they saw and heard *him*, with his engine's racket and flare of bow-wave to give him away. Submarines out of Malta *would* use this route – as well as others – and as Shrimp had surmised, the enemy might very well be aware that the flotilla was reassembling and would be redeploying. Danvers' reaction had been exactly right, Mike thought: stopping engines immediately and ducking smartly out of it – not even risking the klaxon, which in the normal way of things would have been second nature, no more than routine.

'Sir –' Fraser's head up suddenly – 'HE starting up on' – peering at his compass dial – 'red one-oh-five, sir!'

E-boat getting under way, fifteen degrees abaft the beam. Fraser muttering, 'Sort of confused. No – *different* one, that's *two* –'

'Moving which way?'

Concentrating – shifting the knob minutely across the bearing. Then: 'Right to left, sir. Turbine HE, revs increasing.'

'Stay on them.'

Thinking, what one needed to counter this sort of gambit might be night-fighters. Mosquitoes, say – at least when E-boats were on the move, being fast movers with highly visible wakes and bow-waves, which one might guess would make for easy sightings from aircraft on low-flying sweeps.

'Right to left, still. Opening fast, sir.'

'Listen-out all round then get back on them.'

'Aye, sir.'

'Number One, we'll surface in fifteen minutes.'

Three twenty-five, that would be – having made sure of the E-boats putting a few miles behind them. They weren't likely to turn back on their tracks; he guessed they'd try their luck in the approaches to Valetta and Marsamxett, as likely as not plant a mine or two, before coming round to – well . . . At the chart, checking this out: something like 340 degrees would be their course home to Licata. If Licata was where they'd come from – which wasn't unlikely, it *was* an E-boat base, and the nearest. Sixty miles from here, roughly: they'd be reckoning on being home for breakfast. But holding that course at say twenty-five knots while *Ursa* chugged along on 315 at nine – well, let's see. Because if one's instincts were making sense now . . . They were, as likely as not they *were*. Laying the divergent tracks off on the chart confirmed that by the time *Ursa* had the unlit Gozo lighthouse ten miles abeam to port, the Wops on their way home could be overhauling at a range of no more than five or ten thousand yards to starboard.

'Number One – here a minute. And you, pilot.'

Because Danvers would have the watch when they surfaced, McLeod relieving him soon after four; and having lost thirty or forty minutes' progress thanks to the E-boats, that was where she'd be when/if she dived at 0430 – ten miles northeast of Gozo.

'Buggers could well be that close to us – or closer – uh?'

They'd both nodded. McLeod said, 'If they were steering nearer 335 than 340 – dawn coming up astern, at that.'

'Right. Too close for comfort. Forget morning stars, pilot. We'll surface now, dive at four.'

Manoel Island eggs and bacon for breakfast, served up in the wardroom by AB Barnaby at 0740 for Danvers who'd be relieving Jarvis as officer of the watch at 0815. Two hours on watch, four hours off, round the clock and for as long as the patrol might last; *Ursa* at seventy-five feet, main motors driving her at three and a half knots, the Chernikeeff electric log showing this with its blue indicator light flashing steadily and ticking like a clock – actually recording distance run, on the basis of which Jarvis would put a dead-reckoning position on the chart at 0800.

Warmth, low hum of the motors, the boat rock-steady, no motion on her at all. Breakfast would be stirring things up a bit now, but otherwise since the last change of watch sleep would have been *the* off-watch preoccupation.

Danvers however, shaken by Barnaby, was at the table with his plate of eggs and bacon and enamel mug of tea.

'All right, sir?'

'You're a genius, Barnaby.'

'Nice of you to mention it, sir.'

Mike grunted, sliding off his bunk. 'Ready for mine whenever you like, genius.' He looked briefly into the control room before visiting the heads. Would *not* be shaving today, however. Not tomorrow or Friday either or Saturday, Sunday, Monday, etc. – one of the pleasures of this way of life, not having to bother with it. Thinking of those E-boats being in Licata by this time – boats no doubt secured alongside, personnel ashore in whatever luxurious accommodation they might have there – seafront hotels maybe – guzzling up *their* breakfasts. He'd listened-out for them on asdics, for a few minutes around 0430 – or rather had had SD Sharp, AB Fraser's winger, listen-out, reducing meanwhile to slow speed on only one shaft so as to have a better chance of hearing them at however many miles' range they might have been. Sharp hadn't been able to pick them up, but that didn't mean they hadn't been out there somewhere, on course for Licata. Might have passed at a greater distance than he'd anticipated – if they'd been steering a dog-leg course, for instance. He'd have been a damn fool not to have taken the precautions he had, in any case; it annoyed him that he *almost* hadn't seen that rather obvious danger: if he hadn't woken up to it when he had, might have been caught on the hop.

Safety first. By the nature of the job one had often enough to take fairly hair-raising risks, simply to fulfil one's *raison d'être*; all the more reason not to take avoidable or non-productive ones. Might be worth explaining this in answering her letter – a comment on Charles's nonsense, which really did need to be refuted. Especially remembering Ann herself

63

remarking on one occasion – an age ago, in England – 'Not in the safest of occupations, are you . . .'

His brother Alan wasn't either. Millions weren't.

McLeod had prised himself up off his bunk, was at the table looking hungry. Danvers had wolfed his fry-up and was on to bread and jam. Mike pushed the curtain back and pulled out the chair – *the* chair, on this passageway side of the table.

'Morning, sir.'

'Morning, Jamie.' And to Danvers with his clean-scraped plate, 'Feel better for that?'

'Heaps better, sir. We're spoilt, when you come to think of it – I mean, when the Malts are on starvation rations?'

'We're favoured, certainly. Shrimp's farm of course for one thing. And apart from that –' McLeod pointed for'ard – 'for instance, there are a couple of sacks of spuds up there – *real* ones.'

'To go with roast pork. *Naturally.*' Danvers shrugged. 'Hell – pork without roast spuds –'

Mike said, 'All spuds are reserved for submarine crews, as it happens. That's official. Guy Mottram was telling me – he'd been out at Gravy's – Shrimp's chum Gravy Tench, happens to be the food supremo? He was saying it's getting to the stage of a governmental edict for the slaughter of all goats and horses – slight problem being that most owners have already killed and eaten any they had. Gravy's done a census, reckons there are only enough left to eke things out by about a week.'

'Well, crikey –'

'So a convoy operation – and damn soon, at that –'

McLeod had broached this. Mike agreeing but remaining silent while Barnaby delivered two more plates of eggs and bacon. 'Snitched these 'ere out of a batch Cookie was sending for'ard.'

'Enough to go round, surely?'

'Bloody *better* be!'

He'd gone. Thinking of his own breakfast perhaps. Or even Jarvis's. McLeod asked Mike, 'This patrol's nothing to do with any convoy operation, is it sir?'

Shake of the head, while scattering pepper. 'Not as far as I know or Shrimp's letting on.' Adding then, quietly, 'There *is* one in the offing. Has to be, you're right. But not quite immediately, and Shrimp's priority's been to get us out on the job double-quick – after longish absence and the Eighth Army's – well, not predicament exactly, but it *was* being said Rommel could be in Alexandria in three days.'

'Christ.'

'If Malta folded, he probably would be. The Canal, the lot. Oh, it won't happen, *can't*, we can't *let* it, that's the size of it . . . Anyway, answering your question, if we were still on our billet when a convoy operation was launched we might either be left there or shifted to a new one. Alternatively might be recalled, turned around and pushed straight out again. One problem for Shrimp being if we'd had a lively time of it and used up all our fish.'

'Hell, what *about* that?'

'Pray to God they'd have some for us. Magic Carpet working flat out maybe. *Tango* was due in about now with half a dozen – but we're talking of ten or twelve boats, so –' shake of the head – 'God knows . . .'

Had to stop talking then for a while, pay closer attention to his breakfast. Probably enough said, anyway. In his Tannoy speech a day ago he hadn't mentioned the imminence of any convoy operation. Or for that matter the island being pretty well at its last gasp. One had to recognise, in the privacy of one's own thoughts, the *possibility* of running into trouble one couldn't handle, survivors if any being dragged out of the sea half-drowned and/or in shock, whatever – and the plain and simple fact that what a man didn't know he couldn't talk about.

No particular advantage in his knowing, either.

Scraping up the last of this delicious meal, while hearing the watch changing in the control room. 'Relieve helmsman, sir?' Jarvis's standard reply of 'Yes, please' to that, and then to others one by one, men more or less lined up in the gangway for'ard of this point, coming aft as those who'd been relieved came for'ard – 'planesmen, PO and ERA of the watch, telegraphman, messenger. Even then with the swapping of differing weights there'd be trimming problems for Jarvis to put right before handing over to Danvers in about ten minutes.

Incident-free day, all seventeen hours of it. Lunch of bread, cheese and chutney: up to periscope depth before that, for a brief look-round and a check on the weather, also to receive any wireless messages there might be – but had not been, as it happened, not at any rate addressed to *Ursa* – but 'planing up slowly and carefully, after asdics had found no lurking threat, and putting the 'attack' periscope up first for minimal feathering of the smoothly rolling surface. That 'scope being monofocal without any magnification in it, not much thicker at its top end than a Churchillian cigar. Swift check all round before sending it down and putting up the big one for a slower, longer-range search of sea and sky: then back down to seventy-five feet and lunch, and a few pages of *The Moon is Down*.

And think about an answer to Ann's letter.

'Excuse me, sir?'

AB Johnson – LTO, electrician, on battery inspection, one access point for testing the electrolyte's density in number two section being right here, a hinged flap in the deck that was lifted with a special tool, electrolyte then siphoned out of the cell right under it. Mike on his feet, pulling the chair out of Johnson's way.

He'd measured it: was squirting electrolyte back into the cell.

'How's it look?'

He gave him the figure: recording it meanwhile on his clipboard. 'Long enough dive is this, sir.' Johnson, who wore glasses, came from Edinburgh, where before joining up he'd been apprenticed to a company operating trams.

'But we're not caning it, exactly.' Meaning, not treating it all that harshly. Checking the time – 1445, they'd lunched at 1400. 'Seven hours to go, anyway.'

Twelve hours in fact was about long enough for any dive, from the point of view of air and its oxygen content, but today's seventeen hours would be just about matched tomorrow – getting under the minefield, then being so close to Marettimo, not to mention Marsala and Trapani, having no option but to stay down until dark. The longest Mike or *Ursa* had done had been a stretch of more than thirty hours – vicinity of Taranto, being hunted after sinking a large freighter, with depth-charging, some of which had been unpleasantly close, throughout a night which had happened to be moonlit, then in daylight not able to surface anyway. There'd been aircraft in it too, Cant seaplanes – which the Italians were good at using, in conjunction with anti-submarine craft. With the air in the boat getting very thin indeed they'd spread a chemical called Protosorb in shallow trays between compartments – it absorbed carbon dioxide, or was supposed to – and he'd had some guffs of bottled oxygen released at a later stage. McIver's province, that: it had probably helped, although Mike didn't think anyone had noticed much difference. Except one *had* survived, and otherwise might not have.

The thing was, when you were being hunted and having

to take avoiding action, varying courses, depths and speed and necessarily adjusting trim, men taking active part in such manoeuvrings were using a lot more oxygen than they would be if just lying doggo. Whereas a day-long submersion like this one presented no real problems. You just had to take it easy, let the hours drift by.

Take an afternoon snooze now anyway; ration the Steinbeck, make it last.

In March, that Gulf of Taranto patrol had been; *Ursa* had come back from it with a new white bar on the Roger for the supply vessel and a red one for an Italian submarine Mike had nailed the day before. Also one damaged screw, some cracked battery cells and the big search periscope jammed in its housing, as unusable as the bent propeller; and lengthy repairs in the dockyard were no fun at all, under the weight of all-out Fliegerkorps assault at that time. *Ursa* had in fact been darned lucky to get through that period and out of it intact. Just the word 'Taranto' though, in another context altogether, rang a very different bell in memory, had been a secondary cause for celebration on the night of Bill Gorst's wedding – the night they'd danced at the Coconut Grove and he and Ann had made their assignation for the Sunday. News having been released that on the 11th – Monday of that week, Armistice Day of 1940 – Swordfish dive-bombers flown-off from the carrier *Illustrious* had sunk three Italian battleships at their moorings in the port where they'd been cowering since 10 June, the day Italy had declared war on Britain. While incidentally, starting a few days *before* that declaration, Italian naval forces had sown this Marettimo–Cape Bon minefield – a very extensive anti-surface-ship field with layers of anti-submarine mines at lower levels. The Italians had their own safe routes through it, of course.

Mines were reckoned to be responsible for just about all

unaccountable submarine losses. When a boat simply didn't return from patrol, could only be reported as overdue, a mine was what one guessed at.

At the wardroom table, head on his forearms on its edge; he'd been intending to transfer to his bunk-settee, then thought about doing some chartwork first, working out when *Unsung* might make it to Marettimo and the minefield, if she'd sailed yesterday from Gib. Well, four days, near enough, if you gave her two hundred miles a day – which would mean her making virtually the whole trip on the surface, so maybe was an overestimate. Thoughts returning – redirected, say – to Ann then, to that Taranto–Coconut Grove night: her whisper in his ear, through the saxophone's sweetly subdued rendition of 'Where, or When', 'Really *something*, Mike. I mean – heavens above . . .'

The way she'd come to be dancing by that time. Well – as *they*'d come to be doing it, in the crush and semi-darkness. Having only to turn his head slightly to meet her lips: murmuring a few beats later, 'Heaven on *earth*, Ann . . . Not that that's the word exactly –'

'How about tomorrow – twosome?'

'You mean –'

'You know what I mean.'

'But – you *don't* mean –'

'Want to bet?' Moving against him. Soft laugh. 'Not a shadow of doubt *you* do, my darling –'

'But it's simply –'

'Haven't you been thinking of it all evening?'

'Apart from other considerations – look, tomorrow's Sunday, and –'

'The Wellington's open Sunday nights, and very handy for where I'm staying. Know the Wellington, in Knightsbridge?'

'Couldn't dance there *quite* like –'

'Behave ourselves then, won't we. Listen – Charles wants

69

to be back at Blockhouse by lunch-time. The course starts Monday but they're supposed to foregather in advance of that – and I'm to be on my way to Edinburgh – night sleeper reservation, I'm sure I could transfer it to Monday. While as Chloe was saying, you were taking her to Stony Stratford, wherever the hell *that*—'

'Train to Bletchley. Well, she wouldn't much mind, but our father which art in a place called Deanshanger –'

'Let her go ahead, join them on Monday, couldn't you? Emergency in the dockyard affecting your *Ursa*? Urgent message when you get back to the club?' She sang – low-toned, in sultry harmony with the sax – '"The smile you're smiling – smiling then . . ." Ring me mid-morning, Mike? I'll give you the number. Not early, in case he oversleeps. Oh but – better idea – *much* better – couldn't we meet for lunch?'

'Gay Nineties – Berkeley Street?'

'At home in all the right places, aren't you.' Soft laugh, her breath in his face. 'OK, then. Dangerous, but – oh, nuts . . . One-ish?'

Releasing each other as the music died and voices rose. Hardly believing that what had been said *had* been said – or that she meant it, or if she had, still would in the morning.

Surfacing at 2130, after a periscope and asdic recce of the surroundings, gusting fouler air for longer than usual after the seventeen-hour dive. Made you think – until you cracked the hatch and the muck escaped, foul enough to make a cat sick – that that was what you'd had in your lungs these past few hours.

Danvers' stars, anyway, put them twenty-six miles south of Cape Rossello. It was a good fix, Danvers like most Merchant Navy-trained men being a dab hand with a sextant; Mike accepted it as spot-on, and altered three degrees to starboard, to 318.

Distance on this course to the OBB start-line ten miles off Cape San Marco, thirty-six miles. And with seven hours to go before notional first light at 0430, five knots would do it nicely. Pretty well what he'd reckoned on when discussing the route with Shrimp; main thing now being that while the motors pushed her along at this low speed, her diesel-generators with power to spare would be bringing the box right up.

Touch wood, barring interruptions. In reference to which he wrote in his night-order book, *We are only 30 miles SW of Licata, which E-boats use, and the 2130 fix is on the direct route between Licata and Pantellaria. E-boats may well be encountered, therefore.*

As they might anywhere, in fact. Keeping the lads on their toes, was all.

2150 now. *Ursa* trimmed down, with her low profile practically invisible at any range at all, diesels grumbling thickly into the dark, enclosing night.

Supper would be in about an hour, McLeod told him. 2300, roughly.

'So what's *that*?'

Cold pork and baked beans was what it was. McLeod tucking into it while Jarvis who was also at the table rolled poker dice against himself. Mike appreciating, obviously, that McLeod was getting his now because he'd be taking over the watch from Danvers at a quarter past the hour; but cold food, after all, why did the rest of them have to wait an hour?

'Spuds, sir.' Jarvis looked happy enough about it. '*Roast* spuds. Chef's *tour de force*. Number One's rotten luck, so Barnaby's warmed his beans up for him instead. Care for a game, sir?'

Rattling the dice. Mike suggested, 'Why don't we wait for Danvers and make it three-handed Liars?'

Liar dice was *the* wardroom game. In fact poker dice of any kind: when one had the time for it, for instance, Double Cameroon, for which one needed four players and two sets of dice. In other messes the games they played most were Uckers, a form of Ludo, and cribbage. Current Uckers champions were the stokers, individual cribbage king as it happened the Stoker PO, Franklyn.

Intriguing sight, the champ at play. Large, invariably smiling face, huge hands, fingers like great sausages fiddling matchsticks into the scoreboard's little holes . . .

'Barnaby?'

McLeod – he'd finished his pork and warmed-up beans – would have time for a mug of coffee, as long as it took Barnaby no longer than two or three minutes to produce it.

'Two an' a 'alf, sir.'

'Fair enough.' He asked Mike, 'If you're getting this sumptuous repast at eleven, sir, might ditch gash at half-past?'

'All things being equal, go ahead.'

'Gash' meant muck, galley rubbish, and ditching it meant hauling it up through the tower in buckets on a rope – two men up top, two more below and one on the ladder to guide each bucketful up through the hatch. You wanted to avoid spillage, but also to get the job done quickly; ropes and men in hatches, preventing them from being shut, weren't tolerable for longer than was necessary. On the other hand it did have to be done; on a long day's dive the last thing you wanted in the boat was garbage.

He heard the gash-ditching taking place at eleven-thirty, and White watch taking over from Red at midnight. They'd played Liars while the spuds had been roasting, and he'd then flaked out but not slept; wasn't tired, what was more had another long, quiet day ahead. Wasn't likely to sleep at all while traversing QBB 255. As skipper, one had an inclination – instinct – to

72

stay awake. No obvious or logical purpose in it: if you were submerged and hit a mine, you were dead, all of you – unquestionably, instantly, nothing you could do or could *have* done, might just as well have been fast asleep.

Only to be around, was the thing. Present, *with* them – and one might hope, imparting confidence – which in fact one did have, was no bullshit. Steering a course of 300 degrees at 150 feet, as recommended by Shrimp a year or more ago and used time after time since then by all his COs including Wanklyn, Tommo and their brethren – Cayley, Woodward, Norman, Wraith – and a dozen others, faces and boats' names flickering through the stream of semi-consciousness, in one's private, unspoken thoughts recalling Stephen Spender's *I think continually of those who were truly great.*

To be emulated, what was more. As far as one was able. Because to excel in this particular function was as it happened the pinnacle one aimed for. Nothing else came near it, or probably ever would. Not easy to explain, simply how it was.

The minefield business though – *Ursa* had no MDU, mine detection unit, in her asdic equipment; and some COs who did have it didn't use it. The pinpointing of mines or of what looked like mines when the set picked them up served little purpose other than giving one the willies. Much better follow Shrimp's advice – duck under, stay on that course at four knots for fourteen or fifteen hours, then 'plane up into the clean, dark, hopefully empty night. Well – after some further interval. You'd reckon to be clear of the mined area after fourteen hours, but you'd stay under until you had darkness to surface into.

'Four o'clock, sir.'

'Right.' Messenger from the control room, where Red watch was relieving Blue. This was Brooks, Leading Torpedoman, shaking him. 'Thanks, I'm awake.' Up on an elbow to prove it, hearing from the control room 'Relieve lookout, sir?' and Danvers' affirmative down the pipe. Brooks, one of *Ursa's* three Glaswegians, had meanwhile shaken McLeod: Mike telling him as *he* more or less surfaced, 'I'll take over from Danvers at a quarter-past, Number One, dive shortly afterwards on the watch.'

Meaning on McLeod's Red watch, as distinct from going to diving stations and disturbing the whole crew's well-earned repose.

'Right, sir.' At the table, getting it together while fumbling the lid off a tin of Senior Service. First thing Jamie McLeod always did on waking – when on the surface – was light up.

'You, sir?'

'Oh. Well.' It would be the last for quite a while. He'd have switched on the overhead lamp, refrained from doing so in the interests of his night vision when he got up there presently. Jarvis meanwhile snoring like a dog, and some Blue watch men heading for'ard displacing the curtain as they passed. One of them – Llewellyn, who came from Port Talbot, where he *could* have remained in what he said had been a 'reserved occupation', i.e. free from call-up, in a steel works – diminutive, wild-eyed, laughed a lot, sometimes for no obvious reason – giving tongue then over the diesels' racket, 'Bleedin' mines all fuckin' day now, eh?'

'May be, Taff, then again may not.' Brooks, the torpedoman who'd just shaken them. '*Say* there is – never bumped one, did we?'

Llewellyn's cackle fading as he went on for'ard. Scrape and flare of McLeod's match. Mike sitting back from it, thinking again about his answer to Ann's letter. Be less cautious, she'd urged him: OK, so he would. Spell it out the way he felt it, no holds barred – passion, memory, longing – if he could manage that, which he supposed he never yet had, on paper.

74

He stubbed out his cigarette, pushed himself up from the table, fetched binoculars and Ursula jacket – protective clothing designed by the then CO of the U-class *Ursula* – from their stowage behind the bulkhead door. A glance at the clock, and a nod to McLeod: 'Half-past, Jamie, I'll pull the plug.'

5

Coming up for fourteen hours under the mines – most of which time he'd managed to stay awake. 1810 now, by the clock on the control room's for'ard bulkhead, above the helmsman's – Cottenham's – narrow, bald-patched head. White watch on the job although McLeod was still presiding – had spent the last few minutes adjusting the boat's trim; Jarvis would be taking over from him in a few minutes' time, was currently imbibing a mug of tea in there. Mike meanwhile having drifted in to peruse the chart, check *Ursa's* day's progress as recorded in his officers' notations along her pencilled track and in the log. The dive at 0430, and 0600 dead-reckoning position and another at 0800 – breakfast-time, when she'd have been at her nearest point to the Sicilian coast, five miles off Cape Granitola – and at 1230, lunch-time, starting across the southern approaches to the Egadi Channel – towards which he'd then have been turning up if it hadn't been for Shrimp's warning. And now – well, *here*, near enough, ten or twelve miles southwest of Marettimo, just about clearing the minefield's western boundary.

Give it until the half-hour anyway. Then up to periscope depth for a look-around before altering course to north.

Ten miles up that way should do it: You'd have periscope fixes on Marettimo island as you crept up in easy sight of the island's west coast during the last few hours of daylight. Turning his back on the chart, leaning back with his elbows on the table's edge. Needles in the depth-gauges steady on 150 feet again, McLeod behind the 'planesmen with his hand still on the order instrument – switching off at that moment and meeting his CO's eye. 'Good enough for the time being, sir.'

'For the time being' because they'd be going up to twenty-eight feet pretty soon – different kettle of fish altogether then, taking in ballast so she didn't rise too fast. Meanwhile in trim at this depth, following the changeover of watches. With the air a bit thin and the battery distinctly low: would be lower still by the time they surfaced. Time coming up to a quarter-past, and Jarvis sloping in, wiping his mouth on the back of his hand, ready to take over, pink-faced in his greenish-khaki shirt with its torn collar. Nodding to Mike – 'Sir' – and then addressing McLeod: 'On the dot, please note, as always?'

'Bloody hope so. Point of fact, a few minutes early would be better.'

Telling him then – same course and depth, same revs, well enough in trim, DR as on the chart, captain would be taking her up for a look-round shortly. Jarvis nodding: 'Got her, then.' And to the men on watch around them, 'Evening, all!' Impersonating someone or other, Mike realised, some actor or comedian. Arthur Askey, of course – Big-Hearted Arthur, as he called himself. But you'd never have guessed, he reflected, looking round at them, that these men had spent the past fourteen hours in or under a minefield. A basic factor being of course that one tended not to think of it in such stark terms – having been through it before more than once and come to no harm, and now simply repeated that exercise – accepting assurances, incidentally, that minefields deteriorated with the passage of time. Touch wood, they did. Italian ones especially. Shrimp had a theory that Italian moored mines ceased to be effective six months after they were laid – which in the case of this QBB 255, which had been laid more than two years ago, was definitely encouraging – even allowing for the probability that out of every thousand mines you might reckon on there being at least a few exceptions to that generality. Two boats *had* been lost, apparently to mines, in these Sicilian narrows, in the past eighteen months, one 'U' and a 'T'; but there again, since overall losses up to the time the flotilla had taken its recent holiday from Malta *had* been approaching 50 per cent, it was no reason to see this particular transit as more dangerous than any other.

ERA Coldwell asked him, 'About through, sir, are we?'

'Not far off. Give it another mile, in case of strays.'

Stray mines. If mines did stray. Well, loose from their moorings of course they did. But making as sure of it as possible, was all.

Coldwell was about five-seven or eight, with a seamed face and irregular features, jaw already darkening with stubble. Mike asked him, 'Your father still in Heavy Rescue?'

'He is that, sir. Eased off a lot though, compared to what it was. Last I heard, they got him supervising, sort of thing.'

'That's good news. Big relief, eh?'

''Cept it won't keep him out of it – him being *him* like.'

Heavy Rescue squads in the London blitzkrieg – part of ARP, Air Raid Precautions. Coldwell Senior and most of his buddies were '14–'18 veterans, too old for service in this war and not necessarily all that fit, but all volunteers. Coldwell had summed it up to Mike, a long time ago, as 'Just strong. Get in there, take the weight.'

78

Just Strong. Two-word family motto, he'd thought, and it had stuck in his memory as not a bad one. At the chart again, plotting tomorrow's track and distances – Cape San Vito, Cape Gallo, Golfo di Palermo – remembering Coldwell telling him about his father when they'd still been in the yard at Chatham, *Ursa* barely submarine-*shaped* even, at that stage. The blitz on London had been at about its worst in the autumn and winter of '40. Battle of Britain having peaked that summer, but London and other cities and the ports especially still getting it in the neck. Including the weekend of Billy Gorst's wedding – 'Taranto Night' as they'd referred to it on account of the news of that Fleet Air Arm triumph having been released that morning, or 'Coconut Grove Night' coming closer to one's own more private memories. Including the party's ending for himself and Chloe in a jam-packed Tube station in use as an air-raid shelter in the rumbling and flaring small hours of the morning.

And the day after – Sunday. Drifts of smoke over London, even the West End redolent of the night before. Lunch at the Nineties, by sheer luck not seeing anyone either of them knew, then the matinée as she called it, in a flat behind Harrods belonging to friends of hers and Charles's; supper and dancing then at the Wellington, which was geographically as convenient as it could have been, but by no means a late night, partly for fear of finishing up in yet another air-raid shelter – a prospect so dreadful it had actually seemed funny; they'd got back to the flat to all intents and purposes *running*. Coldwell's father, though – where this jumble of reminiscence had begun – well, blitzkrieg more or less nightly all through December, Chatham getting a fair share of it. They'd been going for the docks as much as anything, although the City and its environs had had 10,000 incendiaries strewn across it in one single night, seven solid acres on fire at one stage; the bastards had timed it for low water in the Thames to hamper fire-fighting. Coldwell's father in the middle of all that, Coldwell himself fairly desperate about it, especially around the time of *Ursa's* completion – initial dive in the dockyard basin to ensure she was watertight, brief acceptance trial and a week or so at Blockhouse, then westabout to the Clyde and Holy Loch for work-up.

His ambition, oddly enough – Coldwell's – was to become an *aircraft* engineer. So how he'd found himself in submarines or the Navy at all was a mystery. Mike had an idea that he'd explained it at some stage – or McIver had – but when or in what circumstances –

'Close on half-past, sir.'

Jarvis – cautiously, almost apologetically. Mike grunting acknowledgement, having just switched to the larger-scale chart on which Danvers had marked Palermo's defensive mine-belts in Indian ink. Plenty of time later for a closer study of their extent: one wasn't likely to get close enough to the port itself to bother much with them.

Much better not, in fact. In close proximity to a major port, *those* wouldn't have been left to deteriorate.

He turned from the table and the ticking log with its winking blue light.

'Hundred feet, Sub.'

'Hundred feet, sir.'

PO Hec Bull acknowledging as the brass wheel slid through his hands, putting some dive on the after 'planes to angle her bow-up by dragging the stern down: reversing the 'planes' angle then as Sharp span his wheel to put rise on the for'ard ones. Needles in the depth-gauges initially reluctant to comply, but with the bubble in the spirit-level sliding for'ard of the centre-line – *there*, now – finally responding. Jarvis with his eyes on the gauges and the bubble, a hand rising slowly to the order instrument above his head, ready to tell the stoker on watch in the pump-space aft to flood ballast direct from the sea into 'O', the midships trim-tank.

Ursa nosing upwards. Passing 140 feet. 135. Jarvis now using the telegraph, and whichever of the stokers was spending these two hours cramped in that little machinery space would be cracking the trimline flood-valve, letting in some weight. Steady rise meanwhile, all under control, no excessive angle on her. Mike said, 'Make it fifty feet.'

'Fifty, sir.'

A *thump* from somewhere for'ard. You felt it as well as heard it: by habit and training absorbed, contained, the element of slight shock. Scraping, sawing sounds out there now though: in here, *nerve*-scraping.

'Stop both.'

Jarvis echoed Mike's order as Newcomb, messenger of the watch, jumped to the motor-room telegraphs and jerked them over. Scraping noise continuing from the port side for'ard: but with her forward way diminishing as it would be now –

Mike checked that Jarvis had that trimline valve shut, and told Newcomb, 'Slow astern together.'

'Slow astern together, sir.'

Some kind of secondary impact – again, port side for'ard. He had a picture of it in his mind – his own concept of the likely external state of affairs – even before Cottenham for some reason not immediately evident had begun putting on starboard wheel. Well, to counter a swing off-course, an effort to keep her on the *ordered* course, obviously. Sharp on fore 'planes meanwhile complaining, 'Can't shift 'em, sir, they –'

More of the scraping, grating: Cottenham offering, 'Gotter be snagged or –'

'Wheel hard a-port, Cottenham.' And to Newcomb after a moment's thought, 'Stop port, half astern starboard.' He'd considered going *full* astern on that starboard screw, but was wary of any excessive expenditure of amps, having the present state of the battery in mind. There was a bow-up angle growing on her now: Jarvis glancing at him, on the point of asking whether he should flood the for'ard trimming tank, Mike rejecting this before it had actually been mooted – shake of the head and 'No, wait –' – point being that if she *was* snagged on the wire, pushing an angle into it and her stem sliding up it, for whatever reason – well, comprehensible enough, wire anchored to the seabed 500 feet down from here and fairly rigid, but less so from here on up to wherever the mine might be. *Could* be only a few feet above the casing, in which case a heavy downward tug –

Analysis interrupted then by a *clang* with a shivery deep-water echo to it. Loud, close-sounding, and a tremor that ran all through her. Disconcerting, in its way, but –

Silence, except for the motor's hum, vibration . . .

Jarvis's quiet 'Guess you've done the trick, sir.' Enquiring expression as well as sweat on Hec Bull's pudgy face as he glanced to his right, at Sharp. Mike having envisaged the wire springing free of the port for'ard hydroplane, but aware this might be wishful thinking. If the construction he'd put on it had been wrong from the start, for instance, and whether it hadn't been almost too easy . . .

'Sharp?'

'*Cleared*, sir. Seemed real solid, but –'

'Midships the wheel, Cottenham.'

'Midships, sir –'

'Stop starboard. Ship's head?'

'Three-one-four, sir. Three-one-six –'

To Newcomb, 'Slow ahead together.' Because she'd still have stern-way on. And to Cottenham as the screws' thrust checked that, 'Port ten, steer three-one-oh.' In order to pass at no great distance from that same mine-wire: passing reasonably close to it, touch wood without hitting the bloody thing

82

again, you'd be less likely to hit another. Better the devil one knew, in fact. If one did, if that hadn't been one of a fresh batch, newly laid.

New-laid closer to each other than the originals had been?

Getting clear of it now, anyway. Assume one *was* clear. He nodded to Jarvis. 'Fifty feet, Sub.'

Stay at fifty for – oh, twenty minutes, say. At three knots, two thousand yards. But come round to north before that. This would be keeping to the route as planned, whereas to hold on westward would lengthen it – for no good purpose, there surely being no reason to assume one was still in the minefield, either that the Wops *had* extended it or that one's DR position could be out by that much. Depth-gauge needles circling past 100 feet, Jarvis attending to the trim, and a particular alertness in faces of which one had a view. Newcomb's, for one – small eyes sharp – frankly, rat-like – nice enough lad, the shape of his face not *his* fault, and natural enough that not having previously rubbed up against mine-moorings the possibility of doing it again – well, especially if there might be a greater density even of the old ones at these intermediate depths . . . Amongst the things one didn't know, of course, was the depth of the mine itself below the surface, i.e. above *Ursa*'s casing. And he'd have given a lot to have had a sight of the wire, which if it had been there even a year would be slimy black and streamered with marine growth, or if of more recent origin, clean and shiny bright.

Seventy feet. Sixty-five. Rate of ascent noticeably slowing: although Jarvis would by now have passed the order to stop flooding and shut 'O'. Passing the sixty-foot mark more slowly still: 'planesmen getting the angle off her without having been told to – which Mike would have expected, naturally, of Petty Officer Bull, but not necessarily of Ordinary Seaman Sharp.

Hadn't had time to get to know much about him, this

far. He'd joined in Alexandria, out of the poor old *Medway*'s spare crew, *Ursa* having sailed from Malta short-handed after landing a VD case for treatment.

Fifty-five feet. Fifty-three.

'Fifty feet, sir.'

'Very good.' He told Cottenham, 'Starboard ten, steer north.'

'Steer north, sir.' Winding-on helm. 'Ten of starboard wheel on, sir.'

And Sharp was putting a few degrees of dive on the fore 'planes. Alive to the fact that putting on rudder tended to push the boat's bow upward. For some reason. Well – the turning moment imparting a beam-on, upward pressure of water under the cutaway shape of her forepart, hull-shape for'ard of the keel, was what caused it. 'U's were sensitive beasts, took a bit of understanding.

Three hours after clearing the minefield he surfaced her into darkness six and a half miles northwest of Marettimo, and altered course to 070 – turning the corner into what the Italians might almost legitimately regard as their own home waters. Which of course was where any self-respecting British submarine belonged. Doctrine according to old Jackie Fisher, incidentally – Britain's frontiers being the coastlines of the enemy. Thinking about that, telling the bastards telepathically *And we haven't come all this way just to admire their beauty, signor* . . . Fingers crossed, for targets – preferably whatever the Afrika Korps might be needing badly and going short of. Glasses at his eyes, sweeping slowly across his boat's low, semi-submerged forepart and down her starboard side. Slight chop on the sea, *Ursa* trimmed well down, thrusting through it, rolling a bit at these low, battery-charging revs and such wind as there was on her beam to port.

'All right, Pilot?'

'Fine, sir.'

'All yours, then.' Lowering his glasses. Danvers *not* lowering his, nor the lookouts intently scouring the darkness in their own sectors of white-flecked sea. It was good to see some broken water, after the last two days' glassy calm; on dived patrol the last thing you wanted was a millpond surface, and he'd been hoping it wouldn't last. He stepped into the hatch, climbed down through the tower; in the control room Chief McIver asked him, 'All serene up top, sir?'

'Serene enough, Chief. Little breeze from the northwest – what we need. Donks serene, are they?'

Donks as short for donkeys, slang for engines. McIver shrugging: 'No problems I'm aware of, sir.' The diesels *had* given problems, on occasion. Jerk of the head towards the galley: 'Rabbit stew, he's giving us.'

'Well – sooner the better . . .'

'Canna *abide* fucking rabbit!'

Cottenham would offer him corned beef as an alternative, no doubt.

'Captain, sir?'

Lazenby, PO telegraphist, with a page of signal-pad in his hand. 'Cipher to us, sir.'

Mike took it from him. The former schoolmaster would have decoded it himself in his little caboosh there. This was an innovation of Mike's own: ciphering and deciphering was supposed to be done by officers, but there were advantages in getting the stuff ready for use – as well as satisfying for Lazenby, who was well up to the job and totally reliable. Code and cipher books were kept in a safe, which in *Ursa* was in a corner of the W/T office, not as was customary in the control room. This had the secondary advantage of giving the helmsman more room for his legs than he'd have had otherwise.

Mike asked Lazenby – heading for the chart table and its light – 'From S.10?'

'No, sir. *Swordsman*. On patrol somewhere near?'

'Some way east of us.' From the Gib flotilla, on loan to the 10th and currently about a hundred and fifty miles east, top end of the Messina Strait. Shrimp had mentioned her in his briefing. Mike spread the flimsy sheet on the table's glass top and read the brief message in Lazenby's blue-pencilled copperplate. Telegraphists for some reason *always* used blue pencils.

To: Ursa, repeated Captain (S) 10, Vice-Admiral Malta, C-in-C Med and Admiralty: Italian light cruiser believed Garibaldi class with escort of two destroyers off Cape Milazzo 2050/23 course 270 speed 25. Time of origin, 2105.

Time now, just short of ten. A Wop cruiser off Cape Milazzo approx. one hour ago, split-arsing due west, i.e. *this* way. The stuff a submariner's dreams were made of. Except the bloody thing might stop off in Palermo. Might be its destination, or might put in there to fuel. If it had come out of the Messina Strait – as one could assume it must have – and somehow evaded *Swordsman* – CO Dan Gerahty – who'd either failed to get in an attack or done so and missed. Anyway, reaching for the tools – parallel rule and dividers – conscious already that if Palermo *was* its destination, at twenty-five knots – less than four hours anyway – *Ursa* wouldn't get anywhere near it tonight at any rate. But staying in that port how long, had to be the question. He called, 'Number One – check what we have on Garibaldi-class cruisers?'

Provoking interest and speculation all round – here in the control room, and as always spreading instantly through the boat. Starting close at hand with Jarvis's '*I'll* get it!' Meaning, get out *Jane's Fighting Ships*. Italian section. Mike in the meantime plotting the cruiser's track at twenty-five knots on course due west, noting that she'd be off Palermo in three hours, not four. Reducing speed then for the channel between those minefields – down to ten knots, say – might be anchored or

86

berthed by – oh, half an hour after midnight – holing-up then for the night at least, possibly several days. As likely as anything, though, only calling in for fuel. All guesswork, this, but guesswork being all you had to work on – backed of course by logic, what seemed *likely*, then such petty details as times, speeds, distances. If for instance her destination was Cagliari in Sardinia – even if *she* wasn't in need of fuel, her destroyers might be. Twenty-five knots for – well, *how* long? Might have started from Taranto, even. So – OK, assume it was simply a bunkering stop, in and out of Palermo then back on course for Cagliari. Whereas one's own intentions this far had been to dive at 0430 *here*, five miles northwest of Cape Gallo. Wouldn't do, now – not if the programme *was* Palermo and then Cagliari, as did seem likely. Shrimp's surmise – Wops anticipating a Malta convoy from the west, Cagliari an obvious place in which to lie in wait for it. Could be other units there already, and/or more to come. But this Garibaldi and her escorts (a) could have fuelled and got on their way again before 0430 – the time by which one did *have* to dive, for daylight, should do so therefore as near as possible to whatever would be her track and (b) would be more likely to set a course of something like 280, he thought. Turning on to that course ten miles north of the port, outer end of the swept channel. From ten miles north*east* of Cape Gallo, therefore, working up to full speed on – well, maybe not 280, maybe 275, 278 . . . Pencilling a 278 track on, anyway: guessing they might be on it by about 0600. While *Ursa*, diving at 0430, then an hour and a half at four knots on due north, might reach that track at – well, about six, too.

Might improve on that. Be on it by 0500, say. Early bird maybe not seeing the worm for an hour or two – or longer, depending on how long they spent in Palermo – this *was* plain guesswork, not much else, but –

Could do it anyway, by altering at once. Calling it ten p.m.

87

now – actually five-past, the watch had been changing around him while he was immersed in this – alter *now* to – something like 050 would do it. Or – 055. Alteration of fifteen degrees to port. And still dive at 0430 – with the box well up, and touch wood near enough to the Wop's track to hear them coming. All right, her track as it would be *if* she was bound for Cagliari via Palermo. There was a strong alternative that he'd had in mind since starting on this, and was going to have to work on now, but what he liked about *this* scenario was the 'have-your-cake-and-eat-it' element – *Ursa* in the Italians' 0500 position, then steering the reciprocal of their guessed-at course of 278 – reciprocal 098 degrees – so that if they'd stayed put in Palermo, which they might well have, the top end of that swept channel was where *Ursa* would end up anyway. Getting there at about – well, at the battery-conserving dived speed of four knots, and distance forty miles – early afternoon.

McLeod was hovering, dressed ready to go up and take over the watch from Danvers.

'*Jane's* is on the wardroom table, sir. Two ships in that class.'

'And a fair chance we might meet one of them. When you get up there, alter course to oh-five-five. Look here, though – I'll give you a quick run-down . . .'

He ran over it. Starting with *Swordsman's* sighting report and his own view that the course of 270 suggested Palermo as at least the Wops' initial destination. The rest of it then – 055 as *Ursa's* course from here to intercept, thence 098 to back-track them to Palermo.

McLeod nodded. 'Any luck, meeting them along the way.'

'But suppose she's heading straight to Cagliari, from Messina. Course'd be more like 280 than 270, one might've thought. Although ten degrees this way or that in a sighting report's hardly conclusive, is it? And in somewhat restricted waters there, might've wanted to clear Vulcano by more than

a mile or two, before settling on 280 or thereabouts. So –
could come down to *this*.'

The straight-line course from Cape Milazzo to Cagliari.

'At twenty-five knots they'd be here at 0200, here 0300,
and we could intercept by steering due north and increasing
to revs for seven knots. Dark hours interception on the
surface. Only thing is – if we went for this and it's the wrong
guess – well, diving at four-thirty, we're out in the deep field
and they could be passing ten or fifteen miles to the south
of us.'

'Yes. Yes, I suppose . . .'

'I'm going for the Palermo option. Come round to oh-
five-five.'

The two cruisers of that class were the *Giuseppe Garibaldi* and
the *Duca degli Abruzzi*. Both completed in 1937, displacement
under full load 9,000 tons, main armament of ten six-inch
guns, speed 35 knots; the *Abruzzi* was said to have made 38
on her trials. And what mattered most from the point of view
of torpedo attack was that they drew seventeen feet.

Set the fish to run at fourteen feet. Too deep to hit a
destroyer – the Aviere-class for instance drew only ten or
eleven – but *Ursa's* target was the cruiser, not her escort, and
the aim would be to sink her, which was best achieved by
hitting her a fair distance below the waterline.

Ursa on course 055 now, making five knots and of course
battery-charging. Danvers at the chart, at Mike's suggestion
making his own assessments of possible enemy routes and
timings. Mike thinking, while conscious of the aroma of Manoel
Island Bunny – Chef Cottenham's name for his rabbit stew –
about that cruiser getting past *Swordsman* as it had. Visualising
it: the cruiser coming out of the narrow bottleneck of the
Messina Strait at say twelve or fifteen knots, then abruptly
shoving her wheel hard over and cracking on the revs. Gerahty

sweating blood in an effort to get into position for even a long-range overtaking shot; but with that lot's speed, and the distance from which he might have made the sighting – might well have been several miles to the north of them, in fact – his only chance of getting in an attack being if *they*'d held on northward – Naples-bound, for instance – so he'd have had no chance at all. Another thing, though – they might not have come *through* the Strait, maybe only *out* of it, might have been in Messina itself. Smallish port, but room enough for a light cruiser and two destroyers all right. The eight-inch cruiser *Bolzano* had been in the dockyard there for months after *Triumph* – W. J. Woods – had blown her screws off. But that would answer one other niggling, back-of-the-mind concern, namely whether the bastards mightn't also have got past *Ultra* – Jimmy Ruck, whom Shrimp had stationed off Cape dell'Armi in the Strait's wide southern entrance. *Ultra* would have been on that billet two or three days now.

Better bloody well not get past *Ursa*, was all. He called in the direction of the galley, 'Anyone seen our rabbit?'

He was on the bridge soon after midnight, an extra pair of eyes in the starboard for'ard corner, Jarvis as officer of the watch necessarily on the port side where the voice-pipe was. Friday now. *Ursa* trimmed low in the heave of dark, white-streaked sea, with 'Q' flooded, only 1 and 6 main ballast *not* full. Battery density rising as it should have been, and in the after ends they'd had the compressor running, building up reserves of bottled high-pressure air. It was darker than the last two nights had been, with quite a lot of cloud, stars visible only in clear patches here and there. Not a lot of wind, but with the change of course what there was of it was for'ard of the beam, so that even at these low revs she was kicking the stuff up a bit.

Visualising the Italians smashing through it – while drying the front lenses of his glasses on a wad of periscope paper – seeing the cruiser and her consorts racing westward. In *Jane's Fighting Ships* there was a photograph, taken evidently from a low-flying aircraft, of the *Abruzzi* at what must have been her flat-out speed: calm sea, and the rather beautiful, immensely powerful ship carving her way through it. Mountainous bow-wave, brilliant spreading wake, guns jutting skyward.

Racing *this* way – please . . .

Glasses up again: sweeping slowly across the bow from right to left, circling slowly back clockwise as far as about forty, fifty degrees on the starboard side, covering the sector in which they *might* appear. If for instance they were hugging the Sicilian coast, for some reason – intending to turn the corner either inside or outside Marettimo, making for the North African coast?

Could be. None of this was anything more than guess-work.

Sweeping left again – for maybe the thousandth time. Allowing himself the privilege of watching just this sector, while Jarvis and the lookouts covered the whole three-sixty degrees of surrounding sea and sky. One o'clock now. If one's guess had been wrong and the Italians were on their way directly to Cagliari, they'd just about have passed Ustica, would be something like thirty-five miles northeast, crossing *Ursa's* line of slow advance at right-angles: such a rapid change of bearing that when she dived at four-thirty they'd be more than sixty miles north*west* – in other words, *gone*. He had his own chartwork clearly in mind, was aware that in those hypo-thetical circumstances the nearest they'd get to each other would be at about 0200 – twenty miles apart then, on a bearing of about due north. From then on, range opening.

OK. *Could* be. As well to recognise it, be prepared for it

– while still actually reckoning on their being either en route from Palermo or still there, snoring in their bunks. Which would be perfectly OK. Not as good as running into them at say five, six or seven a.m., but in the long run – a day, two or three days, a week, even . . .

At 0330, near enough, Cape San Vito would be abeam to starboard, distance about twelve miles. One might assume they were *not* coast-hugging or corner-turning: for one thing because it was unlikely – where would they be making for, after all – Tunis, Bizerta? – and for another, the light on that cape might have been switched on for them, if they'd had any such intention. The Italians did often enough switch on coastal lights during movements of fleet units, and San Vito would have been the most useful one in those circumstances.

Maybe wouldn't light the place up for just one cruiser, though.

Danvers had the watch now. Lookouts were Llewellyn and Brighouse, a stoker who came from St Austell in Cornwall and was known to his mates as 'Snozzle' – nothing to do with his nose, which was in no way spectacular, but from the way he pronounced St Austell. He was on the short side, with long arms – which was noticeable when he had binoculars at his eyes.

Three-thirty *now*. Even fewer stars visible than there had been earlier. And one hour to go. Danvers' watch would end at four-fifteen, and as before Mike would tell McLeod to stay below, dive her himself at half-past. Or maybe stay up a bit longer than that, depending on the light.

Red watch lookouts took over at four, Mike sent Danvers down at a quarter-past and the lookouts ten minutes later: had the bridge to himself then, *Ursa* at the point where her 055-degree track intersected with the Italians' theoretical 278.

92

There was a slight greying in the clouded eastern sky, but no discernible horizon as yet. Wind about force 3, west-northwest. The overcast was, as he'd guessed, making a considerable difference – no good reason to dive, as things still were; if there was going to be anything to see you'd see it a lot better – and sooner – from up here, fifteen feet above the surface, than you would through a periscope only a couple of feet above it.

Hardly likely to meet them at this point of intersection anyway. Might, by sheer fluke, but much more likely in a couple of hours, or say mid-forenoon. He called down, 'Starboard ten.'

'Starboard ten, sir!' Then 'Ten of starboard wheel on.' Smithers, gunlayer. Mike told him, 'Steer oh-nine-eight.'

Straightening, as that order was repeated, glasses up again while the ten-degree angle of rudder hauled her round. Wind right astern then, stink of diesel in it. Smithers reporting after a few seconds, 'Course oh-nine-eight, sir.'

'First Lieutenant on the voice-pipe.'

McLeod's voice: 'Sir?'

'Might stay up a bit longer, Number One. How's the box?'

'Close to right up, sir.'

'So stop engines, slow together grouped down, close up asdics, all-round listening watch.'

Diesels' racket faltering, dying away. Motors weren't audible from up here, only the tremor in her steel, butting motion as she drove through the low black foam-flecked ridges, and the sound of the sea flooding aft along her sides and over the pressure-hull inside the casing, thumping around the tower's base. Glasses half up again: but aware suddenly that that broad pre-dawn flush was already something to take notice of – acquiring colour too, enough of it already in the sky to be staining this surrounding whiteness pink.

'Bridge?'

He stooped to it, and McLeod told him asdics weren't getting anything.

'Keep listening.'

Ahead there, what had been a band of colour was now a mass of it – the overhead brightening too although there were clouds still jet-black against it. Dramatic enough, but nothing in it of the kind one had been praying for in the past few hours. And dazzle-effect increasing, so best not goof at it. Best in fact take her down – the enemy having their own submarines, for which one wasn't keen to make oneself a target, in silhouette against that fast-spreading brilliance. He called down, 'Open one and six main vents', shut the cock on the voice-pipe and slid into the hatch, dragging the lid shut over his head and jamming the clips on as the sea flooded up around the tower.

6

Daylight now, sunrise colours faded, the sun itself no longer blinding as it climbed behind ribs of cloud. Nothing of any greater interest visible either in the overhead or seascape, the whole circle of horizon hard-edged, unbroken – no destroyers' or cruisers' funnel-smoke, masts or fighting-tops. Damn-all. But OK, long day ahead . . . He pushed the 'scope's handles up and stepped back, ERA Ellery doing his customary knees-bend in depressing the lever that sent it down into its well: soft thump as it stopped, then only the ticking of the log, the port motor's low thrum at slow grouped down, men's quiet movements on the 'planes, helm, asdics. Red watch, this. McLeod OOW, currently attending to the trim, Fraser on asdics, headphones on his yellow head, Ellery tall, bony-faced, at the panel of vents and blows, Coxswain CPO Swathely on after 'planes and AB Smithers on the for'ard ones, Smithers as always chewing gum. Walburton, signalman, on the wheel, Torpedoman Barnet on telegraphs. Needles in the depth-gauges at 28 feet and as steady as you'd want them, although McLeod was still fiddling at the order instrument. At slow ahead grouped down on only one motor, speed through the water something like two knots, you did need to have the trim about as good as you could get it. After diving he'd blown 'Q' then vented the trapped HP air outboard – to sea – not wanting to build up pressure in the boat, and taking advantage of the then poor light up top – large bubbles breaking into a fairly placid surface being very much a give-away otherwise, if there'd been eyes up there to see it. Aircraft passing anywhere near, for instance. But since then he'd been making minor adjustments via the trimline.

Mike said, 'I'll leave you to it, Jamie.'

'Right, sir.'

Bacon frying. Unmistakable, and mouth-watering. Mike adding as McLeod moved towards the periscope and Ellery brought it shimmering up, 'Might well be the odd shagbat around, by the way.'

'Aye, sir.' Surface-brightness glittering in his eyes as he began to circle. One of the others would no doubt be relieving him presently for his breakfast. Mike pausing at the chart, thinking that air patrols were definitely on the cards – reconnaissance ahead of the cruiser for one thing, but also if they'd picked up *Swordsman*'s enemy report. Wouldn't have needed to *know* anything of its content, only that a signal had been passed at that time and in that vicinity: especially if *Swordsman* had made her presence known, *had* got in an attack for instance. If they had picked it up they'd know or guess that *a* submarine had made it, with the obvious intention of alerting others.

Air-search would be their answer to it. Likely type of 'shagbat' being the Cant seaplane. But surface craft out of Palermo too. Thinking about that, pencilling-in DR positions along this 098-degree track, he noted that at midday *Ursa*'d be within five miles of Shrimp's reference position for this patrol: right on station, despite the cruiser business.

Shrimp back there in Lazaretto no doubt keenly awaiting news of a cruiser sunk.

Tonight, perhaps, the pleasure of sending him that signal?

Meanwhile though, no hurry. Hence the crawl. Conserving battery power for action that might come anywhere along this track, any time. You'd have Cape Gallo abeam at 1900, be off the Palermo gulf when the light was fading, and still have juice in the box. Dived attacks did tend to squander the amps, with bursts of underwater speed often necessary.

He spent another minute, on an afterthought and somewhat grudgingly, checking on where the Garibaldi might be by this time if she'd been heading directly to Cagliari from Messina. And the answer was, at twenty-five knots, at 0530 *here* – out in the middle, well over halfway, with about seventy-five miles to go. Would be in or entering Cagliari therefore – *if* that was the way they'd gone – in say three hours' time.

Unthinkable. Distinctly possible though it was.

Danvers was at the wardroom table, glancing through a copy of *Good Morning*, a mini-newspaper / entertainment sheet produced for submarine crews by the *Daily Mirror*. Copies were numbered, not dated, and the most popular item in it was the *Jane* strip-cartoon. You took a batch with you on patrol and the coxswain distributed them each morning to the various messes. Danvers put it aside: the table was already set for breakfast.

'Morning, sir. Bacon and eggs again, would you believe it!'

'Well, the fragrance does suggest it.' A nod towards Jarvis's recumbent form. 'He's not snoring. Make sure he's breathing?'

After breakfasting he settled on his bunk, thinking to get some rest while things were quiet – in the hope of being busy later. Thinking about the Garibaldi docking in Cagliari though: it wasn't easy to put out of mind. Not that there was any reason to start thinking one had made the wrong decision, only that the possibility continued to exist, would until or unless one ran into them – or ran them to earth in Palermo. Might get a sight of the cruiser's foretop and twin cowled funnels over the surrounding breakwater, for instance – from somewhere near the top end of the swept channel, in high power, with the periscope right up?

'Captain in the control room!'

Alarm call from Danvers, and Mike virtually already there, having in transition become awake enough to realise this was now the afternoon. He'd slept during the forenoon, lunched, read Steinbeck for a while, dozed again: while here and now Danvers had started the periscope down, Mike's arrival checking this so McIver had stopped it and had it shooting up again, Danvers explaining 'More A/S schooners, sir, a pair of 'em off Cape Gallo steering west.' *More* because there'd been some this morning – early, in Danvers' eight-to-ten watch. He was saying, 'As they're going now they'll pass abeam, but not by far.'

'The one right ahead of us wouldn't, Pilot.'

Snort of surprise from Danvers – that there was a third he hadn't seen. Mike admitting, 'Still mostly hull-down, not all that conspicuous.' Changing to air-search in case there was anything up *there* that mightn't have been in sight a minute earlier. Fast all-round search, finding nothing other than broken cloud, then a more careful one and finally back on the three white-painted schooners – wondering why the Italians painted them like that, making them so conspicuous. Maybe so they could recognise each other? For the benefit of shore signal stations, more likely. In any case, better skirt around them. They weren't exactly deadly – had guns on them, of course, certainly machine-guns, hydrophones rather than asdics, and didn't have the speed to have any use for depth-charges. The pair this morning had been to the east of Cape San Vito, in the ten-mile-wide Golfo di Castellamare, well south of *Ursa*'s track, might have come out of Castellamare itself – it was a dockyard port, ship-builders and repairers. Mike had taken a look at the schooners, checked they didn't have a Cant working with them, told Danvers to be sparing in his use of the periscope and gone back to his bunk, dozed until it had been time for corned beef and pickles, chutney etc.

He sent the 'scope down, moved to the chart, decided that a course alteration of just eight degrees would do the trick. Time now, 1510.

The schooners could be making a sweep ahead of the cruiser's exit from Palermo. Alternatively might not have anything to do with it. This kind of anti-submarine activity wasn't in any way unusual; especially in an area like this one, where submarines might be expected – the Egadi Channel, Marettimo corner, much-used route for convoys to the Western Desert – Bizerta, Tripoli, wherever. And they could make quite a nuisance of themselves, those schooners, especially in combination with air patrols, E-boats, whatever.

He told Danvers, 'Bring her to oh-nine-oh. Let me know of any change. When we're past and clear, come back oh-nine-eight.'

Past seven now, and at the chart again. Jarvis, whose watch this was, had put on a 1900 fix by land bearings, and Mike had come through to see where they were and how things might go in the next few hours. *Ursa*'s position being seven and a half miles NNE of Cape Gallo. The precise extent of Palermo's defensive minefields being one consideration: Danvers had inked them on in accordance with information disseminated by Admiralty, but it had caught Mike's eye that for up to about five miles around that headland there was no more than two hundred feet of water; it would surely have made sense to have mined it, at least the stretch along

99

its eastern seaboard above Palermo itself. Hardly believable that they hadn't, in fact: the field as they'd declared it covered quite a large area outside it in any case, in much deeper water.

Mines where they *had* declared them – however long ago but surely renewed / replaced since then – then the swept channel looping out northeastward, further mine-belts to the east of that as far as a minor promontory named on the chart as Cape Zafferano.

Could be a trap there inside Gallo, he thought. Unwary Anglo seeking to nobble Wop vessel in swept channel by firing from allegedly *un*mined inshore water that's as likely as not stiff with the bloody things?

Pull the other one, *signore*.

Tonight in any case one had to (a) assume the cruiser *was* in the harbour, and (b) be prepared for it to come sneaking out some time around sunset in order to make its run to Cagliari during the hours of darkness. Visualising that exit: escorting destroyers emerging first, maybe pinging around a bit as a precaution against ambush, the Garibaldi then pounding out, destroyers taking station ahead and all under port helm, settling on say 330 degrees for a few miles before altering to 280.

How best to cope with this? Which although speculative was realistic; if they were coming out, that was near enough how they'd set about it. So – give them room to clear the channel and form up on something *like* 330, then 280, *Ursa* biding her time in what one might call a stand-off position from which to close in for as near as possible a beam shot on either of those courses. At first sight a little tricky, but probably achievable through knowing from the start that a 50-degree alteration was to be expected, and near enough *when*. He'd aim to get in his attack either well before or very soon after they'd made the turn.

100

After. Definitely, *after*. Accepting, incidentally, that it might be too late then for a dived attack. Surface and close in fast, trimmed right down. Alternatively, if attacking dived and the light went, fire by asdics. One did always have that option. No change of course or speed meanwhile: another two hours like this, and at 2100 you'd be – *here*. Alter then, he thought, to – say, 045. Opening the range a bit, giving oneself more room for manoeuvre – for surfacing, if that was how it turned out – and guessing at 2130 as the time they'd make their move. Dusk in the offing then, sure, but recalling how last night in very similar conditions the light had seemed to be lasting almost for ever then suddenly went to pot. Might reckon on having it until nine-forty or fifty, no later?

Two long hours later, 2100, the light was still good enough to check the boat's position by periscope bearings of Cape Gallo's right-hand edge and the centre of a smoke-haze over Palermo. After sundown, might become a light-haze, he guessed. Some local phenomenon. Not calling this a fix, anyway, only a check, but reassuring in that it matched the charted DR position. He told Danvers, 'Bring her to oh-four-five.'

'Oh-four-five, sir.' To Llewellyn on the wheel then, 'Port ten.'

'Port ten, sir!'

As if delighted to be doing something other than keeping her head on 098, as they'd been doing ever since the deviation around those schooners. Mike told Knox – telegraphist, but volunteer part-time unqualified asdic operator – 'Listen, a minute.' Knox wore a beard – real one, glossy brown, not just the few days' stubble Mike and most others had to show – also had the tattoo of a red heart with a blue letter 'C' in it on his forearm. About which there was some anecdote or other. Oh – that he'd genuinely forgotten the name, what

101

the 'C' stood for. Caroline, Cynthia, Clarice, Clementine? Rival claimants presumably not discouraged – wouldn't be more than one at any one time? Easing the headset off one ear, and Mike telling him, 'We've had Palermo on the beam, due south. Now altering course northeast, putting it on about green 135. If our cruiser's in there, she might break out around sunset – next hour or so, I'm guessing. So carry on listening all round but with particular attention to that sector – green 130 to 140, right?'

'Turbines, would that be, sir?'

'Fast turbines, all of 'em. Cruiser, two destroyers, probably working up to twenty-five knots.'

'Course oh-four-five, sir.'

Knox had the headset back on, had trained to that bearing and was fingering the knob a degree or two this way and that, eyes narrowed in concentration. The set in this listening-out mode was no more than a directional hydrophone, its operator's skill lying primarily in the recognition and inter-pretation of sounds received.

Warmth, quiet, general fug. Own nerves a little taut: really did *want* this cruiser. Meeting CERA McIver's scowl: 'All right, Chief?'

'Reckon the fuckers'll come out, sir?'

'Can't even be sure they're in there. But if they are . . .' A shrug, hand raised with fingers crossed.

'Aye . . .'

He'd drifted through to the wardroom, where an hour or so ago they'd enjoyed a supper of cold tongue and tomatoes, both canned, getting that over early in the hope of having their hands full later. McLeod and Jarvis were both at the table, McLeod reading Edgar Wallace, Jarvis scribbling in what looked like a diary. Diaries were *verboten*, so it couldn't be, had to be his memoirs.

McLeod said, 'No activity as yet.'

'Nearer dark's the more likely time.'

Jarvis nodded: 'That's your Wop for you, all right.'

'On the other hand they may be whooping it up in Cagliari. Could have been there since noon or earlier.'

'*But* –' McLeod – 'to have covered both alternatives we'd have had to be in two places at once, and *either* way –'

'Captain in the control room!' Adding – Danvers continuing, in more or less one utterance as Mike shot through – 'Knox reports fast turbine HE on green 138, sir.'

Bearing of the Palermo exit channel, near enough. Mike said, 'Diving stations.' A feeling of having guessed right, after all. Relief tinged with surprise, oddly enough. Adding as the rush began, 'Well done, Knox.' McLeod was at the trim, ordering half ahead both motors – ensuring sufficient power to maintain control of her during the wholesale shifting of body-weights. Hands closing up swiftly and quietly, looking pleased about it as they always did. Action being what they were here for, worked for, *wanted*, put up with the hazards and fairly considerable discomfort for. Although Fraser the HSD, in headphones still warm from Knox's ears, was looking uncertain as he minutely adjusted the set's bearing, eyes beady on the compass dial while most of the concentration was through his ears. Coxswain and PO Tubby Hart on hydroplanes, AB Smithers at the wheel, Telegraphist Martin on a stool in that corner as telephone link to the fore ends and tube space. Newcomb at motor-room telegraphs, and of course Ellery at the panel – knees-bending to bring the periscope up, Mike having glanced his way with a small movement of both hands. CERA McIver standing back out of it at the moment but ready to play his part if that was the way things went. All in all, in the space available – Danvers taking up some of it at the chart table, Jarvis too, at the Fruit Machine – if you'd had a ship's cat it wouldn't have been

103

easy to swing it round. Mike at the periscope meanwhile completing a quick check on the overhead – sky darkened by cloud but also streaked here and there with colour. He pushed the handles up: having shown as little periscope as possible for as short a time as possible, bearing in mind that at these increased revs it would have been feathering.

'Come down to slow both when you can, Number One.'

'Aye, sir.'

Fraser, then: 'E-boats, sir, not destroyers. On 140, 144, right to left – revs for like twenty, thirty knots –'

'Not transmitting, then.'

'No, sir, too fast.'

'Yes.' Initial chagrin at their not being the destroyers was mitigated somewhat in guessing this could be a preliminary to the heavier ships' emergence. Also recognition that with the light fading as it was, there couldn't be much prospect of a dived attack. Delay therefore essential: two requirements before one could surface being (a) darkness, and (b) absence of bloody Mas-boats.

'Both motors slow ahead grouped down, sir.'

He'd grunted acknowledgement to McLeod. 'Where now, Fraser?'

'Green seven-oh, six-five, sir – still right to left –'

Circling, according to the picture in his mind. Wide, anticlockwise sweep of this gulf, engines screaming, slim hulls crashing across the choppy, darkening water. They were much more likely to be Italian Mas-boats than German E-boats, on this side of Sicily. Similar to E-boats – fast patrol craft, some *very* fast, one type credited with a speed of forty-seven knots – equipped with torpedoes, machine-guns and depth-charges, although they were too small to carry many, depth-charges being heavy, bulky things. The prefix MAS, according to *Jane's*, stood for *Motoscafi Anti-Sommergibili*. *Sommergibili* meaning submarine.

Weren't hunting *this Sommergibili*, anyway. If they'd had reason to believe there might be one lurking in the gulf they'd have reduced speed and begun an asdic sweep – pinging, seeking contact, which at high speed was impracticable. They couldn't even have been listening-out on theirs as *Ursa* was on hers.

He told McLeod, 'Forty feet.'

'Forty feet, sir.'

'Then let's have one motor stopped –'

'Aye, sir –'

'– and switch to night lighting.'

Red bulbs replacing white ones, so his own eyes and the lookouts' would be at least partially adjusted to night vision by the time he surfaced her. Angle on the 'planes, meanwhile, bubble in the inclinometer a couple of degrees aft. With dusk thickening – and as yet nothing to look at anyway – might as well play it safe. Didn't stop one *hearing* whatever might be happening up there.

Fraser's voice intoned, 'Directly towards, sir. Green 75, green 80 . . .'

Having circled the gulf, he thought, now steering west. To round Cape Gallo, maybe? Either that, or they'd turn inside it. At the chart, the moving picture in his mind telling him they'd turn short of the shallower water this side of Gallo, be on course then to return to their starting-point, top end of the swept channel.

Meeting their chums there maybe, ostensibly having cleared their exit route for them?

Stupid buggers, though. What purpose served?

He could hear them now. Everyone could. Similar to the approach of a distant train, sound expanding on a rising note – Doppler effect – starboard side and here already – coming over *now*. McLeod rubbing the back of his neck, reporting, 'Forty feet, sir.'

105

Crashing over. In other circumstances might have been alarming – often had been – but since these were totally unaware of the presence right under them of one of the 10th Flotilla's more distinguished *Sommergibilis* –

Gone over. Falling note now, and contracting – port quarter, anyway somewhere abaft that beam. Helms over now, boys, or you'll be running into Gallo, might regret it . . . Pencil-tip moving lightly on the chart, sketching their likely westward curve, then checking the bearing of the swept channel exit from *Ursa's* position now. He asked Fraser, 'Anything around 142?'

Trying that. McLeod meanwhile proposing, 'Stop port motor, sir?'

'Well, why not.'

Seeing as the less noise you made the better you heard whatever there might be to hear. The Mas-boats' racket had faded to a distant, dying murmur. Presumably holding on, *not* turning inside Gallo.

Making for *where*, then? Trapani'd be in their range, all right. Or Marsala. Cagliari even, but not at anything like that speed.

Fraser told him, 'Nothing on that bearing, sir.'

'Port motor stopped, sir, starboard slow ahead grouped down.'

'Very good.' Saving amps as well as keeping quiet. He told Fraser, when the HSD had uncovered one ear, 'Listen-out all round but concentrate on 140 to 145.'

Time, 2212. At the chart table, pondering the advantages /disadvantages of staying down another twenty or thirty minutes or going on up pretty well right away. It would be dark enough by this time, but a contingency to be wary of was a possible return of the Mas-boats – completion of joyride, tearing back around the headland. Change the whole set-up: *Ursa* being as yet undetected, which was the way to be:

106

once spotted, much less good. Even worse, to be stumbled on in the minute or two of surfacing, blind and helpless.

Would be a relief to get up there, though. Fresh air for one thing, start getting the battery up for another, *and* be ready for the cruiser if it did come out.

As likely now as it had seemed an hour ago?

Knowing the answer near enough, but still checking – dividers set at fifty nautical miles for each two-hour interval at twenty-five knots, and starting now – 2215. Answer being no, they wouldn't make Cagliari before daylight, which one might assume would be the whole point of making a dark-hours passage.

At thirty knots instead of twenty-five, though?

The hell with it. He cocked an eyebrow at Fraser: 'Anything?'

Shake of the head – hadn't needed to *hear* the question. Mike said, 'Twenty-eight feet.'

'Twenty-eight feet, sir . . .'

At the scope – a glance at Ellery – and he had his eyes at the lenses, his body straightening in parallel with the brass tube as its top window broke surface. Tumble of dark water flecked with pearls and diamonds, streaky night sky roofing a close-up of jumpy surface, but horizontally – middle distance or beyond – damn-all. Three hundred and sixty degrees of that. He snapped the handles up.

'Stand by to surface.'

Get up there, breathe night air, get the box in shape for tomorrow's dived patrol. Not forgetting the Garibaldi, but not expecting it either. Facing this now – that he'd had a presentiment growing on him of having missed the bus. Could be wrong, but at this moment it was how he felt – maybe through having expected action and almost seen it coming, then had nothing out of it but bloody Mas-boats arsing around up there. Hearing McLeod's orders and the

107

responses to them: main vents checked shut, HP blows open, etcetera: thinking to himself in the motors' hum and the aura of soft reddish light that if the sod *was* in there he might well be staying put, on station for action against the Gib convoy when that time arrived; in which case air reconnaissance from Malta would be likely to spot him there and Shrimp would leave *Ursa* here to mark him.

So in the end – touch wood . . .

McLeod had put both motors to half ahead.

'Ready to surface, sir.'

2240 now. *Ursa* low in the sea's white-streaked blackness, with four of her main ballast and 'Q' flooded, engines pounding in a way you'd imagine them being heard onshore in Palermo even; but in reality enfolded by the night and by the sea's own murmur, audible to keen ears at maybe a thousand yards, half a mile, not much more. On course due west across the gulf's wide northern approaches, sea-mist limiting visibility in some sectors, despite a wisp of brand-new moon showing occasionally between whorls of high, thin cloud. The Gallo headland from this perspective was like the hump of a whale's back – whale floating in mist though, not water, the mist in fact confusing visibility as much as limiting it.

McLeod's watch – having relaxed from diving stations to Red watch, patrol routine. Lookouts in the bridge Barnet and Simms – leading stoker – both in wool hats, sweaters, oilskins, glasses permanently at their eyes as they slowly swivelled, their backs against the periscope standards. One eternal truth being that maximum efficiency of looking out was a major factor not only in finding targets but in staying alive.

Like the U-boat they'd sunk in the Norwegian Sea in the course of *Ursa*'s work-up patrol from the Clyde. McLeod had had that dived watch, the first dog, made the sighting at medium range in a sea rough enough to have been making depth-keeping difficult. Within minutes of his startled 'Captain in the control room!' Mike had fired a salvo of four fish, hit the German amidships with one of them and broken him in two, the bow section taking long enough to sink for both McLeod and the coxswain, Swathely, at Mike's invitation to have a brief sight of it through the periscope. There'd been no possibility of survivors, and part of the satisfaction had been that it had been outward bound from Bergen to the North Atlantic killing-ground where it would inevitably have made its own contribution to the month's death-toll of British and Allied seamen. And if it had had one sharper-eyed or wider-awake lookout in its bridge, who might have spotted *Ursa*'s periscope of which several feet must have been exposed at the time for either McLeod or Mike himself to have had any view at all over the foam-crested ridges of that force 6 – those noncombatants' deaths instead of the predators'. As it *had* been, forty or more Germans in one torpedo blast, for the want of a better-trained pair of eyes.

'Bridge!'

McLeod stooping above the voice-pipe, still with binoculars at his eyes: 'Bridge.'

'PO Tel, sir. Cipher the captain will want to see.'

'Tell him I'm coming down.'

'Captain's coming down.'

In the hatch, clambering down through the rush of air into the soft light and the jolting warmth. Lazenby was there waiting for him: also Swathely, Ellery, Fraser, all to put it mildly showing interest, the telegraphist offering Mike a sheet of pink signal-pad – pink for Secret – with his own bluecrayon scrawl on it. Mike held it under the chart light, read *To: S.10, repeated Ursa, Swordsman, V.A. Malta, C-in-C Med and Admiralty. From: Unsung.*

Unsung, for Pete's sake . . .

109

Garibaldi-class cruiser torpedoed and sunk in position 38 degrees 51 N. 9 degrees 33 E.

'Be – bloody – *damned* . . .'

Hadn't meant to express his surprise aloud. Mightn't have been audible, in fact: Lazenby was blinking at him as if he hadn't caught it. 'The one would've been *our* bird, sir?'

'I'd say might have been.' Putting that position on the chart. Melhuish had made his kill twenty miles south of Cape Carbonara, Sardinia's southeast corner. The Italian would have been only an hour, hour and a half short of docking in Cagliari – and practically on *Unsung's* eastward track. Which she'd have resumed, of course, would have got this signal out shortly after surfacing.

Bloody lucky. And hell, give the bugger his due, bloody marvellous . . . A glance at Lazenby: 'Our bird if I'd called heads instead of tails. Lucky we had a longstop.'

And now forget Palermo, head for wider-open spaces. At this five knots, at least be out of the way of the Mas-boats if they came back – obliging one to dive, interrupting the battery-charge. Bring her round to something like north by east. On course for Naples, conceivably meeting traffic coming south *from* Naples.

Littorio-class battleship, for instance. That'd do nicely. Or a big, fat tanker. But warships of any kind, threats to the Gib convoy which must surely by now be imminent, or store-ships and especially fuel-carriers supplying Rommel's army in the desert. He put *Unsung's* signal on the clip, glanced at the clock – just past eleven – and moved towards the ladder.

'Tell the officer of the watch I'm coming up.'

'Aye, sir. Bridge! Cap'n on his way up, sir!'

Climbing – thinking about Melhuish and his triumph – flying start to his first operational command and joining the 10th Flotilla. The luck of being in exactly the right place at precisely the right time, of course. Mike telling himself then: *Wiped my bloody eye, is the long and short of it, leave it at that* . . . Out of the hatch now, in his ship's swaying, salt-glistening bridge. Moon – a scrap of it – very low, shrouded in sea-mist but well below the skirting of cloud; would be disappearing into that mist in the course of the next half-hour but meanwhile was creating a danger sector astern where any U-boat discovering *Ursa* against its spread of radiance would have the drop on her.

Of which these three would be aware, of course. Jamming himself into the bridge's starboard for'ard corner, putting his glasses up, searching that threatening stern sector past the squat oilskinned hump of Leading Stoker Simms: clearing his throat before telling McLeod, 'The signal was to S.10 from *Unsung* – on passage Gib to Malta, if you remember. Sank our cruiser – early this afternoon, in spitting distance of Cagliari.'

'Oh, damn it . . .'

Mike laughed. 'Nonsense. Thing's sunk, is what matters. Bring her round oh-two-oh, Jamie.'

'Oh-two-oh, sir.' Into the voice-pipe: 'Control room . . .'

An alteration of a hundred and ten degrees, to take her out of the gulf and clear of Cape Gallo, to start Saturday's dived patrol far enough offshore to intercept passing traffic as well as any to or from Palermo. Something like ten after eleven now, sunrise at about 0500; at this five knots, be about thirty miles offshore when one dived. Which would be a bit too far out, he thought: so alter back to a westerly course after say two hours. Cape San Vito attracted him, rather, looked good for chances of traffic from Naples or points north – Spezia for instance – heading to round Marettimo en route to Tripoli, Homs, Masurata and so forth.

'Course oh-two-oh, sir.'

111

McLeod acknowledging: Mike sweeping slowly up the starboard side, his binocular line of sight passing over Simms' head. Night vision barely up to scratch yet, after those minutes at the chart table. He told McLeod, lowering his glasses, 'Two hours like this, we'll alter to due west at 0100. I'll put it in the night-order book.'

Below, he heard them ditching gash, the watch changing at midnight, Jarvis taking over at a quarter-past and McLeod smoking a last cigarette over a mug of kye in the darkened wardroom. Saturday now. While at the chart table to amend his night orders he'd also roughly plotted *Unsung*'s track to Malta, noting that she'd be passing under the QBB 255 mines tomorrow, Sunday. And berthing at Lazaretto in due course with a red bar on her otherwise virgin Jolly Roger. Which of course *Ursa*'s had too, on account of that work-up patrol U-boat. Quite something – both of those – the breaking of the duck as one might call it. Compared for instance to the lousy start made by the highly respected David Wanklyn VC, who'd done his first few patrols in *Upholder* without hitting a damn thing. Shrimp, as whose first lieutenant he'd served pre-war in *Porpoise*, had been seriously worried as to whether he could justify his old friend's continuance as a CO – considerable expenditure of torpedoes and nothing to show for it, miss after miss. Then Wanklyn had suddenly got his eye in, got the *knack* as Shrimp described it, never missed another trick.

One of the nicest, most modest COs afloat, with a ship's company who worshipped him. Lost in mid-April of last year, somewhere north of Tripoli. Actually, a shocking loss.

McLeod had begun to snore. Probably join that chorus oneself, any minute now. Melhuish, though – rather a high opinion of himself, supercilious manner, in one's recollection of him?

112

Hadn't actually thought about him all that much. Hadn't wanted to – easier not to, in all the circumstances. Hadn't ever discussed him much with Ann, either. Out of resuscitated memory though – at Bill Gorst's wedding reception, Gorst introducing Melhuish with 'Charles is starting his Perisher this Monday as ever is. Doesn't know what he's in for, eh?' And Mike shaking hands with him while actually rather more aware of the man's incredibly attractive wife who was talking with Chloe just yards away – she'd noticed *him*, he remembered – noticed his interest in *her* – or Chloe might just have told her something earth-shaking like 'That's my brother Mike' – anyway, he and Melhuish shaking hands, and Mike naturally enough congratulating him on having been selected for the command course – for which he did look somewhat young – Melhuish answering with 'Thanks, but frankly it's come none too soon – my own possibly biased view of course, but I *have* been in the racket quite some while . . .'

Ann's hand in Mike's, eyes smiling into his: 'You're Mike Nicholson. Your sister was telling me . . .'

Telling her whatever . . . But that had been where it started – right there in the first moment of their meeting, damn-all to do with Melhuish or his opinion of himself.

Milky first light hardening, the sea's ruffled but currently unbroken surface reflecting it in morse-like flashes via the big 'scope's lenses into Mike's eyes as he circled. McLeod having dived her on the watch – at the trim now, confirming 'Twenty-eight feet, sir.'

'Stand by for some bearings.' Eyes off the lenses for a second, a glance at Walburton who was on the wheel – reaching for a stub of pencil.

'Gallo Head lighthouse.' Quick look up at the bearing-ring. 'Red 114.' Blaze of sunrise on its distant whiteness – brick, stucco or whatever – and then 'Right-hand edge Castellammare' – same procedure – 'Red 55.' In both cases Walburton had murmured 'Ship's head 270': true bearings were therefore 156 and 195. Periscope hissing down – Ellery's right hand on the lever, left hand up covering a yawn – Mike moving to the chart to put those bearings on for what would be only a rough fix, the right-hand edge of that promontory being a long way from clear-cut or precise. All one needed, anyway: there being no navigational hazards around, and no problems in fixing her more accurately during the course of the forenoon. Cape San Vito for instance, by about midday. He noted in the log: *Dived 0450, Gallo Head light 156 degrees 7.5 miles.*

'Stop one screw, sir?'

He nodded. 'By all means.' For minimal expenditure of amps, speed through the water no more than a knot and a half, enough to hold her in trim and for the periscope to make very little feather cutting through the surface. *Ursa* simply on her billet, where she was supposed to be – waiting, hoping, two-thirds of her crew asleep.

Jarvis, for one. Mike in the darkened wardroom, settling at the table, hearing a familiar sawing of wood and recalling an exchange between the two sub-lieutenants just recently – yesterday, might have been – Danvers asking Jarvis whether before he dragged some unfortunate female up the aisle he'd have the decency to warn her about his snoring, Jarvis replying that he wouldn't have to, she'd know all about it long before things reached that stage.

'But if she's the kind that won't?'

'Won't what?'

'You know. Do it *before*.'

'Be her lookout entirely, wouldn't it. She'd have had every opportunity, I assure you – and if she was that pig-headed –'

Danvers grinning: 'Determination to remain *intacta* until actually spliced isn't normally seen in that light, old man. In fact it's generally applauded.'

'Not by me, it isn't!'

Pointing at him: 'You reckon any popsie worth her salt getting a close-up of that great red face –'

Barnaby shaking with mirth as he put plates around; Jarvis scowling at him. Mike, who'd been reading, had cut in with 'Any promising candidates in the offing, Sub?'

'Oh . . .' Surprised by the intervention. Shrugging, then. 'Well – I mean, one or two, but –'

115

'That one in the Bay Hotel at Gouroch, for instance?'
Danvers confidentially to Mike: 'Crikey, sir, you should've
seen her . . .'

Cottenham interrupted Mike's reconstruction of that
dialogue: 'Tea, sir?'

'Why yes, thanks.'

'Comin' up . . .'

He didn't feel like turning in again. It had been a quiet
night – no return of the Mas-boats, no alarms. He'd dreamt
of Abigail, woken when McLeod had been altering from 020
to 270 and a White watch messenger had shaken Jarvis, who'd
then spent some time at the table hunched over a mug of
kye. Mike struggling to make head or tail of what had been
a confusing dream.

'Char, sir.'

'Thank you, Cottenham.'

'Shame we lost that Eyetie, sir.'

'Find a replacement, maybe.'

'I'll drink to that, sir.'

During the forenoon there were A/S schooners – three,
white-painted, probably the ones they'd seen the day before
– messing around a few miles inshore of them, and several
times seaplanes flying low along the coast. Natural inclination might have been to use the small 'attack' periscope rather
than the big one, but the advantage of its showing less feather
in the millpond surface was more than offset by its having
(a) no air-search facility – i.e. lenses not vertically tiltable,
which in fact presented a considerable hazard, chances for
instance of there being a Cant circling up there where it
could see you and you couldn't see *it*, wouldn't know it was
whistling-up destroyers, Mas-boats or whatever – and (b) no
magnification, such as the big search 'scope had, which was
extremely limiting. The best answer was ultra-cautious use

116

of the big one, each time with a rapid sky-search first and the ensuing all-round surface sweep interrupted by frequent 'dipping'. It made for very energetic watchkeeping – starting the procedure about every ten minutes, so it was virtually continuous – and absolutely essential, as Mike explained to them, on account of the possibility of a target's sudden appearance from the west side of Cape San Vito. If one showed at all, it *would* be sudden, and asdics would give no warning – the land-mass blanking off one's view of the San Vito – Trapani – Egadi islands area would be no less of a barrier to sound-waves.

Around midday the wind had been coming up a little, McLeod had reported; and when they were having lunch – sardines, cheese, biscuits, coffee – Jarvis put his head around the curtain: 'Stand some *good* news, sir?'

'Try me.'

'White horses developing all over, sir.'

'Ah. Three cheers.'

Thinking about it. Didn't have to go and look at the chart to know that *Ursa* was currently equidistant from the Castellammare headland and Cape San Vito, eleven or twelve miles from each: so he could alter say twenty degrees to port, shave the distance off-cape a little and open up their periscope view of that crucial area a bit sooner.

'Sub!'

Jarvis had stopped the periscope on its way up, Coldwell was sending it down again. Enquiring pink face there again beside the curtain.

'Sir?'

'Bring her to two-five-oh, Sub.'

'Two-five-oh. Aye aye, sir . . .'

One o'clock, that alteration. By four, Cape San Vito was due south and less than five miles away; OOWs could get good fixes on the lighthouse and both left- and right-hand edges, and with a broken surface neither the 'scope nor *Ursa* herself would be all that visible to any overflying Cants. Seascape meanwhile open and empty from fine on the port bow to the nearest of the Egadi islands: Marettimo actually forty miles ahead, beyond visibility range, Trapani down-coast southwestward only half that far. Trapani being an E-boat and/or Mas-boat base and linked by a coastal railway that ran south to Marsala.

Off and on through Danvers' afternoon watch and McLeod's first dog there were sightings of patrolling Cants, and fishing-boats working both sides of San Vito, but the A/S schooners from Golfo di Castellammare must either have gone home or turned back eastward. Periscope watch was still a lot easier than it had been. No less intense: with the Egadi Channel to port and the strategic Marettimo corner right ahead, west by south, a wide expanse of slightly choppy Tyrrhenian Sea open to surveillance from those for'ard bearings clear around to the other quarter – you might have thought the chances of some worthwhile target showing up between tea-time and sundown were as good as they'd have been anywhere.

Damn-all, though. Empty sea, empty day drawing towards its close.

He'd finished *The Moon is Down*. McLeod, having galloped through his Edgar Wallace, had asked to borrow it. Mike now squaring up to the Scott Fitzgerald that Jennie had sent him and he had to tackle now so that in his next letter he could tell her how much he'd enjoyed it. In fact she'd lent him an earlier book by Fitzgerald, and he hadn't got on with it all that well although she'd expected him to; and this one, he saw, was an *unfinished* novel, Fitzgerald having died in the course of writing it.

Give it a go, anyway.

118

At about seven, when they were still within a few miles of Cape San Vito, Jarvis picked up a pair of A/S trawlers on the bow to port, steaming north; they'd come into sight around the bulge of coastline above Trapani. They could have come out of Trapani or from further south; as they were heading now they'd be crossing *Ursa*'s track well beyond the point at which Mike intended turning north at about eight or eight-thirty.

Unless they were an advance guard of something else. Or might shortly alter to starboard to cut around San Vito – in which case he'd go deep, let them pass over. He told Jarvis, 'Watch 'em. Any change, call me.' In fact they passed ahead, their reciprocating engines audible on asdics and continuing north for some while before fading. *Might* acquire nuisance value later in the night, he suspected.

At eight-thirty he had Danvers bring her round to north, pretty well in the trawlers' wakes. Bright, lively evening, more spindrift flying than there had been earlier, and the wind had backed to westerly. The box was still reasonably well up, after this slow, quiet day, and he put her up to slow speed on both motors so that when he surfaced her at nine-fifty she was ten miles northwest of Cape San Vito. Patrol routine then, rolling slightly with the wind abeam, diesels pumping generator power into her batteries for the next day's exertions. Next day being Sunday – a more productive day than this had been, please God.

He was tucking into cold pork – Cottenham had gone so far as to make apple sauce to go with it – when Lazenby came with the decode of a signal that had been repeated to *Ursa* for information, Shrimp telling *Swordsman* to shift to a new billet somewhere on ten degrees east. Mike gave it to Danvers to put on the chart – knowing it had to be somewhere in the region of Cagliari, and having noted that Gerahty was being routed north of Ustica, well clear of *Ursa* – of

119

Unsung too, Melhuish if on schedule likely to be getting his box up in the QBB 255 approaches during the night. Mike had told Danvers to allow *Swordsman* twelve and a half knots surfaced and six dived, and the answers were that her new billet was between Capes Carbonara and Spartivento – pretty well where Melhuish had sunk his cruiser – and that she'd probably be there first light Monday.

Gib convoy on its way?

Swordsman having six bow tubes instead of four – maybe not having got in an attack on the Garibaldi, therefore six in the tubes plus six reloads – thus well prepared for the Wop surface deployments that were anticipated. While in leaving *Ursa* where she was, was Shrimp reckoning on her having her eight fish still – guessing that if Mike had got in an attack on the cruiser he'd have hit her and he, Shrimp, would have known about it? Actually plain common sense, Mike thought – what one might call Shrimp's speciality. Crossing fingers – while requesting Jarvis to shove over the apple sauce – guessing the convoy most likely *was* on its way, and *Ursa* exactly where Shrimp wanted her – i.e. where she'd have a decent chance of worthwhile targets. He'd be shifting Ruck and Mottram, as like as not, while of the boats he'd had in the Bizerta–Cape Bon–Pantellaria–Hammamet southern periphery of the convoy's route some at least would have been recalled, rearmed and revictualled and sent out again in the course of the past few days.

Or that might be happening now. If the convoy was only now entering the Med, say – escort including a battleship and a carrier or two joining it out of Gib, as Shrimp had indicated. Not that such heavyweights were likely to stay with the convoy even as far as this central basin. Destroyers and maybe a cruiser or two would quite likely come through to Malta, but air-cover would by that stage be from the island itself – from Luqua, Ta' Qali, Hal Far.

120

'Sir?'

Breaking out of his thoughts: focusing on Jarvis across the littered table. 'Yes, Sub?'

'Think shifting *Swordsman* to Cagliari might mean a convoy fnally?'

'It might well.'

'Wop fleet movements on the cards, then?'

He shrugged. 'Say your prayers.'

Sunday forenoon prayers, for those so inclined, as in fact requested by several members of the ship's company – notably Stoker PO Franklyn, who'd have liked a hymn or two as well as prayers, only no one else wanted to take it that far. Franklyn had a bass voice which he'd exercised more than once at concert parties, his favourite renditions being 'Yours' and 'Trees'. Attendance in any case was voluntary, except for the men on watch in the control room, which was the obvious assembly point – after end of the compartment, beside the wireless office, leaving the area around the search periscope uncluttered. The muster was at eleven a.m., in McLeod's watch, some watchkeepers joining in while still doing their jobs. Swathely on after 'planes for one, Walburton, Smithers and ERA Ellery as well. For Jarvis and Danvers the question of whether or not attendance was voluntary didn't come into it, they were present simply as a matter of routine.

Mike finished, '– be with us all, evermore, Amen' and asked McLeod, 'Well?'

'A/S schooners still bumbling around inshore, sir, and a Cant last seen flying north towards Ustica.'

Ursa currently a dozen miles north of Cape San Vito and steering northwest, patrolling much the same area she had yesterday – western half of the billet, approaches to the Isole Egadi. Course – unchanged in the past hour – 315 degrees, starboard motor slow grouped down and the other stopped.

121

Prayers now finished, Mike paused at the chart, on which McLeod had put an 1100 fix. It was 1120 now. Mike told him, 'Let's come round to north, Jamie.'

'Aye, sir.' To Smithers, 'Starboard ten.'

'Starboard ten, sir . . .'

McLeod's hand up to switch off the trimline telegraph: churchgoers departing both for'ard and aft had affected the trim, and he'd got it back in hand now. Needles on 28 feet exactly, bubble half a degree aft. The surface was choppy but down here it was absolutely still, the single motor at slow speed barely audible. Mike followed Danvers and Jarvis into the wardroom, with the words of the naval prayer he'd intoned a few minutes ago repeating themselves annoyingly in his consciousness – out of what was virtually lifetime familiarity. *Be pleased to receive into thy almighty and most gracious protection the persons of us thy servants and the fleet in which we serve. Preserve us from the dangers of the sea, and from the violence of the enemy . . .*

Well, they did get violent – when they thought they could get away with it. Could hardly be met with anything but counter-violence. When possible, with added interest. He heard Smithers reporting next-door, 'Course north, sir', and McLeod's gruff acknowledgement. Hiss of the periscope rising then. Jarvis was at the table leafing through the torpedo log and progress book, and Danvers was turning in. Mike reached to the head of his own bunk for the Scott Fitzgerald. Couple of hours on this course, he thought, then spin a coin.

After lunch he'd altered back to 315 degrees, chatted with McLeod for a while then got his head down. Long-range fixes on San Vito and Gallo had put her well out, with plenty of elbow-room, and he thought he'd spend the night motoring due east across the northern part of the billet, midway between San Vito / Gallo and Ustica.

122

He'd been dreaming of Ann, who'd surprised him with the question, 'So what do we *do* about it?' Inference being that Melhuish knew about them and she was putting the ball squarely in Mike's court, although the only way he could know would be if *she*'d told him. Then Danvers' voice – not all that loud, but excited, raised in tone – 'Captain in the control room!' – with the effect of a stick in a beehive, not just his own instant transference but general upheaval, the big periscope halfway down and now checked, rising again, his hands crooked ready for it, swift assessment meanwhile being time 1550, depth 28 feet, course as he knew anyway 315, starboard motor slow ahead grouped down; CERA McIver bringing the 'scope to a halt as Danvers announced – controlled, level tone of voice – 'Smoke on green three-oh, sir.'

Settling the 'scope's annotated cross-bar sights on it. Darkish-grey smudge with a smear extending left to right on an horizon barely crinkled although the foreground and mid-field had as much white in it as light blue. For which thank God. Swivelling the right-hand grip upward into sky-search for a fast sweep overhead and all round, then an equally swift but thorough all-round surface check. Back on the smoke – bare toes stubbing against the iron rim of the periscope's well – bare feet under crumpled khaki slacks, old checked shirt outside them. It was funnel-smoke, all right, but out of *what* . . . ? A movement of the fingers: 'Up.' McIver lifting the control-lever again, deckhead wire purring round its sheaves and the greased yellowish barrel of the 'scope slithering higher, Mike extending with it from a knees-bent position to his full height or near it. Stopped: at maximum extent, top glass something like three to four feet out of water. Focusing on and around the smoke again – and picking up another less dense streamer clear of it to the left. Which confirmed what had seemed a good bet right from the moment of Danvers' summons – either ships in company, convoy or squadron, or one or more ships valuable enough to be escorted.

He folded the handles up. 'Half ahead together. Diving stations. Forty feet.' And through the sudden, fast flux of movement, to Smithers who as Red watch helmsman was staying put – same job at diving stations – 'Starboard ten, steer three-four-oh.' Ship's head currently 315, the smoke had been on green 27, 340 would put her heading within a couple of degrees straight at it, with any luck into periscope visibility-range by the time he poked it up again. Dog impatient to see rabbit now – and expecting to – when you'd seen smoke and you and its source were closing each other, it tended not to be long before you had a sight of mastheads, funnel-tops. Meanwhile the close, fast rush subsiding, familiar figures were where you'd have expected them to be – including McLeod at work on the trim, in this first minute or two coping with changes of both weights and depth. Needles in the gauges just settling on 40 feet – depth-change like the increase in speed being a precaution against losing trim even to the extent of breaking surface, buggering the whole damn thing.

Had been known to happen – though not to *Ursa*. Please God never would.

'Thirty feet, Number One.'

'Thirty, sir . . .'

Mike told Danvers – the rest of them too of course, but Danvers who was at the chart table ready to start a plot which when up and running would provide at least an approximation of target's course and speed, 'Still only smoke but another lot up close.' And McLeod, 'Slow both motors when you can, Number One.' Moving Danvers' plotting diagram sheet off the chart, giving a moment's thought to his own initial concept of the target's likely course – whatever the

124

hell the target *was*. Steering to pass around the Marettimo corner was obvious enough, but whether to hug the turn tightly or take it wide – destination Hammamet for instance as distinct from Bizerta – probably zigzagging, in any case, further to confuse the issue.

'Thirty feet, sir.'

'Make it twenty-eight. Slow both motors.'

'Slow together. Twenty-eight feet.'

Jangle of the telegraph. Cox'n Swathely's murmured echo of 'Twenty-eight'; PO Tubby Hart, lips pursed, tilting his fore 'planes very slightly upward, just momentarily.

'Twenty-eight feet, sir. Both motors slow ahead grouped down.'

Mike glanced at Ellery, opening his hands: periscope rising to them like a well-trained animal. And on target: smoke no more than a distant haze-effect, but masts and a single funnel-top that *was* leaking slightly: more of that funnel than he'd thought though, maybe even most of it – on her stern, growing out of a clutter of deckhousing and he guessed ship's boats shiny grey and low to the sea: and amidships or thereabouts what looked like a fairly massive bridge and accommodation block – 'island' as they called such features. Masts with cross-trees above lengthy well-deck spaces – tank-tops, of course; and a short, raised foc'sl with her foremast at its break, the after end. *Ursa* being say thirty degrees on the tanker's port bow, which would make its course at this moment about 190 degrees. Training right now, though, to get the rest of it – two destroyers or torpedo-boats on diverse courses screening the target on this bow, and – slowly back across her – another . . . No, two others, one thirty to forty on that bow and the fourth much broader, some distance out to starboard. In fact, from the present dispositions of that team he guessed the tanker might be on the port leg of a zigzag: in which case its mean course might be more like

125

210 than 190 or 180. But then, there were zigzags *and* zigzags. While to identify the escorts – training back to the nearer ones for a clearer view – well, identical, each with a single funnel set close up to the rear of the bridge superstructure: also a stubby-looking foc'sl giving a somewhat dated look. Might be *Folgores* or *Dardos*, he thought. Speed – well, the bow-wave thrown up by one which happened to be in three-quarter profile at this moment suggested something like eighteen or twenty knots.

So give the tanker fifteen. In which case at one's own first-sight estimate of range – ten thousand yards, five miles – allowed about fifteen minutes in which to get it all cut and dried. He pushed the handles up.

'Port fifteen, steer two-nine-oh. Forty feet. Group up, half ahead together. Stand by tubes.'

Periscope thudding to a stop, quiet acknowledgements of those orders, *Ursa* already responding to her rudder as well as nosing down. Motor room confirming grouped up, half ahead. You felt it – the deck's tilt and the screws' thrust that would give her six, seven knots. *Full* ahead grouped up would give her nine. Meanwhile, for the enlightenment of a dozen or so intently watching and listening persons, 'Target's a tanker southbound, escort of four destroyers. *Large* tanker – could be twelve thousand tons.' OK, all they needed; he nodded towards the stopwatch in Danvers' hand, told him, 'Start the attack. Six minutes like this. Range provisionally ten thousand, bearing was 339, enemy course south but may be zigging. Give him fifteen knots.' To Cottenham – on Smithers' left, telephone headset adorning the narrow, tonsured head – 'Tell the TI depth-settings fourteen feet, and I'll be firing four torpedoes.'

Full salvo – and Mark VIIIs, thank God. A twelve-thousand-ton tanker deep-laden with oil and/or petrol for Rommel's tanks and Stukas being you might say what torpedoes were bloody well *for*. Taking a glance at the embryo plot as Danvers straightened from it: target at zero minutes / seconds range 10,000 yards and on that north-northwesterly bearing, making fifteen knots, *Ursa* doing her six and a half or seven on this course a little north of west: closing the range, cutting across pretty well at right-angles to the enemy's probably mean course, putting himself where he could then jump either way, depending on how things turned out in the next few minutes. But the Wop wasn't going to turn east, for Christ's sake, you could count on *that* . . . Fraser giving tongue suddenly from the asdic set – because Mike had glanced at him – 'Confused HE starboard side, sir. Trying to sort it, but –'

'We'll be easing down in two shakes, HSD. Target's all of four miles from us meanwhile. Heavy reciprocating, probably about 150 revs, four destroyers' turbines between us and him.' Leaving Fraser with that much, turning to Jarvis who'd ceased fiddling with the Fruit Machine for long enough to get out the Talbot-Booth book of merchant-ship profiles. At the tanker section: 'This a match, sir?' Quick look – checking the time then, less than *two* minutes to go – then back to it, forefinger stabbing at a profile on the facing sheet: 'More like this.'

'*Alessandria*. Fourteen thousand tons.'

'Spitting image.' Checking the time – ignoring murmurs of enthusiasm, asking Jarvis whether the book provided a masthead height – which it didn't, but as a more or less standard proportion of the ship's length might be taken as ninety or a hundred feet. The vertical angle on any known masthead height being measurable in the periscope and providing range.

Which by now would be less than half the originally guessed-at 10,000 yards. He told McLeod, 'Group down, slow together.'

Easing off in order to minimise disturbance before gliding up for a preliminary shufti using the small attack 'scope. He moved that way: ERA Ellery's hand shifting in readiness to the other lever. Power coming off her, the hum of it fading and the motor room reporting grouped down, motors slow ahead. Mike's eyes meeting those of PO Tel Lazenby in his W/T office doorway, and beyond him, on the engine-room's steel step, ERA Coldwell's narrower gaze. Both intent, questioning – with every damn reason to be, too – thirty-two good men, one pair of eyes, 50 per cent chances of survival and mostly dependent on how *you* personally functioned . . .

Back to Fraser: 'Well?'

'Reciprocating HE on green – hundred an' sixty revs – and fast turbine HE green 05 and –' twiddling the knob, finding that other one – 'green 30, sir. Then there's others –'

'Far side of the target.'

A nod of the yellow head. 'Confused, there. All right to left, mostly –'

'Stick to the target and whatever's closer. Any change, sing out.' To Danvers and Jarvis then at plot and Fruit Machine respectively, 'Set enemy speed sixteen. Target bore 318 then, right?' Needles travelling slowly in the gauges – 'planing up, no adjustments to trim, noises of pumping or flooding or any other, in any case *Ursa* was expecting to go deep again shortly for another spurt: but so far, so good. Gauges showing 35 feet – 34 – 33: a glance at Ellery and the small-bore periscope's jerk as it began its upward slide, Mike crouching to take charge of it as the head of it rose clear of the hole it lived in: he had it trained within a degree or two of where the target *ought* to be before getting his eyes to the lenses and the monofocal top glass broke surface – greenish-blue crystals dancing, then clear . . .

'There.' Pirouetting fast then, and back on it – fine on the bow. Destroyers potentially in the bloody light, but – to the attack team, 'I'm forty on his bow.' A nod then: 'Down.' Small periscope hissing down, big one slithering up. McLeod's 'Thirty feet, sir' and Mike's quick 'Twenty-eight. Bearing is *that*, and –'

Chief ERA McIver, close behind him, read it off the bearing-ring, lower part of the deckhead gland – where the periscope passed up through the pressure-hull well above Mike's head, therefore several feet higher than the diminutive Glaswegian could easily read even when on his toes. Straining to do so and somehow succeeding – *having* to, this having evolved as the CERA's job during torpedo attack and if deprived of it he'd likely have cut his throat. Mike taking a range now on the basis of masthead height 90 feet: 'Range – *that*.' Another one for McIver – used immediately by Danvers in his plot and Jarvis in the Fruit Machine – which you fed with enemy course, speed, range, was linked to the gyro compass so already had all of *Ursa*'s own data in it, and gave its operator in return an item known as the DA, Director Angle, meaning aim-off. Holding both Mike and the periscope from wavering off the DA when the time came to be aiming and firing torpedoes, waiting for the sights to come on, was yet another of the Chief's tasks – a purely physical one, for which his arms weren't anything like long enough. He was an extremely competent engineer as well as a thoroughly decent character, under that crusty surface, but –

'*Damn.*'

Having dipped the periscope – standard precaution against over-exposure – in recent seconds, then brought it back up – circling, in air-search – and – Cant. Mosquito-like, port beam roughly, approaching at something like a thousand feet. Well, all right – back into surface-search for another quick range and bearing, then – no, damn it *again* – zigzagging, tanker'd put its damn wheel over, a turn-towards . . . As in fact one might have expected, in fact *had* half-expected, a zig to port – since it must have made one to starboard while he'd been deep, getting over to this side. Now back to the zig's port leg – tanker's length shortening as she swung, destroyers' helms over too, the screen still screening, formation not greatly changed.

Periscope shooting down. Standing back from it, telling McLeod 'Sixty feet' and the other two 'Zigging towards – thirty-degree alteration'll put him on 105, I'll be ten on his bow.' At the plot, showing Danvers: 'Must've altered away at about this point. Distance between alterations therefore –'

'Four thousand yards.' Instant measurement with dividers: follow-up by mental arithmetic no less fast – 'Seven and a half minutes.'

'And the last range was 3100 – call it 3000 –'

'Sixty feet, sir.'

'Starboard wheel, steer oh-eight-oh.'

To open the range – the target's turn-towards having averted the need for another short high-speed dash with the aim of closing it. As Danvers and Jarvis could see for themselves, see the shape of it developing as well as he could – in essence, that one might expect to be firing at a range of two thousand yards or less in five, six minutes. Being safe enough time-wise for seven, in terms of the zigzag. As for the Cant – for now, forget it. Had had the 'scope up for maybe thirty seconds after spotting it – accepting the odds – evens maybe, at best, but *having* to be accepted. You played safe when you could, but –

Fraser blurting out bearings on both target and escorts that were satisfactorily comprehensible and with which Danvers was embellishing his plot.

'– on three-five-two, sir – and nearest destroyer –'

'Target's revs still 160?'

Affirmative. From Danvers then a reminder, 'Four and a

half minutes, sir. Enemy course looks more like one-one-oh than —'

'Set one-one-oh.' Jarvis doing so. Mike construing that the course for a ninety track — torpedoes approaching squarely on the beam, best chance of scoring — would be 200 degrees. Shortest distance-off-track, shortest running-time for the Mark VIIIs. Time just about up now anyway. Go for a ninety track, he thought. Telling McLeod, 'Forty feet' and helmsman Smithers, 'Starboard fifteen.' To McLeod then across both their acknowledgements, 'Stop starboard, half ahead port.' To tighten the turn, *push* her round, save about a quarter of a minute. There'd as likely as not be more than one Cant over the top by now, watching over such an important target in its approach to the strategic Marettimo corner, so obvious a locale for submarine ambush. *Ursa* with a couple of degrees of list on her from the tightness of this turn: he told Smithers, 'Steer two-zero-zero.' McLeod reporting, 'Forty feet, sir', and Fraser giving them a bearing on the target of 338 degrees — Danvers putting that on the plot, Jarvis on the machine — the HSD adding, 'Destroyers between 330 and 345, sir.'

Think about them later. When you have to, when you're up there and you can see the bastards. They weren't transmitting anyway, weren't a *present* danger. A nod to McLeod: 'Slow both motors, Jamie.' She was already most of the way round: Smithers leaving the rest to her, letting the wheel run through his fingers as the rudder centred itself. To McLeod again therefore, 'Thirty feet.'

'Thirty feet, sir.'

'Target bearing, Fraser?'

He was ready with it: 'Two-seven-eight, sir.'

Big change since the last one — but logical, in keeping with the fact one was in at comparatively close quarters now. Depth-gauges showing 33 feet, 32 . . . At the attack 'scope, for a *very* quick look-round — destroyers, for instance, *could* be right on top of you. Smithers reporting, 'Course 200, sir', Mike nodding to that: crouching at the after periscope, unfolding upwards with its business end, a sunburst in his eyes as the top glass broke surface: 'Bearing *that*. I'm – seventy on his bow. And – *damn* –'

Handles slammed up, 'scope on its way down, eyes for a moment on the curve of deckhead – actually to the surface thirty feet above that as he moved to the search 'scope and a destroyer's screws thundered over close. For a second or two he'd had the speeding *Folgore* in close-up, actually looking *up* at it from his waterline perspective: the rush of sound was potentially as unnerving as the sight – *not* in fact right over the top, only as near to that as – well, as his own all-over sweat and doubled pulse-rate told him it had been. Over and gone, anyway, *not* having wiped off either the 'scope or standards, the big 'scope coming up fast into his waiting hands and the *Folgore*'s HE rapidly diminishing. He'd waved down Fraser's startled apology, aware that with HE all round and concentrating primarily on the target he couldn't be held responsible for – well, a destroyer at twenty knots, when there were four of them, *that* one actually the port wing ship of the screen which *Ursa* was now inside. Mike with his breathing back to normal, fairly sure he had it made now: 'Stand by all tubes. Twenty-eight feet. Christ's sake hold her there, Jamie. Bearing is *that*. I'm – seventy on his bow. Range is – *that*.' McIver the gymnast doing his stuff, the peak of his performance to be expected in just moments now, Mike asking sharply, 'What's my DA?'

From Jarvis – metallic clash as he lined up own and target's outline images in his machine's display and called the answer: 'DA green 24, sir!' Mike glancing up at the bearing-ring, checking ship's head steady on 200, shifting the periscope to aim-off 24 degrees to starboard and bloody hold it there. 'Keep me on it, Chief.' Hands like iron clamps on his wrists on the 'scope's spread handles, a grated nicotine-flavoured 'Aye' so close to the back of his neck he felt the draught of it on his ears. Vertical crosswire anyway held rigid: tanker driving at it from the right.

Quarter of a length to go. Slow, steadying intake of breath, and – 'Fire One!'

'Torpedo fired, sir!'

Thud of compressed air blasting it out, sharp jump in internal pressure from sea water flooding into a compensating tank to balance the lost weight and HP air from the now empty tube venting back into the submarine. Fraser having reported 'Torpedo running', and Mike with the tanker's stempost about to cross the wire.

'Fire Two!'

Same thud and jolt of pressure. Fraser's 'Both running.' Tanker's bridge, all that midships superstructure, about to pass the mark: Mike's 'Fire Three!' Three running: distance-off-track, from *Ursa*'s stem to the tanker's iron side thrashing past ahead, 1,700 yards. One to go – and coming up now, black-topped funnel slightly aslant from the vertical of the crosswire . . .

'Fire Four!'

Folding the handles up, Ellery sending the 'scope shooting down, McIver shambling clear. Mike to McLeod, 'Eighty feet. Group up, full ahead together.' Cracking on speed plus some depth for safety before the Wop escort woke up to what was happening, *had* happened, and reacted to it. Danvers with the stopwatch in his palm, estimating 'Eleven seconds, sir.' Eleven *more* – on top of those that had passed already. Mike's eyes drifting over the crowd around him as the 'scope comes to rest in its well, *Ursa* bow-down and her motors fairly singing – shaking her . . .

Those eleven seconds gone, all right. Damn sight *more* than –

Hit. Burst of drowned thunder with a metallic *clang* in it, reverberations echoing away. Relief – well, *joy* – as the reality of it grips. A quiet cheer or two: despite wanting more than *one* hit, which though better than missing altogether was not anything like necessarily a kill.

'Eighty feet, sir.'

'*Half* ahead both.'

Danvers with the watch in his hand and torpedo running-time at 45 knots as the basis of his reckoning has embarked on a muttered count-down: 'Five, four, three, two, one –'

Second hit. It's not a surprise exactly, but there's cheering, laughing. General happiness. Jarvis challenging, 'Any advance on two?'

Mike thinking, maybe not. If those two hits have stopped her – not all that improbable – then number four –

Third hit! And an almost startled renewal of applause . . . Own thoughts however – well, main body of thought, probably – centring on the inevitability of now getting it in the neck.

8

'In contact, sir . . .' Fraser – sadly, as the provider of bad news
– all the worse for coming after a longish run of the other
kind. There'd been more than an hour now – hour and a
half, in fact, *Ursa* creeping west then southwest, Mike and
the rest of them in her control room having in mind
throughout that time how suddenly this kind of situation
could change, fall flat on its face.

As it had now. All hearing it, with no need of headphones.
High-pitched squeaks – asdic pings, changed in character by
distance – Italian-type asdics fingering *Ursa's* hull. *Ursa* on
course 230 and one motor slow grouped down; watertight
doors between compartments shut and clipped, auxiliary
machinery stopped and some personnel dispersed. Chief
McIver aft to his own domain, for instance, young Jarvis
for'ard with his torpedomen. Time – five forty-eight. Had
fired the last of that salvo at four-eighteen, and since then
enjoyed – without really counting on its continuance – ninety
minutes' grace. In the latter stages, to be honest, even beginning to feel one *might* get clean away with it.

Could happen – *had* happened, on occasion, but hardly

to be expected when your target's escort was numerous enough to take care of picking up survivors *and* seek reprisals in the form of your destruction. Mike shrugging and getting to his feet: like others who didn't have fixed positions for their diving stations – asdics, helm, hydroplanes – he'd spent the past hour squatting on the corticene-covered deck.

Shrug, rueful smile: similar reactions from those around him; expressions that said 'Here we go, then' or 'Too good to last, weren't it.' Fraser amplifying his report with 'On red eight-oh, sir, closing. Others is on red one–one–oh and red – one-five-five. Moving left to right –'

'All right.' At the chart, Danvers beside him, Wop transmissions still sporadically audible on the pressure-hull. When they missed a few squeaks it didn't mean the operator had lost her, only that he was working it to and fro across her, some impulses pinging on to fade away in the depths, having encountered nothing to reflect them back. *Ursa's* position by soft-pencilled DR roughly midway between Cape San Vito and the island of Ustica, three destroyers all to the east of her – between northeast and southeast, that sector generally. They'd concentrated their search initially – predictably – on the side you'd attacked from – assuming that having let fly you'd have gone about and legged it back eastward. Also predictably, only three of them at it – as duly confirmed by Fraser – the other one busying itself with survivors, manoeuvring and from time to time stopping engines, around the area of the sinking. That the tanker had sunk was as good as certain: for one thing, three hits, meaning three devastating explosions deep inside her; for another, only the one escort standing by her – no question of taking her in tow as there might otherwise have been – and as conclusive as anything else Fraser's report of breaking-up noises – bulkheads splitting, etc. – which in fact had started shortly after the third hit – *Ursa* by then on due west and at eighty feet – as she still was now, but on 230 degrees – paddling away in the hope of not attracting anyone's attention.

After a while the destroyer that would probably have had a few survivors on board had left at about thirty knots on a straight course for – he guessed – Trapani. Wouldn't be all that many survivors.

'Still in contact?'

A nod: creasing of anxiety around the eyes. 'All three's closing, sir.'

As one might have expected – once one of them had found you. He'd sketched it rapidly and roughly on a blank area of the plotting diagram: the three Italians, this one in contact and on a course converging with *Ursa*'s, in contact but not necessarily aware you knew it. Had to know you *might* be, but his primary concern would be to hold the contact while bringing his chums into it now by voice radio, light or flags – standard tactic then being for one or more of them to hold on to you while others took turns at running over and dropping bloody charges. It wasn't possible to maintain asdic contact while actually attacking.

He pushed himself off from the chart table, nodded to McLeod. 'Time to make a move, Jamie.'

'Sure you're right, sir.'

'Here we go, then.' Another couple of seconds' thought: seeing it as it had suddenly become – and touch wood the solution. Quietly: 'Stop starboard. Group up, full ahead both motors.' And to Smithers: 'Wheel hard a-starboard.'

Orders to the motor room by telephone, telegraphs being shut off as part of silent running. Smithers acknowledging the helm order: 'Hard a-starboard, sir.' Brass wheel spinning, spokes glinting in the compartment's dimly yellowish light. 'Thirty o' starboard wheel on, sir.' *Ursa*'s hull and frames trembling with the sudden onsurge of battery and propeller power – power from batteries already seriously depleted, but that was something else, to be coped with later; here and now the object was to kick up a barrier of turbulence to deflect the asdic probe, leave the Wop confused, with any luck assuming his target had turned sharply away – away from *him* – which it *had* – to dodge away westward behind this burst of speed.

Didn't always work. Had done on occasion. Not in precisely similar circumstances, but the present ones lent themselves to it, Mike thought. Hoped. Close behind the helmsman's stool, watching over Smithers' shoulder the start and then increasing rate of turn, ship's head by gyro threading through on the glowing metal ribbon – 240 – 270 – faster then through 290, 310, 340 – due north – and 010, 030 –

'Midships.'

'Midships, sir.'

Spinning the wheel back the other way while the turn continued, under cover of the confusion now surrounding her. Mike telling McLeod: 'Stop both. Group down. Slow ahead port.'

Still on the swing and with way on but quiet now – *quietening* – emerging from the disturbance that would fizz there for some while. Had been motoring southwestward, caught on to their having established contact and winced away in this abrupt, fast turn to starboard – in *their* view running west now, surely.

'Still transmitting, sir!'

'In contact?'

'No, sir – *no . . .*'

Asdics would get echoes from that turbulence. Not very sharp or clear ones maybe, but still echoes. Which would fade, of course – leading to a report of 'Lost contact'. *Ursa* meanwhile running *under* the bastards, more or less. Effectively, running under them. Steel no longer thrumming, that one screw scarcely audible. Ten to one and please God

138

they'd be frantically trying to regain contact in a westerly direction.

Quietly to Smithers, 'Steer oh-eight-oh.'

'Oh-eight-oh, sir —'

Fingers crossed . . .

Twenty miles on this course would put one somewhere between Gallo and San Vito, maybe a dozen miles offshore. If the sods gave up the search now. Time, 1840. Making only a knot and a half, but that was perfectly all right, when it was taking you east and the opposition were heading west or southwest at — what, ten or fifteen? Rate of progress — from *Ursa's* point of view, rate of *separation*, hard to guess if they were still conducting an A/S search — wide spread, co-ordinated alterations of course, etc. The important thing was that the range was opening and continued to do so. Even if as one suspected these weren't exactly top-notchers, they'd hardly turn back in this direction – purposeless or at least systemless, in their desperation poking around like men with white sticks.

Give it another hour in any case. Up for a look then, and while the light held get bearings of Gallo Head and San Vito. Night patrol then, restful or otherwise but getting the box up as the number-one priority. Northward or northwestward, where the targets seemed to come from.

Immediately though, might be more sense in making real use of this next hour or two. In other words stay deep, or go a bit deeper, and reload tubes.

Having empty tubes wasn't a good feeling. Could meet a battle squadron in the dawn and not be able to do more than keep out of its way. While the argument against reloading tubes right away and in a hurry – well, if the Wops did realise they'd made a bollocks of it and reversed the direction of their search, catching you with your pants down – torpedoes and gear all over the place, tubes' rear doors open, trim all to hell . . .

Wasn't likely they'd be back. *Could* happen, but –

Reload now, finish by eight-thirty or latest nine, surface at about ten – clean air, and battery – all tonight's dark hours for that, after the day's extravagance. Not *enough* hours, in fact, but could manage on it. Diving then at first light somewhere off Gallo Head, and follow one's nose northwestward again – feeling a lot better for having fish already in the tubes.

He shifted around, elbows on the edge of the chart table behind him, asked Fraser, 'Anything at all?'

Headshake and slow blink. 'Nothing, sir.'

Checking the time again: six-fifty, almost. McLeod leaning with a shoulder against the ladder, glancing round, waiting for – whatever . . . Mike nodded. 'Slow ahead both, Jamie. Hundred feet and reload tubes.'

From Sub-Lieutenant Tom Jarvis's illicit diary notes that evening:

Approx 1900 opened up from d/charging, went to 100 feet and cleared fore ends for reloading of tubes. Clearing all the junk out of the compartment an awful bloody sweat, as always. Skipper sent for the T.I., Coltart, while preparations were in progress, and congratulated him on this afternoon's fish having run straight – 'As always, T.I.' The two of them in the wardroom gangway at this stage, standing just about eye to eye – neither of them exactly midgets – and Coltart who usually doesn't have much to say but I suppose wanted to return the compliment about torpedo-maintenance with one of his own, said 'Left that shower looking bloody gormless, didn't we?'

Reloading the four tubes – with Mark IVs, unfortunately – was finished by eight-thirty: which took an hour and a half out of what would have been Jarvis's watch, McLeod consequently standing in for him in the control room – with plenty to do, at that, trimming problems caused by the shifting to and fro of heavy weights – not only torpedoes weighing two tons apiece but the special loading gear that had to be set up, and before that the TSC's entire contents cleared out and stacked in the gangway opposite the for'ard messes. In fact transferring four torpedoes from the racks into the tubes in less than an hour wasn't bad going: the TI and his gang knew their business all right, Jarvis's contribution being mainly to spot blunders before they were committed – like a steel-wire rope led the wrong side of a stanchion, which could set the whole operation back half an hour if it *wasn't* spotted in time – or even a propeller-clamp left on a torpedo's twin concentric screws before that tube's rear door was shut and the inevitable disaster lost to sight. *That* as an outright cock-up being about the worst imaginable. Wasting time was one thing, ensuring that a torpedo couldn't run when it was fired very much another. Plain fact being however that with a dozen hands working flat-out in close confines, such things *could* occur.

Hadn't this time, anyway. And the men who lived, ate and slept in there weren't averse to having some extra space now. Jarvis returned to the wardroom looking pleased with himself, after waiting for the gangway to be partially unplugged, then crawling over the rest of it and coming on aft to report 'Four tubes reloaded, sir.' Mike glancing at the clock, nodding approval; Danvers by this time had taken over from McLeod, who'd got his head down. Jarvis adding, somewhat diffidently, 'Lovely job, that tanker, sir.'

'Could've done worse, couldn't we. Oh, here – Lazenby'll be bunging *this* out, soon as we're up.'

Pushing a signal-log across the table and flipping it open: Top item in the clip being the plain-language version of a signal addressed to S.10, repeated to Vice-Admiral, Malta, C-in-C Mediterranean and Admiralty, reporting the sinking with torpedoes of a southbound tanker believed to be the *Alessandria*, 14,000 tons, in position 38 degrees 31 North, 12 degrees 34 East, at 1630 – zone time and date – destroyer escort last heard searching west of Cape San Vito. The concluding words, *Continuing patrol*, were an assurance to Shrimp that one was still on the billet and had torpedoes remaining.

'Already ciphered, sir?'

'Yes. Get your head down, if I were you.'

Mike liked that signal. Liked his vision of Shrimp scanning it, the gleam of approval in those grey eyes reflecting one's own satisfaction at the thought of such an immense quantity of oil and/or petrol *not* reaching bloody Rommel.

Diving stations now – nine forty-five. Half an hour ago he'd brought her up to periscope depth for a look-round and a couple of shore bearings, which as it happened had put her within a mile or two of her DR eighteen miles north of Cape San Vito. A light overcast had developed in the previous few hours, and the wind had come up to about force 4 – still from the northwest. In these conditions it would be dark enough to surface by ten, so – considering alternatives, over the chart – he'd decided to stay on this course, 080, throughout the dark hours. Best part of seven hours' charging, and making about five knots, say – dive somewhere off the Gallo here at 0500 or thereabouts, daylight patrol then closer inshore and westward. Unless of course one got any better ideas between now and then. But later in the day, a snoop down past the Egades maybe.

At diving stations now anyway – a nod to McLeod, and 'Stand by to surface' – usual checks and reports then following, Walburton opening the lower lid and shinning down again, leaving the ladder clear for Mike; McLeod's 'Ready to surface, sir', Mike giving the order and starting up. It was good and dark up top by this time – final periscope check having revealed nothing but slightly jumpy seascape, even with the help of the two-day-old scraping of moon which had risen in mid-afternoon and would set in four or five hours' time, meanwhile had thickening cloud to contend with. McLeod intoning, 'Twenty-five feet – twenty – fifteen –', Mike right under the top hatch – first clip off, pin out of the second, one hand up grasping the handle in the hatch's centre – not that that would hold it, steadying himself was all – but Walburton now hugging him around the knees, adding his own twelve or thirteen stone to Mike's. McLeod's voice echoey in the tower below them – 'Twelve feet – eight . . .' and the second clip swinging free, hatch crashing up and back, the pressure built up from having fired torpedoes virtu- ally exploding up around them but *not* taking Mike with it like the cork out of a bottle of fizz, which without having taken those precautions it might have done. He'd yelled 'Right!', Walburton had let go and he was clambering out into the dark, salt-streaming bridge.

He'd put a note in his night-order book to be given a shake at 0400, and when Barnaby as messenger in Danvers' watch woke him he felt as if he'd had a full night's sleep. In fact he hadn't got his head down until some time after midnight – mainly on account of his own aversion to moonlight, and cloud-cover being unreliable until about then. Same old contradictory thinking – his officers being entirely capable and reliable, *Ursa* safe in their hands moon or no moon: only one's sensitivity to the fact that just a moment's inattention or misconception, combined maybe with a dozy lookout . . .
  Anyway, had had the best part of four hours' sleep, and wouldn't have wanted more.

143

'Morning, sir.'

McLeod – pulling the chair out and thumping down into it, reaching for a mug, telling him, 'The box has come up quite well. Another hour'll see it about right. Smoke, sir?'

'No – thanks.' Remembering that soon after surfacing last night he'd agreed to cut speed-through-the-water to nearer three knots than five, to get a larger proportion of the generators' output into the battery. After all, one wasn't going anywhere in any hurry, and *had* drained it somewhat, with those high-speed bursts. Hence the amount of movement now – with little more than steerage-way on her, it didn't take much to make her roll. He said – about the battery – 'That's fine, then.'

'There's kye for you on the table here, sir.'

'Initiative of Barnaby's, or yours?'

'Oh, Barnaby's . . .'

Barnaby would have shaken McLeod just before the hour, since he had to get himself ready to take over on the bridge by a quarter-past, while he, Barnaby, would have been relieved by his Red watch counterpart *at* the hour. In fact, come to think of it, one had heard the watch changing, presumably while still comatose. And McLeod must have gone aft right away to check with the LTOs on the battery-state – pausing only to light that cigarette. He was, actually, an extremely competent first lieutenant, Mike thought: never lost his sense of the priorities, definitely *should* be recommended for his Perisher when they got back. In the gangway now pulling on Ursula-suit trousers – which he'd need, she *was* throwing herself around a bit. Up to about force 5, he guessed. On 080 still, of course, wind and sea by the feel of it still north-west, a little abaft the beam.

Very hot kye. In the semi-darkness, sucking noises from McLeod braced against the table – audible even through the boat's gyrations, thump and rush of sea through the casing above

144

their heads, pounding around the gun and tower. Jarvis's snores, surprisingly, *in*audible. Mike at the table now — transference being an easy feet-first slide from bunk to bench — with a hand to his mug ensuring it was still there. McLeod stubbing out his cigarette: 'Dive on the watch, sir, or –'

'I'll join you up there about half-past. Meanwhile might run the blower on one and six, eh?'

'Might indeed, sir.'

One and six being the main ballast tanks that were supposedly empty, keeping her on the surface. With a certain amount of tossing around, air tended to get spilled out of the free-flood holes in their bottoms, and to replace it, buoy her up, you opened one-way valves in the low-pressure air-line and started a machine called the blower, effectively a high-powered fan, ran it for a quarter of an hour or so every few hours. By forcing down any existing level of water in the tanks it made life a bit drier for watchkeepers in the bridge, and reduced chances of the boat diving of her own accord.

He lit a cigarette. The kye was drinkable now. Reflecting that Charles Melhuish should have *Unsung* well on her way to Malta by this time. Having spent yesterday under the mines, surfaced off Cape San Marco last night – then another day and night, to Lazaretto, and – he thought wryly, *See the conquering hero comes . . .* Snide as well as wry, admittedly; but with that cruiser under his belt he might well be a little above himself – having started that way, for God's sake . . . Day after tomorrow anyway, he'd be in: this now being Monday, one week since *Ursa*'s return to Malta from the fleshpots of the Levant. Sailed from there Tuesday evening: not even six days at sea yet, although it felt like more. The business with the Garibaldi had seemed to drag things out a bit. But whether or not the convoy from Gib was on its way, or had been – got through, or otherwise – at least some of them, please God? A few ships in Grand Harbour now, maybe, discharging

145

by floodlights on to wharves or into lighters – please God, *some* at least?

0500 then, down into peace and quiet, *Ursa* steady as a rock even at thirty feet. It had been fairly brisk up there, with the overhead of thin, fast-moving cloud and a lot of the white stuff flying, pinkish dawn spreading like a stain from over Messina and the Italian toe. It had been time to get down out of it in any case, and was certainly a lot more comfortable. He'd dived her on the klaxon – the ear-splitting emergency dive signal, a large press-button just under the rim of the hatch – to remind all hands what it sounded like, since in these five days and nights at sea oddly enough it hadn't been used. It was a hell of a thing to wake up to, a lot more startling than the alternative, a howl of 'Dive, dive, dive!'

All still and quiet again now, anyway. From the rush to diving stations with near-busted eardrums, men drifting back to their various berths and hammocks. Red watch, watch diving, was the broadcast order – and Cottenham had retired to his galley to conjure up an early breakfast. *Ursa* by now steadied on 250 degrees, with Gallo Head on her beam to port, Cape San Vito thirty on that bow. Both motors slow, grouped down. He told Danvers, who'd been cleaning the chart of yesterday's position lines, 'Might take a look into the Castellammare Gulf later on.'

'Closer in than we were last time, perhaps?'

'Well. See how it goes.' He looked up, sniffed: 'Might it be the exquisite aroma of soya links I'm getting?'

A nod. 'Links, fried bread, powdered egg.'

'Marvellous . . .'

Meant that, too – happened to like both soya skinless sausages *and* the much-maligned powdered egg.

★   ★   ★

146

Having had a good sleep last night, after breakfast he got stuck into the Scott Fitzgerald novel for an hour or two. Hadn't been wildly enthusiastic about it to start with, in fact had more or less forced himself into it out of politeness to Aunt Jennie, but in this last hour had begun to find himself caught up in it, especially in the relationship between Stahl and Kathleen. Kathleen in particular appealing to him – he was beginning to think, a variety of Abigail? Not by Fitzgerald's indications physically resembling her, or for that matter really *sounding* like her, but still this sense of empathy.

'Tea's wet, sir, if you'd like some?'

'D'you know, Barnaby, I would?'

'Keep body an' soul together, as they say.'

'I'm sure they're right . . .'

McLeod's forenoon watch, this, Jarvis and Danvers both flat out in their bunks. From next door, familiar small sounds of the periscope watch, backed by the motors' low thrum, that went with the warmth and stillness.

Leave Kathleen to her own devices for a while, he thought, get some shut-eye.

'Char, sir.'

'Thanks.' Dark-brown tea in the usual stained mug. 'Can't sleep, Barnaby?'

'Crash it in a minute, sir, dare say.'

Time now eleven-fifteen. The tea was hot enough to wait while he paid a visit to the control room. Nods or friendly glances from watchkeepers McLeod, Swathely, Fraser, Ellery, Smithers, Barnet. Pausing at the chart – checking the pencilled course with an 1100 position on it. Familiar territory, of course – early Saturday, one had been here. Passing pretty well through the centre of the billet – slightly south of centre today, only just off the thirty-mile-wide opening of the Castellammare Golfo. On Saturday they'd dived with Gallo Head on roughly the same bearing as it had been a few hours ago, only further offshore: the other difference being that with a livelier wind and sea up top, and using both motors to make depth-keeping easier, you were achieving the dizzy speed of two knots instead of slightly less than one and a half. Pass San Vito around four p.m., he thought; might alter to due west for the last few hours of daylight – Marettimo on the bow then, at about twenty-five miles' range.

He asked McLeod, 'Visibility still good?'

'Clear as a bell, sir.'

'No schooners in there today.'

'A few little widgers right inshore is all, sir.'

So – tea, then kip. And while at the tea, maybe another page of the Fitzgerald story. He'd stopped at a point where there's some mix-up over a letter Kathleen's left in Stahl's car: she's been out on a date with him that evening, he doesn't know whether she'd intended him to find it or forgotten about it, maybe had second thoughts on whatever she'd put on paper earlier in the day. So whether or not he should open it –

'Captain, sir.'

McLeod – in the gangway, a shoulder against the bulkhead dividing wardroom and control room. Mike recalled having heard him sending the periscope down a few seconds ago.

'Uh?'

'Some sort of activity inshore of us, sir. There's a Cant circling over the gulf and with the stick right up I *thought* I saw a Mas-boat in there. Can't now, and asdics haven't, but –'

'Let's have a dekko.'

Time, 1125. Reminding himself on his way through that Castellammare would be about eighty on the bow, distance say seven and a half miles, i.e. 15,000 yards, in this sea-state rather long range for spotting Mas-boats. A nod to Ellery, 'scope purring up; needles on 28 feet. Handles down, and

148

starting with an air-search. If Cants anywhere overhead, see the bastards before they see you – they or *it*. Not that you'd expect them to, with this broken, wind-whipped surface. He was on to it quickly in any case – small black excrescence against the clean blue between streaks and whorls of fast-travelling cloud. Well clear anyway, no immediate threat. A mutter to McLeod: 'Your shagbat's there, all right.' Sky-search completed, following it with a medium- to long-range examination of the lively, dazzling-bright seascape. 'Scope well up, as McLeod had had it, on the bearing of Castellammare itself now.

No Mas-boats discernible. 'Little widgers', yes – fishing-boats . . .

Fraser blurted, upright suddenly on his stool, 'HE, sir, red two-oh! Fast turbine. Destroyer, could be. True bearing –' adjusting the knob on his gyro-linked bearing-ring, Mike swivelling fast, instantly aware that with the boat's head on 250 anything twenty degrees on her port bow had to be roughly on the bearing of Cape San Vito – an area of sea which as it happened he'd just searched. Well – half a minute ago, he had. Getting back there quickly, and – '*Christ . . .*' Destroyer, all right. He was about thirty on its port bow. Forty maybe. Destroyer under helm and naturally enough with a lot of movement on her, couple of miles ahead – no, three, could be – toy warship in sight and sound maybe within less than a minute of having rounded that point – helm over again now, pretty well on her ear in a morass of flying sea, making he guessed twenty-five, thirty knots.

Which wouldn't be too comfortable. Had to be some justification – urgency . . .

'Port fifteen. Steer one-seven-oh.'

'– one-seven-oh, sir. Fifteen of port wheel on –'

Mike told McLeod, 'Destroyer entering the gulf. Stop port.'

'Stop port, sir –'

'Christ —'

'I think — two of 'em, sir —'

'Damn right, Fraser!'

Precursors of *what?*

'Two hundred revs, sir. Two-one-oh.'

Shoving the handles up, periscope starting down. Fraser muttering to himself, shaking his head, beady eyes on the asdics' bearing-ring. Smithers reporting, 'Course one-seven-oh, sir.' Mike with the two destroyers in clear sight but otherwise empty seascape all around, nothing else, thinking in answer to his own question *Precursors of bugger-all*, and in search of an explanation deciding to check on what if anything might be happening off Castellammare, where a second or two before Fraser had come up with this he'd *thought* he'd seen smoke. Meaning damn-all, maybe: dockyard, emission of smoke, so what? The more cogent questions being whether these destroyers might be escorting some other vessel so far astern of them it hadn't yet rounded San Vito — which was improbable — or simply arriving on their own, Cant up there to ensure *safe* arrival, McLeod's Mas-boat or Mas-boats real or imagined, but if real also in some way connected with this arrival? *Or*, destroyers here to collect / provide escort for some major unit that might shortly poke its nose out.

Wishful thinking again, with knobs on. But they were here for *something*. So was *Ursa* — even if it might be to sink a destroyer with a crew of something like a couple of hundred men. Or say *two* destroyers, *four* hundred men: nice spread of four fish across the pair of them. *Double* wishful thinking.

'Slow ahead both motors.' Then — 'Thirty feet, Number One.' Because twenty-eight would be a *little* tricky with the surface turbulence. Small movement of the hands, instant upward shimmer of the periscope. To Fraser — 'Destroyers bearing?'

150

Slight pause while rechecking, then: 'Green three-oh, sir – moving right to left – 210 revs –'

'Two in line ahead?'

'Yessir – I *think* –'

'All right.' Three miles clear, even four, six to eight thousand yards. Bright, flickering light in his pupils while making another air-search. The Cant hadn't been anywhere near them but it could be by now – or another could. Anyway, not observably. Back on as much as he could see of the destroyers – which were *Navigatore* class, he thought. Bigger than yesterday's *Folgores* or *Dardos*, and really nothing like them – two funnels apiece, for a start. Not a hope of getting at them as things were right now – range minimally 6,000 yards and opening, and smallish, fast-moving targets. Would have been a lot better if he'd been inside the gulf, ahead of them, rather than trailing them in like this.

Realistically, get one of them on its way out maybe. If for instance they'd been deployed in connection with the Gib convoy, calling in here on their way back now, maybe for bunkers.

'Slowing, sir – revs 150 –'

No great surprise in that: only that if their intention was to enter Castellammare, with still a few miles to go, you wouldn't have expected them to reduce speed this soon.

'One-three-five revs, sir.'

Maybe did *not* intend docking. In which case back to the guesswork, hope that lurked more or less eternal . . . Head back from the 'scope and pushing its handles up, telling Ellery, 'Dip.' Meaning duck it under and bring it smartly back up again: standard precautionary dodge when using a lot of periscope – some Wop pilot supposedly telling himself he'd only *imagined* having seen one. Right up again now anyway: and Fraser with a new surprise – '*Stopped engines*, sir!'

'*Have* they, now . . .'

151

Because if *Ursa* could be got in there, into something like point-blank range, undetected, *might* get the pair of them. Forty feet, say, group up, half ahead, be in a firing position within about thirty or even twenty minutes. Two fish for each of them. No – one each: stationary targets, God's sake – one each, retaining the other pair for whatever else might show up.

'HE in short bursts like, low revs, sir –'

'All right.' In order to stay put, no doubt watching shore bearings. Not *likely* they'd sit there for as long as twenty minutes, but – get in there anyway, give it a go. Knock one or both of them off, alternatively some other, more important target, whatever they were here for. But sinking two Navigatores in one afternoon wouldn't be anything to be exactly *ashamed* of.

He'd checked the line of sight, told Smithers, 'Come three degrees to starboard.'

'Three degrees to starboard, sir. One-seven-three . . .'

'Down periscope. Forty feet. Group up, half ahead together. Diving stations.'

'Diving stations!'

To have her settled and in trim, ready for action before it started. Clang of the telegraphs, hydroplane indicators tilting to put angle on her, motors reacting in no more than a hiccup as the LTOs back aft broke and re-engaged the big grouper switches. *Ursa* beginning to tremble under the increased thrust. McLeod had passed the diving-stations order over the Tannoy broadcast and the rush was already three-quarters over, the control-room team's eyes as ever curious, expectant, hopeful. Danvers stooping over the chart as if he'd never left it, Jarvis blinking like an owl, McLeod reporting while still adjusting trim, 'Both motors grouped up, half ahead, sir.'

'Course one-seven-three, sir.'

Needles slowing in their movement around the gauges,

dive-angle coming off her. McLeod's flat 'Forty feet, sir.' Time, 1142. Mike reached for the Tannoy microphone: 'Hear, there? Captain speaking. Present state of affairs is we're motoring into a bay – gulf, Golfo di Castellammare – Castellammare being a dockyard port on the bay's southern shore. Two Italian destroyers have steamed in ahead of us and stopped engines in the middle. Take us about twenty minutes to get in there – either clobber them or go for whatever they're waiting to escort away. If we go for the destroyers I'll aim to put one fish in each – if they're still lying stopped, that is – but you'd better have all four tubes ready, TI.'

He switched off, hung the mike up. Depth-settings on the fish would have to stay at fourteen feet no matter what, those now in the tubes being Mark IVs, not VIIIs. In general, though, play it off the cuff. There'd been no Intelligence that he recalled of any major target currently repairing in Castellammare; if there had been, Shrimp would have touched on it in his briefing.

1147 now. Give it until 1210. Quizzing Fraser meanwhile with a raised eyebrow, and the HSD shrugging: 'No change, sir. Short bursts at low revs.' Face changing in that moment – a hand jerking up to the headset. 'Sounds like E-boats – Mas-boats, sir. Like them other three –'

First full day on the billet, off Palermo when he'd been waiting for the cruiser to come out, they'd raced off westward around Cape Gallo – reasons best known to themselves . . . 'Bearing?'

'South, sir. One-six-five, right to left. One-seven-five, one-eight-oh. Confused – not *close*, it's –'

'Beyond the destroyers? *They* moving?'

Shake of the head. 'Inshore of 'em, but no, sir –'

'All right.'

Eye on *that* ball, ignore distractions. 1152. Another thirteen minutes, say.

153

'Sir — getting under way. Destroyers. Lost them others, but —'

'Slow together. Group down.' He'd restrained the curses. It had been a spur-of-the-moment, odds-against chance anyway — worth taking, *might* have come up trumps, but —

'Both motors slow ahead grouped down, sir.'

'Thirty feet. What's new, Fraser?'

'Milling around, sir, low revs. One moving left to right, revs increasing —'

'Mas-boats?'

Beginnings of a headshake — but uncertain, hunting this way and that with his receiver without answering. Then: 'Still inshore I think, sir.' A catch of breath: 'New HE — reciprocating —' Counting revolutions, scowling in concentration: 'One-eight-oh revs — reciprocating, freighter I'd say. Destroyers more like 240 — moving right . . .

'Thirty feet, sir.' Periscope slithering up, Mike's hands ready for it while a tentative picture part-formed in his mind — how that lot *might* be sorting itself out. Asking Fraser, 'New target's bearing — and the destroyers' still shifting left to right?'

'All around 170, sir. 165 to 175 — yeah, seems range opening —'

'All right.' Periscope right up and his eyes at the lenses: initially, as confused visually as acoustically. 'Twenty-eight feet, Number One!'

'Twenty-eight —'

'Steer one-seven-oh.'

Destroyers carving great mounds of white. At this moment, damn-all else, but — Cant, to the right of them at less than a thousand feet and flying east. Ignore *him*, for now — or get bloody nowhere, wasting time. Between the destroyers though — could be a mile back, into sight just in that moment and now out of it again — still *had* to be there, darn it!

'Bearing of the new one, Fraser?'

154

'Can't rightly say, sir, it's like —'

There. And as big as a house, in all that schemozzle — dazzling haze, dark centre to it, stuff flying in sheets. *Battlewagon*, bow-on? No — nothing of the bloody sort, optical illusion — no fighting-top, only masts — at least, *a* mast — and yard, funnel smoke spiralling in the wind, certainly not helping — clearing again, thank God. Low, squat funnel: funnels, side by side and rectangular cross-sectioned? *There,* all right, solid, almost clear-cut image hard to make sense of but — training right quickly, and no problems in finding both destroyers well out on that side, three-quarter buried in the stuff *they* were ploughing up. Making say twenty knots and right into it. Just seconds on this assessment, then into air-search to find that Cant. In which no joy, so the hell with it, it'd be blind in the confusion of this seascape anyway — touch wood — and back in surprisingly greater clarity on what he'd called the new one — blocky, specialist transport of some kind; and if it was worth an escort of two Navigatores, Mas-boats and a Cant it had to be worth sinking. Banging the handles up, and a nod to Ellery: 'Dip.' When routine precautions didn't cost you anything, why not take them? Telling himself, snap-attack while the escorts are both conveniently out of the way on the San Vito side of it. Whatever the hell it is. Big, and probably in ballast, making say eighteen or twenty knots. Periscope back up: surprising them all then as he double-checked the whole assembly — including a sight of the Cant — *a* Cant, could be others — limping seaward out beyond the plunging Navigatores — before settling back on the heavyweight, surprising them with 'Start the attack. Target a large steamer, bearing *that.*' CERA McIver gnome-like behind him to read it off. 'Range *that.*' Basing it on a 65-foot mainmast, which was about how it looked. Guesswork, instinct. 'Set enemy speed eighteen. I'm twenty on his port bow. Stand by numbers one, two and three

155

tubes. This'll be a close-range snap-attack.' Head back, and to Ellery, 'Dip.'

Close-range snap attack before the target put its helm over to fall in astern of its escorts – or they shifted over, or the whole outfit altered course – whatever. Periscope back up, his eyes at the lenses and its top glass *in* the froth as much as over it. Wondering about the Mas-boats, telling McLeod '*Half* ahead together. Keep her up, Christ's sake. Depth now?'

'Twenty-nine feet, sir, sorry. Half ahead both motors.'

'Bearings of all HE, Fraser.'

Because of the possibility of Mas-boats, a surprise appearance on this side. Having certainly vanished, but having to be some damn place. Ignore them for now anyway, get *this* sod. Ignoring also the stuff Fraser was giving him, having the main elements of it visually in any case, as far as the sea-state permitted. Further data for the attack team meanwhile: 'Bearing *that*. Range *that*. I'm – oh, thirty-five on his bow.'

Enemy course therefore –

They had it – Danvers on his plotting diagram and Jarvis on the Fruit Machine – over and above which, Mike realised in a sudden clearing of memory, he *knew* this bugger! German tank-transporter *Sassnitz*, sister-ship to the once much-targeted *Ankara* – which *Ursa* as well as several other 10th Flotilla boats had in their time gone after and failed to get. She'd become known as 'the unsinkable' *Ankara*, until eventually sunk by mines laid from *Rorqual* – then under the command of – oh, old Lennox Napier. While *this* one, *Sassnitz* –

It was going to be a ninety-degree shot at a range of about 1,100 yards. Blocky, square-built and *obviously* in ballast, that high in the water. One of the T-class from the 8th Flotilla had claimed her, seven or eight months ago, but she'd then been spotted in Castellammare docks by a Maryland recce flight from Malta and reportedly destroyed next day in a raid by Blenheims. After the sinking of the *Ankara* she'd been the only Tiger tank transporter the Germans had had, so her alleged removal from the scene had been something to celebrate.

Repaired now, after all that, en route maybe to Naples for a load of Tigers – which please God Rommel wasn't going to get?

'Stand by one, two and three tubes.' By the telephone to Coltart in his tube space. McIver here doing his stuff, holding one on the DA – periscope angled out to port by that number of degrees providing aim-off. Heavyweight thrusting forepart of the *Sassnitz* steadily approaching the vertical hairline. Close shot on a ninety track, almost unpremeditated and mostly those stupid bloody escorts' own damn fault.

So don't waste it. Chance in a bleeding million – coming up *now* . . .

'Fire One!'

McIver must have been sucking Fisherman's Friends – or something worse. Target's stem-post passing the crosswire, *Ursa* reacting to the thump of discharge, jump of pressure in one's ears, and from Fraser, 'Torpedo running, sir!' Crosswire by this time on the target's midships section: 'Fire Two!'

'Both running, sir.'

And not *far* to run. Hence the short intervals between shots. Stay up, in the Navigatores' continuing absence, *see* this before going deep. Hairline passing over the ship's raised afterpart, and 'Fire Three!' Third jolt and pressure-rise, Fraser confirming, 'Three running, sir.'

Gift from the gods, it felt like. Twelve-twenty: less than an hour since McLeod had told him, 'Some kind of activity ashore, sir' and he'd responded with a laconic 'Well, best have a dekko . . .'

Hit. The hard-knocking thud, metallic *clang* in it, and a second later the eruption in her forepart, fountain of debris and smoke, gush of flame. That one hit would probably have been enough, with the sea rushing to fill those empty tank-decks. He stepped aside, told McIver, 'Quick shufti, Chief' – Ellery considerately lowering the 'scope by about a foot for him – and a second hit – amidships. Cheers, or the start of a few, here and there, Mike displacing the engineer in order to check on the Navigatores' reactions – the nearer under full helm, by the look of it reversing course, practic-ally submerged in doing so, the other one much the same but beam-on to it, steering to cross the stricken *Sassnitz*'s bows – the *Sassnitz* stopped, shattered, unquestionably on her way down. McIver staggering clear had gasped, 'Fuckin' gonner, *she* is!' but with Fraser's howl of 'Fast HE port quarter!' mostly drowning that. You heard it too – heard *them*, Mas-boats, E-boats – close and closing, crescendo of racing screws over Mike's shout of 'Flood "Q" full ahead, sixty feet!' Periscope rushing down too – those things at forty or fifty knots being perfectly capable of wiping it off, if not smashing into the standards or the tower itself – whether or not the bastards had known they'd been right on top of you, they bloody *had* been. And *might* have been charges coming. Weren't – if there had been they'd have been set shallow and you'd have known it by now. *Ursa* in her plunge passing fifty feet but with the 'planes now hard a-rise to check it, Mike telling McLeod, 'Blow "Q" – group down – slow both when you can' and Smithers, 'Hard a-starboard, steer oh-four-oh.' Then into the Tannoy, 'Shut off for depth-charging. Silent running . . .'

9

'Other's in contact, sir.'

Thanks to the first, whose transmissions had found her ten minutes ago and hadn't been thrown off by a simultaneous ninety-degree alteration of course, change of depth from sixty to a hundred-and-fifty feet and reduction to slow on one grouped-down motor. Before that, for thirty or forty minutes the search had been random, the Navigatores apparently failing to grasp the obvious, that one's natural escape route would be northward into more open water; and the Mas-boats one might guess busy looking for and picking up survivors. That was how it had sounded. But now – both destroyers in contact, one maintaining its range and bearing on *Ursa*'s quarter and the other closing on her beam. *Not* so good.

If there'd been a third, as there had been yesterday, would have been slightly *less* good; and yesterday one had shaken them off all right. These might be better at their job than yesterday's had been, of course. Anyway – sit tight for a while, let them think they had it made while *you* weren't quite on the ball, pick the right moment to make a break for it and this time do it better.

On the deck meanwhile, a position he quite frequently adopted, had yesterday for instance – knees up, arms around them, thinking about how he'd do it and the timing of it, which would have to match *their* moves. Familiar scene meanwhile as the background to such thought – McLeod for instance with his back against the ladder's slope, watching depth and trim, Danvers with *his* back to the chart table, elbows on its edge, eyes somewhat dreamily on the pipe-lined curve of deckhead. Visualising the Italian hulls up there, or at home in Bristol telling his nearest and dearest not to worry, soon be out of this? Jarvis of course was up for'ard with Coltart and company – had taken with him Mike's observations on the *Sassnitz*'s history and the benefits to the Eighth Army of her demise; same with McIver who'd gone aft to preside over the engine-room, motor room and after ends. All hands therefore cognisant of what they'd achieved and might be paying for in the next hour or hours.

Meanwhile, the depth-gauges in front of Swathely and Tubby Hart had been shut off. They were more vulnerable to pressure-damage from exploding charges than was the smaller, 'deep' gauge set midway between them – eighteen-inch diameter instead of about twice that, and less sensitive to small variations in depth. Needle currently static on 150 feet, in that small one. Swathely as always bolt-upright on his stool – muscular, square-jawed – Hart's greater bulk typically relaxed; and behind them and McLeod, ERA Ellery drooping slightly at his panel of vents and blows. All of them damp-shirted, faces sweat-sheened in the warmth and airlessness – as well as in some cases perhaps psychological reaction to this kind of situation.

Which they'd been in often enough before, of course. Been in and got out of, had no reason to doubt they'd get out of this time too. Knowing there might be some periods of discomfort and/or anxiety before they were out of it, but – hell, that this was simply what you were, what you *did*.

Mike on the move finally, getting to his feet: less by the look of it purposefully than as if deciding he'd rested long enough. Asking Fraser, 'Bearings now?'

A nod, as if glad to be asked. 'Red one-seven-oh, sir, and – green seven-five.'

Thin-voiced, and a pinched look around the eyes. Anxiety probably not unconnected to recent memory of Mas-boats having come blasting out of nowhere as they had – with no warning from him, who was supposed to be this boat's ears. Sheer luck it hadn't turned out a lot worse than it had – and maybe worse for Mike not having said a word about it – yet. All his concern in fact being concentrated on the present and immediate future: assuming here and now for instance that it would be the Italian astern who'd run over and drop the first pattern of charges on them, his colleague on the beam who'd hold the contact while that was happening. Or try to hold it, *be responsible* for holding it. Exploding depth-charges drowned-out asdic contact – as did fast-churning screws. Either, if used to best advantage, could provide the cover under which to make one's move.

He told Fraser, 'I want to know when the one astern cracks on revs. Or for that matter –'

'*Now*, sir – *now* he's –'

'Jamie, be ready for full ahead grouped up.'

'Aye, sir . . .'

Tones of voice flat: both conscious of the last attempt having failed but the previous one paying off very well – his manoeuvre after the sinking of the *Alessandria* – and that whatever he tried now could only be a variation of some such tactic – might work, might not, in which case you'd try again – and if necessary *again* – until *eventually* –

161

Lap of the gods: and faith in oneself, even when privately sweating blood. Supported meanwhile by the satisfaction of having put that tank-transport on the seabed under about two thousand feet of water.

McLeod quietly to Newcomb – who'd taken over as communications number, Cottenham having been allowed through to the galley where he was quietly making corned-beef sandwiches – 'Warn the motor room, stand by for full ahead grouped up.'

A nod and a grunt from weasel-face. And Fraser's head up quickly, his rather small mouth opening, a hand to his headset to remove it before depth-charges might burst his eardrums, Mike silencing him with 'Bearing of the one to starboard?'

'Green 78, sir, but –'

'All right.' Because that was all he needed. It was coming now, fast-rising Doppler of the Navigatore's screws accelerating to overtake from astern, volume building and note rising, men's eyes tending to drift up as if to see the menace coming. Reflecting – some, at least – that although the bastards could aim themselves right over the top of you and *might* get lucky, they also (a) lost you at a certain point, the A/S beam not functioning all that steeply downward, so they couldn't know when they were anything like exactly over you, in fact might not be anywhere near it if you'd side-stepped, and (b) didn't know, had no way of ascertaining, what depth you were keeping. Charges did have to be set for depth – to explode at 50 feet – or 100, 150, 200, 250, whatever – the adjustment being to the size of the flood-holes in their pistols – firing mechanisms – which were set off by internal pressure when the sea had filled them.

Five barrel-sized depth-charges in each pattern was the norm. One that rolled from a rack on the ship's stern, one from each 'thrower' lobbing them out port and starboard about the length of a cricket-pitch and carried forward by

162

the ship's momentum – then two more singles from the stern rack, one marking the diamond's centre and the fifth its furthest point. Highly lethal diamond if you happened to be right in it, but odds significantly against that. The accepted theory was that a charge had to explode within ten feet of the pressure-hull actually to hole or crack it. On one or two occasions when a charge had been very close but just not quite *that* close, one had been privileged to hear the *click* of the flooded pistol setting itself to fire about a second before it went off. Tended to be a hell of a long second.

Coming over *now*. Volume and note rising to a peak. Actually very much like a train passing close, which was how people tended to describe the sound of it. Mike telling Smithers, 'Starboard twenty.'

'Starboard twenty, sir!' Flipping the wheel around.

'Steer oh-eight-eight.'

'– oh-eight-eight, sir . . .'

Had been on course 010, would now be steering straight *at* the Italian on this starboard side although neither he nor his chum should know it, all hydrophone effect being eliminated for the moment. And of course worse to come – worse from *their* point of view, better from *Ursa's*. Like the first charge exploding *now* –

'Group up, full ahead both!'

In the motor room they'd been waiting for it. *Ursa* ringing as from a clap of thunder – which still took you by surprise – then the second and third charges, overlapping blasts felt as well as heard, her steel ringing, quivering from them although it was all above and slightly on her quarter – port quarter and *well* above, set for nearer fifty feet than a hundred even, Mike guessed, no catastrophe therefore, not this time. *Ursa* meanwhile flat-out – nine knots, roughly – shaking slightly from that too – and three more explosions over her

163

and to port, smothering however much racket *she* was making in this fast turn to starboard, eastward, to pass *under* the other Wop, get out the other side of him while still in his audially non-receptive area as the droning echoes faded.

Please God. Otherwise they'd soon find you again.

'Group down, slow both.'

McLeod's acknowledgement, and Smithers' murmur of 'Course oh-eight-eight, sir.'

'Make that oh-nine-oh.'

Due east. Still quiet up there. Here, even quieter. Nothing proved yet, nothing certain, hoping fit to bust but still ready for the worst. Which could occur – *had*, to others. You knew it – simply didn't have to think about it. Motors back to their regular hum, echoes of explosions fading into background memory, no trace of any of it in any face. Mike said easily, 'Stop starboard, Jamie.' Had an urge to add, 'Well done, all of you' – out of the pride he felt in them, and had no need to explain – anyway knowing better than to speak too soon.

She'd been well worth sinking, that *Sassnitz*. Better if she'd had a load of tanks in her and been going the other way, but even as it was –

'Sir –'

Fraser. Headset in place again. Mike raised an eyebrow – actually, but not letting this show, steeling himself for – well, disappointment, call it . . .

'HE and transmissions astern and on the quarter – red one-six-oh and – *both*'s transmitting –'

'Closing?'

'No, sir –'

'No problem, then. Next hour or so, Fraser, only give me *bad* news – right?'

It brought chuckles. Swathely raising a hand with fingers crossed, Ellery going so far as to lower himself to *sit* with

164

his back against the panel – long legs extended, slightly self-conscious look on his bony face. Mike deciding, Hear them coming up astern, port wheel and steer north again, try to work my way back westward. Allowing his thoughts to drift then: recalling Ann having asked him in their room in the Railway Hotel in Falkirk very shortly before he'd been due to sail from Holy Loch, 'What's it like being depth-charged, Mike?'

He'd told her, 'Nothing like as nice as *this*.'

Smiling. Moving. Then still moving but not smiling. 'Must be frightful. Isn't it?'

This when he'd been on a final ten-day leave at home in Buckinghamshire, brother Alan and sister Chloe having both wangled short leaves of their own. Mike to his shame had told his father he had only seven days; he'd felt bad about that, all the more so as the week had been a *very* good one, all of them including the Old Man on top form – and Chloe prettier than ever. While Ann had been visiting her parents in Edinburgh – a week or thereabouts, with some lie to *them* to justify a break in it of two nights and a day – duty visit to some boring relative elsewhere . . .

He'd admitted, about the depth-charging, 'Can be. Sometimes it's just noisy.'

'Charles says it's not as bad as one imagines. In *his* experience, he says. D'you think he might have been just lucky?'

'That could be it.'

Never having been really put through it, and preferring not to admit that? Sooner allow it to be assumed that he'd known the worst of it, and – well, so *what*, a few bangs is all . . .

Charles should have a CO's view of it now, in any case. As a skipper, it was the boat and her crew you were primarily concerned for. OK, let them down, you went with them – maybe deserved to. Any case that was the way to think

165

about it. Or better still – as before, the golden rule – *not* think about it. Change the subject, therefore: 'You're stupendous, Ann. Actually, *astonishing*. You're –'

'With *you*. If you find it so. But *only* you. Never like this with *him*. Not even at the start. Never dreamt it *could* be so – so – remember the first time – oh – you said *blinding*, and Mike that's actually –'

'Sir.' Fraser. In that split second, devastatingly. 'Astern, closing on us, both's transmitting –'

'Not in contact?'

'No, sir, not –'

'Port ten, Smithers. Steer north.'

'Port ten, steer north, sir.'

Near *enough* bad news, he thought. A vision of *Ursa*'s painfully slow progress, under helm now to put her on a course more or less at right-angles to her enemies' approach: with a chance of being far enough off their track before the range closed sufficiently for the sods to finger her. But if you pushed it along any faster – which was a temptation, all right – chances were they'd hear you. Smithers already easing rudder off her: otherwise, not a movement, barely a breath, facial expressions set in the strictly non-reactive mode.

Five minutes past two. Thinking ahead to the maybe one-in-three chance of getting away with this, paddling away with a prayer in your mind while the sods probed on eastward. Alternatively if it went bad again, could only try another full-power, battery-weakening rush under them, followed by slow withdrawal westward. *If* the Wop calling the shots up there hadn't by that time caught on to one's thought-processes, instincts, tactics, so that he'd be anticipating exactly that.

Might confuse him by *starting* the rush westward and going silent while turning south at the height of it?

'Course north, sir.'

Looking at Fraser though – Smithers' report overlapping

166

one from him about HE on the port quarter, movement right to left. Drawing a breath before putting the standard, vital question but saved the trouble of doing so by a shake of the HSD's head: no, no contact. 'Transmitting, but –'

'All right.' Eyes on the deckhead: focusing on sound, translating that into visual imagery – churn of screws still right to left, Wops intent on their asdic search, continuous probing when they'd have done better just to be listening, using their sets as hydrophones. Even at slow grouped down on one motor *Ursa* wasn't *entirely* silent. Not silent enough by half: even with the sea-state more or less on her side. In the stillness and quiet down here one tended to overlook *that* factor.

So give it a go . . .

'Port ten.'

Premature, maybe. Passing the order in little more than a whisper: Smithers murmuring acknowledgement, the brass wheel glittering as he span it, Mike adding just as quietly, 'Steer three hundred degrees.'

'Three-oh-oh, sir . . .'

Danvers whispering that course to himself as he ran his parallel rule from the compass rose to *Ursa*'s pencilled track on a plotting diagram. Distances by speed and stopwatch timing, since the log was switched off as part of the silent-running. *Ursa* running northwestward now, Italians holding on eastward still, please God. Mike querying this in a glance at Fraser, getting what might have been a qualified affirmative.

Touch wood – edge of the chart table – Danvers shifting to give him room and a sight of the plotting diagram if he wanted it. Mike thinking, two hours on this course now, if we can get away with it, get well out there in the open, then come round to – oh, 220, say. After *one* hour in fact might speed up a little. Four knots, say, through the rest of the daylight hours. Two-thirty now, so six hours, six and a half. But give it just *half* an hour, then half ahead together instead of slow on just one. Surface about nine and be getting the box up while paddling around Marettimo. And a signal to old Shrimp of course, soon as we're up. He reached for a pencil and the signal-pad, roughed it out for enciphering: *To S.10 — etc. — from* Ursa. *Returning by outward route, only one torpedo remaining. ETA* — but Danvers could fill that in. Then, *German tank-carrier* Sassnitz *sunk in position* — Danvers again, co-ordinates and time — *after leaving Castellammare northbound in ballast with destroyer escort.* Then — as always — time of origin, zone time and date. He slid the pad along: 'Fix that up, Pilot, have Lazenby bung it out when we surface.'

'Aye, sir . . .'

His slightly surprised, pleased look was reflected in other faces. The more or less casual reference to surfacing would be one heartening ingredient, and the intention of returning right away to Malta another. He'd mentioned having only one fish left as the reason for that unilateral decision. Well — proposal — Shrimp would stop you in your tracks if starting back immediately raised problems. If *Swordsman* for instance might be passing through the mines at anything like the same time, or some other boat making the passage eastward. But to stay on patrol with only one fish wouldn't make much sense: he'd only saved that one, using three instead of four on the *Sassnitz*: this way you weren't completely toothless, were still capable of drawing blood if that was how things went.

He asked Fraser: 'Well?'

'Same, sir. Fading on green one-five-five.'

'Fading. *Isn't* that nice.' General agreement, laughter masking relief — and an easing of cramped positions. Another answer he might have given Ann that afternoon in Falkirk, he thought, would have been 'We do our best *not* to have charges dropped on us, you see.'

10

Lazaretto then, a few days later, Mike facing Shrimp across the desk in his newly tunnelled-out office, half an hour after parking *Ursa* out there in the creek between mooring-buoys. He'd surfaced and announced himself to the signal station within minutes of the time Danvers had given as their ETA – not all *that* astounding an achievement, in point of fact, but satisfying in its way – at any rate to Danvers. And of course Shrimp had been there to welcome them, making a somewhat hazardous transit of the floating brow before the boat was properly secured, boarding athletically to shake Mike's hand and congratulate him and all the rest of them, admire the now even more crowded Jolly Roger – which Maltese in *dghaisas* and on a harbour ferry had already cheered. *Ursa* then with her casing party lined up fore and aft, White Ensign as well as Roger flying, motoring in past the head of Sliema Creek and Fort Manoel with the mid-afternoon sun already lowering itself a little over Floriana. The Malts' fierce enthusiasm was always heartening: Shrimp's approbation of course rather more so.

Even a sad Shrimp's – as he was now. *Ultra* having failed to respond to her recall from patrol. Jimmy Ruck's billet had been in the southern approaches to Messina; on his third day he'd reported having sunk an Italian submarine, and since then nothing, no acknowledgement of the twice-repeated call. Shrimp growling to Mike on their way ashore over the floating walkway, 'One of the best.' Stony-faced: anger in it as much as sadness. 'Or say *more* of the best.'

But at his desk now, eyes narrowed against the smoke of his cigarette, and swiftly totting up figures on a sheet of signal-pad. Immaculate in his whites – Mike somewhat less so in seagoing khaki – cocking an eyebrow as he underscored his total. 'Looks like 63,750, Michael.'

Mike had got the same result in a spasm of instant calculation four days ago, within minutes of sinking the *Sassnitz*. Which, Shrimp had reminded them all, in the course of his visit on board, had been the only transport capable of embarking and discharging Tiger battle-tanks that the enemy had possessed, since the mining of her sister-ship the *Ankara*; the Wops would have been sweating blood to get her out of that dockyard and back into service. He'd asked Mike a minute ago whether he realised what *Ursa's* score was now – 'score' meaning tonnage sunk, and Mike looking vague, or trying to . . .

'Must be getting on for – well, crikey –'

'It was 40,750 when you sailed. Add 14,000 for the *Alessandria* and nine for the *Sassnitz*?'

'Be damned . . .'

'Puts you top of the heap, Michael.'

Long breath. Then: 'If Jimmy Ruck hadn't bought it –'

'He'd still have been marginally ahead. Yes. But – fact remains, a highly effective patrol – despite nothing coming your way from the convoy operation.' Stubbing out the remains of that cigarette: he was more or less chain-smoking,

170

Mike had noticed. 'Except the cruiser you made a present of to your friend Melhuish, eh?'

Friend . . .

Slightly over the top – in all the circumstances. But hardly explainable or contestable: so go with it, at least let it go – if that was the impression Charles had given, which presumably it had been. He shrugged, admitted, 'I ballsed that up, all right. Stroke of luck you had him there as longstop.'

'Disappointing for you at the time, obviously, but hardly a balls-up. More of a toss-up. As it was for us here, of course. And a cracking good start for Melhuish. I've sent him to have a go at railway tunnels in the vicinity of Taormina, by the way. *Unsung* like *Unbroken* being blessed with a three-inch gun with proper sights on it – let him get his eye in on *that* – and an inshore reconnaissance of Cape Molini on his way back. But – on the subject of this recent convoy operation, Michael – you'll have heard a few broadcasts –'

'Very little, except –'

'We lost nine merchantmen out of fourteen. Also a carrier – *Eagle* – and two cruisers – sunk, that is. Brought in four freighters and a tanker – the *Ohio*, who did bloody marvellously to get through – well, they *all* did. I'm not sure you'd have realised – but you must have, Gravy wasn't exactly keeping it to himself, was he – how close to the edge we were? We'd darn near had it – food stocks for a week or thereabouts – and thanks to the five who made it we're good for a month now – huh?'

'But nine cargoes lost, as well as –'

'– as well as an aircraft carrier and two cruisers sunk, two others torpedoed, a destroyer sunk.' Shrimp's look and tone were grim. '*Eagle* was hit by all four of one salvo of torpedoes, sank in eight minutes. *Victorious* was hit – bomb, big one – but her armoured flight-deck saved her, and *Indomitable* had *her* flight-deck so ploughed up her aircraft had to land on *Victorious*.

171

Furious had flown her load of Spitfires off to join us here – twenty-nine arrived, I think out of thirty-six. The convoy had very little air-cover left to them by the time they were changing formation for the Skerki Channel, and of course the bastards made a meal of it. E-boats in it too then – from Pantellaria, I'd guess – cruisers *Cairo* and *Nigeria* hit by U-boats – those were the convoy's fighter-direction ships, what's more – and E-boats or Mas-boats got *Manchester* – she had to be sunk next day – and E-boats got another four or five of the merchantmen. Others at about that stage in highly co-ordinated air attacks – 88s, Stukas, Savoias –'

'The lot.'

Shrimp nodded. 'But late in the day, from their point of view. Hence the size of that effort, Michael. *Frantic* effort, might call it. If they'd kept up the pressure back in April – or been *allowed* to – *and* invaded, used their fleet –'

'I remember you were sure they would.'

'Damn fools not to. As by this time they must realise. Anyway – in the Narrows, about the height of it – well, the *Ohio* got a real pasting, but kept going – and a few more were sunk. I think apart from the *Ohio* only the *Brisbane Star* survived that stage. *Kenya* was hit – torpedoed, but held on . . .' Shrimp's hands moved: 'Only bits and pieces this, as I've picked it up, but it gives you the broad picture. The *Ohio* must have come in for it again – stopped, dead-in-the-water for a while – the *Rochester Castle* set on fire and the *Dorset* stopped – so down to three then, and they had the good fortune to find some of our short-range Spits over them by midday or thereabouts. Those being – oh, the *Port Chalmers*, *Melbourne Star*, and the burning *Rochester Castle*. The *Ohio* damn near foundering, but under way again – under tow, nursed in by the destroyers *Penn* and *Robust* and two sweepers. And the *Brisbane Star* got in on her own a few hours later. Just those five, out of your fourteen starters.'

'Without any surface-ship intervention at all, all that.'

'None. Consequently this flotilla didn't get a look in. Except through just *being* here, which may have been something of a deterrent. I had nine boats out there, and not a sausage – except that cruiser. Don't like to risk their own ships if they can help it, do they. Plain fact though, Michael, getting those five in has saved us. If they hadn't made it we'd have been done for, starved into surrender of the island, lost our base – and thanks to them we haven't. All right, there'll have to be another convoy pretty soon; not out of the woods yet, only seeing daylight through the trees – at long last.'

'"Pedestal"'s rated a success, meanwhile.'

'As it bloody well *should* be. Just *some* of 'em getting through makes it so. Huge cost, sure – that's simply to be expected, accepted. As it always has been, if you think about it.' Glancing at his watch, the second time in a minute. Mike put in, 'Changing the subject slightly, if I may –'

'Long as it's quick. I've two boats sailing this evening. Dean's and Grogan's.' Pushing his chair back, Mike asking as he followed suit, 'Torpedo situation, sir – only wondering how that is now.'

'Better than it was, thank God. Mark VIIIs, too. Yes, that *is* looking better. During "Pedestal" we had no less than three deliveries – *Otus*, *Rorqual* and *Clyde*. Torpedoes, ammunition and high octane in their ballast tanks. One thing "Pedestal" confirmed, incidentally, was aviation spirit *can't* be brought through in surface ships. *Ohio* only made it by the skin of her teeth, and she's scrap-iron now. But as for *Ursa's* future now, Michael – barring emergencies you can expect a week or ten days' rest. Only had about ten minutes in last time, didn't you. Then *probably* – for your private info at this stage – a special operation, which to be frank I don't much care for, stunt dreamt up by the Staff in Alex. I'm not what you'd call consulted, only told to lay it on.' One hand on the door, but holding it shut while adding quietly, 'Commando jaunt. Not our own gang either, the intention's to fly in a bunch from Ismailia. As usual, a bugger's rush – on the face of it with good reason, but – look, we'll talk tomorrow. More than just that to talk about, as it happens.'

Heading for the wardroom, to pick up whatever mail there might be, with this lingering image of old Shrimp mastering a sadness to which by this time he was no stranger. He'd said to Mike once, in the course of an evening about half a year ago that had had something in common with a wake, 'Times like these, mine's a foul job. Best chaps ever left the womb – and all of us knowing the bloody odds . . .' Shake of the head – dog coming out of water, shaking it off – 'Had one too many, Michael, getting bloody maudlin . . .' But thinking also about this Special Op – landing commandos, and not the 10th Flotilla's, Shrimp's private army of one officer and however many other ranks it consisted of now, who most of the time were kept kicking their heels with damn-all to do except help in reconstruction, bomb damage etc., and natur-ally didn't look with much favour on others being sent in to do jobs *they* were here for. Which had happened a few times because there was a commando training establishment at Ismailia – down-Canal from Port Said, and first right – turning out canoeists and other cut-throats briefed in the latest tactics and equipment; Staff planners liked to employ them, rather than the old hands one had here.

Mike, like Shrimp, wasn't all that keen on Special Ops. Especially not on stunts dreamt-up by Staff the best part of a thousand miles away.

'Oh, hello there . . .'

Frank Dean – whom Shrimp had mentioned as sailing for patrol this evening. Red-headed, pale-skinned, mid-twenties, one of the newer COs. Shaking hands: 'Heard you were in — and some patrol, uh? Darned great oiler and a tank-transport?'

'They came along, Frank, that's all. Pure luck, nothing else — except the fish ran straight. Where *you* off to this time?'

'Kerkennah Banks, thereabouts. Not my favourite billet, but there you are.'

Tunisian coast — Sfax, Gabès, approaches from the north and northwest to Tripoli. Mike nodded. 'Good luck, anyway.' He'd never much liked those shallows, especially the Kerkennah end of it. 'Off at dusk, are you?'

Heading for *Ursa*'s mail slot; Dean accompanying him across the cavern-like wardroom, apparently to check the contents of his own — getting there first and extracting a message slip which by the look of him he wasn't too happy with. Telephone message, probably. While Mike was finding precisely nothing — pigeon-hole empty, nothing in it for him or for anyone else. Repeating to Dean, '*Very* best of luck, Frank.' There'd no doubt have been mail for McLeod and the others, one of whom must have nipped ashore for it while he'd been closeted with Shrimp. Would have left *his*, though — skimmed through whatever there was, and put his back. As he, being always first ashore, normally did with the others' stuff. Someone might carelessly have taken his with the rest of it? Or asked Walburton to clear the box for them, for some reason. Mike had given his own letters to Walburton — including the much-thought-over reply to Ann's last one, which he'd written during the return passage of the mine-field, and the signalman as per routine would have delivered them with other homebound mail to the appropriate office here in Lazaretto.

McLeod would have sent Jarvis or Danvers to clear this box. All there was to it. Dean enquiring sympathetically, 'No joy?' Mike shrugged: 'Box has been cleared, anyway.' Plain truth being nothing from *her*: which might in fact have come as something of a relief, rather than this disappointment. While as for the others – hell, last time in he'd heard from the Old Man, you couldn't expect him to spend *all* his time writing letters. He nodded to Dean, said again, 'Good luck, Frank.' Dean's boat, *Usurper*, was alongside here at the steps, the 'wardroom berth', with 'Groggy' Grogan's *Urbane* outside her, with the usual chaos – last-minute embarkation of stores etc. prevailing – and Guy Mottram here, presumably to see them off, whatever – accompanied by his own – *Unbowed*'s – first lieutenant, name of Brocklesby. Thin as a rake, freckled, expression of permanent amusement, Mottram about twice his height and girth. Mike stopped, put a hand out: 'Guy.'

'Mike. Heard about Jimmy Ruck, I suppose.'

'Yes.' Shake of the head: 'Shrimp says no clue how or when. A mine, most likely . . . You were somewhere up that way, weren't you?'

'Crotone. Cape Colonne to Punta dell'Alice. Got back this forenoon.' Making way for Brocklesby, who was boarding one of the boats alongside. Mike asking Mottram – change of subject, conventional enquiry – 'Any luck this time?'

'Oh – started well enough.' Shrug of the heavy shoulders. 'Steamer loading at the chemical factory – from a certain bearing one could see funnel-tops and so forth, so I hung around and on day two she came out, deep-laden. Three and a half thousand tons, escort of Mas-boats and a Cant. I fired two fish, hit with one and she blew up. After which, having muddied the waters of course, damn-all for a week except trawlers and A/S schooners making nuisances of themselves. You had another good one, I'm told.'

'Two good targets and no problems.' He changed the subject back to *Ultra*. 'You know Jimmy's wife, don't you?'

'Widow. Yes. I'll write, of course. Saying God knows what that could make it any less bloody for her, mind you.'

'Well – what a great chap he was, and we're all devastated?'

'Something original like that.' A shrug. 'Plain truth, for sure, but –'

'Guy – she's alone, bereft, and you're a chum of long standing . . . Look, why not tell her you're writing for the whole crowd of us?'

'Yes. Yes, *not* a bad idea . . .'

Ultra's record on the flotilla scoreboard was still open-ended, hadn't been ruled off yet. Ruck had sunk a hell of a lot though, the little thumbnail sketches of his kills in the numbered columns of patrols, starting a few months before *Ursa* had joined the flotilla and ending with his one-from-last, one of only two in which he hadn't scored. This final one would have an inch-long U-boat's silhouette pencilled into it: *then* the ruling-off. Mike didn't look at *Ursa's,* for some reason. A mental crossing of the fingers? Leaving the board anyway. The big wardroom was already crowded, and looking around it he could have put names to nearly all the faces, only a few third and fourth hands of newly-arrived boats being as yet unfamiliar: and looking over the heads of nearer groups towards the centre, the massive stone fireplace which was the customary gathering-point for COs and senior base staff – Shrimp not there as yet but his deputy Chris Hutchinson, Commander (Submarines), who'd recently taken over from Hubert Marsham – and who as CO of *Truant* in the spring of 1940 had sunk the German cruiser *Karlsruhe,* in the Skaggerak – was chatting with Guy Mottram, Jack Brodie of *Unslaked* and old Pop Giddings, who ran the Manoel Island farm.

This *was* a wake, though. Expressions mostly sombre, tones subdued. As it tended to be, until the worst of it wore off.

'Evening, sir.'

Jamie McLeod – and Jarvis with him. Mike asked them whether they'd had mail, and the answer was yes, they had,

Danvers had cleared the box as usual, soon after *Ursa* had secured. McLeod added, 'Pretty miserable, sir. I mean *Ultra*.'

'More than that.' He noticed their near-empty glasses. 'Ready for another?'

'Well, thank you, sir –'

'Steward!'

'I was just saying, sir – lucky old Paul Everard, getting promoted out of her just before this patrol.' Jarvis, offering cigarettes. 'There but for the grace of – well, of Ruck, recommending him for that Number One's job –'

Mike was telling the Maltese steward, 'Three, please.' Then happening to see Danvers on his way to join them, called 'No – make that four.' If you didn't specify an alternative, that meant four gins. Back to Jarvis. 'Everard – yes. Went to be Number One of *Tomahawk*, right?'

Paul Everard had been Ruck's third hand, torpedo officer; RNVR sub-lieutenant when he'd joined him, then lieutenant, and very recently transferred to the 1st Flotilla formerly based in Alexandria but now Beirut, replacing that boat's first lieutenant who was being sent home for his Perisher, the command course. Jarvis adding, 'Paul always thought Ruck was tops. As of course he was.'

'Must be weird.' Danvers. 'All your mates gone, and you – you know, still around. Must wonder Christ, why *me* . . .' Looking at their glasses and Mike's lack of one: 'This supposed to be my round, or –'

'It's on order.' Jarvis added reprovingly, 'Generosity of your Commanding Officer.' Adding, 'The *next* round's yours.'

Mike left them before that time came, to join the group now comprising only Mottram, Jack Brodie and Dan Gerahty of *Swordsman*. Brodie, tallish, angular and balding, greeted him with 'Mowing 'em down in droves, we hear.'

'Oh, by the dozen, Jack . . .'

'Seriously, though – a couple of whoppers?'

He shrugged – tired of questions to which the questioners already knew the answers, word having gone round as it always did within minutes of one's return. But he noticed that Brodie was leaning on a stick, and stared at it: 'What's this about?'

'Got stung on the knee – some awful bug. Clearing up now, but crikey –'

'So – *Unslaked* –'

'Hugo Short has the loan of her. Benghazi, or thereabouts. He'd better bring her back intact, that's all.' A hand on Mike's arm: 'Appalling loss, poor old *Ultra*.'

'Yes. Here's to them.'

'Been a lot of *that* going on. Oh, here's the boss . . .'

Shrimp grey-faced, joining Hutch and a lieutenant-commander by name of – oh, lost it – who was taking over as Staff Officer Operations. Gerahty and Guy Mottram were there too. Mike meanwhile accepting Brodie's offer of a refill, Giddings rambling on about two litters of piglets having been born in the course of this last weekend, and the SOO switching to subjects of wider interest such as Generals Alexander and Montgomery having assumed command in the desert, where Rommel was still being held on the Alamein line; Brodie agreeing with Mike's '*Holding* the bugger's not much use', although Mike had immediately wished he hadn't said it – good men were being killed and maimed, just holding him – but before he could take it back Shrimp intervened with 'Give me a minute, Michael?'

'Sir.'

Out past the scoreboard, into the gallery: no boats alongside now, five including *Ursa* out at buoys – which meant about another half-dozen currently on patrol. Strains of *Forces' Favourites* from open fore-hatches out there in the creek. Shrimp said quietly, 'I mentioned that we had more than one thing to discuss. One being this projected Special Op – and

179

I'll tell you about that in the morning – Lascaris at 1100 – right?'

'Aye, sir.'

'It's not exactly imminent, I'd guess we may have a couple of weeks. On the other hand it could come at short notice, we need to be on the top line for it and I want you in on the planning right from the start. The other thing, Michael –' a glance around – 'is that you are now a lieutenant-commander.'

'But – no, I –' beginning to laugh, but seriously baffled – 'can't be, I've –'

'You've five months to go, I know that. But you'll have heard of accelerated promotion? They're giving you six months – in lieu of another gong. Great deal more use, as I'm sure you'll agree. But this is hardly an evening for celebrating, is it.'

'Certainly is not.'

'Why I kept quiet about it earlier, you see. And for the moment let's do that. Give *Ultra* forty-eight hours. Wednesday evening we'll wet the half-stripe. Meanwhile, Michael – warmest congratulations.'

He had supper early, to leave time for writing to the Old Man – who'd be tickled pink. And to Ann? Maybe not: think about it. It was worth a bit though – in the long run would be. The system being that you acquired a certain degree of seniority from the results of your sub-lieutenant's courses, and this set the date of your promotion to lieutenant roughly two years later; normally you did eight years as a lieutenant (two stripes, and equivalent to an army captain) before becoming a lieutenant-commander (two and a half, matching the rank of major), after which there was a further set period before you became eligible – subject to performance, nothing automatic about it – for a brass hat, commander's rank, three stripes on your sleeves and/or epaulettes, oak-leaves on the peak of

180

your cap. With the award he was getting now he could aspire to that eminence six months sooner than he would have otherwise.

If one (a) stayed alive, and (b) kept one's nose clean. The first being in the lap of the gods and the second depending on how one handled things from now on.

He decided on the way up to his cabin that he would not send Ann this news. If he did, she might well comment on it to Charles, and there was only one way she could have got to know about it. Better to let Charles tell her – as he would, having no reason not to. Write just to the Old Man: Something jokey like *Please note when replying to this that the correct form of address is now Lieutenant-Commander M. J. Nicholson R.N. No idea why – wasn't due until some time next year. Probably just a cock-up – but there it is, there's no arguing with their Lordships. Actually I'm having an early night, as I've been away a while . . .*

After a bath and leisurely breakfast, then a visit to *Ursa*, half of whose crew had already been bussed to the rest-camp at Mellieha – where in the blitz period sailors bathing in St Paul's Bay had often enough been individually targeted by Me 109s' cannon and machine-guns. The Messerschmitts had patrolled Marsamxett as well as Grand Harbour and Sliema Creek at two hundred feet or less in perfect safety because the shortage of ammunition had led to our gunners being barred from shooting at anything but bombers. Those men had had to grin and bear it, all right. Recalling those times and – admit it, privately – that degree of taken-for-granted courage – he crossed to the Valetta side by *dghaisa* and climbed Ferry Steps into the old town's narrow stone streets and alleys. Eventually – strolling, killing time, through to Palace Square – the Palace, governor's residence, Governor being Field Marshal Lord Gort VC now in place of the long-serving and generally revered Sir William Dobbie. It was all a lot tidier than it had been a couple of months ago.

He'd been nosing around, taking his time and enjoying it, but still had the best part of half an hour before his assignation with Shrimp; found himself eventually on the Upper Barracca with its superb views over Grand Harbour and Valetta's ancient fortifications. Directly across the water for instance to the Three Cities – Vittoriosa, Conspicua, Senglea, Fort St Angelo a massive foreground centrepiece; and, training right, Dockyard and French creeks with Senglea's docks and the suburb behind them all bombed flat, no more than stone ruins separating the two waterways. A minesweeper at anchor in the approaches to French Creek, sailors moving like white ants on her decks; *dghaisas* like black beetles clawing across blue water, a tug with a string of lighters, and in mid-harbour, off Floriana, the bottomed remains of a burnt-out steamer. That was to his right from here: back this way and right across from him the sun was already high and blinding over St Angelo and more distantly San Rocco and the group of W/T masts at – Rinella, was it? Fort Ricasoli just in one's arc of sight – harbour entrance, eastern side – although the other headland, Fort Elmo, was hidden by the bulge of Valetta's massively-bastioned coastline. Inside the Ricasoli promontory though – seaward side of St Angelo – what he guessed might be the largely submerged wreck of the *Ohio* lay alongside that stretch of breakwater. Something to have seen, he thought – when the tales come to be told. But then before St Angelo, Bighi, the RN hospital, which in the months of round-the-clock blitzkrieg had suffered badly from the Luftwaffe's attentions. They'd gone for all the hospitals – Bighi, St Andrew's, St George's at Floriana – all marked with huge red crosses which had served to make them natural targets for those bastards. Would be like that again too, all of it – if it started again, which in the mess last evening some

182

had guessed it *might*, others preferring not to take the question seriously.

The minesweeper was getting under way, he noticed. And a Sliema ferry – motor-launch with a tall, pipe-like funnel and canvas awning along her sides and afterdeck – was turning in towards the Customs House at the foot of this great stone barricade. Meaning of the word 'Barracca' perhaps? Hadn't occurred to him, until now. There was a landing-place down there and near-vertical flights of steps; *had* been a passenger lift that brought one to the top here but hadn't been working for a year or two. The ferry had passed out of sight, directly below him. These Barraccas, upper and lower, provided the vantage-points from which Maltese by the hundreds, even a thousand or more on occasion, had throughout the siege gathered to cheer the surviving ships of convoys into harbour. Convoy arrivals under attack even, cheers almost wild enough to rival the screams of diving Stukas.

Lieutenant-Commander, for God's sake . . . Come to think of it, would have to scrounge some gold lace from somewhere or other. Had thought of it last night but not since. Get epaulettes complete, ready-made – and preferably scrounge, not buy; but gold lace, half stripes to be sewn-on between the two thick ones on each sleeve of one's two reefer jackets, in readiness for the Fleet's autumnal change from whites to blues – that was something else. But – memory stirring again – there was a shop in Strada Reale – a lace shop that was run by a very smart grey-haired woman named –

No. Lost it. If one had ever had it. Well, one *had*. Abigail French had introduced him to her: which in itself provoked another line of thought – drop in on Abigail, if Shrimp left one with time enough? Anyway, that woman *might* have gold lace in stock, in which case she might do the tailoring as well. Or know of someone who would. Strada Reale anyway

183

– little shop on the right, going back down that way. In fact must have passed it earlier – if it was still standing, of course . . .

Crikey – eight minutes to eleven. Go see Shrimp.

Shrimp told him, 'There's nowhere else, if she can't help you. I think she has nuns who do sewing for her. Carmella Cassar. She certainly does sell the lace they make. Pushing it a bit by this time, but she's still a fine-looking woman. Head on her shoulders too.'

'I'll mention your name, if I may.'

'Mention anything you like. But grab that chart, bring it over?'

In this underground chamber – the Submarine Office, in the labyrinths of Combined Services HQ – there was a hum of some kind of ventilation machinery and when the door was open a rattle of distant typewriters. Mike had been checked in to the old building by a Royal Marine sergeant who'd passed him on to a paymaster midshipman whom Shrimp had recently taken on as his private secretary, and who'd brought him through an outer office to this larger one, announcing him as Lieutenant Nicholson, Shrimp correcting this with 'Actually, Lieutenant-Commander Nicholson, lad.' Adding, 'You weren't to know. One reason and another we're keeping it quiet for a couple of days. But you'd also know of him as CO of *Ursa*.'

'Of course, sir. Er – congratulations – I mean on your last patrol, sir –'

'Thank you, Mid.' They'd shaken hands; Shrimp telling Mike, 'George was sunk in *Medway* and before that in *Naiad*. Michael, you'll need to find yourself some half-stripes, won't you?' Which was how the subject of the lace shop had come up; Carmella Cassar being one of Shrimp's many local friends, apparently. Mike brought him the chart. Familiar enough: central Med, with Sicily and the toe of Italy in its eastern

184

half -- Malta about the size of a pea -- or the Isle of Wight, say -- and the QBB minefield outlined and shaded-in in Indian ink. Shrimp was lighting a cigarette.

'Sit down, Michael. Smoke if you want to.' Touching the chart. 'Won't bother with this for the moment, we'll go over the strategic background, first. Starting with the imperative of feeding and maintaining this island and ourselves. "Pedestal" improved the situation by a total of 32,000 tons -- saving our bacon but only for about a month, at most. Magic Carpet submarines from Gib and Alex are continuing to do their bit, of course, and *Welshman* and *Manxman* are hard at it, bless them.' *Welshman* and *Manxman* being 40-knot minelayers who'd been making frequent solo runs from either end. Shrimp wobbled one hand: a gesture of uncertainty. 'Invaluable, but as far as we're concerned very much hand-to-mouth stuff -- can't realistically count on it for ever, and we need to be able to look a *long* way ahead -- especially as our role here is pretty well bound to become more and more important. That's primarily because Eighth Army under this man Montgomery mean business -- you can count on it, won't be long before we see things moving in the desert, and then the picture *really* changes -- Libyan airfields in our hands, convoys with air-cover and a decent chance of getting through, so then -- well, Sicily, perhaps. Why not? It's the obvious way into Italy. Or -- maybe slightly less obvious, Sardinia, Corsica, Gulf of Genoa -- Spetsia or even Nice -- huh?'

Mike had lit a cigarette. 'Wow.' Eyes on Shrimp's. 'Dependent on an absolutely sweeping success by the Eighth Army -- you say count on it, sir --'

'Tell you this in strict confidence, Michael. The Canal's being closed to shipping off and on for periods of half a day or more while mountains of stuff are lifted over to be deployed south of Alexandria and El Alamein. Guns, tanks, troops, everything. And when he's ready --'

185

'Montgomery?'

A nod. 'With Alexander behind him commanding the whole theatre. I'm told he has a reputation amongst fellow-pongos for not moving until he *is* good and ready, won't be pushed into going off at half-cock – under pressure from Winston, for instance. But in regard to all that speculation – Sicily, Sardinia, whatever – prior to any of that, Pantellaria, perhaps. Or North Africa somewhere. And all or any of this depending on us staying put *here* – and of course continuing to make Rommel's life difficult or better still impossible for him. Which in turn depends, returning to my starting-point –'

'Convoys.'

'And the job being thrust upon us now is aimed at getting one through very soon and if possible intact. Well, anything that could contribute to that has to be worth trying. My own first reaction was less than enthusiastic. We've tried some, haven't we. But if these chaps *could* pull it off, you see –'

'Not another airfield?'

'Three fields simultaneously. Fields selected incidentally by Air Intelligence. Basic idea being to incapacitate all three in the convoy's final stages – small, fast convoy – from the east, this time –'

'Three boats?'

'Yes. *Ursa* as one of them because you're here, due for a week's rest at least and a second one wouldn't hurt you – or a third, for that matter. And of course you've experience of such operations.'

'Not all brilliantly successful, sir.'

'That last one wasn't, but not through any fault of yours. No more than the failure of *Una*'s the other day was any fault of Pat Norman's. If a landing party fails to make the rendezvous – well, rotten luck, but as long as you're in the right place at the right time you've done *your* job. Anyway – airfields to be

186

targeted are Gela, Comiso and Catania. Yes, Catania again. Still home to three Mas-boats, as far as is known – also German E-boats at Augusta. Gela's an open-beach landing with no patrols we know of, although Mas-boats do frequent Licata – what, a dozen miles away?'

'But – in any of those places, sir, what makes them think they can do better than they did at Catania?'

'The commandos are sure they have the answer or answers, and the Staff – well, as I said, *anything* that'll do the trick, or help to . . . Another thing is that so soon after *Una*'s effort it's the last thing they'll be expecting.'

'Well, there's that.' Mike looked up from the chart. 'Comiso, I must say, I don't know at all.'

'Here.' Stab of a blunt forefinger. 'Not marked, but close to Ragusa, which is. Bit of a hike for our pongos – landing *here*, say – open-beach – then all of ten miles inland.'

'Pongos' being a friendly but slightly derogatory naval term for soldiers.

'So that team will need to be landed several hours earlier than the other two – if the assaults are to be simultaneous.'

Yes, simultaneous attacks. Assaults to go in when the convoy's about thirty, thirty-six hours short of Grand Harbour. The commandos'll have their own schemes of course, but as far as landing or launching and pick-up points are concerned we obviously have the final say, nothing's finalised until we've agreed it with them.'

'What about maps, sir – for our own guidance?'

'They're on the way.' Shrimp was stubbing out his cigarette. 'You're right – as an aid to countering pongo bullshit, if any.'

'Well – right . . .' Concentrating on the chart again. 'Random thought, though. We've always gone for pick-ups reasonably close to landing areas. Might be worth a rethink perhaps? Landing-points much farther from targets, land if

187

necessary the night before and lay-up all day, attacking if possible from the blind side –'

'I don't think so, Michael.' Shrimp shaking his squarish head slowly. 'For one thing, the pongos wouldn't wear it. They want in and out double-quick, *always*, on this sort of lark. I can see major problems anyway.' Shrugging, expelling smoke. 'I haven't time to go into it here and now, but all right, see what you can come up with. For all three teams. Settle yourself into a corner of the Ops Room at Lazaretto, tell the SOO he's to let you have whatever charts, pilots etcetera you may want. What else now?'

'Any thoughts on which other boats, sir?'

'Yes. *Unsung* – Melhuish will be back I think on Monday, can't leave it any longer than that. And *Swordsman* – Gerahty's sailing tonight but if necessary I'd recall him – an "S" having a *little* more room for passengers than you do. Depends to some extent on the composition of the teams – if one's larger than the others. But then again, if you and the Chief Pongo hit it off, might make sense to take him and his team in *Ursa*. See how it works out.'

'Aye aye, sir.'

'Give Carmella my regards.'

Up the Lascaris steps into sunlight and the shade of the heap of shattered stone that had been the Royal Opera House until they'd destroyed it in that very bad time in the spring – one particularly bad night for the centre of Valetta, Kingsway in particular, where they'd flattened the Law Courts too. *Ursa* had been in dockyard hands, repairing depth-charge damage, had miraculously survived that and several more nights of the same, although others within virtual spitting-distance of her certainly had not. Although there'd been quite a few bombs that didn't explode, including one out of town that everyone had talked about for weeks afterwards and Mike had (criminally) mentioned in a letter to his father; a large bomb said to be of Italian origin which had penetrated the dome of Mosta Church, bounced off a wall, skidded the full length of the building and ground to a halt without exploding. There'd been three hundred people attending a service at the time. In April, that had been. The vast majority of the bloody things *had* exploded, in the town and elsewhere but especially the dockyard and its surroundings, destroying virtually everything aboveground. That was when Senglea had been reduced to rubble and a number of ships sunk – two destroyers, three submarines, three minesweepers. There'd been a convoy brought in – *some* of a convoy – and the cruiser *Penelope*, which had been part of its escort, had been in dock with frantic round-the-clock efforts being made to complete essential repairs while under constant dive- and high-level bombing. The London press had nicknamed her HMS *Pepperpot* on account of the number of holes in her upperworks; but they'd got her away all right, despite continuing blitzkrieg. Having security and censorship in mind he hadn't mentioned any of that in the letter to his father, only the miracle at the church.

In Strada Reale again now. Down here on the right . . .

11

Carmella Cassar told him that Abigail had 'taken a hard knock': Mike having reminded her that Abigail had introduced them, at some time or other. In fact she did *seem* to remember the occasion, although he didn't flatter himself that this was anything but her natural *politesse*. She was, as Shrimp had intimated, a fine-looking woman: she'd had her shop – same premises – since well before the war, and Shrimp had known her from that time, in his several pre-war visits to the island.

Yes, she had gold lace in stock, and employed a seamstress who'd fix his things up for him. She could provide epaulettes right away – ones abandoned by lieutenant-commanders on promotion to commander. They'd cost him very little, in fact next to nothing; she'd have to look them out, they weren't of recent origin. Congratulations were presumably in order?

Abigail . . . Well, poor darling. But she was back at work now. Colonel Ede had given her a couple of weeks off, and she'd spent that time not in her little flat on South Street but at the Wingrave-Tenches' at St Julian's. Which had been perfect for her, of course. She'd come back to work yesterday, but for the time being was still at the Tench place. She'd dropped by at lunch-time yesterday, as it happened.

She'd paused, Mike had been trying to get a word in edgeways, asked her now, 'What kind of "knock"?'

'Oh. Forgive me. I had assumed you would have heard. But let *her* tell you, Commander.'

'Commander. Didn't stay long as a two and a half, did I?'

'Hah! I dare say you won't. Any case I'm sure Abigail would very much like to see you – and to hear your good news. Do you know where it is, that building?'

'I think so. But if she's only just back at work, poor kid –'

'Don't worry. A person likes to be visited by her friends, especially at such times. Give her a surprise, why don't you?'

Actually he didn't know Abigail all that well. Had met her a couple of times at Pembroke House, the Wingrave-Tench place, and once at the Union Club at a lunch given by her friend Nico Cornish. There'd been an air-raid alarm between the soup and the fish, they'd trooped through the kitchens into the cellar, the raid had gone on for hours and so had the party, and they'd never had the fish. Either it had gone off or someone must have eaten it. Mike had liked Abigail and Cornish too, also a character by the name of Andrew Cohen who was – or had been – oh, impressive title, Deputy Civil Administrator or – no, Assistant to the Lieutenant-Governor; and others including a stunningly beautiful girl, Diana something or other, tall and blonde, whom he'd also met at Pembroke House.

Where on one occasion he'd played chess with Abigail – and lost several times, he remembered. She was about five-four or -five, had rather wild brown hair and blue eyes; she swam and sunbathed quite a lot, by this time of year was deeply tanned, could at first sight have been taken for Maltese – Italian, even, one of the languages incidentally in

191

which she was completely fluent – only wasn't, her family home was somewhere in the Home Counties and she'd worked in the War Office in London before they'd sent her out as a special assistant to the Defence Security Officer, Malta – Lieutenant-Colonel Bertram Ede of the 4th Hussars, the one who must have given her her sick-leave, following the 'hard knock'. For the moment, that was about all one knew about her. Oh, except she was in her mid-twenties, a cipher wizard and a linguist.

This was the building. Hadn't been sure until he was inside it. He told a Maltese corporal sporting thick-lensed metal-framed spectacles, 'Lieutenant Nicholson to see Miss French, please.'

'Miss French expecting you, sir?'

'No. But tell her *Mike* Nicholson, would you?'

'If you would take a seat, sir.'

He did. He'd done a fair amount of walking on Valetta's hard stone pavementless streets, in the course of the forenoon. Must get some exercise, he thought, in the next week or two or however long it's going to be. Thinking also about this Special Operation and especially the reminder that there'd been one in progress during 'Pedestal', that while he'd been disporting himself off Palermo Pat Norman had been landing a team at Catania, halfway up Sicily's east coast. All one knew about it was that the commandos had apparently not made it to the airfield, let alone to their later rendezvous with *Una*, must all have been either killed or gone into the bag. Gloomy enough outlook, therefore.

Although Shrimp might be right in his assumption that the Wops wouldn't be expecting another attempt so soon after that failure; and it was certainly arguable that hitting three airfields at once, if it could be done efficiently – from the military point of view he supposed on the basis of 'lessons learnt' – should have a better chance of achieving its objective or at least *some* of it than just one team of six or eight canoeists against a whole damn Fliegerkorps, or whatever their air-bases' defences might consist of. Couldn't be more than six or eight commandos, plus their folboats, in the confines of a U-class submarine. Maybe numbers didn't count all that much, in the commando science of shock attack, but confusion did: and if they hadn't known there was a convoy on its way – or touch wood didn't get to know of it this *next* time, therefore mightn't be exactly on their toes . . . First step in one's researches, he thought, might be to get all available details of that Catania action, plans, operational orders and of course Pat Norman's patrol report. The commandos, as Shrimp had observed, would have their own intentions cut and dried for implementation after hitting the beach or beaches, and one's aim would be to combine all that with suggestions for less obvious landing-places, withdrawal routes and R/Vs for re-embarkation. Inshore depths – within a few thousand yards of the coast, say – might for instance be only a few fathoms in the southern part of Catania Bay – south of Catania itself – but further north, nearer San Croce, for instance –

'Mike Nicholson. *What* a nice surprise!'

He was on his feet, with her hands in his. She was *very* attractively shaped: and with her tan and the contrastingly light-blue eyes – at this moment actually *dancing* eyes, and slightly trembly lips – '*Lovely* surprise, Mike!'

'Carmella Cassar said you wouldn't mind, and I happened to be in the neighbourhood, so –'

'She was dead right. Mike, someone mentioned you the other day and I said "Oh, he spends all his time at sea." Haven't seen you for *ages*! Of course I know you were all away for ages, but since then quite a few of the others –'

'Got in yesterday. Had thought with any luck I might run into you at the Tenches'. But Carmella tells me you've been in some kind of trouble?'

She'd nodded. 'Perfectly all right now, though. Everyone's been extremely kind, and I've been – well, rather gave in to it, I'm afraid. Mike, if you've say half an hour to spare –'

'Exactly what I do have!'

'– might take a stroll, or –'

'I'd really love that, Abbie.'

'Fact is, I have to go out to Hamrun in about half an hour. Transport's laid on – van actually . . . What about the Barracca meanwhile, sit in the sun for a while? Then you might even come with me to Hamrun – just for the ride? You know – or perhaps you don't – government offices all moved out there – well, before you lot cleared out, anyway, and we've only just moved back in. Hope to God we can stay put now. I'm going out there to look round and make sure nothing's been left in drawers or cupboards that might be of interest to – well, *anyone* . . . But, Mike – ' they were outside, now, she taking the lead, making for a shortcut over the cobbles into Zachary Street – 'you saw Carmella this morning, you say?'

'As a customer, so happens.'

'Let me guess. Lace for the old folk back home, someone's birthday?'

'*Bad* guess. Might not be a bad idea some time, though.'

'She's a sweet woman, isn't she?'

'You introduced me to her. Come to think of it, *you* were buying lace, on that occasion.'

'Isn't much else, is there.' Flipping a hand towards a tall, bomb-scarred building they were passing. 'Information Office. Nico's left us, did you hear?'

'Haven't had time to hear much, yet. But by "left us" –'

'Transferred to Gibraltar, bigger and better job, although he'd have preferred to stay put. He was doing a terrific job, you know. But there you are . . . Mike, did I ever mention my brother to you?'

194

'Brother.' Taking her arm, looking down at her. *This* might be the start of the 'hard knock' story. Shaking his head: 'I don't think so . . .' It had occurred to him that Cornish's departure might have had something to do with her problem. Bit of a coincidence maybe if it *hadn't* – seeing that Cornish had been generally thought to be her lover. On the other hand her boss surely wouldn't have given her sick-leave for that – broken heart, whatever. Not unless the Colonel was a remarkably soft touch as well as more than normally liberal-minded. She was saying, 'Bob – my brother – was RNVR, a lieutenant, in destroyers.'

Was RNVR, he'd caught, guessed from the past tense at what was likely to be coming, and slid an arm round her shoulders. They'd arrived at the Barracca; she turned inside that arm, leant against him. '*Big* brother – twenty-six, two years older than me. Very much like you, in a lot of ways – younger, of course, you're about thirty, aren't you?'

'Twenty-eight.'

'Oh.' Surprised look. 'Anyway you'd have liked each other. I'd thought that when or if he was here I'd introduce you, if you were around. Saying "when or if" because I'd no idea how long he might have been here or in what circumstances, he'd said in this letter "Might come calling one of these days. If I do, what would you like – brandy, champagne, silk stockings?" And I'd answered saying "All three, you stingy bugger, but best of all bring yourself." This was – I don't know, three or four weeks ago, and I was thinking that if he did turn up I'd give a party for him, and who I might have, including you, and at the Gravies' one evening I asked one of your submariner friends where you were then or were likely to be in the near future, and he said he thought you'd be back soon but probably not for long. Bob hadn't given me any date – couldn't have, couldn't even have *known* his ship'd be coming in, only that it was a possibility, which in fact was saying more than he should have, wasn't it? Enough to thrill me in any case – we've always been as close as twins, hadn't seen each other literally for years – for the past year or more he's been in HMS *Robust* –'

'*Robust*. Oh, crikey, the *Ohio*.'

'I saw that part of it happening.' Turning in Mike's arms, pointing with her head. 'I didn't notice that one of them was a peculiar shape. What I've since discovered is that what they call the Director Tower had been smashed, most of it just – you know, *gone*. And *then* I didn't know it was the *Robust*. The other one was the *Penn*. Then when the broadcast got going, you know, the thing Nico used to organise, the new man does it now and not half so well – telling the people here and in the streets what was going on – Spitfires over us too, tremendous noise, you could only hear a few words now and then but I was – well, crazy with excitement. I raced back to the office, tried to get through to Nico's deputy and couldn't, so – cutting this part short, my own boss got on to it for me, had a signal made to the *Robust* asking for Lieutenant French to communicate with his sister at – you know, DSO number on the Fortress exchange, so forth – and after about two hours I got a message to go to Lascaris right away and ask for Lieutenant-Commander Jobling, the *Robust*'s captain. Which I did, and *he* told me – Bob had been killed the day before, at about the height of the convoy battle. He was Gunnery Control Officer, you see, and –'

'The Director Tower.'

One could imagine it, *see* it. Tower gone, chances were the GCO would have gone with it.

'I had some sort of heart attack, apparently. Quite a long period I don't remember at all. Some of that was in hospital. I know I was desperate to go on board and see where – *be* where he – well, senseless maybe, but –'

'Abbie, I'm so sorry . . .'

What was there that one could *usefully* say? Like Guy Mottram writing to Jimmy Ruck's wife – what was the good of saying *any* bloody thing? Still holding Abigail, getting odd glances from passers-by, and as it were letting go, more or less talking for the sake of talking, telling her, 'Abbie, there's damn-all one can say that'd really help. I could say oh, I'm so sad for you, so sorry, but that's nothing, is it – I *am* more sorry than I can say – but so what? Yesterday – listen, similar situation, about writing to the wife of a CO – one of ours, boat overdue from patrol, presumed mined. A man everyone liked, plus his officers and crew, thirty-two of them – well, OK, maybe she'll be glad to have a letter or letters from us –'

'Of course she will. Of *course*, Mike!'

'You'll have written to your parents, obviously.'

'Yes, and telegraphed.'

'They'll be thanking God they still have *you*. Have you thought of asking for compassionate leave?'

'I've written asking them if they'd like me to. Colonel Ede suggested it.'

'What d'you think they'll say?'

'Probably –' she'd moved slightly and he'd released her – '*probably* "come home if you feel you need to, but otherwise not just for *us*". Something of that kind. As much as anything, thinking of Bob, what *he*'d have – you know, expected of us. I'm not being wet over this, Mike, anyway trying not to be, I know there's a bloody war on and – these things happen, no one's immune. *Inviolate*, I should have said. I keeled over I suppose not just from – well, the hideous fact of it, but – the circumstances, one minute madly excited and one's mind full of him, then – *there*, right under one's eyes, sort of –'

'But now you've done your crying.'

Looking at him surprisedly for a few seconds before nodding, accepting it. 'Yes. I have. You're right. Do you have brothers or sisters, Mike?'

'One of each, both younger than me.'

'Doing what?'

'Alan drives a bomber, mostly over Germany, and Chloe's in London training as an orthopaedic nurse.'

'Parents?'

'Father. Retired quack now back in harness.'

'Good for him. One more nosy question?'

'If you like.'

'Well – how about girls?'

'Heavens, this *is* wide-ranging.' He shrugged, smiling. Rather pleased with himself, and surprised at having said something that actually *had* helped, that comment 'Now you've done your crying'. Answering her question about girls with 'A few, here and there. And you – lovers galore, no doubt?'

'At the last count – not even one.'

'That's astonishing.' He'd wondered about Nico, but couldn't have asked, and now she'd answered, more or less. Her business, anyway – certainly none of his. *Absolutely* none of his. There'd been a general assumption that they were lovers, but that was *all* it was; they were together a lot, in fact never seeing her out with anyone else one had treated them as if that was the situation – might well have tried one's own luck otherwise, having always been *attracted* . . . He stooped, kissed her cheek. 'Might play some chess, some time?'

'Oh, let's!'

'Man's a glutton for punishment, you're thinking.'

Laughing: 'Thinking nothing of the sort, Mike!'

'One other thing you might as well know while we're at it. Change of subject, blowing my own trumpet – sorry . . . What I was seeing Carmella Cassar about this morning was gold lace.' He touched one epaulette. 'This stuff. Shrimp surprised me yesterday with the news that I'm now a lieutenant-commander. How d'you like *that*?'

'Well, I'm – oh, I love it! But – you say he surprised you – you weren't expecting promotion –'

'Out of the blue, and completely undeserved. But listen –'

'Am I the first to know?'

'Well, as it happens. Except for Carmella, who's now calling me "Commander" –'

'I'm thrilled for you, Mike!'

'Thanks. But listen . . .'

He told her he wouldn't go out to Hamrun with her, much as he'd like to; he had things to see to at Lazaretto, had only come ashore to meet Shrimp at the Joint Services HQ and would have gone straight back, but having dropped in at Carmella's –

'Awfully glad you did. You've done me good, Mike. I do *hope* –'

'Me too. Chess at the Gravies', to kick off with. I'll let them know I'm hoping to be asked.'

'Easier still, I'll tell them. When, d'you think?'

'Roughly speaking, whenever I'm asked.'

She smiled. 'Good.'

'Possibly tonight. Not tomorrow, anyway, Shrimp's going to announce this promotion, "wet the half-stripe" as the expression goes.'

'Hangover on Thursday, then. So glad for you, Mike. I don't mean the hangover. Why wait until tomorrow, though?'

'Well, I mentioned just now that we lost one of the flotilla very recently. News only came in at the weekend, it was the first thing I heard when we tied up yesterday. Casts a pall, as you can imagine, and – well, a matter of giving it a couple of days to wear off a bit. A very *little* bit – the first shock, you might call it.' He checked the time. 'Where does your vehicle start from?'

'Front of the building.' Glancing at *her* watch. 'God, I must run. Which boat was it, Mike?'

He shook his head. 'Not now. Run, or you'll miss it. Go on – *run!*'

Jimmy Ruck having been a friend of hers. She'd hear of it soon enough, a quick call to some other mutual friend would provide the answer. He didn't much want to be around when she got it, was all. *Ergo*, better not visit Pembroke House this evening, whether or not invited. He thought, making tracks for Marsamxett and Lazaretto, Thursday at the earliest. Programme now (a) check whether there'd been a mail, (b) down to the boat, see Jamie McLeod – or might discuss his departmental agenda over a sandwich in the mess – but check with Chief McIver, and if there were any problems with the flotilla engineer Sam MacGregor, that everything on *Ursa*'s defect-list would be dealt with before the end of the week, and (c) see Bennett or Warne about torpedoes, arrange to land the one Mark IV he'd brought back from Palermo and embark a full set of eight Mark VIIIs, thus be on the top line and not fobbed off later with Mark IVs if there'd been a run on Msida's stocks between now and then – as could easily be envisaged, with a dozen boats in the flotilla now. Could be more than a dozen, he suspected, running names through his memory as he trotted down Ferry Steps: Guy Mottram's *Unbowed*, Gerahty's *Swordsman*, the injured Brodie's *Unslaked*; *Usurper* and *Urbane* back from patrol in say ten days, and surely by that time *Unbroken*, *Unbending*, *Unrivalled*, *Utmost*, *Uproar*, *Una*. Could be others – oh, *Unsung*, for one, nearly forgot bloody Melhuish –

Might have been a mail?

12

Unsung was due in on Thursday evening, the SOO told him on Wednesday. Melhuish had smashed up a train and sunk an armed trawler in a later gun action in the course of which *Unsung* had sustained what he'd called minor damage; not having as yet found use for any of his torpedoes he'd intended remaining on billet, but Shrimp had recalled him and warned Sam MacGregor to have welders standing by to work over the weekend if necessary. That was the kind of damage one might expect – shell damage to bridge and/or casing, which provided good reason for recalling him, flapping or vibrating steel tending to make a submarine noisy when dived, acutely vulnerable to enemy hydrophones. Shrimp had commented in the wardroom that Wednesday when they were celebrating Mike's promotion, 'But he's certainly using that three-inch to good effect.'

According to Intelligence-based estimates, wrecking a train and/or blowing up railway lines, ideally inside tunnels where Wop engineers couldn't get at them all that easily, deprived the Afrika Korps of about 14,000 tons of supplies for every twenty-four hours the line was out of action, and the new three-inch guns with proper sights on them made it comparatively easy, given the right sort of location and conditions.

'Pity we can't all have proper guns.' Jack Brodie, still leaning on a stick but with expectations of resuming command of *Unslaked* on her return from patrol in a few days' time. 'Bloody twelve-pounders, hardly frighten a seagull. Here's to the half-stripe, Mike. You're supping at Pembroke House tomorrow, I hear.'

'I don't know. *Was*, but with Melhuish due in –'

'Oh, come on! You gave him a bloody cruiser, surely that's –'

'Gave him damn-all. Happened to see quite a bit of him and his wife in London at one time though, missed him the last time he was in, doesn't seem to be anyone else knows him from a bar of soap – don't want to seem stand-offish, that's all.'

'Rather seem stand-offish to Miss French?'

He got a laugh, which encouraged him to add, 'Bit short-sighted, I'd say, specially as that Nico character's vanished into the wide blue yonder.'

'Cornish has been transferred to Gib. And she must miss him. They had a lot in common – both noticeably intelligent, similar interests generally. What's your concern with any of this anyway? I'd lay off the innuendo, Jack, if I were you.'

He didn't much like Brodie, and he *had* been thinking quite a lot about Abigail, and more or less convinced himself that that was probably as much as there'd been between her and Nico. But again, that if he was wrong, what the hell? He certainly found her extremely attractive, had enjoyed her company whenever he'd chanced to have it – the chess evening for instance, and once an afternoon's swimming at St Julian's. The Pembroke House Lido, they all called it, a gap in the barbed-wire coastal barrier through which one could get out on to the rocks. All right, at that time he'd seen her and Nico as lovers – everyone had – and if she was now finding herself at a bit of a loose end and making a play for *him* – what was wrong with that?

In two words, damn-all. Actually, rather exciting. In fact not rather, *very*. Not to be thought of as anything more than a temporary or part-time diversion, probably – this week, and some of next – touch wood . . .

'Brown study, Mike?'

Guy Mottram, with a gin in each hand and the affable, Robert Morley-type smile, his eyes going to the second-hand epaulettes Mike was wearing for the first time this evening, in his Red Sea rig. Carmella was charging practically nothing for them and nothing at all for a second pair that were rather more battered and less shiny; actually he preferred them to these. Mottram handed him one of the gins and told him, 'The shoulder-boards are most becoming, old horse. Well done. Seeing you tomorrow at the Gravies', I gather?'

'You'll be there, will you?'

'Most of us old hands will, I imagine. In your honour, of course. Greta's been ringing round. Anyway, here's to it.'

'Cheers.' Blinking – there wasn't much water in this one. 'Beats me how the Gravies got to know about it. Shrimp only announcing it here, tonight.'

'They're his great buddies, aren't they?'

'Doubt he'd have said anything. He told me about it on Monday, it was his idea to give it a day or two – you know, for – oh, did you write to Jimmy's wife yet?'

'Yes. On the lines you suggested. Better than *not* writing, I admit.'

'A lot better.' He'd taken another swallow of his gin, realised as it burnt its way down that Abigail of course was the leak.

★ ★ ★

203

Mike told Jamie McLeod on board *Ursa* next morning, 'I've a splitting headache, and I'm seeing double. So much for bloody celebrations.' He looked at the man who'd stopped in the gangway opposite the wardroom. 'Want me, Hart?' PO Tubby Hart, Second Coxswain, blinking at him: 'Wanted to say congratulations, sir. If that's in order.' Mike shook the large proffered hand: 'Entirely in order. Thank you, I appreciate it.' He'd been congratulated at least a dozen times since coming on board; and as half the ship's company were at the Mellieha rest-camp, there had to be about twenty still to come. Actually he did appreciate it, liked them for it. Liked them, anyway. He asked McLeod, 'Changeover at Mellieha's on Sunday – right?'

'Transport from Mellieha ten a.m., sir, brings the starboard watch and takes this lot.'

'Good. Jamie, I'm on my way to see Shrimp at Lascaris about various things, and one of them is very much your business. Come up top a minute.'

Up through the tower into the bridge. *Ursa* lying between buoys fifty yards off the Lazaretto shoreline, with the last of the engineers' work going on in her after ends, where the HP air compressor lay around in pieces on the steel deck. Commander Sam MacGregor's newly tunnelled-out workshop was in full swing although not yet completed, could cope with machinery defects which before and during the blitz could only have been handled in the dockyard – where there'd been no defences at all, beyond machine-guns in boats' bridges and on the jetties.

Blue sky cloudless at the moment, ruffled blueish water with the sprawl of the old quarantine building reflected palely in its surface; bonfire smoke drifting away from the direction of the farm, overalled sailors moving on the brows that linked submarines to shore. To those with eyes for it, rather a lovely panorama, he thought. He and McLeod both lit cigarettes, but in his own case the first drag on it was enough; he stubbed it out in the pig's ear, a funnel-shaped receptacle into which bridge watchkeepers could pee when at sea and on the surface; a pipe led down to the waterline and was flushed out when you dived her.

McLeod had said, breathing smoke, 'Matter of fact, sir, I can guess what this is about.'

'*Can* you, now. Something that's overdue?'

'Well – arguably. I haven't bothered you with it because frankly I've been – still am – in two minds. Whether to stay with you and *Ursa*, or –'

'Get sent home for your Perisher.'

McLeod had nodded. 'I've thought once or twice, *maybe* –'

'No "*maybe*" about it. I'm not justified in holding you back, Jamie. You're as suitable for command as anyone could be, it's definitely overdue. I may say I had a word with Shrimp about it, a few weeks ago, had to admit I'd very much prefer *not* to lose you –'

'Rather my own way of thinking, as it happens.'

'Good. But talent shouldn't be wasted, a lot of new boats are coming off the stocks and Admiral Submarines is desperate for COs. If he knew I'd been dragging my feet he'd be highly displeased. Anyway, when it came up with Shrimp I suggested that if we were going home reasonably soon that might be the best way to get you there, and he more or less agreed. But since then nothing's been said about us packing up – although we must be in line for it. Anyway I'm going to propose you should be flown home – depending on when the next Perisher's starting, *and* finding a replacement. Which'll be *my* bugbear, of course. Go along with that, would you?'

'Yes. And thank you, sir. I'm sorry –'

'Don't be. It's the right thing to do.' He moved to the hatch. 'Getting our Mark VIIIs tomorrow forenoon, right?'

★   ★   ★

205

Shrimp had been tied up in a meeting with Vice-Admiral Malta, had kept Mike waiting nearly an hour. Bursting in at last, throwing his cap at a wall-hook and missing.

'Blast. And that was *almost* a total waste of time. You look a bit pasty, Michael, serve you right.'

'Have to admit it does, sir.'

'I'll admit it too, then.' Thumping down behind his desk, Mike less vigorously on this side of it. 'Done your home-work?'

'In a rudimentary fashion, sir. Not having the maps they promised, for one thing.'

'What do we have to show them?'

'Only this, sir.' A single sheet of paper: left-hand column headed URSA and UNSUNG, and opposite that, SWORDSMAN. He put it in front of Shrimp. 'Just off the cuff, sir, allocating the Gela and Comiso teams to myself and Melhuish, Catania to *Swordsman* – largely because we'd have sixty miles to our targets and Gerahty'd have a hundred and twenty, and as he has twelve and a half knots –'

'All right.'

'Simple fact being that there's no way we could land them in one place and pick them up in another. I was talking nonsense the other day.'

'Got to come back either to or through wherever they've left their folboats, haven't they. I agree, a fairly simple point. What else are we telling them?'

Mike reached to the chart. 'What I'm suggesting there, sir – *Swordsman* to Catania, sailing a day after the two of us – because (a) she has the extra knots, and (b) her team could be put ashore before midnight on D-day, nearer Acireale than Catania. Depth of water allows this, giving them only three thousand yards to paddle; then subject to the lie of the land – need a map to check this by – they'd circle inland of the airfield, attack from inland, and get back to their folboats by the reverse of the same route. ETA Lazaretto about dawn D plus one.'

'So what's different from *Una*'s effort is the landing-point up-coast and the attack from inland.'

'If the terrain allows it, yes sir. And if they'll wear it − I mean, in the light of their own military principles. Need to leg it a bit, of course.'

'We can try it on them anyway. What about the others?'

He leant to the chart, used a pencil as a pointer. 'Cape Scalambri − Gela, and Comiso. No matter what, the Comiso team has a dozen miles to cover from whatever beach we land them on. And as we can't launch them until dark, and they then have to paddle about a mile and hide the folboats, if the assaults are to take place twelve miles away at 0200 it's less a matter of legging it than split-arsing it. That's irrespective of terrain, obstacles, guard-posts or whatever. Whether they'd take that on − well, their business, and they must have maps and/or special knowledge of the area. Maybe I'm wrong, but Comiso − well, the only way I can see of managing it is to land them the night before − giving them the rest of that night to find a hide to lie-up in.'

'And Gela?'

Shrimp was glancing over the page of notes, while Mike explained them. Cutting in with 'Sending that bunch across-country too?'

'It might make more sense than having them land bang on target, sir, where defences might be on their toes and − anyway, unpredictable as far as *we* know. I'm suggesting we put them down *here* − ten miles west of Cape Scalambri, while the Comiso team's landing ten miles east of it. Giving them − Gelas − about the same distance to their airfield − route up to them to work out.'

'Soundings aren't so convenient for you − or them − at either of those points.'

207

'I know, sir. Have to paddle a fair distance. But closer to Gela'd be worse – in fact much worse. And only fifteen miles the other side of Gela is Licata with its Mas-boats.'

'All right. And after the airfield actions both teams get back to their hides, lie-up until dark and then have – what, four hours for withdrawal?'

'About that, sir. More like five if you include a four- or five-mile paddle and R/V at say 0300.'

Shrimp was checking Mike's figures against distances on the charted coastline, measuring them with dividers. Mike guiding him, with 'R/V positions are noted there, sir. Bearings and distances on Cape Scalambri – the lighthouse – for both of them. Obviously won't be lit, but it's prominent enough. Then for the Comiso team, this headland; Gela force, just a bearing on Scalambri and distance offshore. From mid-week on they'll have a moon – so given a reasonably clear sky – well, may suit them or may not, but –'

'Most likely *not*. But alternative rendezvous twenty-four hours later, same positions?'

'Yes – I suppose –'

'Gives them a second chance which they might well need. Overall, Michael, this is a very tricky operation – primarily for the pongos. I'd imagine that pretty soon after they launch their attacks the whole district'll be swarming with patrols. Even if the attacks coming from inshore confuses the buggers initially. And from our angle we can reasonably expect Mas-boats and E-boats out of Licata for instance, or even Gela. That's on the night of the assaults and the following day, by the second night A/S forces from – wherever . . . Tell me – these pick-ups, the Gela and Comiso teams – if either or both failed to show up, you wouldn't be tempted to close the beach on the surface and hunt around for them?'

'Might well be *tempted*, and they might expect it, but –'

'It'll be covered in your orders – minimal distance offshore to be maintained no matter what circumstances. And I'll make clear to the Chief Pongo – who'll be joining us on Saturday, by the way –'

'*Ah . . .*'

'– flying in from Cairo. I'll make clear to him that in our view and our C-in-C's a submarine and her crew is a lot more valuable than half a dozen soldiers, and that if they don't turn up on time at the R/V your orders preclude any search inshore where it may be impossible to dive. This one does look quite unusually hazardous to me, Michael. I'd say your proposals go some way to make the object of the exercise achievable – *just*, as long as the pongos are bloody good at their jobs *and* very lucky . . . All right, the shoreside stuff's not strictly our business, we're advancing these ideas only for discussion, set out what we can and can't do, see how that fits in with whatever plans they have. Otherwise we rethink, collectively.' Consulting paperwork of his own . . . 'Chief Pongo's a major by name of Ormrod and his 2 i/c who'll be with him is a Captain Haigh. Other parties are scheduled to arrive during the week – twenty-four commandos in all, including Ormrod and Haigh, three teams of eight.'

'Eight . . .'

It meant four folboats, and nowadays they didn't dismantle them. You could get two into a reload torpedo rack, with other gear such as weaponry and explosives stowed inside them. So he'd need to leave two fish behind. Might have thought of this: but no problem, just two fewer for the port watch of torpedomen to load tomorrow – to the satisfaction of Wiggy Bennett and Sunny Warne, no doubt.

Shrimp was saying, 'We'll be accommodating Ormrod and Haigh in Lazaretto, by the way, and the rest – oh, there's another officer, hang on . . .' Flipping through pink signal forms in a spring-back file: 'Here we are – Captain Flood. One officer to each team, presumably. Flood will be arriving a day or two after Ormrod and Haigh, with a staff sergeant, four troopers and weaponry, and finally a Royal Marine colour sergeant with the rest of them plus folboats. That lot in a Sunderland, I'd guess.' He shut the file. 'Three officers in Lazaretto, all the others in Ghain Tuffieha rest-camp, which they'll have to themselves. That's a point I won this morning; another is they'll have RAF transport laid on for them.'

'Does this mean we can put a date on it, sir? On the convoy operation, even?'

'No. And we aren't talking about convoys, Michael. Not even between ourselves. We just had a convoy in, at huge cost, might be a long time before we can mount another. Forget convoys. But – where were we . . .' Checking his own notes again, then shutting the file. 'Anyway, you might join me in playing host to these chaps on Saturday – show 'em round, give 'em a drink or two, set up a planning conference for Monday. There'll be no sea exercises, by the way, they've done enough of that with the 1st Flotilla, apparently, and we want as near total security as we can get. I'll convey the gist of all this to your pal Melhuish when he gets in tonight, but I'll only tell him about his own part in it, not yours or Gerahty's. You'll be at the Gravies', will you?'

'Yes, sir. If I might mention it – just a personal thing – Melhuish isn't a particular friend of mine. I only happened to know him and his wife socially – some time ago, as it happens.'

'I see. Had the impression you were old chums. Not that it makes a shred of difference.' Shrimp was lighting a cigarette, Mike having declined the wordless offer of one. 'So what else? Anything, while we're at it?'

'There is one thing, sir. My Number One – McLeod – is wondering about *his* Perisher. I don't want to lose him, God knows, but in my view he's overdue for it – and extremely sound. I couldn't recommend him too highly.'

'Well.' Surprised look: expelling smoke. 'I think we discussed this not long ago. As I remember it, we agreed that as *Ursa's* time here would very soon be up, the best thing might be to take him home with you.'

'Dead right, sir. But as he's raised the subject himself now, I feel bound to support him in it, we *aren't* on our way yet –'

'I think you might be.'

'Sir?'

Watching, guessing . . . Shrimp explaining, 'I haven't said anything about it until now, but as you know, Ruck was a patrol or two ahead of you, and he'd have been on his way by now. After all, the flotilla's well up to strength, and much as I'd like to hang on to you, you *have* done your time. Our temporary evacuation – and the frightful losses prior to it – put such planning out of mind. But – there it is, Michael. Taking it head-on, how d'you feel about it?'

It was quite a big issue. Which of course he *had* thought about, had known he'd be faced with before *much* longer. Whether he actually had any option, if he tried to exercise one – or even for that matter *wanted* to . . . Ann was somewhere on the periphery of his *private* thinking – or had been. Maybe still was? *Completely* private and incidental though, nothing to do with the issue at stake that had to be decided on here and now – *Ursa* and her crew, the job they'd done and the run of luck *he'd* had, the satisfaction there'd be in bringing them all home intact, *alive*.

More than just a successful outcome, one might say a small triumph, in its way.

Actually not *say* it – but feel it, *know* it.

'You're saying make this airfield operation our last outing, sir?'

'What it comes down to, yes. Unless you've any – serious reservations?'

'Well. No, sir. I don't think I have.'

'Good. We'll take it as read, then. Talk again, obviously, but I think you're wise. In any case it couldn't have been postponed by more than perhaps one patrol. So – coming back to the more immediate future – I should have mentioned that our landing operation now has the code-name "Backlash". Saves frequent references to airfields?'

'"Backlash". Right . . . Will you hang on to those notes, sir?'

'I'll keep them on file for the Chief Pongo to peruse. Better not call him that, I suppose. He *is*, but in the contingent as a whole there are more Royal Marines than soldiers. I think you've done a good job there, Michael, as far as it goes. Can't say I like it, but I don't see any good alternatives either.' He checked the time, added, 'To be slightly more frank, I think it's a bastard. Let's hope *they*'ve some answers. Anyway . . . On your way back to Lazaretto now, are you? May see you at the Gravies' tonight, may not – depends on *Unsung*. I might bring Melhuish along with me, if he's up to it.'

'One other thing I'd raise, sir.' On his feet, and scooping up his cap. 'You said no exercises, which is fine as far as I and Dan Gerahty are concerned, we've both launched and recovered folboats a few times – but *Unsung* quite likely hasn't?'

'That *is* a point.' Thoughtful, rubbing his blunt jaw. 'Yes, damn it, should have thought of that. Well – we'll give him a dummy run with Taylor and a few of his chaps.' Meaning Captain Taylor of the Liverpool Scottish, OC Shrimp's private army, who occupied barracks adjoining the quarantine building and would no doubt be quietly seething at other commandos being brought in to do a job they'd reckon should be theirs. Once they heard about it. They'd have a point, too, Mike thought. Except if they heard the details of it they might be glad they *weren't* being used. Shrimp was saying, 'The decision to do without exercises was based on the security aspect. Similar to hiding most of them in Ghain Tuffieha. But – yes, good thinking, Michael.'

'And about McLeod, sir – I'll tell him we're homebound after this next one, but in the interim will you recommend him for COQC?'

'Yes. You can tell him I'm doing so.'

'Thank you, sir. May I also let him in on the fact this one's a commando operation, folboats and eight passengers? Some practical considerations, and he'll be wondering in any case – leaving two racks empty, for instance.'

'Yes again. But no mention of the operation as a whole.'

Write Ann, tell her 'See you very soon'?

He hadn't heard from her in what seemed like quite a while. Not really surprising – she wouldn't have had his answer to her last one yet, could well be steeling herself against writing again until she did hear.

Hold on anyway, let Charles tell her?

Write again to the Old Man, though, tell him 'Home soon, touch wood.' If one sailed for this operation in about a week, spent say a week or so at sea and another week back here preparing *Ursa* for the trip home – then five days to Gib and a couple *in* Gib – embarking amongst other things a few cases of Tio Pepe – then twelve or fourteen days across Biscay and through the Channel into the Solent, swinging her into Haslar Creek at the top of the tide, the dead water known as the Ten Minute Stand, sliding into a berth on the concrete quay there with the Jolly Roger flying, doubtless some welcoming cheers drifting in the autumn rain or sleet and bitter wind – and no doubt three or four days there before one could get away. So tell the Old Man 'See you in something like seven weeks, d.v.', and to Ann when or if one *did* write, 'Might be a ring on your bell in approx two shakes . . .'

13

Abigail cheered: 'You made it!'

It was a little after four p.m. Greta had left a message with McLeod to the effect that she and Abigail would be swimming from the Lido rocks until about five and he was welcome to join them if he could get away that early. So after a quick late lunch he got the letter done to his father, telling him that with luck and good management he'd see him in about eight weeks. Putting it further ahead than he hoped it might be, so the Old Man wouldn't lose too much sleep if for some reason it took longer. In making such an estimate even in one's own head one tended to shut out awareness that things could go totally, wildly wrong, that there couldn't possibly be any certainty – rather as this morning Shrimp had described Operation 'Backlash' as a bastard from the commandos' point of view while seeing it as nothing other than straightforward, almost routine, as far as his submarines' end of it was concerned. Commandos might not make it to the rendezvous, in which case one or more boats might come back without any; but the 'coming back' wasn't in doubt – or if it was, you didn't take it into account.

You couldn't. The scoreboard in the wardroom entrance told its tale of *other* men's atrociously bad luck, a glance at it stirring a couple of years of memories – names, faces, assorted recollections including some of one's own successes – but *other* men's memorials, last patrols.

Jimmy Ruck's, for instance. Ruled off now, with a U-boat silhouette darkly pencilled in that last rectangle. And again, Shrimp this morning – this was probably what had given rise to the somewhat gloomy (or realistic) thinking – Shrimp not bothering to mention that at least part of the reason for sending one home after a fair stretch of intensive action was that if you were kept at it too long there was a danger of becoming stale, careless or over-confident.

Or just the law of averages asserting itself. You didn't have to be stale to hit a mine. You might even say it had been Jimmy's *turn* to.

'Actually did *make* it!' Abigail, waving from a flat-topped rock and still wet, not having been out of the water long. Slight but very shapely figure in a flimsy blue costume he'd seen before – pale blue, going strikingly with her eyes and dark, gleamingly wet hair. The white-capped head thirty yards out could only be Greta's; he waved to her and she waved back. He'd changed from shorts and shirt in the Gravies' downstairs cloakroom – having come on foot from Lazaretto with Red Sea rig for the evening parcelled in a towel.

'Isn't this superb?' Panorama of sea and rock, the coastline extending south to Sliema, northwest to Spinola, sky lightly patched with thin white cloud, white buildings or just hints of them along the shoreline. Turning back to her: 'Abbie, you look absolutely fabulous!'

'Not so bad yourself, Commander.'

'Sickly white, in fact. Hideous, beside your lovely tan.'

215

'But that's nice – the contrast.'

'In *your* case, heck of a lot more than *nice* –'

'Although you *should* get into the sun while you can, Mike. How long'll you be with us this time? Or did I ask you that the other day – when I finished gassing on about my own boring problems? Oh, my dear – *frightful* about Jimmy Ruck.'

'Yes. More than frightful. Answering your question, though – I can't be absolutely sure, but – few days, a week?'

'Then away again for what – fortnight, month?'

'Never that long, in this outfit. Ten days is about average.'

Greta was on her way in, performing her fast, almost splashless crawl. Long-limbed, dark-haired, but fair-skinned, with blue eyes very much like Abigail's. He waved to her again, told Abigail, 'I need to cool off. Coming?' Giving her a hand up, he kissed her cheek and she turned her head, brushed his lips. He *had* to go in then.

He asked her during supper how she'd managed to have an afternoon off when she'd only recently returned to work, and her answer had been that she'd put in a long morning and been at her desk yesterday until about eleven p.m.

'Crikey. That's close enough to midnight oil!'

'I make my own hours, mostly, according to what's going on.'

'And something was, yesterday?'

'Wasn't half. We work very much in collusion with your Naval Cipher Office, you know. Or perhaps you didn't. But I'd be at my desk all night seven days a week if necessary. Much better than clocking in from nine to five and sometimes damn-all to do except make coffee . . . At sea you sleep a lot, I'm told.'

'As much as possible.'

'And do you read much?'

'When one's slept enough, and things are quiet, yes.'

'Read what? Novels?'

'Mostly. Books one's been lent.'

'Well, I've the beginnings of a small library in my flat. Come and help yourself if you'd like to – before your next disappearance?'

'Abbie, I'd very *much* like to!'

'I'm not using it – the flat – at the moment. I'd come here, as I mentioned, by the extreme kindness of the Gravies, and some friends who're having their hovel done up asked could they borrow it. I'd have moved back by now but the plumbing in theirs is still only a hole in the rock, apparently, another couple of days, they wanted. Mind you, that was yesterday, so just *possibly* this weekend . . . What are you doing between now and Monday?'

'Tomorrow I'm taking my third and fourth hands on a hike across the island – pursuit of fresh air and exercise, which none of us get enough of.'

'Third and fourth hands being your junior officers.'

'Yes. Sub-lieutenants. Respectively torpedo officer and navigator.'

'And you have a second-in-command by name of McLeod.'

'D'you know him?'

'I know a Wren by name of Eleanor who sees him when she can – when *he's* not on the blooming briny. She's great fun, actually.'

'I've met her. Pretty. And Jamie McLeod's a good man . . . But I was saying – on Saturday there's something – oh, Shrimp wants me to help him entertain some transients – military visitors of some kind.'

'*All* of Saturday?'

'Not sure. I'll find out. Might you be available, if I got off the hook?'

'As of now I would.' She frowned. 'I mean yes, of *course* I would. Think you might swing it?'

217

'I'll try.'

The embarkation of torpedoes had been put off to Saturday forenoon, and Mike with this other obligation to Shrimp had told McLeod he could see to it – drive the boat up to Msida, embark five Mark VIIIs instead of seven, and bring her back. McLeod had looked pleased about it – especially coming on top of Shrimp's recommending him for the first Perisher course after their return to the UK.

Abigail enquired, 'What'll we do, if you can, I mean? Come here and swim?'

'Well – if the Gravies wouldn't mind. But they might like to have the place to themselves for a change. Anyway –'

'Let me know.'

'You bet I will. Oh, Lord . . .'

'Who's that?'

'Captain of HM Submarine *Unsung*. Name of Charles Melhuish. He was coming in from patrol this evening, Shrimp said he might bring him. New boy, this was his first patrol, but I knew him slightly before he took the command course.'

'Is he nice?'

'Oh, we're all *nice*, Abbie . . . Must say hello to him anyway. Want to come along?'

Shrimp was introducing Melhuish to the Gravies: Melhuish beaming, telling them what a nice house they had and how kind they were to let him into it, et cetera. Mike was accosted on his way across the room by Guy Mottram, who'd been playing Liar dice with Gravy and some others including Jack Brodie. Game temporarily suspended, Mottram bellowing at Mike, 'You kidnapping her, or vice versa?'

'Not sure, Guy. Could be a bit of both.'

'See what happens when you promote a man before his time . . .'

'Mike, *hello*!'

Melhuish with his hand out. 'Have to congratulate you, I hear.' A smirk at the epaulettes. 'Congratulations, *sir*.'

'Same to you, Charles – for knocking down my cruiser.'

'Yes, I'm told I owe that to you. If I'd known it was yours, might have let the bloody thing go by.' A laugh, and a look around inviting applause . . . 'Ann sends her love, by the way. Three letters from her, and in all three of them she sent it. Can you beat that?'

'Not easily. But you'd better give her mine. Abbie – Charles Melhuish. Abigail French, Charles.'

'Lovely name, as well!'

She shook his hand. 'You've just arrived back, Mike says. How long before you're off again?'

Greta laughed. '*What* a welcome for the poor man!'

'Fortunately, I'm not all that much concerned about it.' Shake of the narrow head. He still had the slightly supercilious look that Mike remembered. Adding now, 'Well, that's not *entirely* truthful, it's been hinted I might be off again in only a few days, for some reason.'

'So Mike's not the only one they push out again as soon as he shows his face. I used to think it was *his* darned fault, Charles, that he volunteered for it or something.'

'No such thing. But hang on –' he patted her arm – 'Quick word with the man who does the pushing out . . .'

Shrimp, sipping black coffee, offered him a cigarette. 'Enjoying yourself, Michael?'

'Very much, sir. We were swimming and sunning ourselves, earlier. Life of Reilly – thanks to Gravy and Greta, who's –'

'Marvellous, isn't she. Admiral Submarines told me to treat my COs like Derby winners, but these two do it all for me.' A glance at Melhuish, who was still drooling over Abigail. 'He won't steal her from you, will he?'

'You know, sir, I rather doubt it.' He shrugged. 'Not that I can claim ownership exactly. Would *like* to, but –'

219

'Really is a looker, isn't she?'

'Bright, too.'

'Does she know your days here are numbered?'

'Not yet. Well, only just getting acquainted, really. I'll have to tell her, obviously.'

'Right. Cards on the table. One thing, for you, though – I invited you to assist in the reception of Major Ormrod and the other one, day after tomorrow – but it's occurred to me that as a Derby winner you might have better things to do, on what might be your last weekend?'

'Well – since you mention it, sir –'

'I can take care of them, all right. Incidentally, Melhuish has been told he has a Special Op ahead of him, and I've recalled *Swordfish*. ETA Monday p.m. And Monday forenoon, let's say ten-thirty, conference with the pongos, my office in Lascaris. We don't need Melhuish at this one. All right?'

'Aye aye, sir. About Saturday, though –'

'Don't worry, I need to be on the base –' a nod towards Mottram – 'for *Unbowed* sailing – no, that's tomorrow – but three others returning from patrol. Pongos can watch it all if they like, and in the intervals I'll – you know, mug it over with them . . . Here and now, you and I'd better mingle – uh?'

Abigail had moved on, left Melhuish talking to Greta and was herself chatting with Mottram and Brodie. She'd thrown him a questioning glance as if wondering whether he was rejoining her – which he wasn't, the thought having occurred that they might have been making their interest in each other a bit obvious, so he just winked at her instead – Melhuish rejoining him at that moment, telling him, 'I got bashed up by an armed trawler, Mike. Vicinity of Taormina, this was. Quite a nasty few minutes, actually. Mind you, the Wop was in a considerably worse state than I was by that time –'

'What damage to your boat?'

220

'Port hydroplane guard, and the casing port side for'ard of the bridge. The walkway around that side too. Gunshield took some of it. Heck of a noise while it was happening, and made a mess of us, but –'

'Sounds like you were under helm while he was hitting you. Turning away?'

'Well, yes. I'd got into rather close range. Good thing I *did* turn away. He was on fire, I might add, we'd hit his bridge a few times then shifted target to the waterline – he actually was done for, just this one gun still at it, something like a Bofors –'

'Gun actions are better not fought bow-on, Charles. Sooner or later you have to turn away, then you're exposing your beam to him. Whereas if you'd engaged him over your quarter –'

'You have only a twelve-pounder?'

In other words, what do *you* know about gun actions . . . Mike nodded: 'Yes, like all the older boats. Wretched thing, 1914–18 vintage, no proper sights . . . Still use it though, on occasion. Ann keeping well, is she?'

'Well – yes. Lonely, of course. Wouldn't be so bad if she had friends among her Mechanised Transport Corps colleagues, but she doesn't. She's not easy to please, you know.'

'Couldn't she switch to something else? Or stick with MTC but ask for a transfer to Edinburgh – where she'd have lots of friends, not to mention her parents?'

'*Could*, perhaps. Not that proximity to the parents would exactly thrill her. Otherwise – well, now I'm *here*, really no reason not to get out of London. I might suggest it. But listen, Mike – Shrimp has me down for a Special Op, landing commandos somewhere. In just a matter of days, apparently – less than a week anyway. That and apparently not knowing exactly where – seems a bit special, doesn't it?'

'Security around that kind of thing's extremely tight. Has to be. If you were a commando paddling in to an enemy beach and not knowing whether machine-gunners were watching you come, you'd hope they hadn't been tipped-off to expect you – huh?'

'But why *Unsung* – when we've only been back five minutes?'

'Well, you're back, haven't put in all that much sea-time as yet, and he might think it'll be good experience for you. We've all done quite a bit of it, one time and another.'

'He's setting up an exercise for us in launching and recovering folboats. Which as I told him I *have* done more than once – not as a CO, admittedly, but –'

'Things change, don't they. Folboats for instance used to be embarked unassembled – timber frame, and the fabric in a sort of parcel. Now we bring them on board intact and carry them in torpedo reload racks. Then usually now don't actually launch them but float them off the casing with the occupants already *in situ*.'

'Well. Given reasonably calm weather.'

'That you do need. Charles – quite a few characters here you haven't met. Guy Mottram there for instance – *Unbowed*, sails for patrol tomorrow. Come and meet him – very old chum of mine.'

'Looks a bit like Robert Morley.'

'Doesn't he, just . . .'

Abigail asked him, 'What was the wink for?'

He demonstrated it again – smooth lowering of an eyelid without any contortion of facial muscles. She tried to do it herself, and couldn't; asked him whether he could do it with the other eye as well.

He tried, and couldn't. 'Funny – never realised.'

'What was it all about, anyway?'

'Good news, is what. Saturday, I'm off the hook.'

'Well, hurrah! What'll we do?'

'Can I ring you in the morning at your office – early?'

'If you like, but –'

'By then I'll have had a brainwave. Even now I can feel it coming on. My God, but you're a wow . . .'

In the morning – Friday now – before breakfast he went to the Manoel Island farm, found the Maltese foreman in Pop Giddings' farm office and asked him whether Vera would be available next day. 'All day – with the trap, of course.'

'I will check, Signo.'

Vera was a donkey, who throughout even the worst of the siege had somehow managed to avoid being eaten. The foreman checked in Pop's diary and told Mike that she had no engagements, wouldn't be wanted for farm work, and as far as he knew wouldn't be working today either. 'So – your name, sir? Lieutenant-Commander –?'

'Nicholson. I'll come for her about nine-thirty – harness her myself. I'll have a look at her, while I'm here.'

She seemed to be on form – tried to bite him when he was examining her hooves – which of course benefited from the rocky terrain, but a farrier had been at them quite recently in any case.

Back in the mess, before going in to breakfast he put a call through to Abigail, and she came on the line at once.

'Abbie – Mike here.'

'Heavens, I only got in this minute!'

'Tomorrow ten a.m. at Pembroke House?'

'All right – I mean yes, lovely. Dressed for what?'

'Country-going – might swim – I'll bring a picnic of sorts?'

'You're on . . .'

Melhuish, who sat down next to him at breakfast, informed him that he was taking *Unsung* up to the Msida torpedo

223

depot to offload two Mark VIIIs. Not having fired any on his recent patrol he'd brought back a full outfit and had to get rid of two reloads to make room for folboats. 'For this exercise and the ensuing operation. Not necessarily the same folboats, for some reason, but four of them for the op – and two commandos per boat – *eight* passengers, therefore – is that normal?'

'There's very little you'd call *normal* on any of those larks.'

'But eight passengers is a bit over the odds in a U-class, isn't it?'

'When we were pulling out, blitz-time at the end of April, some boats took as many as twenty passengers. Engineers, ERAs and so forth, with all their gear. Pass the sugar, will you?'

'I must say, that girl you were monopolising last night's quite a dish. Abigail – right? *What* is it she does?'

'Civilian, works for the Defence Security Officer – offshoot of the War Office. Cipher specialist and linguist. You say I was "monopolising" her, but she happens to be a very good friend of mine. End of gossip, OK?'

'Well, God's sake – hardly *gossip* –'

'One tends not to chatter much at breakfast, Charles – especially about girls.'

'Well. Apologies. If that's what I was doing. Only not having seen each other for rather a long time – and I'll be writing to Ann today –'

'Give her my love.' Gulping coffee. 'Love to her and regards to Sunny.'

'Sunny . . .'

'Sunny Warne. Commissioned Gunner (T). Presiding genius at Msida.'

'But the Flotilla Torpedo Officer –'

'Wiggy Bennett. Lieutenant. Sunny runs the depot. First-class bloke, old chum of Shrimp's. They were shipmates in

L.7 when she got herself stuck on the putty in the South China Sea, back in – oh, mid-twenties, would have been. Christ, now *I'm* chattering.'

Jarvis and Danvers seemed to be in good heart and at least as fit as he was himself. They met on board *Ursa*, crossed the creek by *dghaisa*, passed through Valetta and Floriana, thence by way of Pieta to Msida and Birkirkara, then Lia – on the edge of Ta' Qali airfield, from which a flight of Spitfires was climbing into the northern sky – and on to Mosta, where they paused for a look at the church which the famous bomb had penetrated without exploding. Being Friday, there was a Mass in progress. This wasn't the first sight Mike had had of the place, *was* the first time he'd done anything of this kind with his officers; he'd decided that it was something he ought to do, and they'd reacted well to the suggestion.

They'd been enjoying their shore-time apparently, socialising mainly with Wrens who had flats in Sliema and elsewhere. There were effectively no pubs on the island now, the only drink available anywhere being 'Red Biddy', a concoction that looked like red wine and tasted like paint thinner laced with rum – the rum undoubtedly stolen from naval stores, there was no other way it could have been acquired – and in one bar in Valetta an orange-tasting fizzy mixture allegedly gin-based. But the Chocolate King in Sliema was still open for business, and the Union Club still held dances; one way and another they'd managed to fill their off-duty hours. Danvers interrupting Jarvis's account of Danvers' pursuit of a fat Maltese girl by name of Sara who was allegedly engaged to a policeman, to ask how far was St Paul's Bay from here; the answer was about three miles – 'here' being a few thousand acres of scrub and rock a little northwest of Mosta, a barren-looking landscape where shoats – half-sheep, half-goat – were the only visible inhabitants. Scrawny, scabby-looking animals

225

that gnawed each other's tails. St Paul's Bay was the destination though, and by the time they reached it they'd have covered twelve or fifteen miles of the marathon he'd planned. His intention was to turn east along the bay's southern shore and stop for lunch – corned-beef sandwiches – when the widening distance to the other shore was about half a mile, have lunch before swimming it, then take a southwesterly route passing a mile or two south of the Mallieha rest-camp to Ghain Tuffieha on the west coast, the camp where next week the Ismailia commandos were to be installed. Then south to Mdina and Rabat, Ta'Qali again, and back via Floriana and Valetta – by which time they'd have covered twenty-five or thirty miles.

Mike was feeling good about Abigail – looking forward to tomorrow and his day with her, glad he'd thought of Vera and the trap. Not feeling exactly *bad* at having been promoted, either, or at the prospect of shortly taking *Ursa* home. Reminding himself to make sure Melhuish knew of this, so he'd tell Ann.

Fish pie for supper. *Unbowed* had sailed, *Unslaked* was due in at first light, *Unbending* and *Unseen* later in the day. It would be good to see Otto Stanley and Tubby Crawford again, after an interval of several weeks, comings and goings that hadn't coincided. He nodded, agreeing with Melhuish that it was *very* good fish pie. Since returning from the marathon, he'd written to Chloe and was intending to write to his brother Alan before turning in. It was about three months since he'd done so, actually from Port Said where they'd docked for a bottom-scrape before moving on up to Haifa. Hadn't heard *from* the lazy bastard for even longer. Admittedly the Old Man always passed on any news he had from either of them – so that, for instance, Alan would already know of the promotion and would hear shortly about his imminent return. Mike recognised that the decision to write to him now was to tell him about Abigail. That she existed, had that name and he was taking her for a ride in a donkey-cart, was about all it would come down to.

Actually, a little more than that: that she was worth writing home about. Especially to one's brother, and *not* to the Old Man. Alan would catch on to that, all right.

Charles Melhuish being in the mess, Mike had contemplated giving him the news that *Ursa's* next patrol was to be her last, but decided it would be better to postpone this for a day or two. There was no great rush for Ann to be apprised of it, whereas Melhuish *might* feel inclined to mention it to Abigail, if he found himself within hailing distance of her before Mike himself had told her.

Tell her tomorrow. Choosing a good moment. Hoping to God it didn't spoil the whole day. Soften it perhaps by asking whether she knew when *her* tour of duty might end. Then in a day or two tell Melhuish. Not leaving it too long because he wanted to get a letter of his own away to Ann before shoving off for 'Backlash.'

After supper he found himself drinking coffee in company with Shrimp, and told him how he'd spent the day. Shrimp approved. 'Nothing better. I won't ask you what you're doing tomorrow.'

'Borrowing Vera and the trap, sir.'

'Now that's a splendid idea.'

'She doesn't know about it yet.'

'You mean Vera doesn't?'

He smiled, shook his head. 'She doesn't either.'

'Ah.'

'Very good of you to take on the pongos single-handed, sir.'

'They'll be here about midday. Three boats due in meanwhile, and *Unsung* to sea for exercises. Melhuish still under the impression it's a solo operation, I hope?'

227

'Far as I know, sir. Although to be frank I don't see *why* he has to be kept in the dark.'

'Oh. Well – solo sabotage job, no big deal, but three linked, simultaneous ones – quite different. We've attacked airfields before with the aim of disrupting German Air Force attacks on convoys – with little success, if any, single attempts here or there – and it wouldn't call for a genius to conclude that a triple effort has to be an expansion of the same endeavour, i.e. getting a convoy in. Nobody's saying the island's crawling with spies, but the orders for "Backlash" lay stress on a need for maximum security, which is actually quite difficult to guarantee – for instance, passenger in a *dghaisa* shooting his mouth off, *dghaisa* man's ears flapping . . .' He reached to put his cup down. 'Makes it desirable to restrict the number who are in the know to a minimum, for as long as possible. Damn it, we hanged that Wop spy not so very long ago, didn't we?'

'Pisani. Carmelo Pisani.'

'Well done. But how do we know there aren't a dozen we *haven't* hanged?'

'You have a point, sir. Those Austrian cabaret artistes for instance.'

'They're behind bars, aren't they. But to tidy it all up, Michael – you'll attend our conference on Monday, then with plans more or less cut and dried we'll have what may be a final one in which Gerahty and Melhuish will take part. None of you having known there was any other boat involved, until that stage – no reason to be upset at having been left in the dark – eh?'

Saturday, then. MacGregor's engineers had finished tinkering with *Ursa*'s compressor and other threatening or malfunctioning machinery, McLeod was shoving off shortly for the torpedo depot to embark five Mark VIIIs, and Jarvis was limping slightly. Mike signed a few Admiralty 'returns' that

Danvers as Correspondence Officer had bashed out on the boat's portable, and left them to it. He'd written the letter to his brother last night, and found it still legible in the first light of day; his next one would be to Ann. Plenty to tell her about without any mention of Abigail. He wondered what man or men she'd not find it necessary to mention when *she* got around to writing; and discussed this with Vera while hitching her into the trap.

'Can just happen, old girl, can't it. Especially looking like she does. I dare say in your youth you had similar problems every bloody day. None of that now, uh? Could be why you bite. Whoa-up now . . .'

At Pembroke House, Abigail squawked, 'I don't believe it!'

'Better than foot-slogging, though? In my own case, two days running might be somewhat crippling. And on a fine day like this?' Holding both her hands: had only kissed her cheek, suspecting that Gravy and/or Greta might put in an appearance at any moment. Not, he guessed, that they'd be all that disapproving. Telling her quietly, 'Abbie, you are *lovely.*' Hearing or sensing the approach of Gravy then, adding 'I thought we might picnic and swim at Maddalena or thereabouts – you know, St George's? Oh – Gravy! Thank you so much for Thursday night – *great* evening, and –'

'We enjoyed it.' He was in a brightly striped dressing-gown. 'And good to have you with us again.'

'Careful – the old girl bites, if you give her half a chance. But it was a great evening – you're both so hospitable and generous. Greta OK?'

'Sleeping late. She's fine, yes. Abbie's looking terrific, don't you think?'

'I was just remarking on it, actually.'

'*Actually*, I'm a bit sad. Joan Dewsbury rang – oh, damn, did it wake you, Gravy?'

'I was in the bath.'

'She rang about my flat. Theirs isn't ready, but they're clearing out, got some other place to go – buckshee presumably. So I've no excuse for continuing to play cuckoo here. Much as I love you for all you've done for me –'

'You don't have to leave us just because you have a flat to go to, Abbie.'

'I do. I've traded on your kindness long enough, I'm now restored to what passes for my right mind, and – look, might do church with you tomorrow, *then* scoot off?'

'Vera'd be glad to take you.' Mike patted the grey rump. 'As long as she isn't spoken for, we might come for you early afternoon –'

'No need, Mike, we'll do it in my old rattletrap. How about joining us at church, then back here for lunch?'

'You realise, Mike, he's a bulldog?'

'Church here in St Julian's?'

'No – the Protestant one just off Savoy Hill. Abbie'll show you, if you're heading anywhere in that direction.'

'Well – no, second thoughts. If you don't mind, I'll give church a miss and come straight here. That's if you're sure you and Greta –'

'Certain. Bring swimmers. But off you go now . . .'

'Not a churchgoer, Mike?'

Vera had eased to a walk, on this pot-holed track leading to St Andrew's. He told Abigail, 'Have been known to attend, but not really as a priority. You're keen on it, are you?'

'Well.' Thinking about that: and shrugging – devastating in her orange blouse. 'Wouldn't rate as a fanatic, but yes, I turn up, usually. Out here I think more than one did at home. Probably because the population's a hundred and ten per cent Catholic, one's inclined to fly one's own flag, so to speak. Do you do anything about it at sea?'

'Read a few prayers usually, entirely voluntary attendance.'

'Any idea yet where you'll be going this next time?'

'No, I actually don't.'

'Meaning you wouldn't tell me if you did know, but you truly don't.'

'Roughly that. But – subject of churchgoing – I *would* join you for it tomorrow, but the job I was to have been doing for Shrimp today, he might need some help with tomorrow. I think his guests will still be there, and if it suited him I could give it a couple of hours.'

'Good decision, I'd say.'

'I would actually *like* to be going to church with you. Thinking of your brother, mostly.'

She kissed him, he kissed her back; and the kissing became serious. Vera plodding on, grey head nodding, moth-eaten-looking ears twitching against the flies' attentions. There were people on the road ahead then, which meant the kissing had to stop for a while; Abbie close up against him, his left arm round her small, supple waist, reins slack in his right hand. Vera certainly didn't need holding-in.

'I suppose – well, obviously, you don't yet know *when* you're going, either?'

'Only that it's likely to be before the end of the week. When I know, I'll tell you, right away.' Level with those people now, he nodded to them and called 'Sahha!' – a Maltese 'hello', actually 'health' or 'cheers' – and had the greeting returned, along with waves and smiles; scrawny-looking people who as like as not got most of their sustenance from the Victory soup-kitchens which Gravy had had set up in every village. Gone now, and spreading across the track again.

'But Abbie, speaking of coming and going, all that – fact is, there's something I really have to let you know about.'

Eyes on his face: surprised at first, then worried, then just intent.

231

'Let's get it over, then.'

'Yes. May rather spoil the day, I'm afraid.'

'You're not going to tell me you've left our lunch behind?'

'Oh, nothing *that* bad.' A glance at the bag containing corned beef and lettuce sandwiches, flasks of (a) coffee and (b) cold water. 'Got that, all right – such as it is. Not exactly a Fortnum's hamper. But, Abbie, after this next patrol –'

'Sending you home?'

'Good God – how on *earth* –'

'Jimmy Ruck told the Gravies he didn't expect to be left in peace much longer, and I know – knew – you and he were more or less level-pegging, so –'

'So you just guessed.'

'Had to be something of that nature. And I've wondered about it, how long we'd have. But listen, when you come back from this next one – *last* one – you'll need a week or two, won't you, getting ready for –'

'For the off. Yes. We'll have a week or two.'

'Well.' A shrug, smiling. 'Make the most of it, I suppose.'

'You're great, Abbie.'

'I wasn't a week ago, was I. No *idea* how much good you've done me!'

'Done nothing, except enjoy a few hours of your company. When d'you think they'll send *you* home?'

'Well – God knows. I could be applying *now* for special leave – you know, if my parents wanted me to – which as I told you I don't think they will. And in any case –'

'Wouldn't get *us* far anyway.'

'It wouldn't, would it. Another aspect is that I do have quite a responsible job, whoever took over from me would have his or her work cut out getting into it – *and* need the languages. And with so much coming up in the nearish future . . . Ought to bear left here, oughtn't we?'

232

'Yup. Otherwise be doubling back towards Spinola . . . What all that comes down to, I suppose, is that how long they'll want to keep you here has to depend on how things go in the desert – and so on, so forth.'

'All that. Yes. Touch wood, it mightn't be more than a few months. Could be a year – but once they *don't* need me here –'

'Devonshire?'

'Dorset. And/or London of course, probably War Office. And you – you did tell me, but –'

'Village called Deanshanger in Buckinghamshire, alternatively submarine headquarters – HMS *Dolphin* at Gosport, Hampshire . . . Just as well we aren't going far, old Vera's just about shot her bolt. Find some shade for her, when we get down there.'

'Can we get down on the rocks there?'

'I expect *we* can, with a bit of effort, but *she* can't!'

'Some shade wouldn't do us any harm either. Old ruins or whatever. Quite a lot of those about. If we can find some such place –'

'As far as I'm concerned, Abbie, any place at all.'

14

Monday, the meeting-with-pongos day: disturbingly darkish early morning with a sirocco blowing, the overhead heavy with cloud and a warmish wind gusting down from the Valetta side – originally from the Libyan desert, rocking the submarines at their moorings and jostling the brows that snaked out to them and were easy, being only strings of small rafts, for a wind of any force to slam around. Although – head clearing now, at least to some extent – he'd only been out of bed a minute, was on the gallery in pyjamas – in this sheltered creek the disturbance arose less from the wind itself than from the surge and swell from outside, swell driving in between Fort Tigne and the St Elmo headland, splitting itself on the rocks below Fort Manoel and powering northeast into Sliema Creek and southeast into Marsamxett here. It was a disappointing, somewhat worrying change of conditions after Saturday's calm and Sunday's light southeasterly – recollection of blue sky with hardly a feather in it, Maddalena Bay a virtual millpond edged with a swirl of white on brown rock, its blue not a bad match for Abbie's eyes.

Abbie . . .

He'd shut his own eyes – *seeing* her. Yesterday and Saturday, and the party on Thursday: before that, only a virtually chance half-hour on the Barracca. 'Chance' because if it hadn't been for Carmella Cassar he wouldn't have called in to see her that Monday; had only done so to see if there was anything he could do to help in the aftermath of whatever the 'hard knock' had been. Just one week ago, and in that time several days when he hadn't seen her at all, in spite of this the close-ness between them developing as fast as measles. He'd said something to that effect in the letter he'd written to his brother.

Working Monday now, though. Pongos, plans, precautions. Arrange to fuel and embark fresh water, have McLeod and the coxswain on the top line to store ship in a hurry. And pray the sirocco would be short-lived. Landings had more than once had to be abandoned on account of weather: the kind of canoe they were using nowadays being so light they'd float in ten centimetres of water – not of course with two men and their gear embarked; the problem *then* was they'd be lucky to find they had more than about *five* centi-metres of freeboard. Which didn't make either launching ('floating off') or paddling easy in anything more than a slight lop, *could* make recovery of a team already landed actually impossible.

Siroccos however often *were* short-lived, though. As short as two or three days, even. In which case, no problem – weatherwise.

Ursa looked happy enough down there, not all that much movement on her. She had a steel foul-weather screen around the outer forepart of her bridge which not many U-class did have, and this made her easy to identify even at some distance among her class-mates. Two of which had to be *Unbending* and *Unseen* – originally nameless, known only by their pendant numbers, respectively P.37 and P.51. *Unslaked* was another of

235

that bunch: and *Unsung*, identifiable by her three-inch gun, which so far only she and *Unbroken* sported. She — *Unsung* — had carried out her folboat-launching and recovery exercises on Saturday after dark, had been on her way out with a party of 10th Flotilla commandos in her when Mike had got back that evening after dropping Abigail off at Pembroke House and returning Vera to her paddock — first giving her a good long drink and rubbing her down a little, with nothing in his head but Abigail; Vera could have bitten him without his noticing. He'd told Abbie this yesterday and she'd kissed him for it, admitting that she'd given *him* a thought or two before crashing out. Then in the mess he'd found Otto Stanley of *Unbending*, and Crawford who'd been David Wanklyn VC's first lieutenant in *Upholder* before going home for his Perisher and eventually returning as CO of *Unseen*, and a few others including their own officers, and Hugo Short back from patrol in *Unslaked* — so Brodie had been there too, *sans* walking-stick and overjoyed at having got his boat back not only in one piece but with two new bars, one white and one red, on her Jolly Roger.

After a few convivial libations Mike had expressed surprise at Shrimp not being there on the 'first night in' of three of his submarines, and was told that in fact he most certainly had been, had retired to his office to check over the patrol reports, have them ready for Miss Gomez to bash out on her typewriter on Monday morning. Mike therefore went along and made his offer of helping to entertain pongos instead of attending church, and Shrimp though appreciative told him it wasn't necessary, he was actually shot of them for the time being. They weren't staying in Lazaretto, but in billets in Floriana, and the senior one, Major Ormrod, was delivering a lecture to fellow pongos of the garrison and then lunching at RAF headquarters.

'The RAF have some part to play in "Backlash", apparently. That man Ferrand's acting as liaison officer. Hugo Ferrand, Air Intelligence?'

'Beanpole character who was at the Gravies' on Thursday.'

'Yes. He often is. Great friend of theirs. How was your day out with Vera?'

'Best day ever, sir.' He nodded. 'Truly. In fact if I could persuade you to allow me a few more patrols –'

'Neither patrols nor donkey-cart outings. For sound admin reasons – including Sam MacGregor's report that *Ursa*'s overdue for major refit. That, Michael, I'm sure I don't need to tell you, is an extremely cogent reason. In fact I'm not saying you're stale – not at all, I don't believe you are, surprisingly enough – but it's still in your own as well as your ship's company's best interests – and therefore the flotilla's. You follow me?'

'I – suppose . . . I mean I take your point, sir.'

'How did she react when you told her you were off soon?'

He thought about it, and remembered having felt slightly put out, for a second or two, then having challenged himself with well, what the hell, there's no lifelong commitment here, not even a hint of one! He admitted, answering Shrimp's question, 'Actually, with a surprising degree of equanimity.'

'Has *her* head screwed on, then. All right, Michael.'

Sunday, thanks to Shrimp's temporary disengagement from the military, had justified a late lie-in. Mike could have got himself to the church, except that *Ursa*'s starboard watch were returning from Mellieha at about noon and he felt inclined to be there to say hello to them. In the event he also ran into Melhuish, who was telling people how easy he'd found the float-off and recovery of folboats to be, obviously considered himself a natural at it, but – oh, look here, he'd heard there'd been pongos in the base yesterday, thought it was odds-on they'd be his passengers, and if so why hadn't word of their presence been passed to him?

'I wasn't around, yesterday. But no reason they'd have been *your* pongos. Must be quite a few who aren't. One piece of news for you, though – my next patrol is going to be my last. How d'you like that?'

Blinking at him . . . 'Your last from this base, you must mean. Well – more to the point, how do *you* like it?'

'Don't really care all that much. We've had a pretty good innings, it probably *is* about time to pack it in.'

'What about the lovely lady with the funny name?'

'If you mean Abigail French, *what* about her?'

'Won't be too happy, will she?'

'I don't know. I'll miss *her*. Anyway, keep it to yourself for the time being, will you? Haven't had a chance to tell my crew yet.'

He thought Melhuish would waste no time in passing the news to Ann, and he might as well do the same. Not about Abigail, about going home. Phrasing the letter vaguely in his mind while fetching an air-letter form and taking it down to the boat, where half the ship's company were drifting around smoking and drinking tea, waiting for the truck from Mellieha. Catch them all together, maybe, break the news to them too, before making tracks for Pembroke House.

He drafted his letter in notes on a signal-pad before committing it legibly to the form; telling her he hadn't written in the last week or ten days because he realised she couldn't have had his last one yet and might be waiting to hear from him before *she* wrote, and maybe he should be waiting for that – unless she was being ultra-sensible and laying-off altogether now Charles was here. Which *would* make sense, for sure. For oneself too: despite a feeling almost of *obligation* to write now, and contradictarily enough a lot of the reason for that being the fast-growing relationship with Abigail, whom

238

he would *not* mention, the two items of news to which she was more or less entitled being (1) that he'd been promoted, and (2) that in something like six or eight weeks she might expect that knock on her door.

If when the time came one even approached her door. Pausing on that line of thought: with a sense of surprise at being unable to predict one's own movements or intentions – impulses, maybe. Quite genuine surprise, genuine inability . . .

Fudge it by substituting 'two or three months' for 'six or eight weeks'?

Other bits and pieces in any case: *I'm writing now, anyway, since as you know there are frequent intervals when I can't, so grabbing the chance while there is one . . . And – Have seen Charles a few times. He seems to be in good health and enjoying himself. Enjoying incidentally considerable success, as well. Wouldn't be surprised if you were to get my great news from him as well.*

Not much of a letter, he thought. In fact, rotten. Racking his brain for a moment for some way to give it even a hint of the sense of excitement it so plainly lacked; then adding a PS – *Please* do *write?* Not much, but better than nothing, maybe. He sealed it, stamped it 'Passed by Censor', took it ashore to see it safely on its way, returning on board just minutes before the transport should have arrived. Since it hadn't and for a while didn't, he had McLeod muster the port watch in the control room, told them the next patrol would be their last in this flotilla, and warned them as the initially rowdy reactions quietened that it was possible they'd have only a few days at Mellieha, so make the most of it. Couldn't say for sure, but orders for this last one might come at unusually short notice. None of them had seemed to care much about this – the rest-camps weren't all that marvellous, especially with autumn on its way in now – whereas shaking the stone-dust of Malta off one's feet – well, Jesus, hearth and

239

home well before Christmas! Then the truck arrived and the sun-tanned starboard watch were crowding round to congratulate him on his promotion, at the same time receiving and enthusing over the *big* news right, left and centre.

He was on his way ashore when he re-encountered the TI, CPO Harry Coltart, who'd emerged from the Chiefs' and POs' mess, on his way into the Torpedo Stowage Compartment. Turning as Mike stepped through the latched-back watertight door right behind him, temporarily filling it, as he had, the two of them being much of a size.

'Er – Captain, sir –'

'Yes, TI?'

'Well.' Wave of an arm towards the upper reload racks port and starboard, from which the torpedoes had of course been landed. 'Folboat stowage is it, sir? Special Op, this trip?'

'Christ.' Standing with a hand on the fore-hatch ladder, looking from the Chief to the empty racks and back again. A shake of the head. Back aft there he'd been saying he had no idea what they'd be doing this time. 'Not easy, keeping secrets, Chief.'

'Never was, sir. I won't draw attention to it.'

To Pembroke House then, covering some longish downhill stretches at the double. The Gravies had already returned from church and – well, *wow*, Abigail – taking his breath away . . .

Shrimp's conference with the commandos being set for ten-thirty, Mike left the base at ten, crossing as usual by the flotilla's attendant *dghaisa* and finding himself within easy distance of the Lascaris headquarters with ten or twelve minutes to spare. Brief visit therefore, rather than sit waiting in that outer office, to the Barracca, where one week ago his telling Abigail she'd done enough crying had somehow worked the miracle, certainly added a new dimension to his own life.

Grand Harbour itself had a sombre look this morning, the warmly oppressive wind and heavy overcast dulling and stirring up water that had previously mirrored the surrounding bulk of stone ramps, galleries and bastions built four hundred years ago by the Knights of St John of Jerusalem; the harbour was defended by them under the leadership of Jean Parisot de la Valette against ten times their own number of invading Turks under Suleiman the Magnificent in cahoots with the equally savage Algerian corsair Dragut Reis, in what was generally held to have been the bloodiest siege in history − in the course of it, for instance, the heads of prisoners being used as cannon-balls. And Fort St Elmo falling to the Turks, de la Valette fighting on from Fort St Angelo across the water there, where today Wrens in their coarse black stockings manned typewriters and answered telephones.

But Abigail precisely *here*, one week ago exactly. Hardly knowing her, at that stage: more acquaintance then than friend − let alone lover, for Pete's sake. And yet none of it surprising − neither Maddalena Bay, nor yesterday, when after a cold lunch they'd basked for a while on the Lido rocks and then been driven by Gravy in his Morris to the flat which was in a house near the bottom of South Street, aka Strada Mezzodi. Abbie throwing garments into cupboards and Mike poking through a couple of shelves of books, while Gravy stalked around offering help, pausing at Abigail's narrow windows to admire the views of flat stone roofs and streets like caverns, and the two of them doing their best to disguise their longing for this extremely kind, generous and impressively efficient man to finish his fourth or fifth cigarette and push off.

Later then − just a little later − his own voice asking, 'What's happening to us, Abbie?' and her sleepy answer, 'Don't you *know*?'

★　★　★

241

In the Lascaris submarine office Mike shook hands with the two soldiers – Ormrod with major's crowns on the shoulders of his khaki shirt, a dark, wiry-looking man of about his own age and size, and Haigh who was shorter, square-built, already balding. Also present as well as Shrimp himself were Johnno Broadbent the flotilla's comparatively new Staff Officer Operations, and Shrimp's paymaster-midshipman, who'd be taking notes. Performing introductions, Shrimp had told Ormrod, 'Nicholson is skipper of the submarine *Ursa*, also responsible for the outline scheme I gave you.'

'Sound stuff too, sir, usefully informative for us, we've been reconsidering some details of our own programme in the light of it.' To Mike then: 'Not that there's room for much variation – once you've put us ashore, you know?'

'I'd imagine not. The object was to give ourselves as well as you some idea of special problems we might be up against. I hope I'm wrong, but it still looks decidedly touch-and-go to me, one way and another.'

'From your point of view, or ours?'

'Oh, *yours*.'

Shrimp cut in with 'Let's sit.' A wave of one broad, stubby hand. A pongo each side of him, Mike on the other side of Ormrod and facing Haigh. Shrimp setting things going by asking Ormrod, 'Any comments on the proposed launching points and/or times?'

'Not really, sir. Agreeing the Gela set-down that far east of target, in fact, is the main one of your proposals we're accepting as making better sense, one way and another, than landing closer to the target as *we*'d proposed. Ditto times of launching, since obviously you can't surface close inshore before it's good and dark. Depending on weather to some extent, but near enough 2200 hours in all instances, give or take fifteen minutes, say. Weather prospects don't look too great at the moment, do they?'

242

'At this time of year it's a toss–up anyway. Not all that far into September yet, I know, but the end of August's as often as not a time for change. In this central basin anyway. This sirocco doesn't have to worry us too much – could be as flat as a pond tomorrow or the day after. But if it's looking bad or doubtful when the whistle blows, I'd suggest departures as scheduled, decisions whether to go ahead or abort at the latest possible time, which would be a little after sunset on Dog minus two.'

'Just short of the launch points.'

'Yes. Two days before the assaults as scheduled.' Shrimp explaining this mainly for the note-taking midshipman's benefit, Mike realised. At the same time he'd given himself a cigarette and pushed the tin of Senior Service in Ormrod's direction. Continuing the explanation: 'D-day, D for Dog, Dog-day, meaning the day of the assault. In our own outline we'd guessed at that starting in the small hours, on previous form usually something like 0200, but in the light of *your* presentation, action commencing the day before at 2300 – which therefore becomes Dog–day, the assault actually *finishing* in the small hours of Dog plus one – giving you several additional dark hours for disengagement and holing up again.' He asked Ormrod, 'Am I reading it correctly?'

'Absolutely, sir.'

Mike nodded too: the snotty had also indicated comprehension. Broadbent, SOO, had been jotting down notes which he now ran over as a nutshell summary: 'Dog minus one to Dog plus two, as far as Gela and Comiso are concerned: Dog minus two, submarines move inshore for float-off at 2200, commandos hide canoes and set off for lie-up positions. Dog-day minus one, teams attack at 2300, completing the assaults at about 0200 on Dog-day, when they return to hides and lie-up until dark, start out then for return to beach – Dog plus one – pushing off at about 0300 for R/V positions, submarines standing by to recover them between 0300 and 0400.'

'All right.' Shrimp had allowed a pause for any comments, returned now to the bad-weather question. 'And the final decision whether to proceed or abort will be made by 2100 Dog minus two. Earlier perhaps if conditions are obviously unsuitable. Right?'

'Yes, sir.' Broadbent again, marking his own schedule. 'An hour before float-off.'

Ormrod didn't like it. 'Better make it earlier than that. 2000, latest. We have to get the boats and gear ready and ourselves kitted up, weaponry checked, so forth. Don't want a bugger's rush at the last minute, and I'd sooner not start until I know I'm going through with it.'

Shrimp agreed. 'Deadline 2000 Dog minus two, then.'

'The decision being yours, sir, and applying to all three teams?'

'Of course. The signal – mine – will be addressed to submarines under my command. What would you expect, Major?'

He looked surprised at having been asked the question. Ormrod shook his head. 'Point taken, sir. Only to have it cut and dried.' Mike put in, 'But in our orders, sir, I imagine you'll be calling for a weather report at some slightly earlier stage?'

'Yes. That is, if there's any doubt about it. If there isn't, as touch wood might be the case, we can do without any of that. Next point now – question of which boats for which targets. The obvious choice for Catania, since an S-class is faster than a "U", is *Swordsman* – Lieutenant Dan S. Gerahty, who as it happens returns from patrol this evening. Distances and boats' speeds, incidentally, are noted in Nicholson's screed there. All right?'

'Your choice entirely, sir. But you're for *Swordsman*, Fergus.' Ormrod explained, 'There are factors which tie him to the Catania job, sir. And one aspect of it I'd guess you'll like is that his team won't be looking for a pick-up. When she's put them ashore – not exactly where you suggested, but pretty close – you might have the submarine hang around for a few hours in case of disaster of some kind – we could agree an emergency rendezvous position just short of first light, perhaps. But otherwise she could simply buzz off home.'

'What happens to Haigh's party, then?'

Ormrod was stubbing out a cigarette. He smiled at Mike. 'Good question, but no easy answer except they've other tasks. Might say they simply fade into the wild blue yonder.'

Haigh grinned. 'Vanish singing "*We'll meet again, don't know where, don't know when*" –'

Shrimp observed, 'Might be all right if you could sing it in Italian. But the other two boats now, for Gela and Comiso – any thoughts, Major?'

'Well – I'm opting for Comiso, myself. Originally because it looked like a tall order, that distance inland. Now of course Gela's also a long haul – more straightforward on the face of it, they have a coastline to follow whereas we've got to dodge around Ragusa. But that's it – me Comiso, Billy Flood Gela.'

More notes were being made. Mike suggested to Shrimp, 'I'll take Major Ormrod and his team in *Ursa* – if that's all right, sir.'

'All right with you, Major?'

'Very much so.' A nod to Mike. 'Thank you.' To Shrimp then: 'Leaves Billy Flood – Captain, Welsh Fusiliers – for Gela.'

'And he –' Shrimp put his hand on a clip of signals – 'is due here some time tomorrow, was it?'

Ormrod nodded. 'With a staff sergeant by name of Hazlett and half a dozen Royal Marines plus weaponry and explosives. And the third detachment – which needs to be pretty close on their heels, incidentally – consists of an RM colour sergeant and the rest of them with all our canoes. Wednesday at the latest, I'd guess. Colour Sergeant Gant RM is my own number two in the Comiso team. *We'll* meet both those parties though, and settle them in at Ghain Tuffieha with all their gear – and their own rations for consumption here, by the way, as well as iron rations for use later.'

Mike said, 'And RAF transport in attendance, we were told. So all we have to do is be ready to receive them on board the submarines an hour or so before departure – whenever that's to be.'

Broadbent added, 'Better not be before Thursday – huh? With your third detachment still to come?'

'But both lots might be touching down tomorrow. And as long as your chaps are ready for us –' Ormrod, telling Shrimp this – 'we're fast on our feet, you'll find.'

'I'll ask Cairo when we can expect them, anyway.' Shrimp made another note. 'Otherwise, I think that's covered the broad essentials, don't you? We'll meet again when your man Flood's here, and bring Gerahty and Melhuish into it.' He assured Haigh, 'Gerahty's a very sound man, you'll find.'

'I'm sure, sir.'

Ormrod waited a moment before asking, 'And Melhuish?'

'Oh, Flood 'll find himself in good hands. Charles Melhuish is fairly new as a CO but an experienced submariner.'

'The name's familiar, somehow.'

'Mid.' Shrimp addressing the young paymaster: 'Tell Janet we'd like coffee, will you?'

That evening there was a telegram from his father congratulating him on the promotion – *Blooming marvellous, Michael lad, and so say all of us!*

By now, Mike thought, he might have had the second instalment, news of an early homecoming. Might get another few lines away to him before 'Backlash' – at least let him know I've had this wire.

15

For 'Dog-day' now read Saturday. You could forget the 'Dog' stuff, which was really only useful in the planning stages, like an x, y or z in an algebraic equation, and start calling days by their proper names. This now was Thursday. Shrimp had received the news last night, Wednesday, the duty officer at Lascaris getting it from the Naval Cipher Office in a sealed envelope marked Top Secret and stamped 'By Hand of Officer', sending it on here to Lazaretto by hand of Eleanor Kingsley, 3rd Officer WRNS; Shrimp receiving it and her in his office, inviting her to sit down and smoke a cigarette while he perused the signal and then sent for Mike. Eleanor in fact knew Shrimp and Lazaretto well, working as she did in the Joint Services HQ and often visiting for one purpose or another, not to mention Jamie McLeod being one of her boyfriends – possibly even her main one, at any rate when *Ursa* was between patrols. She was a redhead with an elegantly long, slim neck and slanty eyes. Mike, anyway, having studied the signal and conferred briefly with Shrimp, had suggested that McLeod – with whom he'd been talking in the ward-room on the subject of things to be done in the next day or two — would be the man to escort her back to wherever she'd be heading now — the Lascaris fortress or the Wrennery — and when they'd gone he and Shrimp had discussed Operation Backlash as it looked now with dates on it.

Ursa's domestic plans were reasonably well in hand — McLeod's, as discussed earlier in the evening and amended slightly just minutes ago, the list headed now with getting the port watch back from Mellieha right away. This in fact had been initiated, by telephone. Then, arrange to store ship, and top up fresh-water tanks. Bunkers were OK — had fuelled on Monday and not used any since. Battery-charge — again, McLeod's job, all day Friday, standing charge both sides, in order to sail with the box right up. And check with Ormrod whether he'd like to embark his gear — especially canoes — tonight, Thursday. He probably would, Mike thought — and in that case he'd better leave a couple of his own men on board to keep an eye on it all, especially weaponry and bombs. It would make things easier on Friday to have that done. The commandos were taking two varieties of bomb with them, Ormrod had told him, 'little buggers' for attaching to aircraft propellers, quicker and easier to fix as well as more effectively destructive than the charges they'd used to set on wings or fuselages, and small enough to carry in fair quantity; and heavier, much more powerful jobs they called 'thermos' that were for use against airfield targets such as fuel storage, bomb dumps and the generators that powered flood-lights illuminating perimeters and runways. Ideally you'd get these planted with their time-fuses already fizzing before starting on the lines of parked 88s and 87s, very large explosions and sheets of flame not only wrecking the whole place shortly afterwards but also throwing Wop guards on the field into some degree of panic, with luck distracting them from whatever *you* were doing by that time.

'Guards among the aircraft?'

248

'As often as not two to each 'plane. And *we* work in pairs, usually. One clipping time-fused tiddlers on to props and the other using a Sten and/or whatever else to discourage interference. Number One of each pair has that job as his speciality – to shoot or stab any Wop they're faced with. Grenades for groups of them of course – although that can have its problems. Speed and a fair degree of athleticism's the guts of it, really. And confidence – knowing you *can* do it and get away with it.'

'Because you have done.'

'Well, yes. Not always with the desired smoothness and celerity, but –'

'Got away with it.'

'By hook or by crook, you know?'

'Fascinating. Not quite as fascinating as your last revelation, mind you –'

A laugh, shake of the head . . . 'That, *really* . . .'

He'd asked him to forget it. Having enquired – a day or two ago – rubber-necking in Valetta, Mike having time to kill before Abigail could rendezvous with him at her flat, Ormrod also at a loose end – Tuesday afternoon, it must have been – 'Is your man Melhuish married, by any chance?'

'Melhuish?' He'd been thinking about Abbie, naturally enough; came abruptly down to this much less attractive subject. 'Yes, he is. Why?'

'I may have known his wife. You ever meet her?'

Sharp glance: subject gaining interest. 'Several times.'

'And?'

'Startlingly attractive.'

A nod: 'Getting warm. For "startlingly" might one substitute "compulsively"?'

'As a matter of fact, one could envisage –'

'Not by any chance called Ann without an "e" on it?'

'I'll be damned.' They'd both stopped: on Palace Square,

249

where what had been the Grand Master's Palace faced another ancient and impresssive pile known as the Main Guard. Mike asking, 'Are you honestly saying you – well, obviously you *know* her –'

'Knew. Unless there's another one of that name – absolute dish, and – well, in and around Edinburgh mostly, several years ago, when her name was Ann Morton.'

'"Irresistible" being your word for her, you didn't just *know* her, you –'

'I'd have married her like a shot. Parents wouldn't have stood for it, though. Hers, I mean. Money was the main problem – my lack of it, nothing except my pay. But – we had a training base on the west coast and another on the Clyde, one got moved around a bit, buzzed off to Norway at one stage, things like that – but several leaves in Edinburgh, and there was a pub up near Fort William – well, crikey –'

He'd stopped. 'Forget I mentioned her?'

'Off her own bat, would she have married you?'

'I thought I had a chance, if I stuck to my guns. But there you are, parents felt otherwise. Dreary people, I can tell you; frankly, pompous arseholes. And then out of the blue, damn it, doesn't she write to me saying more or less look here, piss off – in a nice, regretful way, you know, and a week or two later some people I knew in Edinburgh sent me this cutting, "Engagement announced and marriage shortly to take place between Ann Penelope, daughter of these Morton turds, to some submariner name of Melhuish".'

'Who happened – happens – to be rich.'

'Well, I heard that!'

'His father owns hotels.'

'In fact I dare say I'm well out of it. The money angle for one thing, but worse still – well, imagine being stuck out here, and a wife back home who looks like she does – and to be perfectly frank *acts* like she does . . . I mean, out of this bloody *world*, but –'

'She's in London.'

'Yeah, well, there you are – *London* . . .'

'Jim, hang on a minute. Changing the subject rather more than slightly – that marble plaque there? Commemorates Malta voluntarily joining the British Empire – 1815, thereabouts. Napoleon had installed a garrison, Malts didn't like them, asked for our help and got it – actually from Nelson, just after the Nile.'

'Fascinating. And you're right, I shouldn't have brought it up, let alone gone on about her. Please –'

'That isn't *at all* why I rather boorishly changed the subject, only that while we're here –'

'I know. And I shouldn't have *raised* the subject. Such an extraordinary coincidence, that's all. In fact it's not even that – have a run-in with a girl then happen to come across the guy she married? Anyway, please, forget it?'

Food for thought, all right. Not the slightly oblique coincidence – such things did occur, you didn't have to marvel at them – but the light it threw on Ann . . . At which one might have guessed, but conceivably hadn't wanted to? Food for further thought anyway when time allowed – and this Thursday morning it did not. What he'd *intended* doing was calling in on Abigail to break the Dog-day news to her before the eleven a.m. meeting, but in the event didn't have time, having had quite a lot to see to in and around the boat. See her instead when Shrimp's palaver finished, meanwhile hope it started on time and didn't go on for ever. Thing was – or things were – that he'd spent last night in the base just for the look of things – having spent Monday and Tuesday nights with her, on both those mornings clocking in at Lazaretto slightly late for breakfast, and from yesterday, remembering Abbie warm as toast hugging him

251

down to her on the rickety single bed and murmuring, 'I'll find myself branded a scarlet woman', to which he'd replied – spur of the moment, not having given it more than a fleeting thought until that moment when it was simply *there*, the obvious solution – 'Easy to fix *that*, my darling, just damn well get spliced!'

'Oh – that settled, is it?'

'Well – if I were to go down on bended knee?' Kissing her again. 'And look, now I'm a lieutenant-commander, with at least ten bob a month more than I had before –'

'If we ever thought for a moment of doing anything so barmy – which I'm *not* thinking of and you aren't either – I'd want to do it at home, wouldn't you? In the presence for instance of the Old Man as you call him, brother Alan bless him, and little Chloe?'

'And perhaps a clutch of yours?'

'A clutch . . .' Flat tone. He guessed having in mind the one she would *not* have at any such ceremony, the brother she'd adored and whose death had lit the fuse to all this, and whom now she barely mentioned. She'd begun again, 'If we ever did contemplate any such thing –'

'How come we're talking about it, if *not* contemplating it?'

'Talking's just *talk*, Mike, not contemplation. Hadn't you better run?'

And now, Thursday, with only one night left to them he wished he *hadn't* given up this last one 'for the look of things' – having come to believe for some reason that they'd have until the weekend at least. Whereas – well, sailing tomorrow at dusk, the weekend proper starting with Dog minus 2, Saturday, when he'd be diving *Ursa* at about 0500. Please God, in calm or near-calm weather: you couldn't count on that – yet – although the wind was down a bit and cooler, the overhead less heavy. Checking the time as he went down into the stone depths of Lascaris – it was one minute past

252

eleven – and in the outer office finding Melhuish, Gerahty, Haigh and Flood, and Shrimp's paymaster-midshipman greeting him with 'Ah – sir – Vice-Admiral Malta wanted to see Major Ormrod, so –'

'So we're starting late. All right.' A nod to the soldiers – Haigh's easy grin, and the Fusilier's wide, white face and light-coloured eyes, slightly mad look under the dark, curly thatch. Then, 'Hello, Dan, Charles . . .'

'What *is* this, Mike?'

Gerahty's thick eyebrows hooping: 'Three of us? These commando chaps more or less confirm it, but –'

'They should know, Dan. How's it going, Fergus?'

'Something to have a date set, isn't it. And the lads all here. Met Bill Flood, have you?'

'Certainly have. Ah, starter's orders . . .'

Shrimp, and Ormrod with him. 'Sorry to have kept you waiting, gentlemen. We'll try to make up for lost time now. Finding your way about all right, Flood?' The midshipman was telling him as he led them through to the inner office, 'There was a call from Squadron Leader Ferrand, sir –'

'So he can't make it. Doesn't matter, I know what he was going to tell us. Now – Lieutenants Gerahty of *Swordsman* and Melhuish of *Unsung* – Major Ormrod, Captains Haigh and Flood. Charles, you'll have Flood and his team with you, targeting the Gela airfield; Captain Haigh and company are your passengers to Catania, Dan, and Major Ormrod and his team will be taking passage in *Ursa* – to Comiso, that is.'

All sitting – Ormrod next to Shrimp again, Mike putting himself near the bottom of the table and relieved that Shrimp *was* pushing it along a bit, so he'd have a chance of catching Abigail still at her office, not gone for lunch. Checking the time again: already ten past the hour. The midshipman was handing out sheafs of typed foolscap to the three COs –

patrol orders as devised by Shrimp and Broadbent, based on some of one's own ideas, no doubt.

'Smoke if you like. I'll just run over the salient points. *Swordsman* first, since the other two are identical except in navigational detail. As I say, Dan, your destination is Catania, floating off eight commandos in four folboats at 2200 Saturday – in the position given in those orders, two and a half thousand yards offshore.'

'Quick shufti at this stuff before going further, may I?'

'Good idea. Push that chart along to him, Mid. Melhuish, now. Your soldiers' target is Gela airfield, but you'll be landing them a dozen miles to the east of it, between the port and Cape Scalambri. Saturday, you'll dive about 0500, carry out coastal reconnaissance during the day – forenoon anyway – as required by your commando team leader but naturally at your own discretion, basically to spot any potential hazard – including troop movements or new defences around the beachhead area, but of course being damn careful with periscopes. This is the purpose of giving you what looks like a spare day. Anyway – Saturday evening, move inshore to float off canoes at about 2200. Lat. and long. and coastal bearings as in that screed, and you'll pick your chaps up off the same beach on Tuesday between 0300 and 0400. Check all this and the navigational detail in the Ops Room at Lazaretto – I'm briefing you together like this as far as the general outline's concerned so you all have the same overall view of it. An important point for *Ursa* and *Unsung*, though –' Melhuish's head jerked round, from an attempt to read the chart upside-down and from a certain distance – looking for Gela and hadn't yet found it, Mike guessed – 'your team, Melhuish, will be landing seven and a half miles west of Cape Scalambri, *Ursa*'s the same distance east of it, and between the two approaches there's a great gulf fixed, a triangular middle-ground with its apex on Cape Scalambri that's

254

forbidden water to both of you. Broadbent will clarify this when you get down to it. All right?'

Then the weather – Shrimp's own deadline, based on weather reports to be received from the boats – from *Ursa* anyway – as called for in orders, for a late decision either to proceed or to abort. 'Indications are a little better than they were, thank God . . . Yes, Dan – hoisted that in, have you?'

'*Think* I have, sir – but no pick-up? I land my chaps and bugger off?'

'What it comes down to, yes. But I want you to discuss this with Captain Haigh. The proposal being that you spend four or six hours within signalling distance of the beach, in case they run into serious trouble at that early stage and need to be taken off. It's a possibility, apparently. But if that period expires without a call for help, away you go.'

'Aye aye, sir. But may I know what –'

'We don't know what they'll be doing, only that we aren't supposed to bring them back.' Shrimp was very evidently conscious of having no time to waste. With a convoy on its way – as it had to be and pretty well immediately, Mike guessed, to have had the date settled for this outing, he'd have a lot more than just 'Backlash' on his hands – most of the rest of the flotilla to re-dispose as well, presumably. Adding now, 'A novelty our commando friends have brought us is a new kind of torch for signalling through periscopes – communications between shore and/or folboats and submarines. Demonstration at dusk this evening – meet in the Lazaretto wardroom at 1830, all welcome. Until then, any questions?'

'One thing, sir.' Mike – who after a moment's alarm had realised he could get down there for the demonstration then back up to South Street at the speed of light, leaving them to load their canoes without *his* help – 'Minor suggestion for the soldiers – rather than have it all to do tomorrow, might embark gear including canoes this evening?'

That had gone down well, and Shrimp had wound the meeting up with a brief exposition, for Melhuish's and Gerahty's benefits, of the importance of getting the commandos ashore on time and in the right places. '*Then*, it's their pigeon – wrecking those three airfields simultaneously and in so doing disrupting the enemy's air operations right across the board. It'll be a hell of an achievement, if they can bring it off. The weather's still a *little* doubtful, but I can assure you I won't be aborting the operation if it's anything less than downright impossible.'

Gerahty blew smoke at an overhead light, then met Shrimp's eyes. 'Bringing in a convoy, are we?'

'Is that your guess, Dan?'

'Unless we're invading Sicily, or something.'

'Most likely will be, before long. All right, gentlemen . . . Oh, wait – RAF activity you may or may not encounter, during and after the assaults . . .'

Abigail said quietly, 'The intention of working through my lunch-hour and knocking-off early is aimed at – ah – adapting to *your* situation – whichever way the cat jumps?'

He stooped, kissed her neck, told her 'It's jumped – or at least signalled its intention of doing so. I've been at another meeting, couldn't get to you sooner.'

'So what's *our* programme?'

'Well – *mine* is to spend as many consecutive hours with you as possible. What time at Strada Mezzodi this afternoon, for instance?'

'Three-thirty?'

'I can be there by four. Then I'll need to get down to Lazaretto at six or six-thirty, but only for about an hour, back to you seven-thirty or eight. Tomorrow'll be a very early morning, I'm sorry to say.'

She grimaced slightly. 'And the last one, for a while?'

256

'Does look like being so.'

'Yes.' Those eyes on his, from a distance of about two inches. 'You won't be doing anything too damn silly, I hope?'

'Do my best not to.' They'd stopped – more or less out of other people's way. 'For much the same reason you *ask* me not to.'

'You mean – same wavelength. You realise it matters.'

'It's always mattered. Part of my job's to keep us alive. Just that *now* it matters from every other point of view as well.'

'Well, that *is* good news!'

'So what was the niggling about – Tuesday or Wednesday, crack of dawn, I thought somewhat hoity-toity?'

'It was a little early, for a proposition of – I mean, that far-reaching, right out of the blue, one we've never discussed before and frankly I'm not at all sure I'm ready for in any case. Let's not talk about it now?'

He'd got to her a little after the time he'd promised; he was inside and had the door shut and bolted again within seconds. Like surfacing for a gun action, almost. He kissed her. 'Sorry. May say I came most of the way at the double.'

'What else have you been doing?'

'Oh – this and that. Some chartwork was the important thing. Also a procedure known as Requestmen and Defaulters. Then generally squaring things off, solving another guy's non-existent problems for him. Oh, and conversing with various members of my crew. As I say, this and that.'

It had included further discussion of beachhead reconnaissance. And a proposal of more widely separated departure times for *Ursa* and *Unsung*, and varying their routes on both outward and return trips. It had been well worth while, he thought, but he still didn't think much of Charles Melhuish. Abigail had said – in the kitchen and in reference to *Ursa*'s crew – 'I'd like to meet some of them, some day.'

'I'm sure they'd like to meet you, too. When we're back from this one, any time you like.'

She'd made that face again. 'Saying hello, goodbye.'

He frowned. 'Saying hello, goodbye, see you back home.'

'Think we *will*, Mike?'

'If we want to. I most certainly want nothing else. You against it now?'

'Just that here and now it seems a touch incredible . . . What's that?'

'Present from the wardroom messman. Supper – or contribution to it.'

'Is he *allowed* –'

'He's a pragmatist with a kindly disposition. If one's only there for about one meal in ten he concludes one's eating elsewhere, someone *else's* rations, so – Abbie, you're *lovely*. You truly are, you're *perfect*. I have you pictured in my mind all day, and when at last I get to focus on you, you just bloody *slay* me . . .'

When he got back down to Lazaretto, soon after six, Ormrod was telling Gerahty and Melhuish that two of his hates were fishermen and farm dogs. 'Fishermen who don't show lights, especially, as well as those who have a Hun rifleman as passenger. You'd be surprised how often they crop up.'

'So – you're in a folboat, presumably – what can you do about it?' Gerahty pinched out a cigarette stub and flicked it into the creek. 'Could you mount a Bren or somesuch on a folboat's bow?'

'We often do – for other purposes though, not for that. No, all one can do is play it very, very carefully – steer around them, if you've seen them in time, or lie still, dead-in-the-water and holding one's breath until the buggers pass. Otherwise – well, you can let rip with a .45 or a 9-millimetre – may be lucky, if you've taken 'em by surprise. But the

258

problem with farm dogs is they bark. Which is what farmers expect of them, of course, keep the place clear of miscreants of various kinds – including Hun soldiery, as like as not.'

'You shoot them, do you?'

'The dogs? Yes, have done. But a knife's better. Gunshots in the night don't exactly allay suspicion. Mind you, a crossbow has a lot to be said for it as long as there's enough light to see by.'

'D'you carry one?'

Melhuish had asked the question; Ormrod said yes, one did, except on nights that were going to be moonless or so cloudy as to be guaranteed pitch-dark. Otherwise one scarpered – or could crouch, freeze, pray the bloody things would either shut up or come into knife-range. It depended on circumstances, terrain, weather and so forth. You improvised, as much as anything. The conversation ended with Melhuish saying 'Not *my* idea of fun', and Billy Flood arriving with the torches.

Which worked all right, from a motionless submarine secured between buoys. The torches were primarily intended for use when recovering canoes, guiding them out from the beach; you'd see a blue light flashing from shore, set the periscope on it and give the landing-party a few flashes *they*'d see. But obviously when you were on the surface periscopes didn't come into it; and to recover a landing-party you did need to be surfaced. The general conclusion was that there could be circumstances in which they'd come in handy, but that was about the extent of it.

Melhuish said, low-voiced, when he and Mike were making their way shoreward over a long reach of brow, 'When I told you Shrimp had me down for this lark, you must have known we both were?'

'I gave a hand with some navigational planning. Shrimp didn't want the scope of the operation known. His orders

259

stressed the need for maximum security – for the simple reason that getting the convoy in as near intact as possible's about as important as anything could be at this stage, so why risk someone shooting his mouth off? As I'm doing now for instance.'

'Or presumably as *I* might if I'd known about it.'

'*Anyone* might. You and I just *have*. What people don't know about, Charles, they can't talk about. That's not original, I know, but if they don't *need* to know about it, why bloody tell them?'

'That's an old refrain too, of course. But all right, forget it.' Then: 'You hanging on to see the canoes embarked?'

'No. My Number One's seeing to it.'

'Going back ashore, then?'

'Yes, Charles. Going back ashore.'

16

Accompanied by McLeod and the coxswain, he'd completed his usual predeparture tour of the boat, chatting with various individuals encountered along the way – including some of Ormrod's team – Colour Sergeant Gant RM, four other Royal Marines and two Army corporals. In all, forty on board instead of thirty-two. Now, back in *Ursa*'s wardroom, he enquired of Ormrod, who was at the table with a mug of tea, 'Are you happy to stay down here? Bridge isn't exactly spacious.'

'Thanks, I'll keep out of your way.'

'Be a little while. Trim-dive when we're a mile down-channel.'

'Good luck with it.' Looking from Mike to McLeod, who of course was responsible for the trim, slightly complicated this time by the added weight of eight men and their gear. The Major had been around submarines quite a bit, of course, knew what it was all about. Mike checked the time again, and nodded to McLeod. 'Harbour Stations, Jamie.'

For the penultimate time, he thought, on his way up the ladder. *Last* time, as a departure for patrol. Actually her eighteenth. Dog minus 3, in that vernacular, and *Ursa* the last to go. *Swordsman* had sailed at noon, Dan Gerahty having elected to give himself six additional hours in which to cover the 120-odd nautical miles to the vicinity of Acireale, a few miles to the north of Catania. Delays, interruptions or diversions of one kind or another weren't unusual, and having a few hours you could afford to waste was a relaxant. Gerahty had taken Shrimp's admonition to heart, had been thinking about it last evening before the periscope–torch exercise and raised it with Shrimp afterwards, Shrimp according to Charles Melhuish responding in his usual laconic manner with 'All right. Shift in alongside here when *Upstart* shoves off at first light.' Reason for this being that *Swordsman* hadn't finished storing ship, as both *Ursa* and *Unsung* had, and it was more easily and quickly done alongside than out at the buoys; in fact she'd been lying-off, ready to slip into that 'wardroom berth' which *Upstart* had been in the process of vacating, when Mike had arrived for breakfast, telling himself authoritatively *Forget all that* – meaning her damp eyes and warm body, the anxious 'Promise, no longer than a week?'

That was how long he'd told her he *thought* it might be before he got back to her.

Unsung meanwhile had slipped from her buoys and motored out into Marsamxett and the swept channel about an hour ago – before sunset, and the gradual darkening of the water that had been taking place since they'd watched her gradual diminution and disappearance. Very nearly *still* water now, incidentally, and a mainly clear sky, pinpoints of first stars and the square-cut Valetta skyline in grey and then black silhouette against some short-lived brilliance. Staggering the two 'U's' departures had been a suggestion of Broadbent's, his point being that with only a few degrees' divergence between Melhuish's course to the Gela beachhead and Mike's to the offloading-point for Comiso, putting an hour between them

262

rather than only minutes would ensure their being well clear of each other right from the start, thus could concentrate on the essential lookout, forget about each other. Then – another change – at about the halfway mark *Ursa* would be making a detour eastward, as far east as the longitude of Pozzallo, while *Unsung* performed similarly but the other way off Gela. *Swordsman* of course had no such problem, making her enviable twelve or thirteen knots northeastward to round Cape Passero. Anyway, Mike was in *Ursa*'s bridge now, casing party and bridge staff having gone up ahead of him: past sunset, so no ensign flying and no farewell salute to the invisibly watching Shrimp. Jarvis and his team clambering over and down the rungs on the tower's starboard side and thence around it to the fore casing, Tubby Hart and his trio heading aft. Here in the bridge the coxswain ready at the wheel, Walburton close to the for'ard periscope standard, Aldis in his hands, Danvers at the voice-pipe in the port for'ard corner, McLeod on his captain's arrival passing down the order to Hart to let go aft – allowing the stern to drift clear of that buoy and its chain-cable mooring so he could use the screws when he was ready to, making it easier for Jarvis and his lads up for'ard by taking the weight off that lot. Mike telling Danvers, 'Group down, Pilot' – hearing the order acknowledged in the copper tube, and simultaneously from the after casing Hart's report of 'All gone aft!' Via Danvers again then, 'Slow ahead port', and to McLeod, 'They can let go for'ard.' Stopping that screw then: McLeod giving tongue again, and Jarvis's response virtually instant; some time in the past hour they'd have riven a wire in place of *Ursa*'s anchor cable on that buoy, making the job now quick and easy – with her bow already beginning to fall off to leeward you hardly needed the confirmatory yell of 'All gone for'ard!'

'Half ahead both. Start engines. Take her out, Cox'n.'

'Aye aye, sir.' Diesel-generators racketing into explosive,

instant life, Swathely winding on the starboard wheel to pass between two other buoys: *Ursa* on her way, last of the 'Backlash' trio.

Time now, just after nine. Fully dark; trim-dive completed satisfactorily, the boat at patrol routine and steadied on course 006 degrees, trimmed down to half-buoyancy, only numbers one and six main ballast holding her up. The other four filled and ready to drag her down in seconds, assisted by 'Q' quick-diving tank. Press the tit, she'd be under as fast as a sounding whale. Meanwhile her 400hp generators rumbling steadily into the night pumping enough amps into her batteries for the motors to push her along at about eight knots, but in prevailing conditions – being trimmed deep, with that weight of sea to barrel through, as well as having a long, low swell rolling in under her stern – she was making only about six.

Which was OK – if you'd wanted more, you could have had it. With about twenty-five miles to cover before diverting Pozzallo-wards and another twenty-five thereafter. Danvers had this watch – Blue watch, Farquhar and Knox up there as lookouts, Tubby Hart in charge of the watch below, Mike on his way down through the rush of air into the brightly-lit control room.

'Happy to be going home, Hart?'

'Will be when we *are*, sir.'

'Won't be long. A week say for this job, then a couple gearing up for the long haul.' He stopped at the chart table to check the log and slightly revise the entry in his night-order book; asked Leading Torpedoman Brooks, who was on the wheel, whether he'd heard from his fiancée since their return from the last one, and received an affirmative reply – she wrote 'regular every week no matter what', Brooks told him – and moved on into the wardroom, where McLeod was writing a letter and Ormrod reading P. G. Wodehouse.

He'd brought that and another Blandings saga with him, Mike had noticed. Whereas for his own reading he'd borrowed two books from Abigail, novels by Robert Graves, both tales of ancient Rome which *had* belonged to Nico Cornish, the erstwhile Information Officer.

Think some more about that later, maybe. They *had* talked about it – at *her* instigation – and he half-believed her, didn't think it mattered all that much.

McLeod was reading, and Jarvis flat-out on his bunk; any snoring inaudible on account of the engines' racket. Ormrod put a marker in his book and asked, 'Trim-dive gave no problems, I gather?'

'None at all. I have an extremely competent first lieutenant. Have you been offered supper yet?'

'We have, actually. Thought we'd wait for your distinguished company, though.'

'You needn't have.' He called in the direction of the galley, 'Barnaby, we're hungry.'

'Coming up, sir!'

He asked McLeod, '*What*'s coming up?'

Shake of the head. 'You won't believe it, sir.'

'Oh. Corned Dog, as ever.'

'Actually, tongue, sir. Canned ox-tongue. And – no. It's the truth – tongue followed by tinned fruit salad, with which Cottenham is offering *custard.*'

'I'd very much like to believe you, Jamie, but I can't.' Watching Barnaby begin dealing out plates and tools. McLeod had shut his book, which was *No Orchids for Miss Blandish* by James Hadley Chase; Mike asked him, 'Eleanor again?' and he nodded, looking slightly embarrassed; adding, 'And we owe the tongue to our guests, Cox'n tells me. They get the best that's going, apparently.'

'I've always been given to understand that *we* did.'

'Well, same here, but perhaps only by Malta standards?'

Mike asked Ormrod, 'Is he pulling my leg?'

'No, as it happens –'

'Let's keep 'em with us? *Not* float 'em off?' Jarvis, wide awake and pink-faced, sliding off his bunk. '*Grande Luxe* here on in?'

'They flew in some crates of food with the rest of our gear.' Ormrod sounded almost apologetic. 'More or less standard practice – so we don't scoff up all *your* rations and make you hate us is the idea.'

Mike watched the sliced tongue arriving, along with fresh bread, margarine, pickle, etcetera. He said, 'There's also the fact that in a day or two you'll be on distinctly *hard* rations, huh?'

'*Might* be a consideration, but I doubt it.'

'Well.' Mike pushed the tongue over. 'You first. Fill your boots.'

McLeod took over the watch shortly after ten, by which time there was less movement on the boat, which was encouraging, although with a whole night and day to go some further worsening and consequent abandonment of the operation couldn't yet be ruled out. Danvers came down for his supper, which of course he'd heard about. He'd be due back on watch at 0215, moonrise would be shortly after that, with *Ursa* then about halfway to Cape Scalambri – or rather Pozzallo. Ormrod asked him, crossing fingers, 'Swell not what it was, eh?' then commented to Mike, 'Touch wood, we'll be going through with it.'

'Please God. Awful let-down otherwise.'

'*Right.*' The soldier did touch wood. 'Little matter of a convoy to think about too.'

'Oh, *is* there?' Jarvis, speaking from his bunk. 'Did rather think there might be. Otherwise – well, in any case, it's hardly a *patrol* at all, is it.' Danvers cocked an eyebrow at him: '*What* was that?' and Ormrod enquired rather more politely, 'Can't say I'm entirely with you . . .'

'More of a *mission* than a patrol. Land you, pick you up again, bring you back. Single objective, I'd call it a *mission*.'

'While we're ashore, won't you be patrolling?'

'Of course we will.' Mike told them, 'A submarine in enemy waters with torpedoes in her tubes is most certainly on patrol.'

'Well – just sort of waiting, sir? I was thinking we'd be lying low.'

'Not if we run into anything worth sinking.' He added, to Ormrod, 'After all, if we sink something a few miles offshore, doesn't tell the Wops there are commandos a dozen miles inland, does it?'

Ormrod's dry smile. 'I *hope* it doesn't. Also that while you're at it you *do* sink something.' Jarvis explaining, 'My thought, actually, was that if we weren't on patrol we couldn't be on our *last* one – all that carry-on.'

'You mean all that bollocks, Sub.'

Mike saw Ormrod looking lost again, and explained, 'Superstition about submarines' last patrols. One or two happen to have come to grief in the course of them, and – well, a particularly wretched loss was *Upholder* – David Wanklyn VC – end of April, early May. Circumstances unknown, but in fact it was very much a "last patrol", David's twenty-fifth.'

'This one now is your eighteenth, you said?'

He'd nodded. 'Which means we've done about enough. But David was a special sort of chap, highly successful and extremely modest, universally liked and admired, and – well, it stirred up all this cock-and-bull. Just superstition – and that phrase of course, *last patrol* . . .'

'I suppose if you'd had a terrific run of luck right up to that last one –'

Jarvis nodded to Ormrod: 'That'd cover us, all right. *Is* complete bollocks, I agree –'

Danvers put in, 'Someone was suggesting it might be better not to talk about "last patrols", which can have that implication, but "last patrol before going home" – which doesn't. My God, fruit salad now!'

'And custard . . .'

'Not for me, thanks. Think there's anything in that, sir?'

'No, Pilot, I don't. Eat your bloody custard.'

He woke with the feeling that he'd been reading Robert Graves' novel *I Claudius* fairly solidly since supper-time, while the night had been wearing on, *Ursa* grumbling northward with forty men in her and more than thirty of them flat out – including Ormrod on the bunk that was normally Danvers'. Jarvis having the watch at this time and McLeod making use of *his* bunk. In fact, Mike realised, must have conked out quite some while ago. He had the book still open in his hands, resting on his chest, had *begun* to read it after that meal, but in confused though recent memory there'd been a dream of Ann – which was startling, in its way. Although he *had* of course had her in mind from time to time since Ormrod's reminiscing. Reflecting briefly on that now while turning out, dressing for the bridge. Would have been getting a shake in about half an hour for the 0230 alteration eastward, and there'd have been no point just waiting for it. Being now awake, just as well go up for a breath of air and a check on the weather, then maybe a mug of kye and a cigarette.

Cigarette, to start with.

He felt sorry for Ann. Understood her – he *thought* – a lot better than he had until Ormrod had told him all that. The stuffy, money-conscious parents accepting Charles Melhuish as a husband for her because he had an abundance of it – as well as a certain status, of course – not a CO then, but a submarine officer with a medal or two – to *her*, maybe, a certain glamour, but along with that this other ingredient, the appeal of having what it took to get her away from home. Which Ormrod hadn't stood a chance of doing – and Mike Nicholson wouldn't have either, even if he'd felt so inclined, which he hadn't, *wouldn't* have . . . But Charles being noticeably keener on himself than on anyone else, for that and/or other reasons maybe not coming up to scratch – and she being the knockout she was as well as having her own predilections, being more than a little susceptible to expressions of interest and/or actual 'passes' such as were bound to come her way – and had from himself, he supposed, perhaps more blatantly than he'd realised . . . Well – nothing sensational or even original in any of that, but Ormrod's revelations had provided the answer to a question which from the start had baffled him – Charles having on the face of it much the same talents and/or qualities one aspired to oneself, and not being actually ugly, noticeably vicious or mentally deficient, on the other hand having the considerable advantage of being rich – how come she'd have put all that at risk?

Boots, Ursula jacket and hood, binoculars . . . A moment or two at the chart then before telling the helmsman – Nathaniel Sharp, SD – 'Going up', then on the ladder, climbing, hearing Sharp's call through the voice-pipe of 'Captain coming up, sir' and Jarvis's acknowledgement. Rush and roar of engine-air intake, yellowish glow below, brass rim of the hatch, night sky and stars.

'What's new, Sub?'

'Swell's quite nicely down, sir, and moon just starting.'

Moonglow like a thumb-smear on the horizon broad on the bow to port: prime danger-sector therefore abaft the starboard beam – which Jarvis and the lookouts would naturally be aware of. Mike propped himself in the starboard for'ard corner, put his glasses up and began sweeping from right ahead and down the side. The lookout on this side was Parker; on the port side Newcomb, who was mostly obscured from here by the bulk of the after periscope standard. Standards swaying like twin black pillars against sky and stars, and four pairs of high-powered glasses slowly and steadily sweeping, searching. Or say three and a half, Mike's eyes still adapting to the darkness, over sea with a silvery polish on it from the area of the moon's emergence, *Ursa*'s sword-like bow cleaving the dark ahead of her, the whiteness seething aft along her sides and through the casing, bursting and booming inside there, smashing against enclosing steel and the tower's base, churned into foam that spread out on the quarters and lost itself astern. Scent of diesel in the cool night air; *sense* of solitariness and purpose.

Menace, too.

Sweeping back again. Thinking, explain to Abbie what it's like – how it feels – or felt. Qualifying that with *Given the chance?*

He left the bridge before the change of watch, conferred briefly over the chart with Danvers and told him to alter course at half-past to 038 degrees, reducing at the same time, since one was slightly ahead of schedule, to revs for five knots instead of six. And to watch out like a hawk down-moon. Passero was, after all, likely to be a busy corner.

Over kye then he chatted with Chief McIver, finding even that generally dour character in high spirits at the prospect of early return to UK. This operation in his view was no more than a chore that had to be undertaken before they could make tracks for home.

'Old bus'll get us there all right, will she?'

'D'ye have reason to doubt it, sir?'

270

'Commander MacGregor reckons we're overdue for major refit. That's part of the reason they're getting shot of us.'

'Aye, well, I'd no' contest it. But if he said we was to put in another six months ye wouldn'a hear me scream blue murder neither.'

'That's a great comfort, Chief.'

He'd asked McLeod to wake him at 0400 when he was shaken for his watch, and confirmed that all things remaining equal he intended diving on the watch at about 0500. 'On the watch' because there was no point waking all their passengers, better to let the poor buggers sleep while they had the chance. Oh, and before diving there'd be a weather report going out to S.10. Lazenby had already enciphered the brief 'conditions OK' message that Mike had given him. Chancing one's arm on it certainly at this early stage, but what the hell. It would have to be revoked if conditions changed dramatically between now and float-off time, and the decision would in that event be his own, applying both to *Ursa* and *Unsung*. With the convoy on its way by now, as it had to be, it was certainly not a decision to be taken lightly. But then again, as regards this dive, if one had a completely clear sky – there'd still be a moon in it – one *might* opt to get under a little sooner. Didn't intend bothering with morning stars for a dawn fix; any inaccuracy in the 0500 estimated position would soon sort itself out, and there'd be fixes from periscope bearings of Capes Scalambri and Passero and with luck Pozzallo (if there was enough of it to be visible from sea-level) throughout the day, which barring surprises such as the appearance of anti-submarine vessels and/or snooping aircraft would be spent at approximately thirty feet and slow speed on one motor, surfacing well after dark in position Cape Scalambri 140 degrees 10 miles. At about eight-thirty or nine, that would be, followed by a period of very cautious,

271

trimmed-down approach to the float-off position, during which time the commandos would be getting their canoes up through the fore-hatch – as fast as it could be done, because to be at sea with that hatch open anywhere at all, let alone within spitting distance of an enemy coast and the shallows that fringed it, had elements in common with bloody nightmare.

McLeod asked him, 'Depths OK for us, sir, I take it? Where we float 'em off, I mean?'

Soundings weren't as clear as they might have been, the chart having had heavy use on previous occasions, old rubbed-out position-lines not helping much. Danvers should have replaced it – probably months ago – from the RN chart depot in Fort St Angelo. Might have tried and failed, in which case he should have reported the situation to Mike – who perhaps should have been keeping a closer eye on such matters. Nothing of the sort had occurred before, and he'd make damn sure it didn't again. Well – it wouldn't, of course; after this one you'd be using charts from entirely different folios. Edging over to give McLeod a closer view of this one, and pointing with a divider-tip: 'Might turn her so we're lying bow-to-sea. Other hand, might not. Either way that's in mini-mally sixty feet of water. OK for us, and gives them four thousand yards to paddle, which the Major describes as a piece of cake – would you believe it?'

He'd studied the chart again before turning in for perhaps another hour's repose, had it all in his mind by then, that stretch of coastline and the varying depths, some reasonably good notion of where shore lookout stations were likely to be, and possibly submerged detection apparatus such as had been encountered recently in other locations – in the vicinity of Cape Vaticano for instance, and a different variety on promontories on the Wop mainland from Cape Spartivento

272

northward towards Taranto – lights in pairs that were horizontal while in a searching mode but swung to the vertical when they caught you in some kind of direction-finding beam. If you held on as you were going it tended to be only a matter of minutes before an E-boat came tearing out along that beam – so you didn't, you dived, and before long heard the sods race overhead. Having to watch the eccentric behaviour of shore lights was a nuisance, of course, a distraction you didn't need.

As well to assume there were no such installations on this stretch, he thought. Be alert to the possibility but otherwise not waste time on it. And in respect of *submerged* D/F, one answer might be to bottom her, when you could, when you'd done the beach recces the commandos wanted, bottom and lie doggo, hoping the Wop hydrophone operators might decide you'd never been there in the first place.

That might be a good solution. If in daylight, bottoming in at least a hundred feet of water, deeper than a Cant can see. And warning the commandos, who'd be preparing their canoes and weapons during the afternoon and/or early evening, not to drop any tools or oil-cans, burst into song or even flush the heads, during that crucial time.

Time now, three-fifteen. Abbie fast asleep, he hoped. Tucked up in her iron-framed single bed which she'd said would feel like a double and lonely as hell without him in it. 'Thrashing around and wondering where you are and what you're up to.' He'd told her something like 'Chances are I'll be asleep as well. As I think I said, one does a lot of it, on patrol. Rest of the time I'll be thinking of you – when I'm not *dreaming* of you.'

'Mind on the job though, Mister? Ordinarily I'd hate it if you *didn't* think of me more or less exclusively and continuously, but –'

'Just don't worry about anything like that, my darling.

I'm sure I *will* be thinking of you a lot of the time, but that's for me to take care of, and I will. Seven days is really a very short period of time, you know? *Try* not to worry. I tell you, I'm so sure it won't be longer than a week that I've been thinking I should only have taken one of those Robert Graves books, not two. They're fairly substantial, aren't they.'

'They were Nico Cornish's, as it happens.'

'I know. His name's in them.'

'Oh. *Is* it. Well, when he was clearing his place out for the move to Gib he had stuff to get rid of and thought I'd like them. I haven't read either of them yet, but he said they're terrific.'

'I'll give you *my* view when I bring them back.'

'In a week or less.'

'Definitely. Read or unread.'

'He wasn't my lover, you know.'

'Well – I *didn't* know, but –'

'He wasn't, that's all.'

'All right. It never occurred to me that he might have been.'

'A lot of people thought he was. The Pembroke House set, as some of them call themselves. The fact of it is he was more like an elder brother.' She'd smiled. '*Uncle*, even. Highly entertaining, companionable, and – you know, *fun*, but –'

'I quite liked him too, the few times I met him.'

'Mike.' Clinging to him. Lips against his face. 'I love you. People say things like "you'll never know *how much* I love you", but that's balls, isn't it? – when it's *real* you either love someone or you don't – you know?'

Ursa was throwing herself around a bit but not enough he guessed to deter the commandos or make the launch anything like impossible. He looked in at the stuffy, hot-metal-smelling W/T office and told Lazenby to get that signal off to S.10

right away – 'Quick as you like, PO Tel, we'll be diving shortly' – and joined McLeod on the bridge a little before 0430. He'd dreamt of Abbie again but she was out of his mind now, she'd have been pleased with him. Or *would* she? Dawn's left hand was in the sky all right but there was cloud as well, a lot of the time hiding the moon at that, so there was no great hurry to get under. His eyes seemed to have been adjusting themselves quite rapidly to the darkness: had already made out a faint shine on the surface-lop to starboard, where a false dawn was threatening to become real but taking its time about it. There was no visible right-hand edge of land yet where Cape Passero had to be – which was what he was mainly looking for, expecting to get a sight of it at a range of as much as twenty miles, with dawn poking up not far behind it. Whereas the Pozzallo coastline, which would be more or less right ahead but lower and flatter, might even be enshrouded in dawn mist, mightn't show up even at half that distance.

'Bridge!'

McLeod had dipped to the pipe, and the helmsman told him, 'PO Tel reports message passed to S.10, sir.'

'Very good.' Straightening. The binocs not having left his eyes during this interruption. 'Your weather signal passed, sir.'

'Yes. Good.' His own glasses sweeping right to left across the bow, and starting down the port side. The weather really wasn't all that bad: and Shrimp might have been getting anxious, waiting to know whether or not his show was on the road. Quite a number of authorities in fact would be relieved at having that signal repeated to them – recipients ranging from C-in-C Med through Vice-Admiral Malta and the AOC – *and* the convoy's commodore and escort commander, no doubt. Surprising, when you thought about it, on the face of it such a *small* thing.

A grunt from McLeod: 'Scalambri, sir – red seven-oh!'

'Stop engines, port ten, slow ahead together, lookouts *down*!' Sudden and uncanny silence as the diesels cut out and she began to swing, responding to her helm, motors alone driving her now. He was on it too, the Cape Scalambri light-tower — not lit, of course, but suddenly not at all difficult to make out — and indicative of the fact *Ursa* was likely to have been approaching an area of shallow patches. Not in any danger surfaced, but as one was going to have to dive within minutes, on account of increasing light —

'Well sighted, Number One. Tell 'em steer two-four-oh.'

McLeod passed that down. The lookouts had gone like sacks of coal down a chute. Boat under helm: 240 degrees would steady her on a seaward track, clear of those shallows — *any* shallows. He'd heard the order acknowledged from below, told McLeod, 'Go on down, Jamie. Thirty feet, I'll dive her now.' Last quick look all round — moonless but lightening sea and McLeod as it were melting into the hatch; Mike called down 'Dive, dive, dive!' and as he shut the cock on the voice-pipe heard numbers one and two main vents crash open and the powerful escape of air. On the ladder then, pulling the lid down over his head, the boat by then submerging — submerged, by the time he'd engaged the first clip. Second one then, and a shout of 'Hatch shut and clipped!' Clomping on down — not in any rush now, hearing McLeod tell his Red watch 'planesmen, 'Thirty feet', and Danvers' surprising comment, 'Almost in bloody Sicily.'

17

By mid-forenoon they'd done all the reconnaissance that Ormrod had wanted, using the small-calibre 'attack' periscope from about three miles out, switching to the big one with its fourfold magnification when a closer look was wanted. Mike hadn't refused any such request, but he'd been making sure that neither 'scope was overused. There was a breeze down-coast from the northwest, frisking-up the surface, and he hadn't been greatly worried about aircraft; in fact the first one they'd seen was this Cant limping to and fro ahead of an armed trawler and two landing-craft which had come into sight from behind Cape Passero and turned west, were steering to pass to seaward of them, making he guessed for Pantellaria. They'd spotted the Cant – Danvers had – half an hour before the little convoy it was escorting.

'Not exactly crowding us.'

'Wouldn't seem to be, sir.'

'Except the Cant might drift a bit close.' He dipped the periscope, gave the situation a few moments' thought. Then, 'Forty feet, Number One.' McLeod had taken over the watch from Danvers, and Mike had been discussing Ormrod's suggestion that having some hours to spare they might give each of his team a good sight of the landing beach – using the big periscope and from fairly close in. It would mean accepting the kind of risk he'd sworn to avoid, but seemed only fair to the canoeists, before asking them to paddle 4,000 yards to that beach in pitch darkness. Even if there was still a clear sky by then, there'd be no moon at ten p.m. As things stood otherwise, they'd have a course to steer and their individual compasses with luminous dials – which didn't amount to much, especially in a sea-state that was a long way from flat calm and might worsen before float-off time. He rejoined Ormrod in the wardroom, where they'd been talking about it over mugs of tea and he'd drunk only half of his own; 'All right, let's get on with it. Sneak in there while we have the time *and* the inclination.'

'Good thinking, skipper.'

'Well – paddling two sea-miles in the dark to a beach you've never set eyes on – crikey . . .'

'How we earn our living.' He glanced around, added more quietly, 'Tell you, though, I'm glad I drew this billet and not young Flood's.' Mike stared at him, realising he was talking about *Unsung* – or rather Melhuish. Which was improper but in fact inconsequential, as he was the only one there to have heard it – Jarvis being asleep, Danvers still fiddling at the chart table, and McLeod with the trim to watch, in the low hum of the motors . . . Well, of *one* motor . . . He shook his head: 'Not entirely with you there. But let's say giving each man ten seconds? Have the 'scope ready trained on your beach, he gets his shufti, then down periscope for two minutes while that chap goes back for'ard and the next comes aft – trim's not endangered, periscope's not over-exposed, and the whole process'll take about – oh, fifteen minutes. All right?'

'Very much so. I'll have a word with Gant.'

'Approx one hour's time. It'll take that long getting in there.'

The commandos – Colour-Sergeant Gant, Corporals Thomas and Carlyle, and Marines Newton, Block, Denneker and Larkin – had had their privileged scan of the beach before Cottenham served up lunch. *Ursa* then retiring seaward still at slow speed on one motor, depth thirty feet and course 175, almost but not quite the reciprocal of the track on which she'd be nosing back on in about eleven hours' time. The landing-craft convoy had gone on its way, and the sky was empty. After lunching on sausages, tomatoes and packaged cheese Mike got on to his bunk with the intention of reading *I Claudius*, but in fact thinking about Abbie – primarily that she and Nico Cornish had not been lovers.

Partly because he didn't want them to have been. And/or his instincts told him they hadn't. Not just instincts – *judgement*. Their own situation was entirely different, practically and emotionally unique: he *knew* it. There'd been no artifice or self-consciousness in her denial of the Pembroke House set's beliefs; she'd raised the subject calmly, matter-of-factly, a plain statement of fact which she'd had no reason to doubt he'd accept.

'Captain in the control room!'

Mike's well-practised bunk-to-control-room high-speed transition in response to OOW's (McLeod's) alarm call; time just gone five, search periscope hissing down agleam with grease and salt water, thudding to a stop and Ellery bringing it purring up again as McLeod reported, 'Several Mas-boats green six-five course east, sir. Our course one-eight-oh – as they're going now they'll pass astern, inshore of us. Doing about twenty knots.'

'All right.'

Twenty knots indicating (a) they were in a hurry, for some reason, and (b) were not using asdics or other listening gear, at that speed, therefore weren't hunting. And judging by that course, might well be coming from Licata, which was one of their favourite haunts, about ten miles west of Gela. Might even, exercising one's imagination, en route have come slap over the top of *Unsung*. Periscope's top lens breaking out in a blue-green dazzle giving place to a blueish lop streaked with white and – training left now – *four* of them – in rough quarterline, course easterly, and – yes, twenty knots was about right, they *would* pass astern. Light beginning to fade a little, incidentally, a pinkish tinge developing. He folded the handles up, stepping back, Ellery sent the brass tube gliding down into its well and Mike told McLeod after a glance at the nearer depth-gauge, 'Forty feet.'

'Forty feet, sir.'

Hydroplanes tilting to put down-angle on her. Swathely on after 'planes, Walburton on the for'ard ones, Knox on asdics raising a finger suddenly – 'Comin' over, sir.' Audible then to everyone within about a minute – screws not exactly 'coming over', more like belting across perhaps a cable's length astern, the note rising towards a scream then peaking and the volume too beginning at once to fade. Swathely growling to himself, 'Easy come, easy go.'

'Depth forty feet, sir.'

A matter of killing time and keeping track now – several hours of both, to culminate in *Ursa* surfacing in about four hours' time ten miles southeast of Cape Scalambri. That was if he followed the orders which he himself had originated but which had subsequently been revised by Broadbent the SOO at Shrimp's behest, had left one now with *too much* time to kill. He asked Knox, 'Hearing them still?'

'Faint, sir. On one hundred, one-oh-three –'

'All right.' He told McLeod to bring her back up to

280

thirty feet; then gestured for the big periscope again, swept sky and horizon before taking bearings of the Scalambri light-tower, right-hand edge of Cape Passero and smoke rising from Pozzallo. He sent the 'scope down, and the fix when charted was good enough to believe in, only three-quarters of a mile from the DR. So – work on this . . . Aligning the parallel rule between this position to the one ten miles southeast of Scalambri, which he'd marked on earlier in the day, he found the course to it would be 348 degrees, distance 3.9 miles, which at the current rate of progress – one knot – would take as near as dammit four hours. Might have been pretty good if the light could have been expected to last that long – which of course it couldn't.

'Bring her to three-four-eight, Number One.'

'Three-four-eight, sir.' To Smithers, helmsman: 'Starboard ten.'

'Starboard ten, sir.' Brass spokes flashing. Smithers of course chewing gum. 'Ten o' starboard wheel on, sir.'

'See here, Jamie.' Touching the chart. 'Position now. Won't get a new fix for another couple of hours – at the outside – so –'

McLeod cut in hurriedly to Smithers: 'Midships, and steer three-four-eight. Sorry, sir –'

'Need to float 'em off at or by 2200. And calling the safe limit for fixes – well, hour and a half, say – seven o'clock'd be the time to get here – *here* – and bottom. Otherwise could end up flying blind. Come up to slow on both motors now.'

They were in position, or within a few yards of it, by 1900. The failing light had only permitted a fix, using two of those points of reference, shortly after Jarvis had taken over the watch at 1815, hadn't been good enough for any of those rather long-distance bearings twenty minutes later; Mike had allowed her to run on until just before the hour, when the log showed she'd covered the required distance, then sent the crew to diving stations and stopped one motor, used the other only in short bursts while settling her on the bottom in what he'd expected to be about ninety feet but turned out to be a hundred and fourteen. Having bottomed, he anchored her to the sand by flooding 'Q'.

Seven-twenty now. As good a time as any for supper. He asked McLeod, 'Which watch was it?'

'White, sir.'

'White . . . Well, hang on. Major Ormrod, spare me a minute?'

Ormrod came from the wardroom: 'Stuck in the mud, are we?'

'Sand bottom, hereabouts. If supper can be laid on for about eight, Major, how'd that be for your crowd?'

'Excuse me, sir.' At diving stations as they were now, Cottenham the cook was Spare Hand in the control room and currently stationed on motor-room telegraphs. Mike looked at him, and he said, 'Beg pardon, sir, but if you wanted I could dish up in ten minutes.'

'Could you, indeed.' Back to Ormrod. 'Same question, but –'

'Gear's on the top line, ditto canoes. A bit of personal tarting-up's about all they'd need – face-blacking, so forth. In fact if you wanted to get rid of us sooner –'

'Suit you, would it?'

'Make it nine instead of ten if you like. From our point of view, yes, be just the job. For instance, an hour in hand for getting the boats really well cached, find or build a good one. If it suits *you*, skipper –'

'You're on. Float-off at 2100. Supper at –' a glance at the clock – 'seven forty-five. Blue watch sooner if that's possible, Cottenham. What are you giving us that's so quick?'

'The rest o' that tongue, sir, and spuds I boiled last night, need ten minutes to hot up like.'

282

McLeod had the Tannoy microphone in his hand, clicked it on. 'White watch, watch diving. Blue watch to the galley in ten minutes, diving stations at eight.'

After the meal Mike went for'ard with Ormrod to say goodbye to the troops and out of curiosity see their equipment. Four canoes on the deck now, middled between the torpedo-reload racks and crammed with gear ranging from paddles and bailers to tommy-guns, food, drink, medical stores including Benzedrine, bombs of different kinds, grenades, fighting-knives with nine-inch blades, entrenching tools, hand-guns according to individual choice – Ormrod's choice for instance being a long-barrelled, silenced .22 pistol.

Mike asked him, 'What, no cheese-wire?', and he nodded towards Colour-Sergeant Gant: '*His* speciality.' A shrug: 'Funny, everyone asks about cheese-wire.'

'A leatherneck speciality, might say?'

Gant smiled politely. Leatherneck being slang for a Royal Marine, and cheese-wire in this context coming in a noose with wooden handles that was primarily for silent assaults on sentries. Used skilfully, it amounted to beheading. Gant had a pleasant smile, and looked young for his rank. Shrugging: 'Bit of a knack to it, sir, really.'

Ormrod agreed: 'Certainly is.' He was buckling a waterproof luminous compass to his left forearm. He hadn't blackened his face yet or donned the dark-wool hat he'd shown them earlier, remarking 'Absolute *must* for Ascot, this.' They were dressed as they pleased, looking mostly like farm workers or mechanics, nothing like members of any armed force. Mike shook hands with them all and wished them luck, told them he'd see them on Tuesday; and they were joined at about this stage by the TI, Coltart, who'd be running things in this compartment when it came to removing the strong-back from the hatch then getting it open and the boats out – up the ladder and

283

out on to the casing, where Jarvis with Tubby Hart and a few others would be waiting to assist as necessary.

'All right, TI?'

A grin, and a mocking look at Gant: '*I'm* all right, sir . . .'

Ormrod muttered as they went for'ard, 'Good fellow, that.'

'Torpedo Gunner's Mate, CPO. He was a boxer – fought for the Navy's Portsmouth Division a year or two pre-war. More importantly, knows what he's doing and keeps on doing it.'

Ormrod had stopped, in the gangway opposite the POs' and Leading Seamen's mess, where for the moment they were on their own. Speaking quietly – on the seabed with no machinery running it was *extremely* quiet – 'One thing, skipper . . .'

'Uh?'

'If when you're home you happen to run into that girl – as you might, uh?'

'Not impossible, I suppose. Not likely either, but –'

'Give her my love?'

'Well . . .'

'Just that, nothing else.' He started forward again – between the galley and the heads now, still no one noticeably in earshot – only Cottenham the master chef whistling between his teeth while dishing up, potatoes steaming in pans . . . Ormrod continuing, '*Should* you happen to run into her, Mike –'

'I'd give her your love – in the unlikely event, et cetera – but no passing of messages either way.'

'No, wouldn't ask you to. How did you happen to meet her, though? I wouldn't have thought you and Melhuish were the closest of chums?'

'I met them both in London at another submariner's wedding, as it happens. But now listen – I wish you all the luck that's going.' He put his hand out. 'We'll be saying prayers. Just bloody well *be* here on Tuesday – uh?'

She'd lifted off the sand a few minutes before nine p.m. and McLeod stopped her with fifty feet on the gauges while Harris the HSD listened-out carefully all round and confirmed no HE, no foreign body hanging around to make a nuisance of itself. Before they'd blown 'Q' and then some main ballast he'd reported he wasn't getting anything, but on the bottom she'd been lying with her snout in sand and weed, and the asdic dome was in her forefoot, the leading edge of her keel; he'd had to make sure of it. He told McLeod now, 'Surface!', waited for Walburton to open the lower lid for him, climbed into the tower.

McLeod's reports from below him, then: 'Twenty feet – fifteen': he had the first clip off the upper lid at the count of twelve, and the second at ten, the signalman's weight latched on to him and holding him down by the final shout of 'Eight!', and with the aid of the internal pressure had the hatch open and slamming back, himself up and out, arriving solidly in the front of the bridge: voice-pipe open, and yelling into it 'Group up, half ahead, steer north', then 'Up casing party and folboats.' *Ursa* pitching a bit as well as rolling, in the white pool of her emergence, but the canoeists were ready for that, twenty-four hours ago had been expecting worse. He was sweeping all round with binoculars – Walburton too, and stars well in evidence, which would help the casing party as well as canoeists – casing party now in the still streaming bridge behind him, Jarvis asking 'Go on down, sir?'

'Yes, please.' Jarvis, Hart, Brooks and Barnaby, over the star-board side there, down the outside of the tower, necessarily quick and sure-footed in not *quite* total darkness getting around it and for'ard past the gun, piling into the break in the casing that gave access to the hatch; Jarvis's rap on it with a wheel-spanner would have told the torpedomen and troops inside that they and the boats were awaited topsides.

'Hatch is open, sir!'

Walburton, sounding surprised. Well, it *had* been quick, well synchronised. Mike too had caught the splash of yellow light, and now a radiance partially obstructed by bodies getting the canoes and in eight cases themselves out on to what was effectively a mobile steel platform with free-flood holes in it, holes that would be serving as hand-holds as well as securing-points for ropes' ends that would really come into their own when the folboats were in position and manned. In a few seconds, that should be: one pair of them well forward of the hatch, between the hydroplane guards – invaluable at this juncture – and the other pair abaft them, less easy to hold in place – and movement around the hatch again – two of the casing party having slid into it, leaving only Jarvis and Hart *out*side, slamming it shut, extinguishing the yellow glow, a howl from Jarvis of 'Fore-hatch shut!', the pair of them then pounding aft. Mike told Walburton, 'Down you go', and called into the pipe, 'Stop both motors.'

'Stop both, sir. Both motors stopped.' Jarvis and Hart were back in the bridge, panting like dogs. 'Fore-hatch shut, sir, canoes ready to float off.'

'Well done. Go on down.' Into the pipe again then, 'Open number two inboard vent.'

Main ballast tanks other than numbers one and six didn't have outboard vents, you could *only* vent them inboard. With this conning-tower hatch open you weren't building up any internal pressure, and you could stop the venting and flooding process as you wanted – flooding number two now sufficiently to weigh her forepart down, drowning the fore casing and allowing the boats to float off. Calling down 'Shut number two main vent' and watching them drift away, until they were well enough clear of one another to use their paddles.

286

18

Tuesday now, Dog plus 2 as it had been, time 0120, McLeod in the course of being relieved as OOW by Jarvis, Mike down for a break after spending recent hours up top. Crucial stage approaching, *Ursa* on her way inshore to make the 0300–0400 rendezvous. Please God. She was banging around a bit, wind north-by-west, on the bow and making it damp on the bridge; he was hoping there'd be some degree of shelter further in, enabling one to embark the men at least, though probably not the boats. *If* the men had made it to this point: the double uncertainty was what was making one bloody sweat. He'd been on the bridge most of the time since they'd surfaced, would be up there again before much longer, was meanwhile taking this break at the wardroom table with a mug of kye that had been organised for him by the PO Stoker, 'Caruso' Franklyn, who for some reason was standing in for Hec Bull as PO of this watch.

McLeod came down: pausing in the control room to accept an offer of kye from Franklyn, who sent Newcomb to the galley for it. Mike heard McLeod agreeing with something Franklyn had said: McLeod's response being 'Yes, Spo.

Bloody hell, yes.' Responding to something like 'Hope to God the poor sods've made it, sir', no doubt. The same hope or fear having been expressed at least a hundred times a day since the float-off. McLeod came on through then, shedding a wet Ursula suit and looking for a cigarette, remarking as he accepted one of Mike's, 'Been a hell of a long three days, sir.'

'Tiring, rather.' He yawned. 'Anxiety neurosis, could be.'

Actually three and a bit days, not three, since he'd watched the canoeists with their circling paddles getting clear of *Ursa*, then turned her seaward and restored her to a normal trim while putting another mile between her and the beach – on her motors still, to keep her departure as quiet as her arrival had been. He'd had to wait longer than he'd expected for the blue-flash signal confirming they were ashore, but it came all right; he'd started the generators and altered to southeast, with Cape Passero thirty on the bow and revs to push her along at five knots as well as bring the box up.

Then, what one could think of as three days not entirely wasted. They'd snooped along this stretch for instance for fishing-boats, and found none where it would matter. Between Pozzallo and Passero had been the greatest regular concentration, day *and* night. But that first night he'd got a signal off to Shrimp confirming that the Comiso team had landed, and Sunday forenoon in the control room as well as offering up the customary naval prayers he'd asked God to protect the commandos, further their endeavours and bring them safe home again. The 'Amens' had been fiercely insistent, and every man not on watch had been present, creating trimming problems for McLeod – whose watch it had been anyway – and Mike was asked several times during the rest of the day whether *he* reckoned the commandos stood any real chance of making it back. He couldn't say more than that Ormrod had been quietly confident, and that they were highly trained and experienced in the work they were doing; they truly had given the impression that for them it was nothing out of the ordinary. In the boat generally though, there'd still been a lot of speculation and anxiety; most exchanges were on that subject, and *still* were. Just about everyone was on tenterhooks. Which was unusual. Submariners had never been worriers by nature. They were saddened when another boat was lost, often desperately so, but they didn't anticipate calamity, shorten the odds before they had to. If you'd been inclined to you'd have been scared on your own account, consequently not much use. Which was not to say that being depth-charged for instance didn't scare you. It did – anyone half normal. When it was really close and sustained it scared you rigid, and you knew better than to show it because – well, you *didn't*. Which was infectious, no one did, you could say it 'wasn't done'. You made jokes, if you could. He felt sure Ormrod would have made jokes.

McLeod, who'd been on a visit to the heads, sat down at the table across from him and reached for his kye. 'Not going to be easy getting 'em on board, sir.'

'*Them*, we'll manage. Not the canoes.'

'Not going to try?'

'No. One, bloody difficult if not impossible; two, time-wasting; and on that score the sooner we get off this coast the better.' He thought of adding, 'Besides which it's our last patrol, remember?' Didn't, because everyone knew he didn't believe in any of that stuff.

Coming up for 0300. In the bridge, he and Walburton concentrating on forward bearings, the smeary-dark vagueness of land from which at any moment one might –

Might?

They'd both seen it, fast blue pin-pricks from two miles

away in the scrambled grey-and-whitishness of the shoreline; a commando would have scythed the seascape with his lamp, *his* horizontal mark or guide the wave-tops. Mike had called out '*There we go!*', heard Walburton's simultaneous reaction as a squawk of 'Blue light-flashes – something or other' and was surprised at the levelness of what had been his own tone, considering the importance of the moment. They'd had a shot at stirring things up about a minute and a half ago, the signalman pivoting his own blue-lensed lamp in a sweep of the surf-line, not exactly counting on the lads being there ahead of time and keeping their heads down until given some such encouragement, but *hoping* for it – and lo and behold, even if they'd taken their time about it . . . Mike telling Walburton to switch on again and hold it on that bearing – poor sod already doing so, hadn't needed telling – and stopping both motors, putting the starboard one astern, to help her round then hold her more or less *in situ*; and now displacing Danvers at the voice-pipe, telling McLeod 'Casing party stand by in the control room. Bare feet, Mae Wests and heaving lines. Cox'n stand by for casualties. Blankets, food, tea – in half an hour, twenty minutes.'

Guesswork – distance two sea-miles, canoes surely with nothing like the amount of weight they'd had in them three days ago. Most likely only the weight of the men themselves – and these were skilled swimmer-canoeists, incidentally with the wind behind them. And the double flash again now, Ormrod telling him *Here we come* – meaning they'd be carrying their canoes down over beach, rocks and surf into clearish water where they'd saddle-up and start paddling . . . Mike mentally acknowledging *Quick as you like, and eight of you, please, preferably all in good shape.* And to Danvers, loudly, 'Stop starboard, slow ahead port, starboard ten' and then 'Midships', and the course to steer . . . Once in the canoes and paddling the commandos had this light to steer on, so by holding her

290

as she lay now, counting on the one motor being enough to hold her against the wind, and the lamp high enough to be visible at that distance – but not much further, and strictly on target, so as not to attract enemy attention from any wider area – this light twenty-five feet above sea-level reaching canoeists' eyes at a height of about eighteen inches . . .

Anyway, and thank God, the canoes were in sight with the aid of binoculars after less than thirty minutes, and to the naked eye not all that much later. Paddles had to be going like hell – driving them as he'd now realised slightly *across* the wind: *Ursa* of course bow-on – her shoulder to it as it were, and her 600 tons by no means static. Jarvis, Hart, Leading Torpedoman Brooks and Torpedoman/wardroom flunkey Barnaby, in wet-weather gear and equipped with coiled hemp heaving-lines, crowded into the centre of the bridge between Mike and Danvers in the curve of its forepart and the lookouts abaft them – and no point their going down on the casing until the canoes were in reach of their lines or nearly so.

Three canoes. Two canoeists in each of them, all right, but –

Needing only three?

'Sir –'Walburton at close range in his ear:'Only six blokes, sir!'

Jarvis then: 'Christ – three canoes, Second, not four.' Addressing Hart as 'Second', normal abbreviation of 'Second Coxswain'. Hart responding with a growl of 'Bloody hell . . .'

'All right we go down, sir?'

'Yes, go on.'

Barefooted, as the best way of *staying* on – of staying on *board*, in fact. More than enough men had drowned off casings in foul weather. The two front-running canoes weren't far out of line-throwing range now, even against the wind. Walburton perched up in the bridge's forefront with his

Aldis, shifting its beam between the three wildly tossing boats, the beam's silvery fallout also illuminating the scene as a whole – at this moment a line arcing blackly through it to fall just short of the nearest – and Mike yelling through a megaphone, 'Leave the canoes adrift! Only yourselves! Not embarking canoes!' One boat had already secured a line and was being hauled in, the second just this moment catching its own, bowman snatching a turn on a towing-cleat. First one though – might have been the leader, the one they'd missed with that first line – soaring bow-up almost to the vertical and turning on the swell, smashing down then beam-on and bomb-like against *Ursa*'s side, its crew spilling out or *had* spilled out but still mixed up with it, crabbing and floundering at the casing's edge then actually – miraculously – on board, and moments later helping – Barnaby, it looked like – sending their own or another canoe's wreckage on its way – over the port side, gone. Elsewhere, casing party and canoeists fighting their way aft – not by a long chalk easy . . . One in particular – canoeist – who'd collapsed on the casing after being hauled on board, but then by the look of it made this solo effort, then slumped again, been saved from washing on over by Brooks and another hand lifting him like a corpse. By no means anything like easy, with this much movement on her: for one man, would have been impossible, you'd have gone over with him. In fact surprising he hadn't: that *they* hadn't. Out of sight now anyway, close below the forefront of the bridge. The gun would be a useful staging-point – for a moment or two's pause hanging on to it while grabbing a breath, and/or a wave crashed over, then a quick dash and scramble to the tower with its iron rail around it.

Six were as many as you were getting. Two absentees – casualties – out of eight. Could have been worse maybe – *had* been, on previous occasions – but –

Hadn't seen or heard Ormrod yet. And – he'd been aware of this for a minute or two – one *would* have, surely.

'Cor strike a fuckin' light!'

'Who's there?'

'Beg pardon – sir. Marine Block, I –'

'Better get below, Block. Hatch *there* – see?'

'– across my shoulders, right? Brooks – here . . .' Voice of Jarvis, at the base of the tower or on the rungs, talking not about Block but that casualty. Others heaving into sight and sound – including Hart in his immensity looming amongst them, but *this* was –

'Captain, sir?'

'Yes, Sergeant –'

'Colour-Sergeant Gant reporting with five men, sir. Major Ormrod's dead. So's Marine Denneker. Report later, sir, may I?'

'Yes. Go on down. I'm *bloody* sorry, Sergeant.'

'Yessir.' He'd saluted in the noisy dark, moved to help with the man or body Jarvis was getting in over the side of the bridge, might have a job manoeuvring down through the tower. All extremely lively. Mike hadn't asked how it had gone at Comiso: *would* have asked Ormrod, but Gant's 'Report later' would substitute for that. Meanwhile, for Christ's sake, Ormrod *dead*. And one other. He told Danvers, 'Start engines, half ahead together. Port twenty, steer – what was it, one-seven-five?'

175 degrees it was. Setting out on the one-night return trip with approximately twelve miles between oneself and *Unsung*, and she according to the orders steering 185: about twelve miles between them, plus the ten-degree rate of further separation. Good enough if Melhuish had recovered his commandos and was pushing it along. The importance of *Unsung* completing her pickup on schedule was that if for

293

instance that team didn't make it until say 0400, with moon-rise about 0430 and sunrise half an hour after, there wouldn't be a lot of time to spare, and you could bet there *would* be A/S forces off this coast tonight. He left Danvers with the watch, and went on down. Blue watch on now, Tubby Hart again in charge in the control room. Mike told him, 'You and your party did a needle job up there, Second.'

'Turned out all right, sir, didn't it. An' seems they done that airfield a fair treat!'

'Is that so?'

'What they're saying, sir.'

'Well, *is* it.' He went on through to the wardroom, thinking about the signal he had to send Shrimp now, and wondering whether the convoy had got through, or was getting through. According to Lazenby there'd been surprisingly little signal traffic. He asked McLeod, 'What about the damaged one?'

'Nasty-looking head-wound. Bullet or shrapnel, Cox'n isn't sure, but he must have done himself further damage on the casing. He was mobile, apparently, didn't want them carrying him.'

'But *paddling*?'

'I know, sir. Amazing. Marine Newton. Cox'n's got him in the POs' mess. Gant's there too, sir.'

'Right.' Looking at Jarvis, who was smoking on his bunk. 'You all right, Sub?'

'Right as rain, sir, except for a few bruises.'

'You did a good job.'

'Thank you, sir. Damn shame, the Major –'

'Yes.' He went for'ard, to the Leading Hands' and POs' mess, which had been evacuated by its usual inhabitants. Marine Newton was unconscious on the after thwartships bunk with his head parcelled in bandages, not much face visible, and a blanket over him; Cox'n in attendance, also Colour-Sergeant Gant and the two corporals.

'Been able to do anything for him, Cox'n?'

There was a general shifting around, letting him in from the gangway. Swathely, who as cox'n was keeper of the boat's medical stores and had done a course of doctoring, was saying, 'Did like for other wounds – cleaned it, then this new stuff. But I don't know . . . Be in about sunset, will we, sir?'

'Better than that – afternoon or first dog, I hope. Battery's low, unfortunately. I'll ask for an ambulance to meet us. I've a signal to make to S.10 before we dive – and that's something else, Gant, they'll be wanting to know how it went at Comiso – short answer, success or failure?'

'As near success as in your right mind you'd hope for, sir. Except for losing the Major.'

'Was he shot, or –'

'Yeah.' A nod. 'He –'

'But hold on – aircraft destroyed – rough idea how many, what kind?'

'Better 'n we ever done, sir. 88s, mostly – couple o' dozen, could be – 87s too. Maybe a third of what there was – and a field generator blown up – the Major done that right at the start, put the lights out for us. Then a fuel store – my aunt, *didn't* it go up!'

'Object of the operation achieved, might say?'

'Could say we wrecked the field, sir.'

'What I will say, then. Congratulations!'

Although no one seemed to be smiling much. On account of Ormrod, he supposed. Gant adding at that moment, 'Fact is, sir, it was Major Ormrod's plan, start to finish, he'd worked it up to really something. It and *us*, to put it square and honest.'

'Well – he'd have been proud of you, too. Tell me though – the disengagement, early hours Monday – did the RAF come up to scratch?'

'We had 'em dropping shit on us an hour or more.

295

Good old ruckus, and they timed it right. Yeah, took the pressure off of us, like he'd wanted.'

'We didn't hear any going over, but they were taking a roundabout route, weren't they – so one didn't know. He'd have been glad that came off.' To Swathely – change of subject – 'Breakfast after we've dived, Cox'n – all right?'

'Good and ready for it by then, sir, speaking personal.' A glance down at his patient. 'Be comfier for this lad once we're under.' A nod to Gant: 'Heads down until lunch then, eh?'

Mike went back aft, looking forward to getting his own down before long. After breakfast, yes – go deep, sleep like a dog, with any luck dream of Abbie . . . In the wardroom, McLeod had fallen asleep over his thriller and Jarvis was flat out, snarling rhythmically. Mike sat down with a signal-pad and pencil to note down items to be conveyed to Shrimp by W/T. *Ursa's* diving position at five, and her ETA Malta – before sunset anyway. Comiso airfield reported wrecked, fuel store and numerous Ju 87s and 88s destroyed. Major Ormrod and Marine Denneker killed, remainder on board including Marine Newton unconscious with head wound, hospitalisation urgent on arrival.

That would about do it, he thought. Abbie would be happy too – he'd promised her no longer than a week, and it would have been five days. In fact he'd told her a week thinking that with luck they'd do it in five days, but in the knowledge that if Ormrod and his team didn't make the first RV there'd have been another in the same place twenty-four hours later; and the seven-day forecast would have covered that.

It was pretty good, in fact, to be on the way back to her, having concluded this business that had had to be seen to first, and which incidentally *had* been his last patrol – he was clear of all that now – that was it, clear of just about everything except Abbie and the way he and she felt about each other.

Goofing at his notes, realising it wasn't a feeling he'd had before.

'Uh?'

'Sorry, sir – clumsy – woke you –'

'Wasn't actually asleep. Putting this together for Shrimp. Our ETA plus glad tidings of Comiso.'

'The buzz was right then, sir, they made a job of it?'

'Did indeed. Except for losing Ormrod. Successful action attributed incidentally by Colour-Sergeant Gant entirely to his – Ormrod's – planning and leadership.'

'Decent of him.'

'Yes. Epitaph, might say.'

Abbie was still in his head, though. Get back to her in a minute, with luck. He'd heard McLeod say he only hoped it had gone well for the convoy, adding after a moment, 'Might get in half an hour's bunk-time before my watch.'

'Good idea. Shake me before you go up.'

He'd been sound asleep but the dream had been of Ann. He didn't remember much about it except that she'd been making plans for his return, which he'd found exciting, and now of course embarrassing. Well – *dreams* . . . He turned out immediately for fear of dropping off again: time now 0415, moonrise 0435 – whether or not cloud-cover let any of it through – and anyway he was going to dive on the watch at 0500. On the watch again in preference to sending the hands to diving stations or breaking eardrums with the klaxon when those poor bastards were getting their first sleep in four days. Which sounded impossible – he guessed they'd surely have cat-napped in their hide. Also they'd had Benzedrine. Although actually, he thought, it was *astonishing* what they'd achieved and come out of – most of them . . .

Three-quarters dark in the wardroom now, with the gangway curtain drawn and no white lights, only one red bulb in the lamp above the table, for the sake of one's night vision. Which admittedly he'd be setting back now by visiting

297

the wireless office – where Telegraphist Martin, the younger of Lazenby's two operators, confirmed that the signal to S.10 had been acknowledged. Less good was that nothing had come in. He'd hoped Shrimp might have had news to give him of the convoy, and that Melhuish, to whom he'd repeated his own signal (as well as to Vice-Admiral Malta, Commander-in-Chief Mediterranean, and Admiralty) might have come up with something. Such as where he was, *his* damned ETA – even how Flood's commandos had done at Gela. But with not a peep out of her, one could only assume that he was where he was supposed to be – twelve-plus miles west or west-northwest, and like *Ursa* diving before first light.

Sooner, maybe. Might not stay up and risk the moon. The battery was lower than one would have liked it to be at the start of a day's dive; but then, another half-hour's charging wouldn't make much difference. With the urgency of getting Marine Newton into hospital and surgeons' hands he'd have *liked* to have been able to go deep and crack on at something like full speed – which of course was out of the question; even four or five knots might bleed her dry.

Danvers, down from the bridge, said there was no hint of moon yet. Fair amount of cloud. He thought at a pinch it might be OK to stay up until five-fifteen or even the half-hour.

'Won't be pinching anything, Pilot. These chaps have wrecked an airfield, Wops must know they'll have come in by submarine and survivors picked up by now. Whatever anti-submarine forces they have handy they'd have been daft *not* to have deployed in this direction.'

'Take your point, sir. Just fold the old tent and silently creep away.'

'That's the obvious thing. Accent on "silently".' He'd been on his way up to the bridge, but didn't stay up there long; the darkness didn't look or feel long-lasting, after five.

298

He made a last binocular-sweep all round, said to McLeod 'Let's get out of this', and came on down, leaving him to dive her. Time then 0509. Breakfast followed, consisting of Manoel Island ham and powdered egg on toast, with double rations for passengers; *Ursa* steady as a rock at forty feet with both motors at half-ahead grouped down, the log recording speed-through-the-water of four and a half knots – which he decided he'd now increase to five, and if the battery looked like giving up the ghost he'd surface with all due precautions wherever they happened to be, go over to generator power – nine knots, or near it – and radio for air and/or surface escort. With the island's air-defence situation pretty much in hand these days, they'd surely spare a sweeper and maybe a couple of Spits to get a man into hospital who might die if they didn't, might *not* if they did. He'd called McLeod through from the control room to explain this to him, and they were discussing it when the first depth-charge erupted.

First of a pattern of five. Some distance off, but not all *that* far. Starboard bow, somewhere. Mike had said with his mouth full, 'Those weren't intended for us', and McLeod said on his way back into the control room, '*Unsung* getting it in the neck, no doubt.'

All it could be; but it would mean she was a good few miles off-station. Mike was on his feet, following more slowly, entering the control room as the last of the batch exploded – standard pattern from Wop destroyers being either five or nine, and that had been the fifth, all right: one waited for more but for the time being that seemed to be it. Fraser the HSD having come to the same conclusion sliding the asdic headset back over his ears and yellowish head, and after a minute or so searching around telling Mike, 'HE between two hundred and two-three-oh degrees, sir. Destroyer HE, fair way off . . .'

19

Still at watch diving and for the moment staying there, despite an instinct to go to diving stations. With, after all, some Wop A/S vessel or vessels sowing the waters with bloody dynamite. Maybe a fair way off but going by the sound of it close enough to one's route as planned – if one stuck to that route, staying deep or deepish and – OK, diverting around the problem area but then getting back on to the southerly track, and for obvious reasons making no larger a diversion than was essential – reasons including the state of the box.

Fraser said, 'HE moving right to left, sir, bearing one-nine-seven, one-nine-six, range 3250 yards. Second lot – geared turbines too but lower revs and bearing nearer two-one-oh, sir . . .'

Picture filling out, but not usefully. In general terms, bearings around 200 degrees and distance one and a half miles. Confusing, though, no clear pattern to their movements. And no transmissions. Just listening, presumably; start again when they picked up *Unsung*'s HE. He told McLeod, 'Slow both motors.' Giving the order time to reach the motor room and be acted on, begin to take effect. Thinking about *Unsung* being bloody miles from where she should have been and that however much trouble she might be in, his own primary responsibility was to keep *Ursa* clear of her and it. Despite having some natural interest in *what* one would be steering clear of.

'Thirty feet, Number One. Easy does it.'

Meaning for Christ's sake let's not rush it, risk any loss of control – breaking surface, showing periscope or standards a Cant might happen to spot, maybe lose sight of in the next second but still *have* spotted, know a second submarine was in the offing. If it *was* Melhuish who was being hunted, not a 'non-sub' contact – wreck, rock, school of fish, whatever.

Unlikely. But even if their target was *not Unsung*, no reason there shouldn't be a Cant or two up there – Wop having *thought* they'd made contact in the first light of day, and lost no time in whistling-up support.

If Melhuish had hung on for too long before diving – been spotted in *that* time?

'Port ten. Steer one-five-five.'

'One-five-five, sir.' Smithers, Red watch helmsman, acknowledging and winding the new course on – southeast instead of south. Hart, Mike noticed, was on after 'planes, although he should have handed over to Swathely at the start of this watch. Swathely no doubt attending to his patient. Walburton was on fore 'planes, what should have been Hart's place. Gauges creeping towards thirty-two feet, and hydroplane indicators more or less horizontal, Mike crouching to meet the 'scope's head as it emerged from its well, and get his eyes to it, adjusting the lenses' width-apart as he straightened with it and started a swift preliminary search in that sector referred to a minute ago by Fraser – and circling on round, before switching into air-search. Full daylight now, brilliant in the east, pale sky cloud-littered, jumpy seascape patched with the clouds' long shadows.

'Dip . . .'

Brass tube slithering down a few feet and then back up again, *maybe* by its brief disappearance having weakened some imaginary Cant pilot's belief in the periscope's 'feather' he might have thought he'd seen – if he existed, up there in the new day's glitter and scattering of cloud. Might well do, sooner or later, but as of that moment clear all round – sea and sky, no hint of any enemy activity at all even just seconds before the boom and reverberation and this time *sight* of what was to develop into a second pattern of five. *Then*, an area of sea swelling, lifting into a white-capped mound of darkish then all-white foam, upper part scattering white but the bulk already subsiding; he was training left for the explo-sions of charges numbers two, three and four (centre of the diamond pattern) producing similar effects over that wider area in which *Unsung* might be, or have been, might now be reeling – or even – well, if so, whose extraordinary cock-up? But then, *he* should have been dipping this periscope again, wasn't doing so only because his attention was held by those eruptions – charges that must have been shallow-set, incidentally – this last one collapsing into itself, presenting him with a destroyer-shape in miniature and on its beam-ends several cables' lengths beyond it; heeling hard, wheel obviously hard over. He'd muttered to himself 'Thar she blows', and seen the second, identical shape there – roughly bow-on – of which the one under helm had just cleared his view. Another thing taking one by surprise was that the range had closed dramatically and unexpectedly – he'd been heading more directly for them than he'd intended, on courses almost reciprocal to the outcome of their manoeuvrings.

Slowing, that one. Might even have stopped engines. Disappearance of white splodge under her forefoot indica-tive of this. Small destroyer or torpedo-boat – in fact, a Partenope. Both of them Partenopes. That one stopping as for instance one might on sighting evidence of a kill. Bubbles, or one large bubble, flotsam, bodies, oil. The next thing might be a lowering of boats − if that *was* what was happening, what *had* happened. Might not be, only in the circumstances − Melhuish, etcetera − one was rather specially conscious of such a possibility. He pushed the 'scope's handles up, leant back from it, and Ellery sent it down.

'Forty feet, Number One. Starboard ten, steer one-eight-oh. Half ahead both motors.'

'Forty feet, sir . . .'

And so forth − acknowledgements of orders stemming from a notion hitherto unpremeditated but inspired by that little ship's suddenly losing way and stopping; linking that to the by no means rare experience of A/S vessels taking it in turns to hold a contact while the other runs in to drop charges, purpose being to minimise the incidence of lost contact, a tactic last seen as recently as two or three weeks ago on the Palermo billet, and obviously the game they were playing here with *Unsung*. Were, or *had been* playing. He thought it had to be. Get in there oneself, therefore, while they worked up towards their next attack, or maybe the one after. If Melhuish's luck held out that long − or had held out *this* long, even. Then, intervention of third party − a beam shot from a few hundred yards, one torpedo, ninety-degree track if possible, one Partenope a sitting duck and *Unsung* consequently off the hook.

McLeod, never all that slow on the uptake, asked him quietly, 'Diving stations, sir?'

Danvers had recorded in his navigator's notebook, *0556 Diving Stations: Course due south, motors half ahead grouped down, depth 40 feet.* On Mike's orders he'd passed the diving stations order quietly through the forward compartments while Cottenham as Spare Hand had done the same from engine room to after ends – the aim being to let sleeping commandos sleep on, as most of them were doing.

Mike asked Swathely whether his patient was any better.

'Was taking notice, then give up, sir.' Shake of the head. 'Dunno there's an 'ope.'

'Well. Please God.' Moving to the chart for a look at the DR Danvers had put on it when they'd dived and since then extended to a new one for 0600, based mainly on fairly minuscule differences between log-readings. He asked Fraser, 'Bearings and distances of HE now?'

'Two-four-six and – lost that one, sir. Transmitting, could be in contact. *Was* moving left to right, both of 'em. Two-four-six and –'

'Time for a shufti anyway.' Shufti being Desert Army slang for a look, squint, recce, most common everyday usage being 'Shufti bint' meaning 'Get an eyeful of that piece of crackling'. Point of taking another squint now being that largely through the Partenopes' own manoeuvres – manoeuvres of one of them at least – they were or soon would be in much closer range – had set this up themselves, *Ursa* had only to let them come. He told McLeod, 'Slow both, thirty feet', and Jarvis, 'Stand by numbers one and two tubes. Depth-settings eight feet.' This in keeping with his confidence in those two being Partenopes, whose draft was listed as eight feet but with a wartime load on – such extras as ammo, torpedoes, depth-charges – would be several feet more than that. A glance at the depth-gauges – needles creeping up towards thirty-three feet – and he moved over to the small 'attack' periscope – the after one, monofocal – and nodded to Ellery. 'Up.'

McLeod reported, 'Thirty feet, sir.'

Daylight in only one eye. Also – extraordinarily – one perfectly good target in it. Little grey destroyer-shape lying stopped – as of this moment, stopped.

'Port ten.'

'Ten of port wheel on, sir . . .'

Wouldn't get a ninety shot, but nobody could expect to get absolutely *all* the luck. As it was – to have come up with a chance as good as this . . . Calling for an alteration of just a few degrees – and one's own presence on the face of things quite unsuspected.

'Midships and meet her.'

'Meet her, sir . . .'

'Steady!'

On target, and steadied. At least, steadying . . . Asking Fraser whether he had either HE or asdic transmissions on or near that bearing. Reply negative, although he *should* have had. Passive, hydrophonic listening, presumably. Target static, except for pitch and roll; *Ursa* more like on its quarter than its beam, but still roughly how one might have prayed for it – without dreaming any such prayer might be heard or answered. *Could* still go for a 90-degree shot, but doing so would have involved quite a lot of manoeuvring around, and to risk buggering up a chance as good as this – range a thousand yards, call it, a torpedo's running time at forty knots about a minute and a half – and no third pattern yet dropped on *Unsung*, but there could be at any second and it would put an end to this, the first touch ahead on the bugger's screws would be all he'd need to save himself, whether he'd know he was doing so or not.

Well, he wouldn't.

'Stand by numbers one and two tubes.'

Doubling one's chances by using both. Jarvis having received the TI's confirmation of one and two tubes ready, and Mike telling Smithers to steer a single degree to starboard.

'One degree to starboard, sir.' Applying what was little more than a slight hint to her rudder. The range could be nearer nine hundred yards than a thousand, he thought. So, running time less than a minute and a half, more like –

'*Damn!*'

Messerschmitt 110 – in a dive from slightly to the right of his target – agleam in sunshine and a blurry streak of Wop colours, slicing seaward at the periscope 'feather' or whatever its pilot had spotted, flaming staccato of its guns as it smashed over –

'Fire One! Flood "Q," hundred and fifty feet!'

Hundred and fifty because those *Unsung* charges had been shallow-set and *Ursa* might be receiving similar attentions shortly. It was a toss-up, of course. Hearing from the HSD 'Torpedo running, sir', and sending the other one after it as the flooding or 'Q' dragged her bow down – 'Fire Two!' Almost certainly wasted – three thousand quids' worth gone beyond recall – and there'd been some kind of detonation, a bomb from the Me being the only thing it could have been – felt as well as heard, a hit on or in the after casing as the most likely thing, he thought – or a very near miss astern there. Screws, hydroplane, rudder not very far under there. The attack 'scope was on its way down and the boat tipping bow-down. He'd yelled at McLeod, 'Full ahead group up!' – bow-down angle of about fifteen degrees calling for her screws' full power to drive her down into it – and 'Port twenty' – now both fish were on their way. In the last minutes one hadn't been able to touch the helm, only trust to Smithers holding her like glue to that firing course. Now, however, port wheel with the intention of settling her on something like southeast, meanwhile announcing over the Tannoy broadcast, 'That was a near-miss aft, bomb from an Me 110, report damage if any.' Presenting as fact what was actually not even supposition, more like hope, the least alarming explanation one had been able to come up with. Telling Smithers then to steady her on 130. Jarvis had gone aft. Danvers, stopwatch in hand, was looking at Mike queryingly, and in the next second reacting not only sharply but you might say *ecstatically* to what might have been a clap of thunder on the bow to starboard. Torpedo-hit – *not* wasted, not that one anyway. Mike had almost forgotten that a hit was to be expected either this soon or not at all. Danvers confirming in a whoop, 'Minute and twenty seconds, sir!' Hardly believable, but plain fact; everyone knowing what a torpedo warhead sounded like. There were other sounds now, including cheers, McLeod looking at Mike and shaking his head, grinning, and the coxswain growling '*That*'ll learn 'em . . .'

'No damage anyone's aware of, sir.' Jarvis, back from his visit of inspection aft. 'But – crikey . . .' To Danvers, a mutter of 'Just about takes the blooming biscuit.' Mike telling McLeod, 'Group down, slow both.' Thinking of the depleted battery and the probability there'd be disproportionate demands made on it before long. Not thinking so much of one's output of sound, at that stage, not being aware of any close enemy attention until Fraser's sudden 'Fast HE on green four-zero, sir. Closing – moving right to left – turbines, sir . . .'

Turbines, so *not* a chance encounter with *Unsung*, but the other Partenope – which in recent minutes had not been in evidence, barely even in one's cognisance, but now cutting in on the bow from starboard – knowing the direction from which one had fired, of course, seen the bloody Messerschmitt's performance too – well, for sure . . .

'Shut off for depth-charging.'

None too soon either. Watertight doors thudding shut all through the boat, other things happening as well. McLeod taking in reports from the now isolated compartments before making his own, 'Boat shut off for depth-charging, sir' – this coinciding with Fraser's yelp of 'Transmitting, sir! On green three-six – three-five –'

You could hear it. Not only transmitting, but in contact

– the first squeaks at that moment, electronic bleeps on the steel of her hull: and McLeod's further report of 'Hundred and fifty feet, sir.'

'Bearing now?'

'Green three-two – in contact, closing –'

'Starboard fifteen.' Turning inside the Wop's line of approach. And, 'Stop starboard.' To tighten the turn in altering to either south or southeast. Thinking about this sequence of events, though – the second Wop having got on to them so extraordinarily quickly. Attributable he supposed to having sunk the other one pretty well under this one's nose – so they'd have known the direction from which one had fired and then withdrawn – or begun to – and certainly the line of one's escape from the Me's attack – speaking of which there were two other possibilities, both stemming from that bomb – *could* be –

'Lost contact, sir. Slowed, and – ceased transmitting, that's –'

'Yes.' Meaning, he's just listening; and thinking that *Ursa* might have a singing screw – propeller damaged by that bomb. This was one of the two possibilities. The other might have been an oil leak – there being both oil-fuel and lub oil tanks back there, and if the bomb had burst either close alongside or actually in contact, in either case several feet under, well . . . But a damaged screw was the most likely. Hydrophone Effect at its lethal worst, in that as long as they had ears they couldn't lose you. Ears meaning asdics in the listening mode. Only *reassuring* thing at this stage being they didn't know your depth, could only guess at it. It was a thought worth holding on to. But also, here and now, if he was right about the bomb having bent or cracked a propeller-blade, maybe there *was* an immediate solution. If one could handle it right and had a modicum of luck, *might* be.

He told Smithers, 'Stop port. Slow ahead starboard.'

Praying it had been only the port screw, not both of them. Five or six feet underwater, it was conceivable that the blast could have damaged both.

'Ship's head?'

'One-eight-eight, sir.'

'Steer two hundred.'

'Port motor stopped, starboard slow ahead, sir.'

Thoughtful expressions, here and there. Working most of it out for themselves. It was in fact more a response than a solution, didn't by any means solve *all* the problems, might only save one's bacon if a few other things went right. Smithers centred his wheel, reported quietly, 'Course two-zero-zero, sir.'

If the Wop would drop some charges, the disturbance would give one the chance as it almost routinely had of getting away under cover of the furore. Whereas like this, one was achieving nothing . . . Except – having stopped the port screw, if the Wop began transmitting again, mightn't one assume that that was the one that sang, had been all the contact he'd thought he needed?

Slow HE on the port quarter now, according to Fraser. Low revs passing up the port side and out on that bow.

'Transmitting, sir. Red seven-oh, opening.' A pause, and then: 'In contact, sir!'

He nodded. Seeing the case as proven against that port screw, and guessing the crunch was coming pretty soon now. The attacker had to be moving at a certain speed to be able to drop charges that wouldn't cause damage to himself, would start his attacking run from out there where he was going now and drop the charges which would explode at whatever depth had been set on their pistols and some safe distance astern of him – and from the throwers, out on his beams. And the other thing as well as not knowing one's depth was loss of asdic contact prior to actually passing over, so he was then

309

temporarily blind and deaf and you had your chance – using starboard screw only, for Christ's sake, and hoping to God this one wasn't in the habit of putting *deep* settings on his charges – if it had been the *other* one dropping that shallow-set pattern on *Unsung*.

'Same?'

Fraser had confirmed that the Partenope was still moving out that way, at only a few knots, on a course diverging from *Ursa*'s by twenty or thirty degrees. The same thing was clear from a glance at Danvers' attack diagram: *Ursa*'s course just west of south and the Wop's now southeast, pinging into empty sea.

Or sea that might have *Unsung* in it. One's own mental picture was of her creeping away probably southwards out of trouble, barely comprehending events of the past half-hour, simply getting out from under while through some miracle she had the chance.

Alternatively, it was possible Melhuish might have *had* his chances.

'Going round to port, sir. Red three-five, right to left, transmitting.'

So all right – if the bugger imagines you're out that side of him . . . Not a sound, let him lose himself out there, and after a while come gently round to west then – after a while – back on course for home. Meeting Danvers' hopeful glance, raised eyebrows, thinking, well, it's possible, it's what *is* happening . . .

'Transmitting, sir.'

Instead of continuing into the wild blue yonder the Wop had circled away to port and for some time been lost to them, now turned up overhauling on *Ursa*'s own course at revs for nine or ten knots. Transmissions not yet audible to anyone but the HSD, via his headset. But it *would* be coming now, surely. Reminding himself that only a very short while ago he'd been impatient for it – for the chance to evade, slip away. But the Wop now suspecting he'd gone wrong, unsure how to play it from here on – having no partner in this now, solo maybe for the first time ever?

Well – wishful thinking, probably – was not only transmitting, by sheer luck – *his* – was back in contact. Jarvis had just whispered, 'Squeak-squeak-squeak' – pointing at the sweating white enamel on the deckhead, somewhat clownishly drawing Danvers' attention to asdic pings that had suddenly become audible – as were the destroyer's churning screws, sound that had started out of nothing only seconds ago and was rapidly getting louder. Charges set for about fifty feet, please God? Anyway, make one's break to port, and use both screws, just that minute or maybe two minutes of extravagance. The Wop wouldn't be hearing any of it, so what the hell, give it all she's got – all right, might not have all that much more of – and since in order to be at any rate *slightly* removed from its centre before the first charge exploded you'd be putting the wheel over a fraction early, the Wop if he was on the ball getting what he might interpret as notice of which way you had it in mind to go, hold that rudder on her and take her all the way round, full circle through the welter of it and out the way he would *not* think you'd be going.

Like the Flying Scotsman pounding at you.

'Stop starboard. Group up port *and* starboard.'

'Group up both sides, sir –'

'Hard a-port, full ahead together!'

In one's mind's eye seeing it happen up there. First one, set to however many feet, out of the rack on his stern, up there in the sunlight, then the throwers lobbing theirs; next one off the stern again to splash in midway between those two, fill the centre of the pattern. *Ursa* into her turn by this stage, trembling from the effort while the barrel-shaped charges sank down towards her through a steadily darkening however many fathoms.

This one doesn't go for shallow depth-settings anyway. Makes you bloody *wait*, recognising that if they'd been set shallow they'd have been going off much sooner than this. Than this, *now* – first thunderblast much too close for comfort and then it's like going over Niagara in an oil-drum only not as much fun as that, first describable effects being lights gone, gyro alarm a completely deafening scream in pitch darkness, men and objects being flung around – he'd gone sprawling himself, cracked his head, back of it sticky-wet – the boat steeply bow-down and going deeper, repeated blasts out there like very heavy blows to which her steel was ringing, cork chips raining from the deckhead. The cork was in the paint, meant to absorb condensation. Glass splintering – battery-tank, that was, under one's feet – and fuses blowing like rifle-shots. He'd called for number one main ballast to be blown – which Ellery had done, in that initial darkness, checking the vent shut before finding the blow also by feel – to get her bow up, check the dive – Mike having already stopped both motors and grouped down, put first the starboard one then both of them astern. With this much bow-down angle on her, the last thing she wanted was forward power to drive her deeper. Tested depth being 250 feet, which wasn't all that far below 150, and she was below that now. Blowing number one main ballast should have got her bow up, but as yet had not, nor had the screws running astern had much influence on her. He'd realised they were only at *slow* astern, and increased to half grouped up: she'd be just about hanging on them now, and maybe not far off running out of juice.

Emergency lighting had come on – a considerable improvement, thanks to the LTOs – and McLeod's torch centred on

312

the depth-gauge showing 214 feet, indicative of an alarmingly fast descent in the space of no more than a minute. The dive *had* been checked now, though, and she was slowly righting herself; he told McLeod to get her up to a hundred feet as soon as possible, also to reduce power when he could get away with it. It had come as a huge relief when the gyro alarm had shut off. But asdics were defunct, according to Fraser, ERAs and others were checking steering, hydroplanes, all telemotor controls and functions – periscopes for instance, the big one wouldn't rise – and hull-glands. The heads here had a leak on them. More importantly, the after ends had reported by sound-powered telephone that the propeller-shaft glands were leaking badly, on account of which Stoker PO Franklyn had the after ballast pump sucking on the bilges, but the pump was running hot, not making much of a job of it and obviously couldn't be relied on. Stokers were working on those glands.

At 170 feet now. He asked Smithers, 'Ship's head by magnetic?'

Gyro compass being still out of action. Hec Bull working on it, flat on his belly on the corticene. Smithers had come up with 'North fifty-two west, sir.'

'Well . . . port ten, steer due west.'

'Port ten, steer west –'

Bull's Welsh-intonated voice from the recesses: 'Soon have her up an' running, sir.'

'Good man.'

Not that it mattered much, no great inconvenience getting by on magnetic. Worst of it was the probability that about as soon as you did have it – or anything else – up and running, that thing would be over the top again with more of those bloody charges. He'd be searching now, plainly *had* been fooled over which way you'd gone, but he'd only to reverse his course, come back and listen for you; might be doing so at this moment. Or if he thought he'd sunk you he'd want evidence of it, a sight of whatever might have come floating up. Might try to *stir* some up; alternatively, find you and have another go. Probably do that anyway; and *Ursa* wasn't in shape to stand much more of it.

McLeod reported, 'Hundred feet, sir.'

'Well done, Jamie.' He told him, 'We'll hold on like this for an hour or so if the bugger'll let us.'

'I'll drink to that, sir.'

'And His Majesty'll provide the hooch.' He smiled at the quiet cheers, in semi-darkness and the odour from the batteries, the smashed foul-smelling cells. It wasn't unusual for a jar of rum to be smashed in the course of a serious depth-charging. Rum was one of the coxswain's responsibilities, Admiralty required him to account for every ounce; he'd write a jar off, and Mike would order a splicing of the mainbrace.

Once this was over.

The breakages that most concerned one were of battery containers. There was no way of telling how many had been smashed without actually getting into the battery tanks, opening them up, which could only be done when you were home and in dockyard hands. There were two tanks – batteries – number two here under the control room and number one for'ard of it, under the ERAs' and POs' messes, each containing fifty-six cells, glass-enclosed and standing waist-high with cross-sections about sixteen inches square, each cell needing at least two men and usually a crane, to lift it. In the two steel tanks, 112 of them. When the glass containers were cracked or broken the acid content of course leaked out, and was contained in the tank; it smelt, and could be set on fire, but worst of all, if salt water got into it – the tank itself holed for instance, acid escaping into the bilges – you got chlorine gas, which kills unpleasantly.

314

For the moment, the battery was still providing power. If it could keep on doing so until dusk — and of course the Partenope and others stayed away . . .

Well, they might. That was a matter of pure luck now. The real threat was the battery. If it chucked its hand in, the answer might be to bottom. Simple evolution made slightly tricky by the echo-sounder being out of action. Although it might be better not to use it anyway, with the risk of having its impulses picked up on Wop hydrophones. But bottom, anyway. How much water you were in you'd find out when you hit the putty. Then shut down everything, lie bottomed until nightfall, when you'd blow some main ballast, float her to the surface, start the generators and head for home — getting a signal out if possible, although wireless might not be operable — experience telling one that the main aerial might well be done for. If on the other hand it was OK he'd ask for air-cover to be provided at first light. Alternatively, trust to luck — plug on homeward through the night and probably the first hours of daylight, eventually identifying oneself by Aldis light to the Castile signal station on arrival in the swept channel.

'Number One.'

'Sir?'

'If we're left to ourselves now, we'll turn south in about an hour, and if the box conks out we'll bottom, sit tight until dark then surface and get cracking on generators.'

'Home like a bat out of hell.'

'As near as possible like that.' Thinking, *albeit slightly crippled bat* . . . 'Here and now, though, we'll open watertight doors. Cottenham issue tea and buns, whatever, you and I'll confer with the Chief, and no doubt there'll be a run on the heads — if Ellery here passes them as OK to use.' He'd glanced at Ellery, who muttered 'Long as I get first crack, check 'em out.'

315

'Outside ERA's perks, fair enough.' Turning to the chart, checking soundings in the vicinity of the last DR position, he startled himself with the news that bottoming was right out of the question: you wouldn't find bottom at much less than 400 or even 600 feet anywhere within about fifty bloody miles. Well – *ten* miles, you'd have a chance – but ten miles, at this present rate of progress, which one daren't exceed . . .

0840, and peace and quiet still prevailing. Had even read a few pages of Robert Graves' *I Claudius*, to take his mind off other things – which oddly enough it wasn't doing, and he thought he'd probably give it up. He'd only persevered with it – as far as he had – for Abbie's sake, he realised – and there was no reason she'd actually give a damn. He wished he hadn't given Ormrod's two P. G. Wodehouse titles to Colour-Sergeant Gant; but he had, and it was probably a good thing to have done.

Ursa now on course 200 – gyro duly fixed – running on her starboard motor at slow grouped down, which he reckoned was giving her about a knot and a half – and at eighty feet in the hope she'd be invisible to overflying Cants, while not suicidally deep in terms of sea-pressure and her injuries, especially the shaft-glands. He thought a hundred would be unnecessarily deep, sixty maybe dangerously shallow.

And bottoming now out of the question, no matter what.

He'd put Abbie's book down, and McLeod looked up from Miss Blandish, asked him quietly as their eyes met, 'If the box jags in, sir, what's the solution?'

'Might better put it as *when* the box jags in, Jamie.'

'Well . . .'

'What would your answer be?'

'I think bottom. Praying for a shallow patch and – well, continuance of our famous luck, maybe?'

'Spotted any *charted* shallow patches?'

'No, sir. Small ones often aren't though, and —'

'Fancy the idea of trimming her down further and further past her limits knowing that eventually something's going to crack?'

'Don't *fancy* it exactly, no —'

'She's already damaged, she wouldn't stand for it, would she? Imagine those shaft-glands blowing in like champagne corks. The only realistic option's to surface, take *that* chance.'

McLeod held his stare for a moment. Then: 'Taking on the Partenope and its four-inch guns maybe.'

'Partenope or whatever else.' After two hours it was a fact that the Partenope was very much less of a danger than it had been, but he didn't need to tell McLeod that. He said, 'Tactic then might be to turn tail and run.'

'At eight knots.'

'Yes. Well, exactly . . .' Voice down to a murmur – knowing he could have been heard from the galley if there'd been anyone in it, or the wardroom if any Blue watchkeepers had been tuned in – Danvers, or the helmsman who'd be either Farquhar or Llewellyn, or 'planesmen Hart and Brooks – since some of these prognostications were likely to be dire enough. One didn't want any of this to be overheard, was all. Continuing with 'Likely as not, Jamie, we'd find ourselves on our tod and remain so, continuing on generators – well, as you say, eight knots with luck, depending on that screw – Lewis guns in the bridge, of course – hell, Stoker PO Franklyn up there singing "Land of Hope and Glory", if you like . . . If on the other hand when we break surface we find ourselves in close company with Wops of any kind –'

He'd been going to say – murmur – 'Probably nothing for it but abandon ship, send her down with the hatch open' – but instead was silent, listening – eyes on the deckhead port side aft, HE having quite suddenly become audible from that quarter. Not *fast* HE – overhauling, obviously, but a target running at not much more than one knot didn't take a *lot* of overhauling, and this whatever it was would be listening-out on hydrophones, hence the low revs. He called to Danvers, 'Silent running, Pilot. Diving stations when the bastard's left us.' Then in a flash of inspiration and – all right, change of mind, lunacy or tactical innovation – told McLeod to take over the trim, stop starboard and see how she coped with that – whether she'd be able to hold her depth for the few minutes it might take this Wop to pass on by.

20

The convoy had made it intact, been brought in on Sunday, consequently were still discharging cargo, those at moorings in Grand Harbour here using their own gear to discharge into lighters alongside, others' masts and upperworks visible across the water in French and Dockyard creeks. One Union flag, two Stars and Stripes, one Dutch red-white-and-blue. And at anchor in midstream the cruisers *Orion* and *Euryalus*, dotted around in other berths half a dozen Hunt-class destroyers. Others of the escort had already started back, apparently, and the light cruiser *Arethusa* who'd been torpedoed in a night attack by Savoia-Marchettis had made it home to Alex under tow. She'd had 155 of her men killed in that attack, Shrimp had told Mike in his office in Lazaretto an hour ago. It was past midday now, a fine, cool day on the Upper Barracca, Grand Harbour actually a thrilling sight, illustrative of the turning of the tide after the long period of siege. Ships' boats all over, smoke drifting from merchantmen's and warships' funnels, ensigns fluttering, *dghaisas* busy as fleas on a dog's back. Not that sight-seeing was primarily what he was here for; after the meeting with

Shrimp he'd telephoned Abbie at the Defence Security Office and asked her when she came on the line, 'How about the Upper Barracca in about thirty minutes, you incredibly lovely creature?'

'Oh. Well.' Then: 'I suppose I *might* manage it.' Further pause, and '– Whoever the hell you are.'

'Can't guess?'

'Don't want to seem stand-offish anyway. OK, I'll take a chance. Nearer forty-five minutes than thirty, though?'

Could hardly have been a happier time. To have got back was one thing, imminence of reunion with her another. Shrimp hadn't exactly hauled him over the coals, and just a few minutes before he'd called her there'd been a message from Colour-Sergeant Gant, who'd gone in the ambulance with Marine Newton, that the surgeon who'd be operating on him later in the day had told Gant there was no reason the patient shouldn't come out of it as good as new. So after the call to Abbie he'd nipped back aboard *Ursa* to pass this to the coxswain – who'd been overjoyed, not only at the news itself but at having been apprised of it. Also on board at that time had been Commander Sam MacGregor, the flotilla engineer, making decisions, lists and notes, with Chief McIver at his elbow disputing practically every point. MacGregor had said, 'You put her through the wringer this time, didn't you. We'll have her in dock at least a couple of months.'

They'd discussed this. It was roughly what Mike had expected. As well as the things they'd known about before she had a cracked engine bed-plate, which had made itself known when he'd surfaced her in the late afternoon and started the generators. The need to take it easy had slowed them down considerably in their night's passage on the surface.

He'd asked the engineer, 'What about *Unsung*?'

'Oh, two or three weeks'll have her in shape. So we'll fix her up first. Do her here mostly, shift this one to the dockyard.'

'Right.'

'Rotten luck, Nicholson. Bagged a destroyer though, I'm told.'

'A tiddler. But with respect, sir, outstandingly *good* luck, overall. We were at 150 feet, this was just one pattern of five charges, and I heard the clicks of pistols cocking themselves. Despite which the Chief and I are here talking to you . . .'

'Enormously to your credit.'

'Bloody lucky.'

'That too. Still a remarkable achievement.'

McIver had growled, 'An experience I personally could'a done wi'oot.'

There'd been letters, including one from his father which he'd opened and skimmed through in case it contained news of Alan – which it did, but not the kind against which one habitually steeled oneself. Much to the contrary – Alan had been promoted and was being moved to an air station in Sussex. The letter was back in Mike's pocket, to be read more thoroughly later, and meanwhile he thanked God . . . If one didn't, next time it might be *bad* news.

All right – more out of superstition than fear of the Almighty. But if it went any distance towards averting anything so absolutely frightful – well, thank Him night and day and twice on Sundays.

'Why the grim regard, Signo?'

Abbie. Looking – well, actually he'd forgotten *how* fantastic . . . Was on his feet, were then in each other's arms. Telling her he didn't know, in any case couldn't possibly be looking grim *now*: only staggered, overwhelmed, happier than he'd ever been. 'Just the sight of you, Abbie. You're *blindingly* attractive. *Beautiful* if you like, but it's more than that, it's

321

something else entirely. Even more so than I've had you pictured for the past five days. *Five*, please note?'

'Oh, duly noted!' Laughing, or could have been crying, or a mix of both. 'Crazy for you, Mike!'

'Enough to marry me?'

'For that one doesn't have to be crazy at all. One can be just sort of medium stupid.'

Laughing more, hugging; he still had his arms round her and they were attracting notice. With Grand Harbour as busy as it was now there were a lot of spectators lingering on these stone galleries – people enjoying their lunch-breaks in the fresh air, children out of school, so forth. She'd stopped laughing, told him seriously, 'Straight answer right between those anxious eyes of yours because I've been giving it quite a bit of thought – yes, more than crazy enough, if we still want to when we're home, that is. But you'll be going home now, won't you – and OK, so will I, *one* day, maybe in six months or a year – by which time they'll have sent you to Japan or –'

'You're going to have me around some while in any case, my darling. *Ursa*'s going to be in dock about two months – so I was informed half an hour ago –'

'More wrong with her than there was before?'

'What I'm pointing out is if we were to announce our engagement it would make things a hell of a lot easier –'

'What I *asked* was have you been in some kind of trouble in these past five days?'

'Well, yes. Haven't been at my most brilliant.'

'What happened?'

He'd grimaced. 'Got depth-charged. Does happen, on occasion. Sooner not talk about it, though. Not supposed to, either. I do terribly want to kiss you, Abbie. To be frank, I don't think I can wait. Scoot along to Strada Mezzodi, might we?'

'Oddly enough, *I'd* thought we might. And we'd better, if you're going to start behaving badly. Did you get in last night, or this morning?'

'If I'd got in last night, my darling, I'd have –'

'All right – first thing this morning, then –'

'Not quite first thing. Mid-forenoon. Then there was a lot to see to, and the usual grilling by old Shrimp, and I was *looking* for Charles Melhuish, who'd got in a few hours before I did, but he'd turned in, apparently. Shrimp did mention he'd seemed all-in. I expect I'll see him this evening. Abbie – Strada Mezzodi now?'

Shrimp had said when he'd come on board after Mike had secured *Ursa* in the Lazaretto wardroom berth in mid-morning, 'Had us in a blue funk, Michael. Your radio given up the ghost, or something?' It had, of course, they'd simply turned up in the swept channel, identified themselves by light to the Castile signal station and come on in, been directed to this berth. Then after Mike had told him most of what there was to tell, he'd summarised it with 'So your patrol report will tell me that you achieved the primary objective – put 'em ashore and brought 'em off – incidentally they most certainly did *their* job –'

'Deep regrets about Ormrod, sir.'

A nod. 'Damnable. But then you saved *Unsung* from getting a worse pasting than she did get – could have been a *lot* worse, apparently.'

'But I have to admit I shouldn't have been anywhere near her, sir. Should have cleared out, left her to it.'

'But Melhuish shouldn't have been where *he* was. You took a hell of a chance, and you're right, you had no business doing anything of the sort, and – well, I don't have to read you the riot act, all you'll be doing from here on is taking *Ursa* home when she's mended. On which subject, Michael,

I'm still not saying you're stale, in fact you're obviously not, but – a touch overconfident, perhaps?'

'I'll admit to an error of judgement, sir.'

'You also happened to sink a Partenope, you say.' Shrimp had shrugged, glancing at his watch. 'Let's have it on paper, Michael. See Miss Gomez gets it for typing first thing in the morning.'

'Aye, sir. Possibly before the close of business.'

'How long were you *in daylight* on the surface?'

'About four and a half hours, sir. Had no option, the box had had it. Aircraft I thought were going to be the main danger – had the Lewis guns rigged of course – but not a bit of it. Earlier I'd thought of bottoming and waiting for dark, but –'

'Bottoming in what depth, Michael?'

'Well, exactly – with shaft glands leaking even at eighty feet. But having confessed to that, sir, mind if I brag about one I'm quite proud of?'

'Brag all you like.'

'At eighty feet on one motor slow grouped down, and having realised I couldn't bottom – in fact I'd just told McLeod we might wind up taking our chances on the surface –'

'Time of day?'

'Forenoon. Nine, ten . . .'

'Not such good chances, then.'

'No, sir. But it wouldn't have been all that great if they'd caught us as we were, either. We had no asdics, incidentally. She couldn't have stood much more rough stuff – or gone deep or used the port motor – and battery mostly broken glass – and then bloody hell, there's HE coming up on the quarter. Turbines, but low revs, obviously its ears flapping –'

'So?'

'We couldn't afford to be detected, and as likely as not we would have been, so I stopped that screw, she turned out to

324

be heavy aft, went down by the stern. Couldn't use the after ballast pump incidentally – *had* been doing so but it was noisy and running hot, so –'

'Despite all of which you got away with it.'

He'd nodded. 'Not what you'd call a stop-trim, exactly – she was at about a hundred and forty feet with a twenty-one-degree stern-down angle on her by the time we'd lost all sound from our Wop and put the motor ahead again.'

'And it – complied.'

'Well, yes. Hadn't been too sure it would. But it did, and since nothing else came near us –'

'You deserve to be alive, Michael.'

'Thank you, sir. I won't put all that in the report.'

'Why ever not?'

'Rather a lot of typing for Miss Gomez?'

Finally, Shrimp had told him that *Unsung*'s commandos had done a good job on the Gela airfield but that only three of the eight had made it back to the rendezvous, the other five either killed or taken prisoner. And that Melhuish's reason for having been so far out of station and still on the surface when he'd been put down by the Partenopes had been a whole crowd of fishing-boats he'd had to get round, and did so that way about because earlier on there'd been Mas-boats the other side of Gela. 'Yes, it's a little complicated.'

'Miss Gomez will have her work cut out. Any news of *Swordsman*, sir?'

'Oh, yes. Gerahty put his team ashore, they ran into no problems he was aware of, and he's now off Cape dell'Armi – with three or four days to go. Will you be in the mess this evening, Michael?'

She padded away damp and naked, came back with two small towels and gave him one of them.

325

'Really *something*, Mike.'

'Understatement of the season. And you're beautiful all over.'

'I've missed you dreadfully.'

'So marry me.'

'Mike, darling.' Drier, she sprawled beside him. 'I was beginning to explain — about an hour ago? You back home in — what, four or five months now? — me perhaps in a year, and in the course of that interval you've been sent to Australia, Singapore, Shanghai, or —'

'Don't want to lose you, Abbie.'

'Think you would? For lack of a damn *ring*?'

'I never had the least inclination to be married to anyone at all. Believe me, never even thought about it — until now, wanting *you*. Marriage itself isn't the thing, it's us belonging to each other and making no bones about it, including making love, all of them assuming it's what we're doing anyway — as in the case of whatshisname — I know, wasn't going to mention him again, you told me and I do believe you, I was thinking about it at sea —'

'Apart from any other consideration, Nico Cornish has a *wife*, Mike.'

'And?'

'I was thinking when you were away, I should have pointed this out before — it's something I don't do and never would. We talked about this, if you remember — not about Nico, in general terms — the Sunday I moved back from the Gravies', wasn't it. I think I brought up the subject — morality of having affairs and so forth, and I said as long as people aren't doing the dirty on other people, meaning wives and husbands, I saw it as a matter of personal choice, both in principle — whether to do it at all — and the specific, individuals concerned and circumstances. My thinking there included him — Nico, married man I liked and enjoyed as a friend, which I can tell you wasn't all *he* wanted. In fact

326

I suppose that's how it is with most of you. I mean, if I
had a husband in England or somewhere it wouldn't stop
you trying, would it?'

'Abbie, I fully agreed with you that afternoon –'

'So you did.' She laughed. 'So you did, my darling!'

'How's that funny?'

'Despite screwing the living daylights out of the wife of
the submarine captain you mentioned a while ago?'

He'd frozen. 'What are you talking about?'

Her slim hand stroked him, on the damp, rumpled single
bed. 'Exceedingly good-looking woman by the name of –
oh, Anne, I think?'

'Ann . . .'

'Morals of an alley-cat, by all accounts. Oh, I don't mean
it *that* way, I mean it's not all that incomprehensible, you're
attractive, all right, even fairly devastating. Don't look so ashen,
darling, it's partly what drew me to you – alleged *proficiency*,
might call it. Actually I suppose I was *drawn* already, but—'

'Allegation by whom?'

'You won't be horrid to her for having told me?'

'Who?'

'Please *don't* say anything to her about it, but – Eleanor
Kingsley. You do know her.'

'Not all that well. Girlfriend of my first lieutenant's.'

'The doughty James McLeod.'

'Yes, and I think you've mentioned them before, but how
the *hell* –'

'He told her. In what circumstances, I know not. Usual
routine, though, not a word to anyone, etc. He's devoted to
you, apparently. But he'd met this female at a submariners'
shindig she attended with hubbie – back home, this was –
then saw you together at some pub in Scotland when you
were supposed to be elsewhere – no doubt of it, apparently,
and he was certain it wasn't a one-off. I don't know how,

327

didn't take in all the details – rather doubt Eleanor had either. You must have been pretty damn careless, Mike.'

'And young McLeod –'

'He admires you for it,' Eleanor said. 'Thinks you're the bee's knees in any case. The lady's a stunner – right?'

'With your principles about people not cheating on each other –'

'– with which as you've just mentioned you agree root and branch. In this instance you must absolutely have *forced* yourself?'

'I don't know *how* it started. In any case that was *then*.'

'If you were in London *now*, though –'

'No. Absolutely not.'

'Even with you and I neither married nor engaged?'

'*She's* married – and I do agree with you on that issue. That's one thing, another is I'm in love with you. No one else even bloody well *exists*. Believe me, Abbie –'

'All right, I will. I do.'

'Thank you. In fact thank heavens.'

Melhuish ran *him* to earth that evening. Mike had been looking for him again and drawn a blank again, had reread his father's letter and was in his cabin changing into Red Sea rig for the evening when Melhuish came knocking on the door, looking both sick and slightly hostile.

Maybe they'd always shared what might be described as a natural coolness for each other. He couldn't remember any time he'd actually been glad to see him.

'Hello, Charles.'

Stiff nod, expression still not exactly amiable. Melhuish was jealous of him professionally, of course – for some reason or reasons unknown. And Ann might have spoken well of him at some time? While from one's own point of view there was an impression of excessive self-regard reflected in a some-what supercilious manner.

Saying now, 'I had rather assumed you'd be ashore.'

A crack at his relationship with Abbie. Mike nodded equably, 'I was, for a while. Also spent some time looking for you — as it happens. Heard you'd turned in. Around midday, that was. Sit down, Charles. You had the legs of us last night, uh? But Shrimp mentioned that you'd seemed fairly knackered.'

'Slightly touch and go for a while, wasn't it. One of the things I'm here for is to thank you for what you did. Even if I'd come out of it in one piece, I'd have been well and truly put through it. Well, I *was*, but thanks to your — intervention . . .'

'I was curious to see what was going on. Curiosity darn near killed the cat — *this* one — and by chance happened to get you out of your tight corner. I'm glad of that but I never *set out* to do anything of the kind.'

'You had a good hammering, I'm told.'

'Don't know what was good about it. That Wop had his depth-settings spot-on, consequently damn near got lucky. A bloody Messerschmitt actually set the ball rolling. I was asking for it, I suppose. Look, if you'd like to compare notes over a gin or two —'

'Not this evening, if you don't mind.'

'Only I told Shrimp I'd be down there — and later I've a patrol report to concoct . . . Are you all right, Charles?'

He looked awful. Eyes dull, with dark rings around them, face pasty-grey, sweaty-looking. Sitting now, at last, fumbling with a silver cigarette case.

Fumbling because his hands were shaking.

'I had a letter from Ann, Mike.'

Staring at him: declining the offer of a cigarette. Thinking

329

Oh Christ – reacting to the tone of that announcement and the fact Melhuish was still looking down at the rather ornate case he was fiddling with, sooner than meet Mike's eyes.

Denounced by Abbie earlier on, now about to hear *Ann* had dropped him in it?

He'd managed a smile. 'Only *one* letter? I thought she wrote them in threes?'

No answering warmth. Flare of a match, then, 'What's called a "Dear John" letter. If you know what that is. Look, I'm only telling you this because you know us both – or did – quite well. Would you have thought it even possible? That she *could*? When you saw how we *were* together? And – well, imagine it – feeling a bit rough, opening a letter thinking oh how marvellous, bless her heart – and – well, Jesus –'

'Dear John meaning she's – leaving, *breaking up* with you?' It *had* taken a moment to sink in. Shaking his head: 'Didn't occur to me that could be – what you meant . . . I can hardly believe it, Charles. I'm – I was going to say shocked, but it's you must be in shock. Very, very sorry, Charles – Christ, what else can one say? What is it, some other –'

'Care to see what *she* says?'

'No, not really. Your *very* private business –'

'Some Yank Air Force colonel. The greatest thing ever happened to her, she says, she's never felt so intensely about anything in her whole life – three pages of it begging me to understand, forgive her – and *him*, would you believe *that*?'

Staring at the letter open in his hand, head wagging like a metronome. Mike with a hand on his shoulder: thoughts a compound of personal relief and wondering what Ormrod would have made of it. 'Look – Charles, come on down and have a stiff one . . .'

★   ★   ★

330

In the wardroom that evening they were talking about the desert war, Montgomery's breakthrough at El Alamein which had been imminent a week ago when *Ursa* and the other two had been on the point of departure with their commandos, and was now a *fait accompli* – Rommel in full retreat and the Eighth Army on his heels, church bells ringing in English villages.

Melhuish had had a few gins, become near-maudlin and finally told Mike, 'Not up to it, I'm afraid. Any case, thanks for the support. I'm going to hit the sack.'

Shrimp then, joined as he invariably was by his right-hand men and technical specialists, the new Commander (Submarines), others including Mike and at least half a dozen other COs wanting news of their brethren's latest successes radio'd in from sea. There was a lot going on, and when you'd run out of that you had island gossip. Mike heard Shrimp questioning Sam MacGregor on the subject of *Unsung*'s defect-list, Shrimp then asking, glancing around, 'Charles Melhuish not with us this evening?' and Melhuish's first lieutenant, Showell, piping up with 'He's a bit out of sorts, sir. Was going to polish off the patrol report and then turn in.'

'Skipping supper?'

Showell had been a brand-new sub-lieutenant in Shrimp's anti-invasion flotilla at Harwich in which Mike had had his own first operational command; he was stocky, red-headed, freckled. He'd looked at Mike, shrugged slightly as if saying 'Search me', and Mike told Shrimp, 'He was here, sir, had a couple of snorts then skedaddled. But –' he'd lowered his tone, and there'd been an interruption at that stage, a message to Shrimp from Gravy. Shrimp returned to the subject a minute later: 'Michael – what were you going to say about Melhuish?'

He checked that they were more or less on their own. 'Only that he's out of sorts for private reasons, sir – had a "Dear John" letter from his wife.'

331

'Dear John . . .' Getting there, then. 'Oh. I see. But — was this to be expected? You knew them both, I think you told me.'

'I did, yes. Extremely pretty girl. You'd know Billy Gorst, sir, I expect?'

'Don't tell me *he's* the —'

'No.' Mike laughed. 'Only that I met the Melhuishes at his wedding.'

'Is Melhuish likely to get over it reasonably quickly?'

'Honestly can't say, sir. Most sincerely *hope* —'

'Damnable, in any case. By the way though, Michael, how's the delectable Miss French? Over the moon at having you back?'

'Seems quite pleased about it, sir. Entirely mutual, I may say.'

'You won't find it *too* arduous being on the beach eight blooming weeks, then.'

'Don't suppose I will, sir.'

'Greta was asking after you a few days ago. The water's still swimmable at their Lido, incidentally. Anyway — Lascaris at noon, right?'

He told Abbie next day, 'Would have been undiplomatic to have spent the night here. First night in — and Shrimp had asked if I'd be in the mess. After all, Lazaretto's where I'm expected to hang out when I'm not at sea. In the week or so before this last trip I wasn't there much, was I. Might be what he was thinking about when he asked me that. He's under orders to treat COs like Derby winners, but I think one shouldn't take too much advantage of that — for instance have one's mess-mates ask "Where's Mike?" or "Where's bloody Nicholson?" and get the answer "Oh, screwing his girlfriend." Bad for discipline, my darling, and not terribly good for girl-friend's reputation. But there's nothing wrong with mornings and afternoons, is there — actually I'm all for them.'

'Me too. As a working girl —'

'If we were engaged, you see –'

'We're not, and as I've told you once or twice –'

'If we *were*, the hypothetical reply to "Where's bloody Nicholson?" would be "Ashore with his fiancée, as usual." Totally different sound to it. That's the point I'm trying to explain.'

'I wouldn't say that in practice it'd make much difference. Very weak reason for getting engaged, in any case. To my mind we're fine as we are – for now, at any rate.'

'Well, I think the only reason you're taking the attitude you are taking is that you don't trust me. The Ann Melhuish business – my feckless womanising? Well, I'll give you the latest – Ann's husband, Charles, has had a "Dear John" letter from her. She's leaving him for some Yank. Doesn't that tell you something about her natural tendencies?'

'No. Even if it's true – the timing's a *little* coincidental – wouldn't mean she's swept *him* off his feet – some sod on the make –'

'Well, *thank* you –'

'Not referring to you, you know perfectly well I wasn't. Mike darling, leave it, *can* we?' Her arms slid round his neck, her breasts against his face. 'Unless you want to make me love you less?'

Shrimp, in their patrol-report meeting in the Castile at noon – Melhuish had been and gone by then – had run his eye over the three or four typed foolscap sheets and had little to add to his previous comments.

'Shouldn't have been there in the first place. Well, you're aware of that. But you made up for it in several ways; and the extensive damage to *Ursa* is not a major issue, since she's only to be fixed up for the passage home. And that's that. Next question – what to do with you for a couple of months. First, you'd better take a week off. Then, the obvious and most useful thing's the Lazaretto Ops Room, backing up Johnno Broadbent.

333

He could use you, all right – heck of a lot going on, and now a biggish show in prospect, in which we'll be heavily involved. I'll be away shortly, by the way – Cairo, by Dakota, with a temporary replacement here. Anything else, meanwhile?'

'I'll be working with Broadbent, but also Spare CO?'

'Technically, but Hugo Short's ahead of you for any seagoing replacement. He's been sitting around grinding his teeth for months . . . That all?'

'Except that I don't need a week, sir. Two or three days, perhaps?'

A nod. 'Fix it with Broadbent, Michael.'

He hadn't said anything to Abbie at this stage about his projected few days on the loose or the work he'd be doing at Lazaretto thereafter because he had yet to see Johnno Broadbent and tie it all up; and since concluding that rather hurried Castile interview with Shrimp had been giving thought to his best options and / or preferences as he'd put them to the SOO when he did see him. To start with, he needed to be available in his capacity of CO of *Ursa* for a day or two – paperwork mainly, sailors' personal documents and the forwarding of requests, dozens of lesser items requiring his signature. This would take him to the weekend, which he'd spend with Abbie if she wasn't working or whatever – and then – well, Monday to Wednesday he'd take as his three-day leave, and stay with her in her flat. Nights anyway; days, might hike around the island. She might even get a few days off herself. But once he'd started work as Deputy SOO – Thursday onward – he'd be living at Lazaretto. Have to be – so Broadbent could be off the hook occasionally – or when he wanted – and this might not help in the situation *vis-à-vis* Abbie. Looking down at her sprawled, *lovely* body, tanned arms and shoulders and a leg thrown across his own; most certainly not wanting to make her love him less, but realising it might happen.

21

Swimming – at the Lido, Pembroke House, practising his crawl to quite a long way out while Abbie and Greta sunned themselves on the rocks. It wasn't exactly a cloudless day and from time to time they covered themselves, but the sea was still warmish from the long hot summer. The Gravies had invited them – this was a Saturday, Abbie hadn't been working, and Mike's colleague Johnno Broadbent had been prepared to look after any crises occurring in the Ops Room, especially with Mike in easy reach by telephone to/from Pembroke House.

Broadbent, lieutenant-commander, was several years senior to Mike but confined to shore duties on account of a problem with his eyes which had been caused by a torpedo warhead exploding in its tube, in 1939. He was an easy-going but very intelligent man with a scarred forehead, prematurely greying hair and a wife and two small children of whom he had leather-framed portraits in his cabin. Mike had co-operated with him in the planning of Operation 'Backlash', and they got on well.

Shrimp had been gone a week and there was no date yet

for his return: he was with the planning staff in Cairo. His temporary replacement, Captain Andrew Swann DSO, having had only three days taking over from Shrimp was of course heavily reliant on his senior staff, also tended to keep to himself, especially in terms of appearances in the wardroom. Naval tradition was for a ship's captain to live and mess on his own, whereas Shrimp believed in living amongst his officers, knowing their personalities and problems as well as ensuring that they were aware of his.

Nothing wrong with Andrew Swann. Only that in this flotilla Shrimp was *not* actually replaceable.

Mike wasn't seeing as much of Abbie as he'd have liked. She'd understood from the start that he wasn't going to be able to spend whole nights out of the base, and maybe because they were getting about a week together before the new routine commenced it hadn't seemed so bad. She'd been able to take a long weekend, that first one, so they'd had Saturday to Monday and then the Tuesday and Wednesday nights. They'd swum twice and dined once at the Gravies', made a trek across the island, over the same route he'd taken with Jarvis and Danvers. Abbie missing Vera the donkey, who Pop Giddings had told Mike was slightly lame. Abbie had asked Mike to visit the animal and wish her an early recovery, and he'd said he would although as yet he hadn't. He *had* taken Abbie to the base, though, shown her round a visiting T-class boat and spent some time with Johnno, whom she'd liked and had met a couple of times at the Gravies'.

That trip across the island, though – during their stop for picnic lunch and sunbathing etc. before swimming across the head of St Paul's Bay she'd murmured at a certain point, 'Vera *should* be with us. Not just for transport – essential scenery, remember?'

'Beauty and the beast and Maddalena Bay as background to something not far removed from heaven – yes, I remember.'

'I will all my life.'

'Good. Mind you, there've been other – times, moments, not easily forgettable – at least I'd –'

'– remember them all –' a hand freeing itself for a sweeping gesture indicating their surroundings, situation generally: then – 'Oh, Mike, *blimey* –'

They'd returned to Valetta by a more direct route than he'd taken with the lads, thus shortening it by a mile or two. But it had been a good day. It wasn't in fact easy now to be out of touch with the base for more than an hour or so. The picture was changing fast as the Eighth Army powered westward, 10th Flotilla boats effectively blockading the desert ports to starve Rommel's forces of food, fuel and ammunition, and surface forces from Malta in it too now – Force K, primarily, cruisers and destroyers intercepting Axis convoys – a few nights ago ruining / wrecking one completely, by all accounts half a dozen freighters and their escorting destroyers blown out of the water, *gone*. On other nights they – Force K – were bombarding the island of Pantellaria, obviously in preparation for its capture. That would be an important E-boat base eliminated, and an essential step towards the projected invasion of Sicily; before which was to come an even more massive assault, the operation Shrimp had referred to vaguely and was presumably why the planners had wanted him in Cairo. It was likely, Mike thought, that he'd be consulted on plans for ensuing operations as well. Sicily, for one thing, as a prelude to Italy; and as the desert advance pushed on west into Tunisia and Algeria – well, if the 10th Flotilla moved west it would need a base, and the obvious place might be Cagliari: which would mean invading Sardinia.

He'd have *Ursa* back in the UK by that time, he thought. Would have handed her over to her builders in Chatham for virtual rebuilding. If U-class submarines were still wanted then. Meanwhile they were wanted *here* all right: and doing as well as ever. Shrimp would be proud of them when he got back – any day now. There'd been two boats lost since his departure: sickening, as always, but also to be expected, in all the circumstances, particularly in view of the greatly improved effectiveness of Wop A/S forces. Mike's own recent experience in *Ursa* had been an example of that – quite possibly some new development in target depth-assessment – and if so, probably of German origin, the Germans in recent months having taken a hand in their allies' training and re-equipping, according to Intelligence reports.

He stopped swimming, put his legs down, found the beginnings of the rocky foreshore and climbed up to join the girls. The sun was hot now and they were both flat out on their backs, Greta with a straw hat covering her face and forehead, protecting that fair skin. Removing it, to squint up at him: 'You were miles out. Much fitter-looking too than you were before.'

'Something to be said for the sedentary life.'

'Which Abbie tells me you're not having.'

'Actually not. Things are somewhat frantic.'

Abbie was saying she'd like a cigarette, when his hands were dry, and Greta asked, 'What's frantic that you're allowed to tell us about?'

'Damn-all really – I mean that's discussible. Current *local* news is that *Unsung*'s completed her sea trials – which is a good thing, she'll be off in a day or two. Guy Mottram's due in this evening, in *Unbowed* – he knocked down a fair-sized tanker, very much to his credit – but Johnno and I are on our own now, Hugo Short having got away in *Thane*.'

'*Thane?*'

'T-class from Beirut, en route Gibraltar.'

'Just Gib, or all the way home?'

'Home. Done her time. CO landed with a burst appendix.'
He squatted beside Abbie, lighting cigarettes for her and for

himself. 'Greta – sorry – didn't ask – have you still given up?'

'Yes – still don't. By the skin of my teeth. But when you've smoked those, might get ourselves some lunch? Gravy'll be home any minute, *may* want a dip before scoffing, but –'

'The two of you are blooming *marvellous*.' Abbie, exhaling smoke. 'You really are. *So* hospitable, and –'

'Balls. We just enjoy our friends, and are lucky enough to have this rather super house. Tell me something, though – why don't you two get married?'

That had been Saturday. Sunday he'd been in or around Lazaretto all day, Monday he'd spent most of the afternoon with Abbie at her flat, and on Wednesday, business being slack and Broadbent happy to cope with it on his own, he took Abbie in the ferry from Customs House steps to Sliema, had a few glasses of Red Biddy and a fish supper at the Chocolate King.

While sipping the fairly atrocious, rum-flavoured 'wine', she asked him why at Pembroke House on Saturday, when Greta had asked why didn't they marry, he'd remained silent, not looking at either of them, only gazing out to sea – leaving it to *her* to tell Greta that they'd discussed it all right but – 'Look – Mike'll be off home when *Ursa*'s ready. Not much more than about a month now. I'll be here another *six* months at least. By the time I'm back he could have been sent anywhere. I mean, what's the point? When the bloody war's over – how long, a year, three years – *if* we still want to –'

'So you do want to?'

She'd shaken her head. 'What I'm trying to explain – I *don't* want a fiancé on the other side of the bloody world!'

At that point Mike had about finished his cigarette, flicked the stub away across the rocks, smiled at Greta. 'Lunch, you said?'

Abbie asked him, 'Does it mean you're leaving it to me now, don't give a damn, or what?'

'It means I disagree with you strongly, but on your insistence agreed not to quote go on about it, unquote, which is why I haven't raised the subject since, and I certainly wouldn't want to start a row with you in front of Greta or anyone else.'

'You could express your opinion, without actually –'

'Not discussing it is the only alternative to quarrelling. You know, I quite *like* this appalling brew . . .'

The fish, straight out of the sea, was very, very good. And Abbie, in the glow of Mediterranean dusk, unbelievably lovely. The sun was already a dying influence when they caught the last ferry out of Sliema Creek and around the point, back into Grand Harbour. The climb up to the Barracca, more or less vertical and something like a couple of hundred feet, was enough to make him regret having had quite that much Red Biddy. At the top, the upper level, sagging in exaggerated exhaustion against the railing, she suggested that he should go on back to the base on his own, leaving her to make it on *her* own to South Street.

'I'll do no such thing.'

'As you like. What a damn bore, though.'

That he had to go back 'aboard' – i.e. to Lazaretto, rather than spend the night with her on her rattly little bed. She was saying it again, or words to the same effect, when they were almost at her flat and saw the light, also a motorbike parked on the cobbles not far from her door.

Royal Marine commando's khaki battledress uniform. A corporal in 'Shrimp's private army' whose name Mike happened to know. Crash of heels as he saluted.

'Evening, Perriman. What brings you to these parts?'

'Evening, sir. Evening, Miss. Urgent dispatch, sir, from Lieutenant-Commander Broadbent.'

'What's it about?'

340

'I think you're supposed to read it, sir.'

'Am I. Well, inside, in the light. Abbie, you might make him a cup of tea?'

'If you'd like that, Corporal?'

'Wouldn't half, Miss!'

'Come on up, then.' She'd let them in. Asking Mike, 'What *can* it be?'

'Haven't the foggiest.' Switching on lights. 'But if you have coffee –'

'What passes for it, yes. Corporal – ?'

'Tea for me, Miss. But if I might use your –'

'In there.'

Mike had ripped open the khaki OHMS envelope. Inside he found a sheet of signal-pad on which Broadbent had scrawled: *Mike – sorry to do this to you. As you know,* Unsung *sails tomorrow at dusk. As you did not know, she'll be doing so under your command. Charles Melhuish tried to kill himself this afternoon – did not succeed but has been removed to hospital.*

He let Abbie read it.

'My God. Poor devil. But – oh, God . . .' The kettle was boiling in her tiny kitchen: she'd gone to it. Sound of the plug being pulled. Mike snapped out of a thirty-second trance, told the corporal 'I have to get back to Lazaretto. Might cadge a lift on your pillion?'

'You're welcome, sir.'

'One tea, two so-called coffees. Sugar in the tin if you want it, Corporal.'

'Much obliged, Miss.'

'Well, sit there, look – I just want a very quick word with Commander Nicholson. Won't be a minute. Mike?'

'Yes.' In the bedroom, holding each other. 'No point hanging about, you realise?'

'Of course. You'll need to be there first thing in the morning – if not before.'

'Neither of us would sleep, in any case.'

'Or much else, either.'

He kissed her. 'I'll be back, don't worry.'

'Well, of *course* you will!'

'I mean in about a fortnight. If in doubt about anything, ring Johnno.'

'You know what you'll be doing, do you?'

'Oh, yes. But tell Greta you're on your own, and – just hang on. Eat properly, sleep well –'

'I'll dream of you.'

'Ditto. I love you, Abbie. No, none of that – no business crying, no reason whatsoever – *remember* that now . . .'

Showell, *Unsung*'s first lieutenant, joined him at breakfast. He was properly concerned for his own CO but apparently glad to have someone he already knew as the replacement. There was no news of Melhuish, only the assumption that he was still alive. Johnno Broadbent had said last night that Charles had had a second letter from his wife in a mail that had come that morning; it had been filed with his other papers, in readiness for whatever kind of inquiry might be ordered. It seemed likely that the answers would be found in those two letters. Mike would have tried to visit him, but even if they'd allowed it he wouldn't have had time. He'd collected his patrol orders from Shrimp's office after breakfast; he'd drafted a good part of them himself, so it was no great revelation that *Unsung* was to join two other boats patrolling off Taranto. A very large landing operation was about to take place in northwest Africa, and emergence of Italian surface forces from their main bases was considered likely – from the Royal Navy's point of view, sincerely hoped for.

In taking over command of *Unsung* there was a lot to check on and discuss. Everything from charts to torpedoes, including the boat itself; variations in design which one should know about and could lead to problems if one didn't; signals and W/T gear, asdics including a mine-detection unit of which he'd had no practical experience; and of course personnel – meeting and needing some time with his officers, heads of departments and technicians. He'd said to Guy Mottram during a quick snack at lunch-time, 'A week's work in one day.'

'You'll catch up on it at sea and on the billet, old cock.'

'Dare say I will, but the more one can do now –'

'Anyway, good luck. I'll be there to wave goodbye if I can. Six, six-thirty?'

'Aiming for six.'

Unsung was in the wardroom berth, alongside, and storing ship had been in progress then, under the supervision of Showell and the coxswain, a Chief PO by name of Gladwich, thin as a boathook and about nine feet tall, Geordie accent, Conspicuous Gallantry Medal. They weren't a bad lot at all, was his first impression. None of them said anything about Melhuish.

Storing ship was completed by five and the light beginning to change by six. He'd written and posted a quick letter to the Old Man, spent half an hour in conclave with Captain Swann, and was on board a few minutes before six, bringing his old seagoing rucksack containing as much gear as he'd need. It was precisely six when Showell reported all hands on board and ready for sea. Gladwich and the signalman, name of Horrobin – slight stutter and in need of a haircut – were already in the bridge, Showell ditto, Mike and his navigator – a sub-lieutenant whose name for the moment he'd forgotten – now joining them in the rapidly cooling evening air. He told Gladwich, 'When we've cast off, Cox'n, I'll get her clear of this lot and you can then take her out.'

'Aye aye, sir!'

Obviously pleased. Which was a good start. He told

343

Showell, 'Leave me the back spring to turn on, get every-thing else off her.'

'Aye, sir.' He left him and the casing party to it, called down to the control room to group down.

'Group down, sir.' Ready for when the ropes and wires were off her and he'd put one motor slow ahead, swing her stern out. For the moment, glancing across at the softly-lit upper gallery, from where there'd been a call in the voice of Guy Mottram of 'Good luck, Mike!' There were other well-wishers too – a considerable gathering – including *Ursa's* officers – along the forefront of the old building. Swann, Shrimp's replacement, more or less central to it, flanked by Commander (Submarines) and Sam MacGregor. Movement amongst them now – in the centre there, Broadbent pushing in, and Mottram making way for – Christ – *Abbie*?

Abbie. Incredibly . . . In the care of Johnno. Made no sense but –

Waving, and laughing – *she* was – at his surprise, he supposed – and Johnno beside her cupping his hands at his mouth and bawling, 'Mike, she told me about your engage-ment not having to be secret any longer, and asked just this once might she come see you off. Captain S/M very kindly agreed, so –'

'Congratulations, Nicholson!'

'Thank you, sir. Thanks a lot, Johnno. Abbie – *bless* you!'

Fore spring gone, and the after breast. Fore breast cast off and being hauled in ashore. Enormous amount of cheering and clapping from the gallery. Nice of them: and *brilliant* of her. Life-lastingly brilliant, what she'd done. Must have called Johnno earlier in the day; his manner at lunch *had* been a little furtive. Mike had called down, 'Slow ahead port'; he asked CPO Gladwich, 'Ready to pipe, Cox'n?'

'Aye, sir.' Showing it in his palm – strangely-shaped tin whistle of a kind that had been in use in English fleets since

344

the Middle Ages. Mike had stopped that motor and ordered both of them slow astern – nodding to Showell to have the casing party take that spring off her. She was beginning to slide away from the building stern-first now. He told Gladwich, 'Pipe.'

All of them at attention, he and Swann at the salute, for the 'Still' – a thin, high note that was supposed to last eight seconds, then the 'Carry On', a similarly high but then steeply falling call cutting out abruptly after five. Formalities observed, and *Unsung* backing away quite fast now, dark water swirling; he'd ordered 'Stop both motors', and Showell was passing that down, while for a last sight of his fiancée he focused his glasses on her, saw her still waving frantically, and under that yellowish overhead light a glistening on her cheeks that couldn't be anything but tears. Explicitly forbidden, on more than one occasion – but surely not to be held against her. *Nothing* to be held against her, *ever*.